PLANET SONG

BOOK ONE OF THE FAHR TRILOGY

T.K. BOOMER

Planet Song

ISBN 978-0-9951667-1-4 (paperback)

ISBN 987-0-9951667-0-7 (ebook)

Dedication

This book is dedicated to Barb Galler-Smith.

Acknowledgments

Cover Design: Ben Baldwin. Editors: Nicole Luiken, Constantine Kaoukakis, and Kevin Quast. Writers Groups: The Scruffies, The Edmonton Writers Group, The Cult of Pain, and the Sherwood Park Critique Group. Notable Individuals: Karen Probert, Lea Kulmatycki, Robin Young, Lou Sytsma, Bruce Ehlert, Ann Marston, Brad Oates, Tim Anderson, Ella Beaumont, Jennifer Leface, and Randy McCharles. Also a special shout out to the When Words Collide writer's festival in Calgary.

Author's Note

The back of this book has an appendix, and the first page of that appendix has a physical description of the aliens you're about to meet. I tell you this because the text of the novel has no such description.

Act One: The Seeking

Teracia

Teracia unfolded herself from the flaps of the manta and waved it off. The giant ceph jetted away, moving far faster empty than it had with a passenger. She watched as it rose toward the surface, spread its diaphanous wings, and soared the ocean currents. Teracia felt a twinge of guilt for interrupting its day.

She turned and looked across the swimway at Song Corp's headquarters, a giant teal-blue dome that mimicked an aroused male diaphragm. Centrix city had many palaces and impressive government buildings but none like this. Teracia felt the ballow on her forehead inflate and its neutral beige morph into a swirling tempest of rage red and fear yellow. She fought to control it, drawing water through her gills to force a return to the beige.

Three security guards floated in a line behind the entrance to the building. Fit and young fahr, they showed no signs of song addiction. Each held a pitch wand. Behind them a coral garden beckoned with a collection of radiant trophy fish and a few gauzy shrimps.

Teracia swam forward. "I have an appointment."

"You're the femfahr?" the one on the right asked. His pitch wand moved to within a few inches of her diaphragm.

Teracia said nothing but felt the beige yellow and then to pink into irritation. The pitch wand caused severe pain when touched against the male Fahr diaphragm but would have no effect on her. She glared at the guard until his ballow inflated and mauved into embarrassment.

"Of course, she is," said the second one. "If you would follow me, Mamini."

Someone had taught him the ancient form of femfahr address. Teracia allowed her gill slits a small ripple of pleasure. It was a nod to a time when the fahr expressed their sexuality, when males noticed females. Now the femfahrs were little more than objects of curiosity, mistakes made in the reproductive labs, pitied because songs could not arouse them, and males had no interest.

The guard led Teracia past the coral garden and into the stunted kelp forest beyond. A blue-green jelly, a favorite food, pulsed into Teracia's peripheral vision, she snag-tongued it, pulling it into her mouth and swallowing.

"Not many job applicants would poach in the Song Corp forests on the way to meet Lord Greyling," the guard said.

"Not many job applicants are called in to meet him personally," Teracia replied allowing just enough gold into her ballow so show a hint of arrogance.

"True enough, I suppose," he said but pinked into irritation.

They swam deeper into the kelp forest. Somewhere amid all the greenery the board met, a secret group of well-placed fahrs that controlled Song Corp. Apart from Lord Greyling himself, no one was sure who belonged to this group, although there were plenty of rumors.

The kelp forest gave way to a sandy clearing with a small population of sharks and rays. Teracia looked up. The teal dome of the Song Corp building still loomed above her but the current against her scales and the plankton in her gills made it feel as if they were in the open ocean.

"It's bigger than it looks, isn't it?" said an old voice.

Teracia turned. "Lord Greyling," she said, willing her ballow to purple with respect, though she could feel the small shards of fear yellow. Then she tried willing this toward confidence green, but the shards persisted.

Greyling spoke to the guard. "You may leave. I'll be safe here."

The guard disappeared into the kelp forest and the old Fahr turned back to Teracia. "Don't call me Lord. A simple Greyling is fine. Money should never give rise to titles. It's their doing," he gestured dismissively at the kelp forest. "Indicative of power, I suppose, but I don't like it."

"Greyling," Teracia said, studying the legendary merchant. At close to one hundred millennia, he was the oldest fahr she had ever met. Still she was surprised how thin and frail he was. His scales showed maintenance that only the rich could afford, meticulous cosmetic repair, but the result showed wealth and not vitality. He had multiple implants in his fins. His diaphragm, though sagging and showing the scars of previous ruptures, was clean and glowed a healthy teal blue. He could still be aroused, even at his age.

Greyling gestured to the structure they were in. "Anyone can do this, given enough ambition." His gills rippled, and he turned to Teracia. "The board is curious about your application. You can't be interested in song."

"No. I expect to profit from this," Teracia said, a lie she had practiced for hours before a reflector, getting the tinge of her ballow a perfect shade of confidence green.

"Most song collecting expeditions don't make money," the old song merchant said. "I assume you know that? Occasionally we make a major find and then everyone is well compensated. Crew members are motivated by the quest, however long that may be. And because they get front-line exposure to virgin song should they find any. That's not a well-kept secret, I'm afraid."

"No," Teracia agreed.

"So then, if profit is unlikely and virgin song has no effect on you, why do you want to go?"

"Curiosity is a secondary motivation, I suppose. New worlds are always interesting."

"But profit is still the primary one?"

"Yes."

Greyling's aging ballow was green with a confident splatter of gold. "We've filled the position you've applied for, that of exobiologist in charge of sapient species research."

Teracia was stunned. "When?"

"A few days ago. A bright young fahr, Derath I believe his name is. I'm sure he'll do well."

"Then why did you bring me in?"

"You are an anomaly. A femfahr with an interest in the activities of Song Corp? You must know how strange that seems."

Teracia flattened her gills. "Strange? I seek lucrative employment. How is that strange?"

"Ah, yes, your stated motivation. Profit. We like that but then what corporate entity wouldn't? Profit is the engine we all run on, isn't it? But, that's what anyone in our position would want to hear from a prospective employee and anyone seeking employment with us would know this."

She had to be careful. "Are you suggesting that I have another motivation?"

"Do you?"

Teracia studied Greyling. The CEO of Song Corp didn't bring her in just to tell her they would not hire her, so there must still be a chance. "There are fourteen of us," she said guessing that the issue was her sex, "fourteen femfahrs out of a population of twenty-five million. Hardly a significant group. The truth is I've only met two. The rest are reclusive, rarely venturing out. If you had such a target on your abdomen, you might feel the same way." Teracia looked down at her small diaphragm. "So, you see, I'm no threat to Song Corp. I may well be the only fahr applying to the corporation who has a single motivation."

Greyling's gills rippled. "Well played. But even if we assume that profit is your sole motivation here, there are multiple ways in which you might profit from this situation that would not be in Song Corp's best interest."

"Spying for the competition?"

Greyling said nothing. The green of his confidence had deepened.

"I've done my research, Sir," Teracia said. "Song Corp has three times the success rate of any other company. You're powerful enough to have done thorough checks on any applicant, and I'm sure you have done so in my case. I wouldn't have been called in if you had found anything."

"That's just it. We found nothing. You live an incredibly modest lifestyle for someone so interested in money."

"Money is power, sir. You of all fahr know that. But if one spends it on trivialities one weakens that power."

"Ah, so you're one of those rare individuals who doesn't feel the need to show off one's wealth."

"I am a femfahr. Why would I seek even more attention?"

"Another good point," Greyling said. "But that still doesn't tell us what you plan to do with the money."

Teracia went pink. "Do you ask that question of all your employees?"

"We know what most of our employees will do with the money: bigger houses, menageries, extensive loop collections, visits to exotic pet spas. They're a predictable lot. We like predictability."

"And I'm not predictable?"

"Exactly."

Teracia would have to give him some truth. "I have an interest in ancient artifacts," she said. "I'd like to take an occupation off and devote myself to the study of them. No paid positions exist for that kind of research so, to survive a millennium with no income, I will need money in reserve."

"Khards," said Greyling nodding his head.

Teracia blanched. He knew, but how much did he know? "That's right," she said. "How did you know that?"

"We didn't, but thanks for confirming it. We know that you have been seen in the presence of the Holy Son and we know that he has an interest in ancient religious texts."

Teracia said nothing.

"Well," he said, "Studying ancient texts is a benign enough activity, I suppose. All right then, we're prepared to offer you a position."

"But you just said you gave another Fahr the position I applied for?"

Greyling studied her. "Most applicants understand that the application process is more open than that. Most will accept whatever we offer them."

Teracia flattened her gills.

"We keep our plans to ourselves," Greyling said. "Our antiquity gives us certain advantages over the competition. We have records of expeditions going back half a billion years. Some of those early expeditions visited planets where all factors were in place to ensure the evolution of singers, but they hadn't appeared yet. Too early in their evolutionary history. So, we plan a return expedition when the planet has matured. It increases the chances of success and gives us a decided advantage over the competition."

"So, you're saying that this is one such an expedition?"

"I did not say that."

Teracia allowed her gill slits a slight quiver. "What is this position?"

"Exobiologist."

Teracia studied Greyling. The old fahr was trying to maintain control but his gills were betraying his amusement.

"A song chaser? You want me to be a song chaser?" Song chasers were exobiologists, but their focus was entirely on the finding of alien singers.

"Well, you have to admit it's an interesting idea. When we thought about it, we realized you are quite possibly the best insurance policy we could have. A song chaser who can't be impaired by song. A song chaser without lust. A song chaser whose sole motivation is profit."

"The perfect corporate employee?" Teracia asked.

"Precisely."

"Your reputation is justified, Lord Greyling".

"So?"

Teracia flattened her gills. The position was not ideal. Most song chasers had the well-deserved reputation of being song-addicted louts. They would not be pleasant company. Still, she would have achieved the goal of getting on board a Song Corp ship. "The bonus would be higher?" she asked.

"Triple the standard crew percentage. We like to keep our song chasers happy."

"Triple?"

"Yes."

"I think you've just hired yourself a song chaser," Teracia said.

Occeane

Occeane, the Holy Son, met Teracia a few weeks later in the bowels of his official residence. There he knew Song Corp could not listen in. They would see her coming and going though, a risk that Occeane was prepared to take. The Holy Son was of the Elite, genetically engineered to be taller and more regal than the common Fahr. For Teracia this made him attractive in ways she wasn't supposed to feel.

"Did you get on board?" he asked her.

"Yes, Holy Son."

"And did he reveal the venture?"

"He did not confirm it was a return expedition, but I think it is, yes. He was sure of the profits."

"And you will be able to protect a sapient species, should one be encountered. This is good."

"Not quite. I wasn't hired as the sapient species specialist. They've found someone younger with no experience."

Occeane was silent for a moment. His ballow reddened. "This is typical of Song Corp. I thought your condition would give us an advantage, but apparently not."

Teracia went silent, her ballow graying into sorrow.

"I'm sorry," Occeane said, his ballow purpling, "I didn't mean to reference it in that way." His ballow shimmered into a soothing alga green.

"No, it's all right," she said. "Sometimes a chance word will pull me back into emotions I haven't felt in ages, emotions I've long since moved beyond."

She went silent again. Occeane waited.

"It's curious how they call one's first millennium an occupation, isn't it?" she said. "Because you're not employed, you're a child. And they never put your first millennium on your PDM because you're supposed to recall your childhood at will. Because it's a defining part of who you are. I recall it. Two-thirds the way through, the blood flows to the diaphragms increased and, as they enlarged, the minders came and took my friends away. They were adults then, at least in their bodies, and alive to song. So, they were led to sonically controlled environments where they would learn to cope. One by one they went until I was the only one left."

"Is that when they brought you to be my companion?"

"No. First, they did tests. What happened after that was odd. They didn't tell me the results; they changed the pronouns. Instead of 'he' and 'his' it became 'she' and 'hers'. But I knew what it meant. Song could not arouse me. I was a throwback to the old sexuality. Now I see it as freedom, then it was a shock."

Occeane darkened. "I too would be song deaf if I had such an option."

Teracia nodded. "But you would be more than just song deaf."

"Not if I, like you, had the original sexuality." His ballow lightened and blued pleasure as he looked at her.

Teracia shivered. It was the first time Occeane had ever expressed such a wish and the first time he had ever looked at her in that way. There had never been a male reversion. The First Modificate had destroyed all remnants of the original male genitalia. Occeane could not feel for her what she felt for him, but that did not prevent her from...

It hit like a wave, a full body flush that rippled back and forth beneath her scales. Her ballow blued and then rainbowed. She tried to steady herself.

"Are you all right?" Occeane asked.

"Yes," she said. "I felt a little unsteady for a moment."

"Are you sure?"

"Yes."

Occeane nodded. "So, tell me, what will you be doing on board that ship?"

Teracia's gills rippled. "Song chasing," she said.

Occeane, the Holy Son, nearly swallowed his tongue.

Greyling

His space within the kelp forest was little more than a small clearing. That was all any other fahr would see if they chanced upon it. The ancient algorithms would open its true purpose only if Greyling were to arrive alone.

He swam into it and felt the gentle swirling waters rise to support his aging body. A holographic image appeared before him, a ghostly scene of hundreds of ancient fahr, soft focused so he could recognize none of the faces.

"Have you hired her?" a solitary voice asked.

"Yes," Greyling replied. "She has agreed to be a song chaser on the mission, as we planned."

"And can she be managed?" another voice asked.

"She will be one fahr swimming against the corporate tide. She has assets we can use even if she opposes us. Yes, we can manage her."

"And her patron, the Holy Son?" another voice asked.

"He's no threat to Song Corp," Greyling said.

Baronth

The Fahr scout-class ship was a small interstellar ocean, one that could self-sustain for two millennia without replenishment. It was the perfect pet collecting vessel with a containment area adapted to any aquatic singer they might find.

Junior Navigational Officer Xyros was one of the youngest crew members on the ship and Chief Navigational Officer Baronth had the misfortune of being assigned mentorship.

"So, we're now approaching the target star system?" Xyros asked.

"We've been approaching it for three hundred years."

"Yes, but now we're actually approaching it?"

Baronth said nothing.

"I mean; won't we have to make adjustments because we'll be leaving interstellar space?"

Baronth's ballow displayed just a hint of pink and his gills slits rippled diagonally. He wasn't sure Xyros even understood condescension. "Yes," he almost hissed.

An appropriate response for Xyros would have been the mauving of his ballow but instead he pinked. "The ship's astrophysicist is down," he said with flattened gills.

"We have plenty of time."

"Ah yes, the tyranny of time!"

"It's hardly a tyranny if we have so much of it." The Chief Navigational Officer floated before the wall screen and stroked his Personal Digital Memory. In it, he had cached the memories of his sixty-three previous occupations.

"You're going into your PDM?" Xyros said, a hint of exasperation in his voice.

Baronth ignored the question. The wall screen showed an itemized list of the eras of his life. In his 17th occupation he had been an astrophysicist and there was information from that period in his life they needed now. He reached out and selected it.

"Seventeenth occupation selected," the ship's voice said in its flat and toneless timbre. "Astrophysicist level one. Approximate download time 29.3 minutes. Proceed?"

"Proceed."

Xyros watched as his mentor entered into receiver mode. Baronth's body went into a horizontal free float and tendrils dropped down from the ceiling to secure him in place. He was in mental stasis, aware of his surroundings but only enough to react if something were to endanger his person. The parasitic fish were quick to latch on for a blood feed.

The young fahr swam up to the panel and studied it. Xyros had yet to be fitted with a PDM and therefore retained his full mental capacity, no part of his brain needed to lay fallow in anticipation of a memory transfer. Procedures for entering a star system were tricky but well within the capacity of his young mind. He set to work.

Baronth could tell that Xyros was accessing the panel but, since this was not a threat to his person, the memory transfer continued. When it finished, he turned to the young fahr.

"What did you do?"

"I did a preliminary scan of the approaching star system, calculated the likely distribution of obstacles and their orbits, and then increased the effectiveness of the space debris sensors. That's standard procedure when entering a star system, isn't it?"

Baronth displayed red, gestured to the screen, and returned the sensors to their original settings. He turned to Xyros. "There's a reason you are being mentored and why you should not do things on you own initiative."

Xyros's ballow became a swirling mix of purple and red.

"Now watch and learn." Baronth spread his tentacles toward the screen in a wide arc and waved to the upper left side of the panel. It responded by glowing and then showing the ship's current speed. Baronth then made a claw-like motion downwards until the panel indicated the desired speed.

"The deceleration will take 14.6 days," said the ship's voice.

Baronth turned to Xyros. "In 14.6 days, we will increase the debris sensitivity by the precise amount needed by this star system." He tapped his PDM. "We slow the ship first, then increase debris sensitivity. That way we preserve power."

"And you got that from your PDM?" Xyros asked.

"I had done a detailed analysis of the dynamics of this star system in my 17th occupation."

"The ship's computer could not have given you that information?"

"Of course, but it would not have had a feel for this star system."

"Feel?"

"You are so young."

Xyros turned away, trying to hide the reddening. The area around navigation was a coral reef; alive with all manner of fish and crustaceans and the micro fauna and flora they fed on. These were silent animals bio-engineered to communicate by display and not sound. The colors were vibrant and watching them was a good way of neutralizing one's ballow. Baronth knew what Xyros was doing, trying to control his anger.

"When will they surface?" Xyros asked after his ballow had beiged.

Most of the crew would not come out of stasis until they were close to the planet. "Moving through the star system at this speed, it will take us ten years to reach it. So about five years from now you'll see them."

"And then you will go into stasis," Xyros said.

"When we get to the planet, yes. I'll miss all the excitement," Baronth said. "And you will get your first real test, landing this thing on a planet, assuming there's something to collect."

"I've been through the simulations hundreds of times. They're boring except for the ones where the automation fails, and you have to land manually."

"Pray to the Giver that doesn't happen," Baronth said. He

studied Xyros. "You cannot have taste. Do you understand that? Even residual impairment from recreational loops is dangerous. Taste is out of the question."

"I thought direct exposure to the singer was necessary for taste? For that to happen we'd need to be on the planet."

"Sometimes atmospheric microphones can pick up virgin song. It's rare, but it happens. Avoid it if it does. Impairment is out of the question if you're going to land this ship."

Xyros said nothing. Getting taste was what being on a pet expedition was all about.

Teracia Surfaces

Surfacing, in Teracia's experience, was like slowly becoming aware that you were ascending through a murky yellow sea. Her eyes opened. Her first visual was of the attendant, his ballow inflated a soothing alga green and his gill slits rippling.

"Happy surfacing, Teracia," he said.

Teracia gestured a greeting. Her tongue would require loosening before she could speak clearly.

"I've contacted nutrition and they'll be sending your first meal shortly. I imagine you're famished," the attendant said.

"Yeth," said Teracia.

"The post-surfacing nutritional protocol on board is pretty tasteless, I'm afraid, but it'll have your energy back in a few days. Then you can eat whatever you want. In the meantime, I'll draw your attention to the major difference between surfacing in space and surfacing on Centrix." He gestured to the walls. "This room is sponged. We'd like you to stay in here for a couple of days until you've got your coordination back. Coordination returns a little slower in artificial gravity. It wouldn't be good for you to go crashing into expensive equipment when we don't have the option of sending out for parts."

"Oh, aye," Teracia said. She wanted to ask if they had detected any radio or digital signals from the target planet but didn't think she could form the words.

Maragheh

In its day, the Maragheh Observatory in Persia had been world famous, even attracting scholars from as far away as China. But the Mongols had stolen the library, and an earthquake had stolen the buildings. The murals had sustained even further damage from the aftershocks. There were now great cracks in them and bits and pieces of the constellations had fallen from the wall. These lay in a dusty rubble on the floor awaiting repair, but there was no money.

Sadr al-sharia al-Bukhari had spent years there studying the heavens. He could identify every constellation and every star, however minor, just by looking up into a clear night sky. It brought him peace to look at it, glorying in Allah's creation. This was a dark clear night with no moon to dull the stars. He smiled with pleasure, allowing himself to bask in the Creator's glory.

Then he saw it. Something dark was moving through the sky, blocking the light as it passed in front of each star. It was too solid to be a cloud and oddly geometrical, a floating black rectangle. He watched with apprehension, wondering if a new evil had made its presence known.

Sapient Species

It took ten years for Baronth to navigate the ship through the star system. When he had parked it in orbit above the planet and had begun the five-month fast before his downing, Derath came to him.

The young fahr was one of about seventy mission specialists who had surfaced in the last few years, the sapient species specialist, if Baronth remembered correctly. He was not a fahr with whom Baronth had had much interaction and, in his fast-induced haze, Baronth couldn't remember if the youngest member of the crew had ever called on him before. Having to deal with Xyros was bad enough without having to deal with someone even younger.

"Hello?" Baronth said, a question not a greeting.

"Navigational Officer Baronth," Derath said. "My apologies for coming to you during your fast but there's something I thought you'd like to see before you go down," the young fahr gestured to the panel on Baronth's wall. "May I?"

"There's not much I haven't seen," said Baronth. It was the standard response older fahr made to any attempt by the young to show them new things.

"You didn't see this," Derath said.

The panel displayed a high-resolution image, an aerial view of part of the planet's surface. At first Baronth wasn't sure what he was looking at, a bit of cloud cover, a desert, and a river. But then he saw them. Grids. Cultivation. The planet had a sapient species, early stage one and terrestrial. It was rare to see one this primitive. On approach, the planet had looked so pristine he had not bothered with the standard tests, but here they were. Contact with such a species was unwise and would complicate things.

"It seems you have a reason for being," Baronth said.

Derath said nothing but his gills were rippling.

"Has the commander surfaced yet?" Baronth asked.

"They're feeding him," Derath said.

"Well, I'm sorry I didn't catch this but, as you can see, I'm too far into the pre-down fast to be of any use to you now. He would have to take over in any case."

"I thought you should see it," Derath said.

Baronth allowed his gill slits to ripple. "You'll be down before I surface, but I'll check the logs to see how well you've done." He turned from Derath to let him know the conversation was over.

Prostallen

Commander Prostallen was only a few millennia away from elderhood and on his 57th occupation. He was focused in his choice of jobs, with only a dozen being outside the corporate sphere. The rumors about his wealth hinted at a large personal menagerie, and at an illegal loop collection hidden somewhere on the ship. Derath thought he was likely to be impatient with sapient-species protocol.

"Report," Prostallen said when Derath was ushered into his presence.

"The species went undetected, Commander," Derath said. "It was only after the first few high-definition surface scans we knew they were there. Early stage one. Terrestrial biped."

"Stage one and terrestrial?"

"Yes."

Prostallen swam around the command center, raggedly, accompanied by more than his share of parasitic fish. Derath had few opportunities to study the commander at close range. His wrinkled ballow sagged to one side. He had patches of discolored scales and his spine had an arch to it that contributed to his swimming problems. His last down time had not fixed this. The final decline had begun and Derath doubted if Prostallen would see one more occupation, two at most.

"I suppose it's pointless to ask about transmissions?" asked the commander.

"None," Derath confirmed.

"So now we just go round and round this ball while you do your little experiments?"

"This is a great opportunity to study a sapient species in its earliest stages of development," Derath said.

"The oceans are singing! They're SINGING! It's been millions of years since we've heard the like of this and we have to worry about contaminating some..."

"The Giver..."

"The Giver? Religious crap! That's what that is!"

Derath said nothing keeping his ballow as close to neutral beige as he could manage. He knew Prostallen would have to comply. Not doing so would put his wealth and position at risk. He watched as the commander swam around the space, his damaged ballow shifting between shades of red. When he came to a stop, he looked at Derath.

"What? Are you still here? Get on with it!"

Derath backed out the room and left. He had the freedom to do his job for now, but he also knew Prostallen could make his life miserable. He would have to do his work quickly or risk the consequences. It was rare that time ever became an issue for the Fahr. They considered near-infinite patience a high virtue under normal circumstances, but these were not normal circumstances. When the promise of virgin song was at hand, decorum was always at risk.

Pickers

They were in the exobiology lab. Prostallen had seconded Teracia, along with the five other song-chasers, to Derath. Teracia could not believe her luck. She was doing exactly what she wanted, even if she didn't have the position to go with it, but the others were not happy. With an ocean teeming with new singers, the last thing song-chasers wanted to do was waste time studying a primitive sapient biped, but that was the protocol.

"The first thing we need to do is map their settlements and determine the population," Derath said to them.

"And how exactly do we do that?" one of them asked.

"Analysis of surface structures," Derath said. "There are certain topographic features you can learn to recognize. These vary depending on the species but once you determine how and why they build the structures they do..."

"Oh, we wouldn't be any good at that," said another.

"We're trained to look at sea beds not land masses," said another. "We wouldn't have a clue what we were looking at."

"Well, of course, I will train you."

"We're song-chasers, boss. That's what we do. Now if those little bipeds become aquatic and start singing, then we can help you."

Five sets of gill slits did a wild ripple and Derath reddened but he was too intimidated to say anything. Teracia watched as they swam around in circles joking with each other and snag-tonguing fish and jellies.

"Release them," she whispered to Derath. "They'll only get in your way."

Derath looked at Teracia then turned to the others. "Teracia is the only chaser I need at the moment," he said. "The rest of you are free to go. I'll call you when I need you."

"Right, boss!" one of them said, and they all swam out moving in exaggerated deference to mock him.

Teracia knew where they would go, straight to the observation deck where they would try to listen to the oceans below. The filters would be on so all they would get was mild titillation, but this would fuel their impatience.

"The pickers are ready," Teracia said.

"Good," Derath said, his eyes drawn to Teracia's diaphragm. It was child sized. The big surprise was that Teracia was on the ship at all. What reason would a femfahr have to seek virgin song? That she was song-chaser was even odder. Her presence, however, gave the whole expedition one huge advantage. A femfahr could not be aroused by song but neither could she be impaired' She could work without filters.

"They're in the chutes then?" he asked.

"Ready to go."

"All right then..." Derath gestured toward the panel and waited until it showed the ship to be on the night side of the planet. Then he spread his claspers wide, flicked them at the screen, and watched as the ship released hundreds of capsules.

"You'll stay for the return?" he asked her.

"Of course," Teracia said.

The capsules would descend through the atmosphere until they reached a level a few hundred feet above the planet. Then the outer covering would retract inside the picker's exoskeleton and its wings would take over. These were atmospheric pickers, each programmed to snatch a specific target animal, anesthetize it, wrap it in a protective cocoon, and return it to the ship, all under the cover of darkness.

Having Teracia around proved almost unnecessary. One mammal produced a kind of musical howling that was filtered for safety purposes, but the birds were quiet on board.

"That was kind of disappointing," she said.

"Disappointing?" Derath said. "I was relieved."

"Not sure how you would respond?" she asked.

"I've never been exposed to virgin song, never."

"That's right," she said. "I keep forgetting how young you are."

"It's different for..." he said and then regretted it.

"I can still enjoy the songs," she said. "They just do nothing to me. That's why I wanted to hear the birds. I like bird songs. But I guess they only sing when they want to."

"Well, it makes things simpler," Derath said,

"How's that?"

"The mimics," he said. "If the animals don't always vocalize, then the mimics can be mute. If we don't have to reproduce the song, then it will be easier, quicker and..."

"Safer," Teracia finished.

"Well, it is annoying wearing those stupid filters even when you're only dealing with artificial song."

"What if the sapient species expects them to vocalize in certain situations?"

"They'll be suspicious, I guess. We don't have time to make this perfect. You know that."

Derath might be the only fahr on board, aside from Teracia, who had never experienced extreme arousal. He wasn't sure he wanted to. He didn't like the way the experience seemed to drive the others.

Demon

Brother Cornelius was a scribe, a copier of religious doctrine, and a calligrapher in Latin. His fingers were ink-stained, as was the shaved bald spot on the top of his head, the unfortunate result of his habit of resting those same ink-stained fingers on his scalp while deep in thought. Outside the monastery, they regarded him as a learned man, but the truth was his skill was in the calligraphy, not in the understanding. He had studied Latin but only long enough to gain a basic knowledge of what he would do as a copier of the sacred texts. His teachers had spent far more time on his penmanship than they ever had on his understanding. Many of the words he copied were meaningless to him as meaningless as the stains on his sleeves of his robe. Still, he thought he should understand. He thought long and hard about the words he put down, willing them to have significance even if he was wrong about what that significance was.

His religious vows were more about self-preservation than they were about faith. He carried with him the same fear of the afterlife most people had, to be sure, but he had a far greater fear of the world outside the monastery. Out there, one could starve if the crops were poor, or be killed or imprisoned for walking down the wrong road or swearing allegiance to the wrong prince. Religious vows required him to learn the prayers and rhythms of the monastic life, to do what was expected when it was expected. That he could handle—well enough to get by at least—and if by this small bit of service, he gained entrance to paradise, so much the better.

Cornelius did not notice the dog until he had finished the page and hung it up to dry. He did not remember it entering the room and wondered if it had been there all along though that seemed unlikely. It was not a dog he recognized, but he paid little attention to the semi-wild pack that hung around the monastery. It was time for evening prayers and he could not leave the animal in the room with the pots of ink and manuscripts. One spill could ruin a day or even a week's work. He went to shoo the dog away, but it stood up slowly and appeared to study him. The tail was not wagging, but neither were the teeth bared. The animal just stood staring at him, its eyes locked on his. These lacked the softness Cornelius associated with dogs. These were precise, attentive, and unnerving. He reached out towards the animal palm downwards offering the dog a chance to sniff him. It did not, but the eyes moved to his hand. The monk moved his hand slowly towards the dog's back and went to pet it. The animal moved away and again locked eyes. Cornelius reached out again and this time the dog did not move away.

The fur had a stiffness he did not expect, and it was cold. Cornelius pushed his fingers deeper into the coat and still found no warmth. The dog was no longer looking at him. Instead, it had fixed its attention on the drying manuscript page. Then it moved away from him closer to the page until it was staring straight up at it. The page hung about six feet off the floor and out of the animal's reach. Cornelius wondered if anything in the manuscript would interest a dog, nothing of food value. As he was considering this, he noticed a soft whirring sound, like the rapid flutter of a bat's wings or perhaps a large humming bird. Then he watched in horror as the dog's neck extended itself, lengthening towards the page like a long tongue.

"Daemon!" Cornelius screamed. "Daemon!" He grabbed the chair he had been sitting on and crashed it into the dog's neck.

The whirring stopped, and the dog's neck and head swayed back and forth twice before shattering. The headless body stood amid a debris field that looked like a collection of pottery shards and feathers, with two elongated metallic eyes lying on either side of the torso. There was no blood, just light wisps of white smoke. Cornelius looked down and saw some of the feather-like material clinging to his robe, where it quivered and shook. He screamed, ripped the robe from his body, and ran naked from the room.

The Abbot was not above using the superstitions and fears of the people when it suited him, but he was rarely patient with the same behavior in the monks under his charge. They were a scholarly order, given to the study and copying of books, and he encouraged a healthy skepticism in all matters concerning the occult. So when Brother Cornelius ran naked and screaming into the chapel claiming to have seen a demonic dog, of all things, the Abbot was not pleased.

Now, as he stood before the remains of the creature, he could understand Brother Cornelius's fear. Whatever this was, it was not a dog, not a living-breathing dog at any rate. What it was, however, was another question. There was no blood, no gore, and no entrails, nothing that looked like death. If this was demonic, one could expect an aura of death or at least organic corruption of some sort. Cornelius had talked of smoke, but that was gone if it had been there. There was no smell to speak of, just this strange rubble and a carcass. It was like no carcass he had ever seen. He reached down and touched the feather-like things on the floor. They had a silken texture. Running his hand across the rump of the carcass produced no familiar sensations.

"This is not a demon," he pronounced to the wide-eyed monks around him.

"Then what is it?" One of the monks asked.

"I don't know but I intend to find out," the Abbot said. He

pointed to the rubble on the floor. "Sweep this into a box and then bring it with that thing up to my quarters."

"But Lord Abbot..."

"This is not a demon. It will not hurt you. Do as you're told."

Later that night the Abbot discovered intricate gearing systems far more complex than anything he had ever seen before. Then there were the eyes, the shiny metallic eyes.

Plague

Teracia used all of her spare time to watch and study Homines. It was a fascinating lesson in early sapient species evolution. She loved the creative ways they organized their societies, and their errant but amusing attempts at cosmology, where imagined gods willed everything into existence over impossibly short periods of time. She loved the little things like their animal husbandry techniques, the funny songs they sang, how they blended, mixed and—horror of horrors—cooked their foods! They had fragile bodies and an enormous range of coverings for them. Their sailing ships harnessed the prevailing atmospheric winds. But most of all she loved their families, the way their children were coddled and nurtured and the consequent bonds that formed. There was no equivalent in Fahr society.

There were darker things too: the incipient tribal conflicts that drove them to violent confrontation; the way the ideological and religious authorities stifled original thought in favor of the errant conformity; the social stratification of their societies allowing one individual to own another. And then there was the whole problem of disease.

Teracia went to Derath's quarters. "They're dying," she said.

"Dying?"

"I've detected a pathogen, a virulent strain," she said. "It's carried by small rodents and is transferred to individual homines by flea bites. In some places, they're showing a ninety percent mortality rate. They do not understand how to protect themselves."

"How widespread is it?"

She gestured to Derath's wall. A high-resolution map complete with topographical features appeared, and she pointed to two highlighted areas. "These affected villages are part of the Mongol empire and they're in the middle of a major trade route. Many of the inhabitants are already dead and there have also been outbreaks in these major ports," she said pointing to them.

"So, it's spreading?"

"Projections have it infecting as much as ninety-five percent of the population on the largest northern continent within the next five years. They also show it spreading to the largest continent in the southern hemisphere. Depending on the mutation rate, it could be disastrous."

"So, contamination by us might be the least of their worries?"

"We could send down pickers with an antibiotic."

"No, we can't," Derath said. "We would be interfering in the natural evolutionary process, in defiance of The Will of the Giver."

"The Will of the Giver is all about preserving the evolutionary process, allowing it to continue. What is the point of being an advanced species if we can't help?"

"Pathogens are part of the natural evolutionary process," Derath said.

"And what are we then? An entire species bio-engineered in defiance of natural evolution."

"All of that happened before The Will of the Giver. We've allowed no changes since."

"Really, Derath? We do it every time we enter the stasis chambers, or don't you understand they're using cultured stem cells to regenerate body parts, in complete defiance of natural evolutionary aging? Or that we're using our PDMs to archive memories even our regenerated brains couldn't possibly contain? That part isn't even organic. Or how about reproduction? Done in labs where evolutionary natural selection plays no part. We couldn't have survived as a species without interference in our own natural evolution. Without our bio-engineered extended life spans, we would never have survived the journey from Aquafahr when its star became unstable. In comparison sending out an antibiotic to help Homines along to the next stage in its evolution seems like a small act."

"It's also an illegal act," Derath said. "Get caught and we would spend the rest of our lives vegetating on Centrix."

Teracia pinked. "Who would know? We send out pickers to collect the fleas, infect them with the antibiotic and return them to the surface. The effect won't be dramatic, but it should reduce the mortality rate."

"No."

"It's not like something like this would show up as an unnatural leap in their technological progress. There would be no sign of them being pushed by us."

"If they caught us..."

They shared a long silence. Teracia watched as Derath's ballow morphed from red to yellow and finally green.

"If we were careful, we might be able send out dual-purpose pickers. How large are these fleas?" Derath asked.

"Tiny."

"How will we create the antibiotic?"

"In my 19th occupation I was a micro-biologist. I think we have all the equipment in your lab that we will need but I'll need to revert to know for sure."

"Better do that then," Derath said.

"Then you're in agreement?"

Derath took a moment to answer. "I believe that every sapient species in the galaxy makes us richer. When I chose this occupation, I thought I'd be lucky if I could study a new one, let alone be involved in an act that might help preserve it. You can't let the other seekers know about this."

Teracia's gills rippled. "Just send them to the observation deck and tell them to count the ocean-going ships. They'll love it."

Derath said nothing but Teracia watched as yellow bled into his ballow. She touched his gills. "We can do this," she said.

Push

"Report," Prostallen said.

Every one of Derath's debriefings began with the same word. Report. As if in that minuscule amount of time Derath and his team could have put together a definitive analysis of the diverse Homines population, one that hadn't even been hinted at the month before.

"As I said the last time we met, Commander, this species is primitive and tribal. We have thousands of languages to analyze and most of these are pre-literate. And we've only been at this for seventeen years."

"The same seventeen years during which I haven't received a single shred of useful information?" Prostallen asked.

This was a rhetorical question, one of many Prostallen had asked over time, but on this occasion the delivery was different. His ballow was a mellow green. Gone was the jitteriness and impatience Prostallen had shown in the past. Something had changed. Derath chose not to answer.

"All right then, I will give you a new directive," Prostallen said. "You will tell me, in five years, the likely impact of us putting this ship deep into that ocean. I want to hear with absolute certainty whether we are likely to contaminate these bipeds."

"Sir, according to protocol, I cannot make that decision based on incomplete information. We have just begun to understand some of their cultures. If we do this properly it will be a wonderful addition to... "

"Who, on this ship, is the ultimate interpreter of protocol?" The control was gone, and the green bled into red.

Derath did not answer but, as his silence continued, it became obvious Prostallen would wait for his answer.

"You are, Sir," Derath said purpling.

"And you will give me an answer about those bipeds in five years."

"I don't think that's enough time. It would mean learning more in the next five years than we've learned in the last seventeen."

"I have given you help, all six exobiologists."

Derath was tempted to tell him that five of the six were next to useless.

"And you may use the navigation computer," Prostallen said. "As of this moment, I give you access to the most powerful computer on board."

"The navigation computer? But it's not programmed for cultural analysis."

"You have Teracia, the femfahr. Her last occupation was as a data specialist, I believe. Program the navigation computer."

"But..."

"Five years, understand?"

"Yes, Commander."

"Good, now get on with it."

"We call them Homines now, sir."

"Homines?"

"Yes, Commander."

"And how did you come up with that name?"

"One of the more dominant cultures seems to use it as an inclusive term, though they also exclude some less-dominant cultures. We think..."

"We'll call them Homines, then. And you will tell me, within five years and with absolute certainty if contamination of the Homines is likely to occur. And Derath?"

"Yes, Commander?"

"Do not become attached to these bipeds."

Resistance

The images on Derath's wall were of mass graves, places where victims of the plague were being dumped by the wagonload. The happiness in the families Teracia had seen only a year or two earlier had been replaced by grief, fear, and distress. Most of the largest continent in the northern hemisphere was in chaos.

"The thing I find the most difficult about this," Derath said, "is that it would have been much worse if we hadn't intervened. It's hard to look at this and conclude that the antibiotic did any good at all, but the survival rate is still much higher than projected. They have a future."

"Can you imagine a push event on top of this?" Teracia said.

"Prostallen wants his songs. It will be hard to argue a fireball in the sky followed by a landing in that ocean will push anything under these circumstances. The Homines infrastructure is crumbling."

"There are other cultures, other tribes that aren't on those continents."

"Yes, but they're not as advanced as the ones here," he said gesturing to the images, "and this will be a major setback to their species."

"The death of a third of the population isn't a bad thing, not in the long run. Sometimes it creates opportunities for the survivors they may not otherwise have had."

"That's optimistic," Derath said.

Teracia was silent for a moment. "What's amazing is that none of the other song chasers have figured out what we're doing," she said.

Derath turned and looked at her. "They don't even suspect?"

Teracia's gills flattened. "They all spend their time trying to listen to the ocean. It's like they're drooling. If they knew about this, they'd go straight to Prostallen."

"Why did you come on board as a song chaser?"

"Do you think they would have let me on board as a sapient

species expert?"

Derath blanched. "You applied for my position?"

"Lord Greyling actually brought me in for an interview. I was quite surprised. But it turned out he'd already given the position to you and wanted to pitch me on being a song chaser."

"But your qualifications are better than mine. I've seen them. I assumed that you wanted to be a song chaser because the bonuses were higher."

"I feigned an interest in the profits to be made, right from the beginning. Made it sound like it was my priority. And most of the song chasers are also addicts, which reduces their efficiency. Lord Greyling liked the idea of a sober profit-driven song chaser."

"Then the real reason you're on this expedition is?"

"The Homines, or whatever other sapient species we were likely to find because, at the time we didn't know."

"We didn't know we'd find anything. Most expeditions don't."

"They knew."

"Knew?"

"Song Corp has been around long enough they're now revisiting promising planets. One hundred million years ago, this planet was evolving singers. They made a note of that and planned a return trip when the planet was more mature. They knew they would find singers, perhaps not sapients, but they knew they'd find singers."

Derath thought about this. "I didn't think we were likely to find anything and that I, therefore, wouldn't have much to do. It was like a training exercise. I couldn't believe my luck when we actually found Homines."

Teracia's gills rippled. "Did you know it used to be a requirement that they have three sapient species experts on every expedition? Three? A little lobbying before the High Counsel by Song Corp and its competitors got rid of that requirement, and the requirement that the sole adaptive species expert be experienced."

"I know my stuff," said Derath with pinkish irritation.

"No one is questioning your qualifications. They couldn't hire you if you weren't qualified but what those qualifications don't require is any kind of expedition experience. And, because they're only required to have one sapient species specialist on board, you're not being mentored. Look around you. Do you see any other junior position on board not being mentored by senior staff with more experience?"

Derath thought about this. "How about Xyros? No. He has Baronth."

"Xyros is actually older than you, isn't he?"

"Not by much."

"But he's still older and no one in their right mind would turn over the navigation of this ship to him with his level of inexperience. It wouldn't be done. Which is why he's being mentored. And yet they're entrusting the welfare of any sapient species we might encounter to you, the youngest and least experienced fahr on the ship."

"I know my stuff," Derath repeated.

"And who do you report to?"

"Commander Prostallen."

"And does he have any expertise with adaptive species?"

Derath said nothing.

"Major pet finds are rare and, when they happen, the last thing Song Corp or any of its competitors want to deal with is a native sapient species. The quicker they can collect the singers and get them and their songs to market the better. But they have this ethical obligation to preserve the sapient species and not push their development. Here's the problem. We're a long way from Centrix. We're a long way from any kind of meaningful enforcement of that obligation."

"But Prostallen hasn't..."

"Yet. But he's pushing you, isn't he? And he has given you an ultimatum."

Derath's gill slits flattened. "You're taking a risk talking about this aren't you?"

Teracia swam in small circles around the room. "You're not tainted yet," she said.

"Tainted?"

"Witness my fellow song chasers. Do they appear to you to have any concern for Homines?"

"No."

"Ever ask yourself why?"

"But Prostallen is..."

"Prostallen is worried about how things will look if he doesn't take the proper precautions. That's his concern. He can't rush right in and collect the singers with no regard to the effect it would have on Homines. If he did, the High Council would never let him fly again. That's why we've been in orbit above this planet for twenty years, but do not deceive yourself. He has every intention of collecting those singers."

"But if the High Council will discipline him for doing so, why would he do that?"

"It's not the reality that matters, but how it looks. If it looks like he's tried to get it right, then he'll get away with it. It's the perception that matters. You are the only fahr who can stop this."

Derath's gills stood straight up. "Me? But you've just pointed out I'm occupying a junior position here and I report to Commander Prostallen. He can override me. He has that authority."

"But if he overrides you and then things go badly, the blame will fall on him. You will be on record as opposing the collection. That's why he needs your agreement."

Derath considered this. "He wants me to give him the go ahead and you want me to say no. I'm not stupid. If I say no, I won't just be dealing with Prostallen. Every crew member on this ship is lusting after those songs."

"But if you say yes, we will expose Homines to advanced technology and that could push their development along at a destructive rate. Given what's already going on down there, this could destroy them. Sapient species need time to grow morally into their technologies. You know this! You can't plunge a ship of this sophistication into that ocean without the Homines noticing!"

"Probably not," Derath admitted. "So, I have to tell Prostallen 'no' even though it's not likely to be good for me?"

Teracia studied him. "Sometimes you have to put The Will of the Giver before your own personal survival," she said.

"That assumes that my personal survival is not The Will of the Giver," Derath countered. "All right," he said. "We have two years to build a strong case for leaving this planet as we found it." He regarded Teracia. "You're mentoring me, aren't you?"

Teracia's gills rippled. "You're not supposed to notice."

Exposure

"Report," Prostallen commanded.

The time had come for the decision and the commander had surrounded himself with all his senior officers. It was an intimidation ploy of the highest order. They would not like what Derath had to say.

"We have determined, according to your instructions, Commander Prostallen, that proceeding with the expedition would contaminate the evolution of Homines, the resident sapient species on this planet," he said with as much authority as he could manage. "Therefore, according to protocol, I have to recommend that we abandon this mission."

Prostallen's gill slits rippled. Derath was not expecting this. The commander seemed pleased with what he had said.

"There," Prostallen said. "That wasn't that difficult now was it? All I wanted from you was a definitive answer and now I have it. This is good work and I will put you forward for a commendation." The commander swam towards the door. He gestured for Derath to follow. "Before I do that, however, I'd like to show you something."

Derath followed the commander down a long hallway he knew led to the observation deck where Teracia's fellow song chasers spent their time drooling over the oceans. It was a place Derath avoided. The deck itself amounted to a bulge on the side of the ship. It gave an unobstructed view of the planet and incorporated high-definition magnification systems for the study of specific parts of the surface. As they entered, the magnification systems were on and the view was of a vast stretch of open ocean.

Prostallen indicated Derath should move forward so he would get the maximum view possible. As he did so, Derath noticed the filtered songs emanating from below the water's surface. His body tingled with pleasant soothing warmth. The effect was minimal, but he understood the attraction. He moved forward again and everything intensified. He had just enough time to look behind him and see the commander and all the officers now wearing personal filters. A huge rush went from one end of his spine to the other and every muscle in his body vibrated. He pitched forward, and he lost control. Glorious ecstasy!

Permission

The menders had Derath in a harness to keep him from drifting. Ten days after his exposure, the young fahr had yet to regain full control of his person; his gill slits rippled randomly, his ballow morphed between hues and the fins on the right side of his body twitched. Teracia wondered if Derath would even recognize her, but he did.

"Ter-ah-ci-ah," he said pronouncing each syllable in her name.

"You're healing," she said, not at all sure that this was true.

"Healing?" Derath said. "Oh no. I'm not ill. I feel wonderful!"

"So, why are you with the menders?"

Derath looked around at the menders and then at the harness that held him upright. "OK, I'm a little..." He stopped and looked at Teracia and his ballow began to purple. "It was wonderful," he said.

"So now what?" Teracia asked.

Derath's gills flattened, and the purple deepened. "The commander came to see me," he said.

"And?"

"I told him."

"Told him what?"

"That we had to get those singers," he said.

Teracia studied him. "Did he ask you or did you tell him?"

"I thought about all the fahr back on Centrix. I thought about how much they would enjoy this. How much they would want this..."

"Did he ask you or did you tell him?" She repeated as she pinked.

Derath stopped. "He wanted to know about my experience, about how wonderful it was. Then he told me how privileged I was to have it, and didn't I think more fahr should be exposed to something that wonderful. I agreed with him." He purpled and turned away from Teracia. "That was a mistake wasn't it?"

Teracia reached out and touched his gill slits. "We'll talk later," she said. She could wait to tell him about the loss of the mimic, but the immediate problem was Prostallen; a problem she was in no position to solve, at least not yet.

Taste

The atmospheric microphones had picked up plenty of birdsong from the planet. As always, the filters were in place and it was these filtered versions that found their way into the ship's loop library. The effect was pleasant but little more. One of the song chasers had given Xyros a solution for that.

When he swam into the library, security stopped him. "Extend," the guard said.

Xyros extended both his tentacles out to their maximum length for a visual inspection.

"Pass through," the guard said after the search. Xyros swam across the detection grid. Nothing.

The guard nodded. "Proceed," he said.

The library proper was the ship's largest garden. It mimicked the shallow-depth coral reefs on Centrix except it had none of that reef's native singers. Like the rest of the ship, every sound in the library was controlled and sonically neutral. Any species roaming free was mute, but each was also a beautiful creature, one that could be watched for hours with a slight level of impairment.

Xyros wasn't interested. He plucked a loop player from the wall, found the desired bird song loop, and made his way to an isolation booth.

The first thing he noticed entering the booth was the security camera system disguised as a barnacle. He looked around and found what he was looking for, a sea slug slowly making its way across the sandy floor. This he picked up and placed over the offending barnacle. Considering the creature's speed, he would have at least five minutes to alter the loop player.

He tongue-searched inside his mouth until he found the chip, embedded in a thick layer of scanner-resistant mucus in his cheek. He took it out, popped open the back of the loop player, and disarmed its security system. Then he removed the filtration chip and replaced it with the one he'd smuggled in.

Taste at last! He'd waited millennia for this!

Flagellants

Frederic pulled himself painfully upright in his bed of straw. This put him in the breeze blowing in from the room's sole window. The cooling was welcome, but the air was not fresh. It carried with it the stench of death mingled with rotting vegetation, human and

animal filth, and a wisp of coal fire smoke. He couldn't imagine anyone preparing food under these circumstances. Frederick touched the
swellings on his neck. They had gone down during the night. He
pulled back his tunic and looked down at his groin. There too the
swelling had gone down and there was no sign of the black flesh he'd
seen on his wife and sons. It was small comfort. It meant in him the
disease had not run its course and it might spare him. Spared him for
what?

He glanced at Else, his daughter, and the last to succumb. She
slept ragged and raspy against the back wall. The corpses of his wife
and sons lay on the straw near the door. The previous evening, he had
been too ill to move them. Fredric stood testing his strength. He had
some now, but not much. Still, their bodies would have to be moved.
They could not stay where they were. He found some water, drank,
and then looked down at them again. In the distance, he could hear
the squeak of the cartwheels.

In his weakened state getting their bodies out the door and into
the street was almost more than he could handle. No one else would
touch them. His neighbors all kept their distance when it came time
for him to bring out his dead, just as he had kept his distance when
they had brought out theirs.

The man pulling the cart would not help. He had not even
looked back as Frederic struggled to add to his load. Fredrick loaded
them face down, so they would not stare back at him as they went on
their final journey. Then he collapsed against the side of the house
and watched them go.

None of the priests gave his wife and sons their last rites. The
Black Death was everywhere, and they also counted priests among the
victims. The wrath of God was a terrible thing, but Frederic wondered
how the dereliction of their priestly duties could do anything but
worsen their lot when they came to stand before the judgment seat.
He should have been angry. Instead there was a kind of hollowness,
as if his illness had scooped out his emotions and left him without the
ability to feel anything, even sorrow. But he could hear sorrow. Else
had woken and was calling for her mother and brothers. Frederic

would take care of her as she had tried to take care of each of them, a duty abstract and mechanical.

By the third day, she was over the worst of it and it looked as though she would survive. Frederic walked out the front door at dusk just as the cart for the dead passed by again. On this day it contained the body of one of the village priests, his face a mask of agony. Was there no one left to bury him at the church?

Walking the cobblestone road to where it stood was exhausting. Frederic wondered if he would ever regain his stamina. He fought his way up the twelve steps to the church's massive oaken door and found it ajar. From the outside he could hear the cries but when he pushed his way inside, there were no priests, just a throng of people lighting candles and prostrating themselves before the altar. Perhaps the priests were all dead. By now the sky had dimmed to the point where little light was making its way through the stained-glass windows depicting the stages of the cross. These were recent additions that had cost a fortune, all of it paid for by the church's impoverished parishioners buying their way into heaven. Many of them were now dead and hopefully getting what they had paid for. He had his doubts. Some terrible sin had to have been committed for God to bring this Black Death. Why would he do this and then welcome them into paradise? Who had committed this sin?

He felt a sudden and welcome rage. To his right were the stairs leading to the second tier. Frederic dragged himself up and threw open the west window seeking the face of God in the sky above the town. Who had done this? Who was the author of this sin? The sun had long since gone down, but now, skirting the horizon, was a large red orb trailing bright arms of flames behind it. A Jewish menorah! He watched it sink beneath the edge of the world until it and the flames were gone, and the sky had returned to normal. Everywhere he looked the bright ghost of the menorah remained etched on his vision until that too faded away.

His eyes were still on the sky when he first heard them, their fractured holy songs punctuated by the snap of whips. Even in the poor light he could see the wounds on their backs, but it took a few moments before he realized these were self-inflicted. A group of perhaps one hundred men of varying ages were staggering into the church square clad in rough white linen from the waist down. From the waist up they were naked and bleeding, their right hands gripping multi-strand whips they lashed across their own backs every few paces. Following them, at a respectful distance, was a crowd of hundreds more. They carried torches, praised God, and lifted their hands up in reverence.

Frederic looked down and realized the people who had been in the church now flooded into the square, joined by more from the adjoining side streets. With new energy, he staggered down the stairs to join them. By now the flagellants had formed a circle in the middle of the square. Their leader held up his bloody whip and shouted, "Join in! Join in all you who have sinned! Share the sufferings of our Lord! Share them for the payment of our terrible sins! Join in to the sufferings of our Lord who died for you! Take the pain of Jesus upon your back! Take the scourge of Christ upon you! Join in!" With that the men in the circle lashed themselves in unison.

One man crumpled to his knees as fresh blood streamed down his back. A woman rushed forward, pressed her hands into the flow, and smeared the blood over her face. She collapsed on the ground in ecstasy. The crowd praised God and lifted their hands towards the sky.

Frederic saw the lash in the man's hand had small iron nails. He turned to the leader. "I saw a Jewish menorah burning across the sky!"

"Yes!" The leader said. "We all saw it! A sign from God! A burning menorah, that's what it was! You are a prophet! God has given you this understanding! Join us! Join us and be purified through the sufferings of Christ! Join us in removing the scourge of Judaism. Join us!"

"They have poisoned our wells!" someone shouted out. "They have brought the plague!"

"They have killed our Lord!" said another.

The crowd shouted its rage and Frederic shouted his.

Landing

A strobe flashed throughout the ship; the landing was imminent. Teracia yellowed, pushed herself into the restraining sponge and tried to relax. It nearly engulfed her, but she still had a clear view of the panel on the opposite wall. It showed the descent in units of time. She would spend the next hour immobilized, protected by this living restraint. Chief Navigational Officer Baronth was down, putting the landing in the hands of his protégé, Xyros. Teracia wondered at the wisdom of this, but planetary landings were automated. He only had to initiate the sequence.

As the display decreased, she felt the ship shudder and lurch. It was unnerving. Her memories of atmospheric turbulence where all contained within in her PDM, experienced in occupations from her distant past, so she could not draw upon them now. She knew the ship's hull would be super-heated and it would appear as a fireball to anything watching from below, to Homines. That was one part of the contamination that Prostallen could not avoid, but it was unlikely that any homines would understand what it was seeing. If the landing went smoothly, the ship would disappear into the depths of the ocean, out of sight and out of mind.

It was now a matter of seconds. She braced herself even though she knew she was safe, but the impact was far greater than she expected, and the sponge nearly lost her. As it was, it pulled her deeper into itself, cutting her off from the rest of the room. A strange acidic smell leaked into the water from within the sponge. She remembered accounts of similar situations when the animals had released stress hormones during rough landings.

Teracia wiggled her way out of the sponge and surveyed the damage. The panel display, normally protected behind a thin sheet of transparent glass, had broken through. It was now powered off and detached from the wall. Various bits of personal debris and a dozen stunned fish floated around her room. She fixed the panel back into its place and turned it on. A few gestures later, she was looking at the view outside the ship.

Steam engulfed the ship. This meant Xyros had attempted a manual dive and had failed. The ship was now on the ocean surface, in plain view of any homines in the vicinity. It was worse than that though. A landing of this type would have caused a serious disturbance in the surface of the ocean itself. This was a large ship.

Tsunami

Kanaloa, god of the ocean realm, had sent them a gift. Perhaps. Iekika, the young Hawaiian shaman, was wary. A baby whale had beached itself and lay in shallow water by the sand bar. In the twilight it looked like a giant black slug. A runner had been sent to get the King. In the distance, Iekika could see him coming with his sons. Until they extracted the teeth, no one could touch the animal.

The women were building fires for light, their daughters bringing wood from the forest. The tribe would have to butcher the young whale at night. By morning the tide would be in and could wash the animal back out to sea.

The old king lumbered up to the carcass and grinned. He had a small necklace of whale's teeth he wore as a status symbol on ceremonial occasions. This would add to that. It was a good day. He nodded to his oldest son, who took out a knife and removed the teeth. They said no prayers. They gave no thanks.

Iekika gritted his teeth. His grandfather's death earlier that year had made him shaman, but the King had no respect for a holy man so young and now all but ignored the rituals. There was great peril in offending the gods, but this king didn't care.

The young prince finished extracting the teeth, dropping the last into a white abalone shell and then presenting it to his father. Everyone cheered and then one of them gasped. The man pointed at sky. A large fiery ball had appeared on the horizon.

"Pele!" someone gasped. Everyone dropped their tools ran screaming away from the whale.

The king looked at Iekika. "Do something!" he said and then he too ran.

Iekika stood alone before the whale, trembling. The sky was now ablaze. He had never seen Pele so angry, but why? His body erupted in sweat and he had to fight the urge to run like the others. The whale had been a gift from Kanaloa. Why was Pele so angry? Was this some kind of conflict between the gods? Regardless, he would have to deal with the more immediate threat. Iekika took several deep breaths and then found the knife the young prince had dropped. He cut a piece of the blubber away from the animal and held it up to the sky.

"This we will give to you, Pele, god of fire!" he shouted. He ran down the beach toward the lava flow that Pele had laid down during the time of his grandfather.

It took Iekika an hour of hard climbing to reach the highest fissure. During the ascent his feet were cut in several places by shards of volcanic rock, but he knew this only by the blood and not through pain. There had also been at least one burn, but he knew only by the smell. He had ventured too close to one of the lower fissures and part of the thick callus on his foot had smoked, but again he had not felt pain. Shamanic purpose had driven him and kept his mind focused and the pain away. It wasn't until he had offered the blubber into the highest fissure that he turned back to the sky. The flames were gone.

Now Iekika felt the pain. Not only were his feet injured, but there was a rawness to the back of his legs and his underarms not unlike what he had felt as a child when he had spent too much time running in the hot sun. But this was not the sun; this was Pele.

Dawn was breaking by the time Iekika limped back to the

beach. He found the others butchering the whale. The high tide had pushed the carcass further up the beach. He stood at a distance and watched, too tired to join in, nauseated by the smell of the now rotting animal, but elated his small offering had had its desired effect. His action was not part of shamanic tradition; it was sacred improvisation. His grandfather had told him sometimes he would have to do this, sometimes he would have to trust his instincts.

Movement on the shoreline caught his eye. The water was pulling out, way out. In the distance he could see some of the larger fish thrashing about where they had been abandoned by the waves. *Kai mimiki,* he realized. *A tidal wave is coming*! Had he angered Kanaloa by making an offering to Pele?

"*Kai mimiki*!" he shouted to the others pointing out to sea. "*Kai mimiki*!" But they either didn't hear or they ignored him. He shouted again and this time they heard him and waved back. Then one of them looked out to sea, shouted to the others, and they dropped what they were doing and ran in panic towards him.

Higher ground was a long way back from the beach. Iekika looked around for the largest and strongest looking palm he could find. This is what his grandfather had told him. "If you are on beach and you see the *kai mimiki* run to higher ground or climb up the strongest highest palm you can find because the *kai e'e* will come and it will wash away everything." Most of the larger palms on this part of the beach were old and did not look strong but he found one that had a better look about it, a little shorter perhaps, but stronger. He began his ascent and realized that the damage to his feet was greater than he thought. The cuts and the burns had reduced their flexibility and he could not grip the trunk, as he wanted to. He felt himself slip and then his foot struck something. He looked down only to see the surprised face of the king.

"Sorry," he said and then pulled around the backside of the palm to let the king past.

"Do not follow me!" the king said as he climbed past Iekika.

Iekika looked around to find another tree but what he saw were the other villagers trying to scramble up anything available. Then he looked seaward as the wall of water picked up the remains of the whale carcass and bore it right at him. He threw himself into the air and landed in a cushioning mass of putrid blubber.

Singer

Commander Prostallen barely acknowledged Teracia. She was just another song chaser, one of the half dozen on board. But less than two hours after the landing she was summoned to him. Could it be her connection to Derath, she wondered? Could the young fahr have told Prostallen of her desire to scuttle the mission? She took a moment to get the yellow under control. Showing some was to be expected. She was being summoned into the commander's presence without explanation, but she must also appear to be under control.

"I checked the records," he said as she swam into the room. "You are the first femfahr song chaser in recorded history. Did you know that? It never occurred to me in a millennium a femfahr would apply for the position. I couldn't believe my luck, actually. Of course, there is the whole matter of your annoying interest in the resident bipeds. Could that be the real reason you came on board I wonder?" His gills rippled. "I know about your qualifications, but we'll let that pass for now. I have a special task for you, a task not unrelated to your concern for Homines."

Teracia swallowed. "Commander?"

"You have, by now, noticed that we are on the surface of this body of water and not below it. It's one of the poorest landings I've ever experienced, and I am not pleased. Whatever possessed young Xyros to attempt a manual landing I don't know. As I'm sure you realize, it leaves us in full view of your little bipeds, should any be in the vicinity. That increases the likelihood of contamination. We need to get underway and under the water as soon as possible, but there is a problem." He paused and studied Teracia.

""A problem, Commander?" she said.

45

Prostallen flattened his gills. "Small leaks caused by Xyros's incompetence, not serious enough to affect the integrity of the ship we think but with increased depth and pressure one never knows. However, the biggest concern is this damage could allow for sound leakage. The problem is in the observation deck. Now, any fahr who ventures there is at risk of unintended and unfiltered exposure to song. Not immediately. The landing has sterilized the area around the ship, but it's only a matter of time before singers arrive so we have to get the deck sealed."

"I see," said Teracia feeling relieved, "and because I can't be impaired, I'm the logical choice to do that job?"

"Exactly. And we must keep this quiet. I don't want crew members straying in the observation deck in search of virgin song. It's far too tempting."

"Understood, Commander."

The observation deck itself was submerged, about three fahr lengths beneath the surface. Teracia wondered what she would see there. An ocean surface zone, under normal circumstances, should be full of life, but the ship's awkward landing had super-heated the water for hundreds of fahr lengths in every direction. Not much would have survived. It would take a day or two before the creatures, those that had been further out, found their way into the area around the ship. The boiled remains of those that had lived there would provide a feast for the scavengers among them. How quickly they would arrive depended on their mobility and no one yet knew how fast these creatures could move.

The ship's internal water had the typical yellowish cast of Centrix and it was thick. The ocean water of this planet was thinner and mostly a translucent blue, at least at depths where it was exposed to stellar light. It should be easy to see if one was leaking into the other and where this was occurring but there was nothing obvious. This meant that the leaks were small and easy to fix, providing she could find them. Sound would be the better tool for this. Teracia swam over to the panel and switched on the filter's diagnostic program.

Everything was functioning which meant no damage had been done to the filters. Now she would need to turn them off and that meant any crew members in the area surrounding the dome would have to leave.

Prostallen had been discreet when he had given her this task, but it was still possible some members of the crew knew where she was and what she would be doing. If anyone guessed that she would have to turn the filters off, then there was a risk they would linger around hoping for "accidental" exposure to virgin song, especially after what had happened to Derath. This planet had the potential to be a major find, but only if Prostallen could keep his crew filtered and disciplined. The commander may be an addict, but he was a corporate loyalist and great profit could be made here. Teracia made the call.

After about twenty minutes, a filtered security guard appeared at the entrance. "I have cleared the area around the observation dome," he said.

"Then I would get yourself well away from here too," Teracia said. "There are no guarantees a personal filter will protect you."

"I am a professional, Mamini," the guard said.

"I'm sure you are," she said, her gills rippling. "You have about ten minutes to be out of the area."

After he had left, Teracia turned her attention back to the dome. She tried to listen while the filters were still on. There was song out there, rendered indistinct by the filters, but there nonetheless. There was also something she could feel, a presence at a low frequency. While in orbit, the high-resolution surface scans had given them occasional glimpses of large animals coming to the surface to linger momentary, passing the tops of their bodies through the atmosphere. On a few occasions, they'd observed these animals throwing themselves out of the water to crash back down hard on the water's surface. These were huge beasts. No one yet knew if they could sing but something had to be generating those low tones.

Once the security guard had been gone for about fifteen minutes, she moved again to the control panel. When the filters were off, she would have to discipline her hearing, trying to isolate the sounds of leaks from the songs she was about to hear. Work now, enjoyment later, she told herself and gestured to the panel.

The dome shook. Whatever was generating this sound was close and powerful. She wondered how it could have survived the ship's impact, but then realized an animal of that size might have the speed to swim into the area from the outside after the waters had cooled. Still she could see nothing and tried to put it out of her mind as she listened for the telltale hissing sounds of small leaks.

There were five and, by the sounds, easy fixes. She used her echolocation to find each one and apply the sealant. It wasn't until she had finished the last one that she looked into the ocean again.

It was almost motionless and parallel to the ship. The eye that met hers was on the side of the head, set above and towards the back of a huge black jaw encrusted with what looked like hard fungal growth. The shape of the jaw gave no hint to the animal's diet and there were no visible gills. How did it breathe? The jaw ended near a long slender flipper, black on the top and white on the bottom, a color scheme that matched what she could see of the animal's body. This body was so long that the end of it was not visible in the window. She assumed some kind of fluke but could not see it. The animal just hung there gazing at her as fascinated with her as she was with it. Then she noticed the silence. There was no song now, and she wondered if this was the source of what she had heard earlier. If so, the ship was not big enough.

Song

With the repairs done, the ship dove just deep enough to be undetectable from the ocean surface. The fragile wooden vessels that Homines used to navigate their seas hugged the coasts and were rarely seen this far out in the open ocean, but on the off chance one found its way to their location, it would pass overhead none the wiser. For the next half-century, the expedition would collect, catalogue, record, and study the singers on this rich world, a world they had now dubbed "Planet Song." When they were done, they would return to Centrix with a trove of songs and singers large enough to make even the lowest ranked among them wealthy. But before all that, they would have what most of them had been waiting for since the discovery of Planet Song's oceans: taste.

Just the idea made Teracia's ballow go white.

Prostallen noticed. "You don't like this?"

"I'm sure everyone will enjoy themselves," she said.

"Except you?"

"I'll be fine, Commander. I'm concerned about that one song."

"Which one?"

"We haven't isolated them, so I can't yet point to a specific song or animal. But, if you remember Commander, when Derath was exposed we were still in orbit. The feed was from an omni-directional atmospheric microphone flying above the surface of the ocean. So even with distance and atmospheric distortion, he was still in the care of the menders for three weeks after his experience."

"It was his first exposure to virgin song. Many have extreme reactions the first time. He's fine."

"Is he?" Teracia asked.

"Yes. And lucid."

Teracia could feel Prostallen studying her. She had flattened her gill slits and her ballow continued to pale.

"I'll tell you what," he said, "if you're concerned, I'll put you on the filters. You can turn them on if things get out of hand. Just remember the whole point behind this is celebration. For many of the fahr on this crew this is all about taste; it's all about that huge rush that comes with virgin song. Some of them have waited thousands of years for this. They will not be happy if they are denied and neither will I."

Taste would be had in the observation dome. That way the

participants would see the singers and hear them, but the location concerned Teracia. The dome was the ship's weak link. The filtration system there was compromised. Designing the dome for observation meant that light and sound were allowed in. Designing a filtration system to keep sound out of a space designed to allow it in meant certain compromises. There had, however, been no recorded instances of dome filter failure and it seemed to be working during the repairs. She tried to relax.

Commander Prostallen divided the crew into groups of thirty. Those lucky enough to be in the first group had arranged themselves in two floating half circles facing the ocean, their gill slits rippling, and their diaphragms engorged. Prostallen, his own diaphragm enclosed in a personal filter, swam in ragged little circles close the filter panel. His excitement was also palpable.

Teracia could hear the muted songs of the various singers through the filter, but with none of the low-frequency tones she had heard earlier. She waited for Prostallen's signal. He gave it, a quick slicing motion through the water. She disengaged the filter but did so slowly, thinking gradual impairment and arousal was preferable. Prostallen looked at her sharply, pinking as he did. He made the slicing motion again. She sped up the disengagement.

Songs filled the observation dome with varying degrees of intensity. Everyone in the group drifted into free float, their gill slits rippling. Their ballows were pulsating and changing hues, but the effect was less than Teracia expected. Impairment, while evident, was not extreme. This was a much tamer version of what she had seen in the past, but it took Teracia a few moments before she realized why. These fahr were being exposed to virgin song in a live ocean environment, not to optimized loops, so the intensity of the various songs depended on the distance the singers were from the ship. This was a much more organic experience.

Teracia relaxed. This was less intense than she had expected and, although she could not share in the arousal and the high that the others were experiencing, she enjoyed the unfiltered exposure to the ocean's ecosystem. The area around the ship was rich in fish, and though their songs were simple and repetitive, the mix was charming. There were larger animals that sang to each other in playful chirps and squeals; these would bring a high price when sold into the menageries on Centrix. She looked over at Prostallen who was pleased that his crew members were enjoying the experience. Teracia knew the commander planned to join the next group, a group composed of the ship's senior officers. They would have a longer exposure. He would have his taste, perhaps multiple times if his reputation was any indication.

The first thing she noticed was a slight blurring to her vision. Then everything, even the water, throbbed. The note was so low her diaphragm could not detect it. Prostallen went into an immediate free float, his gills rippling, and his sagging ballow pulsing random colors.

Deafening squeals, thick hollow calls, and stuttered clicks - ricocheted around the room. Teracia spun around and looked at the others. They were throwing themselves at the bulkhead and into the window. Outside the ship, she caught a quick glance of the creature she'd seen earlier, floating upside down in the distance.

She hurried to the filter control panel but one of the others arrived first, crashing into it. The panel buckled and went dark. The fahr that hit it bounced away twitching and convulsing, blood clouding the surrounding water. Teracia turned and looked back into the room. In every direction fahr were in distress, bleeding and broken. Those who could still swim continued throwing themselves into the bulkhead and windows.

Commander Prostallen was in a state of total ecstasy but, otherwise, appeared to be unharmed; his personal filter protecting him from the extremes the others were experiencing. Teracia dragged him to the door, opened it, and pushed him through into the filtered passageway beyond. She closed the door, sealed it, and turned to face the chaos.

Things were slowing. Only a few of the remaining fahr still swam. She caught glimpses through water now clouded with blood. A severed tentacle floated past her. She vomited and then tried to regain control by drawing water through her gills, but there was too much blood in the water. It only made her retch again. She found a corner where the blood had not yet reached and took several long pulls, calming herself. A quick swim through the rest of the room confirmed the worst; every fahr within it was dead or dying.

She went to the COM system to call the menders, but the creature's continued singing stopped her. How long would it go on? Until the song was over calling the menders was pointless. Even if they wore personal filters, they would be too impaired to help. She swam to the window and looked out at the creature. It had no idea of the carnage it had just caused.

Vortex

Prostallen had instructed Teracia to filter the most lethal frequencies but leave the power of the song intact. She had done that. The song would not kill him, not immediately.

She swam into his quarters and gave him the loop. His diaphragm was engorged, and his gills were rippling but his ballow was purple as if he felt he had to apologize for his arousal.

But he did not apologize.

"Is it safe?" he asked.

She nodded. "It's a powerful song. Be careful how you use it."

He swam over to his loop player and, with a wave of his tentacle, dismissed her.

She waited until she was outside his quarters before allowing her gills to ripple.

The song was insidious. It sucked him into a vortex of overstimulation and arousal out of which he could not swim. Every time he tried for normalcy, his body and his mind screamed for the arousal and stimulation only the song could provide. Sobriety became a monotone hell. He put off his down time by one hundred years during the return voyage to expose himself again and again. The menders had to drag their blubbering commander into the stasis chambers.

Act Two: The Preparation

Crowd Control

Serving as part of the Centrix constabulary was mandatory for Fahr citizenship and had to be done during one's ninth occupation. Roont was nearing the end of his time as a niner.

The members of the constabulary were required to be song deaf during their service, which meant the continuous wearing of personal filters. And not just any personal filter; these were constabulary-issue filters known for their ability to cloak the wearer in a bubble of absolute song silence. All sound was filtered and passed though as monotonal. Roont had spent nine hundred years listening to a single pitch with no possibility of impairment or arousal, a near-millennium of alert drudgery.

Today's assignment was the one he liked the least, crowd control while Chancellor Agastin gave one of his public pronouncements or, to be more precise, gave song. No one much cared what the chancellor had to say. It was all about the loops. The chancellor knew this and kept his words few. Roont's first task was to float, pitch wand in hand, waiting for the inevitable chaos.

The chant started as soon as the crowd saw Agastin's transport, descending through a cloud of golden jellyfish. "Give song, give song," they intoned as the chancellor swam out of the transport. With a broad sweeping gesture, he motioned them into silence.

"Good fahr," he said, gills rippling. "I wonder how many of you know of this day in our history. One hundred million years ago today our ancestors found this world, realized that it had all the attributes to be our new home and set in motion the processes that would make it habitable. So, we have reason to celebrate!"

"Give song, give song!" the crowd responded.

Roont tensed up. This was a big event even if the crowd didn't care about its historicity. Agastin would respond accordingly.

The chancellor inflated his ballow deep gold, blending in with the surrounding jellies. The crowd cheered.

"I have, in my menagerie, a family of opedasaurs," he said.

"Give song, give song!"

Roont tried to remember which animal this was, but he could not. Not that it mattered. Agastin did not keep animals that would not arouse and impair him personally, and if they would do that to him, an elite fahr engineered to be resistant to impairment, they would seriously affect common fahr, even filtered. Roont braced himself.

"And so, in honor of the one hundred-million-year anniversary of finding Centrix." Agastin gestured to the transport, and the roof opened, releasing the loops. "Accept this gift from those who love you!" He turned, swam to the transport and got inside, on his way before the crowd snagged any of the loops.

It began. The loops' natural buoyancy drew them toward the Centrix atmosphere, rising through the water. With a crowd this size, few of them would make it to the surface. The fahr surged upwards, jostling each other.

"Any of you know anything about opedasaurs?" Roont asked his fellow niners as he watched the scene unfold.

"They're marine reptiles and there's a territorial component to their songs. Strong stuff. Can be bad news depending on who's listening."

"So, wands up?"

"Always."

Of all the elite, only Agastin provided virgin loops this strong and all the common fahr loved him for it.

The ones that got to the loops first were the most vulnerable. They fed them into their players and then drifted off, floating in out-of-control ecstasy and into everyone else's way. It was the quickest route to injury Roont could think of, short of actual combat, and it was already happening. The niners surged forward grabbing the floaters and stiff pushing them towards the ocean floor and away from the lusting frenzy at the surface. Some of them were trailing blood as they went down.

Roont pulled his attention back to the surface and realized opedasaur song was bad news. Several fahrs had gone rogue, reacting to the song not with floating ecstasy, but with song rage, attacking the hapless floaters. He rushed to the surface only to have one rager meet him head on. One deft fin movement got Roont out of the way and a quick flick of his clasper brought the pitch wand against the rager's diaphragm. The resulting scream made it through Roont's filter intact. It took a moment to shake it off.

When he did, he found the rager floating beside him. The fahr was studying the wound to his diaphragm, a white flash-point mark against the teal background. The sound shock had robbed him of his high.

"Did you have to do that?" the rager asked pointing at the wand.

"You were charging me."

"Was I?"

"Yes."

"All I wanted was the song stone."

"It's my duty to inform you opedasaur song is now restricted in your case."

"Couldn't afford it anyway," the rager said, his ballow mauving. "Thanks for stopping me. I wouldn't want to hurt anyone. I didn't know I'd react that way. I always come out when the chancellor gives song. It's a wonderful thing he does for us, you know? Very generous. But that was the first time I've ever gone rogue." He rubbed the injury on his diaphragm.

Roont pointed to the menders who were treating the wounded on the ocean floor. "They can give you something for that," he said.

"No charges?"

"No one gets charged when the chancellor gives song."

"Yeah, he wouldn't let that happen, would he? He's the best chancellor we've ever had," the rager said, beginning a slow painful swim toward the menders.

Most of the crowd was now floating in ecstasy, a state they would remain in for hours. The other niners had subdued the few remaining ragers. There were multiple injuries.

Roont grabbed a floater who was bleeding from a wound above his diaphragm and towed the oblivious fahr to a mender. The mender, an older fahr who showed the discolored scales of song addiction, rippled his gills when he saw the wounded floater.

"Well, first off, he won't be needing this," the mender said pulling the song loop out of the floater's player and tucking it behind his own filter. The menders wore the same constabulary-issue filters as the niners but, unlike the niners, they could remove them when their job was done. Roont had watched them steal loops from unconscious floaters countless times, the principal perk of their job. The mender gave Roont a knowing look and applied a balm to the wound. "Don't you have something else you should do?" he said to Roont.

Herding. Once the initial frenzy was over, there was still the matter of taking care of hundreds of song-stoned-ecstasied floaters. Left alone some could stray miles from the site and even get dragged out into the open ocean before they regained their faculties. So, the niners took up positions around the floaters and kept them safe, prodding them back into the group when they strayed. It was boring, irritating and had the unfortunate side effect of reminding the niners of how much fun they were missing. Roont took up his position on the periphery of the floaters and looked back at the menders.

He had considered becoming one when his constabulary stint finished but he'd had his fill of crowd control. He wanted the perk but there was another way of getting it. One could sign up for a pet-collecting expedition.

Agastin

The Chancellorship Monolith was a three fahr-length high slab of granite with one smooth face. On that face was an engraved image of a male and female fahr—pre-Modificate—floating before an ancient coral reef on Aquafahr, the original Fahr home world. The image was so eroded one had to know what one was looking for to recognize the figures. Chancellor Agastin knew what to look for and it always reminded him of how little patience he had with the ancient practices of his race.

This one was most annoying. Agastin would float in place before the Monolith for hours in total silence. The petitioners would be in the room before him but unable to speak because of protocol. The ancients, who devised this system, thought significant time spent reflecting in the presence of absolute authority would lessen the frequency of inconsequential matters being brought before it. In practice, everyone who sought an audience with the chancellor considered their particular issue to be of utmost importance. They would float before him for hours to make their particular point, keeping him away from his precious songs. His stasis time was coming, and he wanted to enjoy them while he could.

Agastin was familiar with the six individuals before him. They had been in recent broadcasts. Their concerns had something to do with the acquisition of tracks of ocean floor for the extension of a public park. Why he, the chancellor, would be involved in such a decision he had no idea. This was the province of municipal politicians well below his rank, but his minders had scheduled this audience. In their judgment, something about this case required his attention. He would have their hearing if they were wrong.

As the prolonged silence ended, the first of the six swam forward. His ballow displayed the mauvy purple of contriteness. *He's already feeling apologetic*, thought Agastin. *Surely, I haven't waited four hours to hear a confession.*

"Lord Chancellor," he said. "Thank you for this audience."

"I trust the time has been well waited."

"It has, Lord Chancellor."

"Then please tell me your name and your concern."

"My name is Wassot, and I and my colleagues represent The Citizen's Coalition of Greater Centrix City, Lord Chancellor."

"And the concern?"

Wassot's ballow turned a deeper shade of the purple and his gill slits did a sloppy ripple. "As you may know, Lord Chancellor, The Citizen's Coalition is working towards the expansion of the existing civic park system."

"Which is a matter not normally brought before the Chancellorship Monolith."

"This is true, Lord Chancellor, except the expansion we have in mind concerns you."

"How so?"

Wassot drew a long stream of water through his gills. "The proposed expansion," he said, "borders on the Chancellor's Menagerie."

"The Menagerie?"

"Yes, the proposed swim way surrounding the park would be next to the Chancellor's Menagerie for several hundred fahr lengths."

"And?"

If anything, Wassot's ballow was now an even deeper purple. "The creatures that are kept in the Chancellor's Menagerie are quite vocal."

"They're singers, Wassot," Agastin said. "Get to the point, please."

"Well, Lord Chancellor, as singers they have the potential to arouse and impair park users."

Agastin stared at Wassot as his ballow pinked. He then looked at Wassot's five companions who were now also displaying deep purple. "I hope, Wassot, that you are not about to make a request of me you will regret.

"Wassot talked quickly. "It's a logistical issue, Lord Chancellor.

There are two ways in which we can solve this problem. The first would be to erect large filtration barriers between the Chancellor's Menagerie and the park which is by far the most expensive and unsightly option. The second is to have the menagerie keepers restrict the movements of the singers so they cannot approach the area next to the park. I'm sure you will agree, Lord Chancellor, that the second option makes the most sense."

Agastin's ballow was now inflated and approaching rage red. He did his best to restrain himself. "The Chancellor's Menagerie has been designed to provide the singers we have collected with the most natural environments possible. These environments encourage the natural production of song as it would occur if these singers were on their home worlds. A lot of time and research has gone into getting it right. And, as you well know, Wassot, I have been generous with the Fahr public in providing loops of these singers. Everyone enjoys it. I will not be altering the menagerie to accommodate a public park expansion."

Wassot floated in silence before Agastin, but the hue of his ballow was changing. Purple was morphing into red. It was rare that any common fahr would dare display anger in front of the Chancellorship Monolith. Agastin's peripheral vision assured him his security fahr were in place.

Wassot began carefully. "With all due respect, Lord Chancellor, it is common knowledge the Chancellor's Menagerie is, at the present time, far from reaching its full capacity. Less than half of it is being used to accommodate singers. At the moment some of those singers are housed adjacent to the purposed swim way, but given the space available, it would be a simple matter to move them outside the arousal zone. The Citizen's Coalition of Greater Centrix City is prepared to cover the expenses of any such move."

"Are they?" asked Agastin. "And do you suppose, Wassot, that the Lord Chancellor of all Fahr, the near perpetual head of state for our great race, would have any actual need of financial assistance? I am fully capable of funding anything I choose to do. I choose not to change The Chancellor's Menagerie because it suits my purposes to have it the way it is."

"Well, Lord Chancellor, strictly speaking, The Chancellor's Menagerie belongs to all fahr."

Agastin had heard enough. His ballow was bursting, inflamed with the deepest red. He rose well above the heads of the six petitioners. His tentacles extended and, with all eight claspers spread as widely as possible, he gestured an arc above their heads. Security staff rushed forward to grab the petitioners. Once they were restrained, Agastin studied Wassot's diaphragm. *A pity*, he thought. *It looks to be in good shape.*

"Put them all in song isolation," he said to the security staff. "And that one," he pointed at Wassot, "will know permanent silence."

Wassot's ballow receded into his head, turning fear yellow. Chancellor Agastin had just ordered his diaphragm surgically removed.

Safe

Occeane, the Holy Son, disliked going out in public. At best, he would have a few moments before they ruined everything for him, but it was still predawn and few fahr would be in the park. He looked out the transport window. Suspended globes of tiny iridescent fish gave off a shimmering light, enough for navigation but not for sightseeing. They would be released at dawn, when the planet rotated into the light of its star, and then recaptured at dusk, lured back to the globes by food.

"Pull over here," Occeane told the transport driver, "and stay in the area. When they gather come and get me. Did you bring the loops?"

"Yes, Holy Son," the driver said, coming to a stop.

"Good. I never think to do it," Occeane said.

He got out of the transport just as the edge of the star hit the horizon. The fish were released, and they swam off into the park in a jerky sparkling school. Occeane tried following them. If he could get into their midst, he might be less visible, but the fish were too quick. The Fahr were built for floating, not swimming. He spread his fins out, floated about four fahr lengths above the ocean floor, and turned away from the star rise.

With the ruddy dawn light now behind, the aqua vista spread out before him. The rays shone through the yellow water giving an orange tint to the submerged mountain range at the far end of the park. He rarely rested his eyes on such a sight. Parts of the range appeared to be covered in clouds, but these were most likely schools of fish, congregations of jellies, or chemicals rising from the thermal vents, perhaps all three. The peaks were too far away to know for sure. Where there was no obstruction, he could see bands of spiky vegetation and, nearer the water's surface, rainbow coral reefs self-arranged in terraces. This was home to some of the planet's few native singers and off limits to the common fahr. The Holy Son could go there if he wished and often did, but the best views were from this end of the park.

Occeane looked up where ragged volcanic cones broke through and emerged into the Centrix atmosphere. These were among the few bits of dry land on the planet. Swirling tides driven by Centrix's three moons played havoc with the shoreline, grinding down the volcanic rock into coarse black beaches, then sculpting the sand into dark mushroom-like formations before the storms came and washed them away again. Nothing much lived there except small sand crabs and, further up, yellow green mosses and rusty lichens clinging to the basalt. It still amazed him they had found planets where complex ecosystems had evolved on land. The Giver was inscrutable. The Holy Son allowed his gill slits to ripple with pleasure. All this visual wonderment came at no cost to Fahr physiology, unlike that which was heard and not seen, but he knew he wouldn't be able to enjoy it for long.

They gathered.

Everywhere he swam the common fahr would defer to him, but

his presence in any public place always meant a gathering above, below, and around him. They kept a respectful distance but were there waiting for him to act and cutting off his view of any sight he might want to enjoy. Visual stimulation was free of consequence, but he could never enjoy it for long. The gathering fahr would have expectations.

"Give song, give song," they began in their flat toneless voices.

Occeane was from the same genetic pool as the High Priest Barracute, engineered to be a mono-occupational mystic. He was an elite fahr, one of only four alive. That, in the common mind, meant that he was a bestower of songs. Never mind that he owned none of the singers and had no involvement in their collection. They expected it of him.

"Give song, give song," they repeated, their voices getting louder and the ballows on their foreheads showing a pinkish irritation.

The Holy Son looked for the transport and saw it coming in the distance. He extended his tentacles and made a wide arc above his head. His ballow inflated and displayed the gold of his elite status.

The toneless chanting stopped, and the gill rippling began. Occeane gestured to the transport as it came to a floating stop beneath and to the right of the assembled crowd. The driver pulled the latch on the roof and up they floated, thin buoyant silvery strands catching the red star shine as they rose. The crowd raced forward to snag them.

Occeane gestured the arc again to try getting the crowd's attention. "Good fahr," he said, "accept this gift from those who love you. But remember playing loops in public spaces is not permitted. Go home and enjoy your gift."

"Yes, Holy Son," they said, but the rippling in their gill slits betrayed their intent.

Occeane knew that loop players would come out as soon he departed, and the park would become the scene of arousal and public intoxication. He got into the transport. As they were pulling away from the scene, he looked at the driver. "Which loop did you choose?"

he asked.

"It's paranax song, Holy Son," the driver responded. "The singer is a small marine amphibian from Pont in the Daralique system. It gives a pleasant even warmth and mild intoxication. Everyone will be safe as you wished."

"But not satisfied," Occeane said.

"No, Holy Son. I saw no need to call the constabulary. No one will go rogue here and no herding will be required."

Occeane was silent. There was great risk to his personal popularity in what he was doing. The elite maintained their favor among the common fahr by giving song, but those songs had been gaining in intensity. Public intoxication and aggressive behavior had increased and, with it, addiction, but so had the popularity of Chancellor Agastin who was behind this policy of giving stronger song. Things were getting worse.

Da Vinci

Brother Francisco found the monastery's guest fascinating, but the Abbot did not share this. The old man's walking stick clacked against the stone floor, broadcasting his approach every time he was in the studio's hallway. Francisco steeled himself. It wasn't as if he could escape. The studio only had one door.

The Abbot entered and squinted as his eyes adjusted to the light. He glanced at Francisco and then brought his attention to the easel in front of him.

"Have you seen Maestro Leonardo today?" he asked Francisco.

"He is about, Lord Abbot," Francisco said.

"I meant in here," the old man said.

"No sir, not today."

"And the last time?"

"The last time I saw him in here?"

"Yes."

Francisco thought for a moment. "A week, maybe ten days. I'm not here all the time, Lord Abbot. I have other duties."

"Yes, you do, and apparently not enough of them." The Abbot reached out and touched the painting and then looked at his fingers. "Dust," he said. "There's an actual layer of dust on this. That's how long it's been since he's worked on this!"

"Should I find him for you?" Francisco said.

"So, I can listen to further excuses? No. I should have listened when they told me he was unreliable." The Abbot turned and clacked out of the room. "He'll get no more money out of me," he said as he left.

Brother Francisco stared yet again at the unfinished work. He had never seen anything like it. It was supposed to be a painting about the visit of the Magi to the Christ child and it was that, but there was a lot more going on in the work than one would expect in such a commission. It had some kind of battle going on in the upper right-hand corner, a ruined building on the left, and a strange rabble of finely drawn characters surrounding the Magi and the Virgin Mary with child. A self-portrait of Leonardo himself was on the lower right-hand side. These distractions fascinated Francesco, but they had not pleased the Abbot. The old man regarded them as unnecessary complications preventing Leonardo from finishing the work. The young artist had already established himself as a significant talent and the Abbot wanted to add his work to previously commissioned paintings by Botticelli and Lippi. Having a completed painting by the notoriously unproductive but brilliant young painter would enhance the status of the monastery. The work's size, at eight-foot square, would make it the largest easel painting the young Leonardo had ever attempted.

Payment for the commission was dependent on the completion of the work. Leonardo had spent an inordinate amount of time deciding on which themes, angles, colors, perspectives, and techniques to include in the painting. Once he had made those decisions, he seemed to lose interest. Now it sat, more or less abandoned, waiting for the artist to come back and apply more paint, paint he could not afford.

Brother Francisco found the young Leonardo sitting on a bench in the monastery garden. The artist was sketching what looked like some kind of machine though Francesco had never seen its like before.

"Maestro Leonardo," he said. "You have an interest in engineering?"

Leonardo looked up startled. "I uh... Yes. It is an interest of mine. Most certainly."

"Then I should show you something we have locked away," Brother Francesco said.

"Locked away?"

"One of the previous abbots—he died over a hundred years ago during the Black Death—had collected a curiosity. None of us knows what to make of it. Come. I'll show it to you."

Brother Francesco led the artist down the back stairs and into the wine cellar. There, in a corner, hung an ancient curtain. He pulled this back to reveal a dusty dark brown chest. Francesco opened this, and they both squinted at its contents in the poor light.

"What is it?" Leonardo asked.

Brother Francesco went to the table to fetch a candle and brought it over. "It appears to be some kind of mechanical animal," he said.

Ecstasy

The green came, opaque and trailing filaments. He wondered why these strands of algae would be moving, waving as if caught in a current. Then, as his mind became sharper, he realized he was surfacing and the current was his own circulation system. The vahume were there, gathering at the furthest edges of his peripheral vision. It was happening again. He would have to watch these tiny snails munching in interlacing patterns through the opaque green of his under lid for hours, back and forth, to and fro, with nothing else to occupy his mind but increasing irritation. It always left him in a foul mood when the surfacing was over.

Agastin was known for this, and, if they could, all the attendants avoided him when he surfaced. The vahume moved at the speed of sea slugs even when they were in a hurry, but they were always gone before he could see anything. What usually came into focus first was the face of a concerned attendant, the one who had lost the lottery. This time, however, he found Lord Greyling, the aging merchant of songs, the dealer in pets. Greyling's gills slits rippled from side to side.

"Happy surfacing, Chancellor" he said.

"Thith haa be'er be good, Greyling." Agastin slurred, his tongue trying to re-familiarize itself with the inside of his mouth.

"Only the sweetest song you'll ever hear."

Agastin stuck his long tongue out and whiplashed it around the space in front of him, avoiding the merchant. The tongue was coated with rancid accumulation of organic material and the action did little to displace it, but at least the flexibility of the organ was restored. Agastin knew the smell of it could overpower but Greyling pretended not to notice. Agastin pulled his tongue back into his mouth and studied Greyling. "You realize I have a well-deserved reputation for being disagreeable when surfacing?"

"I'm willing to take the risk," Greyling said. "The transmission came in just before they scheduled me to go on my pre-down fast. It was beautiful, just beautiful! I wanted to play it for you."

"What have you found?" Agastin asked.

"I could tell you, Chancellor, but the recording speaks for itself. It will be a wonderful thing to experience right after surfacing."

"But I haven't gone through the nutrition protocol," Agastin said.

"I'm sorry. Are you hungry, Chancellor?"

"No, no I'm not," Agastin admitted. He used to be ravenous after surfacing but not since entering elderhood. His body was now less active when he was awake and therefore stored more fat for the down. There was still the problem of the taste in his mouth, however, and eating something always helped. Then he noticed the bowl the lucky attendant had left behind. He picked up the sparkly-leafed plant it contained and stuffed it into his mouth. This wasn't food in the traditional sense of the word but the leaf's coating contained tiny bioengineered crustaceans. These would now roam through his mouth, consuming what had accumulated there, another ancient symbiotic relationship. The process was not unpleasant, a bit like teeth tickling and a tongue and gum massage rolled into one. When the crustaceans were finished, he would swallow them, though the nutritional value was minimal.

"I should tell you, Chancellor, that this recording is not virgin song," Greyling said.

"Not?"

"In its virgin state this song could do serious damage, especially to an elder who has just surfaced."

"I have never yet been exposed to virgin song I could not handle."

"I understand that, Chancellor, but Commander Prostallen transmitted this in a filtered state. For precautionary reasons, he said."

"Prostallen?"

"Yes, Chancellor."

"That old fool will expose himself to anything."

"All I know is that he sent it in a filtered state for the reasons he mentioned," Greyling said. "According to him, it's so dangerous they chose not to have a copy of the virgin song on board for fear it would get out and decimate the crew. It's that dangerous but it's also incredible."

"You've heard it?"

Greyling's gills rippled. "I sell nothing I haven't tried. But I should tell you there will have to be a strong therapeutic element when I go down this time."

Agastin studied Greyling. "Well, you've piqued my curiosity.

Perhaps this will make up for those damn vahume."

"I will have to wear a filter, Chancellor," Greyling said. "It would not be wise for this old body to re-expose itself to this loop. It's set to trigger at your command."

Agastin waited until Greyling strapped the filter around his abdomen, covering his diaphragm. Greyling was now deaf. Agastin inflated the bladder in his lower back and floated a few feet off the floor. It was his preferred listening posture, suspended away from anything fixed. That way he could both hear and feel the song with less distortion, nothing to get in the way. He gestured with his tentacle before pulling it into his body.

The room filled with deep resonant sounds, long looping melodies, and squeaks, squeals and stutters that seemed to chase each other right through the center of his being. His spine tingled and his various body bladders pulsed and vibrated, creating a wonderful building warmth. The visuals showed large graceful animals ranging over vast areas of pale blue sea. Sometimes they jumped out of the water and smacked their bodies against the surface. There were at least three distinct songs, each one long, complex, and amazing. When sung together, the counterpoint was dazzling. He felt the control of his gill slits, ballow, and fins slipping away. The songs became indistinct, lost in a fog of extreme ecstasy, releases coming and going then coming again.

It took Agastin an hour to get his bearings afterwards. When he did, he looked at Greyling. The old fahr was no longer wearing his filter and his gill slits were rippling. Agastin joined in. "How big is the ship?" Agastin asked.

"It's a scout class," Greyling replied, stilling his gills.

"Are there any on board?"

"They had space for a few but not enough for a breeding population. And they have to be heard in a group or the effect is, well, diminished. The males sing to the females or perhaps to the other males. We're not sure. But we know it's a social thing. The songs are group dependent."

"So, all you have is the recordings?"

"Yes. We'll need a much larger ship to bring them back in sufficient numbers."

Agastin allowed his gill slits to flatten, a sign of irritation but nothing more. Greyling expected an outburst of anger but that would accomplish nothing. Scout-class ships were standard for this kind of mission, and usually adequate for the task. It was too expensive to send bigger ships on pet expeditions, but they would need a bigger ship, perhaps even a military cruiser, to get these animals. That much was clear.

"And you will get these animals?" Agastin asked.

"I'm too old for interstellar travel," Greyling said. "And Prostallen is not well, so we will have to find..."

"Then I will go to this planet," Agastin said.

"You? But you're The Chancellor!"

"It has happened before. Chancellors have gone on interstellar journeys in the past."

"Not for about 200 million years!"

"They've been waiting for my son to take over for a millennium," Agastin said. "I can't understand why. He's half my age and spends more time down than I do, but maybe it's time, a trial run if you like." Agastin's gill slits rippled again. "I want to see and hear these creatures in their natural habitat."

"There are three small matters I should tell you about."

"Tell."

"Well, first if all, these animals are surface breathers, a kind of mammal. Probably evolved from a terrestrial animal that returned to the sea. The atmosphere of the planet is eighty percent nitrogen and twenty percent oxygen. Ours has less than twelve percent oxygen and it's unlikely they'll react well to its high methane content."

"So, we're going the have to construct an off-world environment for them?" Agastin's gills flattened again. "This could get pricey. What else?"

"The planet has a stage-one sapient species, primitive but still..."

"Aqueous or terrestrial?" Agastin asked.

"Terrestrial," Greyling said. "A small land-based biped. They call themselves Homines." His gill slits rippled. "They're not even aware their planet orbits a star; they think it's the other way around."

"Homines doesn't sound like much of a challenge."

"But they prey on the singers, some of the singers anyway—the smaller ones—not the one you heard today. The exobiologists think it only a matter of time before they can also kill the one you heard." Greyling said. "So that's the third thing. They have a vested interest in the animals."

"Possible conflict," Agastin said. "Could we trade with them?"

"It would go against The Will of the Giver. The technological gap is massive. There is no way we could interact with them that would not push their development."

"How massive?" Agastin asked.

"I haven't read all the reports, but the summary said the pace of their development was slow. No significant advances in the hundred years we were on the planet. They get around on boats driven by the vagaries of atmospheric wind and by riding on the backs of animals. Their weaponry is mechanical, with a few primitive chemical devices. No electronic or digital machines so they have no ability to communicate over distance. They're still in the tribal stage. Even if you wanted to negotiate, there'd be no unifying world government to talk to."

"And so, you're sure that this adaptive species is no threat?"

"Well, we were on the planet for a hundred years and came away unscathed."

"Were they even aware of us?"

"There was no actual contact. A few of them saw the ship arrive and depart, attributing what they saw to astrological phenomena and superstition. In between, we were operating too deep in their largest ocean for them to be aware of us, or we were watching them from orbit above the planet. They have no telescopes," Greyling said

"And how far away is this planet?"

"About eighty light years."

"That's close. Why didn't we know about this before?" Agastin asked.

"This was our second visit. The first time we went there the planet wasn't mature enough for singer evolution. That expedition originated from New Aquafahr," Greyling said.

"So that must have been over 100 million years ago?"

"About that, yes. It was one of the last pet expeditions before the migration."

New Aquafahr had been the Fahr second home world where they had lived for 2.5 billion years until it too had to be abandoned, like the original Aquafahr, when the star became unstable. "That would have been a long expedition," Agastin said.

"About four millennia."

Agastin did the math. Fahr ships travelled through interstellar space at about one third the speed of light, much slower when they were in a star system. "So, it is now about 300 years since the scout ship left the planet?"

"Yes."

"And it will take us 300 years to return there and get the animals?"

"Of course," Greyling said.

"That's 600 years for Homines to develop a telescope and a lot of other things. But, if they are as you say, 600 years will not be enough time for them to develop to the point where they could mount resistance, to the point where we would have to negotiate with them. A stealth mode would be advisable. Get in, take what we want while they're not looking, and leave. That way we also avoid contaminating their development," he said with a slight ripple to his gills. *As if that matters.*

There was a pause in the conversation. The images from the recording still lingered in the water between them.

"Can you handle a 300-year journey, Chancellor?" Greyling asked.

"I can handle it," Agastin said.

"You'll have to go down at least twice before you arrive. Some would choose to do it the whole way."

Agastin grunted. "Surfacing after 300 years and in space. No, thank you."

"It's not that bad. The lower gravity makes muscle recovery less painful than it would be on Centrix."

"I will need to be awake at least part of the time so I can get the logistics of this thing right." Agastin extended a tentacle and lightly touched Greyling's gill slits. "You've done me a great service, Greyling, and you will be well compensated. Now you had better rest before I have to have you carried out of here."

"Thank you, Chancellor," Greyling said before flattening his gill slits and swimming backwards out of the chamber.

Agastin watched the old merchant go and then restarted the loop. "Six hundred years will give us plenty of time to build a habitat," he mused aloud.

High Counsel

For at least three hours Greyling had floated before the Centrix High Counsel. Tradition held that any fahr who came before the council had to float before the Chancellor's Throne for at least one hour before he would be acknowledged, longer if the situation was weightier. So, he had now been there for over three hours, floating before the throne Agastin would soon vacate. Of course, the chancellor himself was not there. Probably he was on his third or even fourth time through the loop, but he would not have been expected to take the throne until after he had gone through the post-surfacing nutritional protocol. Under the circumstances, Greyling thought it unlikely Agastin had yet eaten anything.

Agastin's co-chancellor, the High Priest Barracute, now occupied the place of extreme authority. The holiest of all fahr, Barracute was the religious head of state and held the throne while Agastin was down. He was the only fahr, besides the military, who wore clothing, if a small gold breastplate emblazoned with the DNA double strand could be called clothing. Barracute was also the only fahr who was never seen in public without his ballow bright gold and inflated. This was a status thing, Greyling knew, but the few times Greyling had kept his own ballow inflated for extended periods had always resulted in a terrible headache. The old merchant wondered if the same was true of the high priest. If so, it would explain his testy disposition.

At the three hour and forty-five-minute mark, Barracute looked down on Greyling. "And so, my dear merchant, did you accomplish what we sent you to do?"

"Agastin has just been exposed to a filtered version of the longest and possibly the finest song we have ever collected," Greyling said. "Of course, he wants to hear it in its virgin state."

Barracute flattened his gills. "You're being coy, merchant. Is he or is he not going?"

"He plans to turn over his chancellorship to Petar." Greyling said glancing at Agastin's genetic son. He could see the rippling gills on all the other members of the counsel, but the high priest's remained flattened.

"That was a direct question, merchant. It requires a direct answer!"

"Yes, Your Holiness, he is going," Greyling said.

"And is there any chance he will survive the exposure?" Barracute asked.

"Commander Prostallen lost thirty members of his crew the day he gave taste. Those fahr were a lot younger than our chancellor, but they were also not bio-engineered for his level of resistance," Greyling said. "It's hard to say whether he will survive."

The high priest's gill slits did not budge. "So, we do not have certainty here?"

Greyling studied Barracute. He had to be careful how he answered the question. This was the high priest he was talking to. The Will of the Giver was the central factor in his life and what Prostallen had done defied that will. The whole matter hinged on how badly the priest wanted to be rid of Agastin.

"Commander Prostallen has taken a precaution to increase the likelihood of a satisfactory outcome," he said.

"A precaution?" Barracute asked.

"When they arrived at the planet, they discovered an early stage-one sapient species. Primitive and not detected until the ship was in orbit."

"So, they should have just turned around and come back," the high priest said. The bladder on his head was now a deeper red.

"Except, as you know Your Holiness, they discovered a rich trove of songs at about the same time. And, keeping in mind the cost of such expeditions and the rarity of such finds, they felt obligated to at least explore the possibility of extraction."

Barracute studied Greyling. "So, what is the other precaution you are referring to?"

"Perhaps precaution is the wrong word," Greyling said. "Perhaps advantage would be a better word because the Homines population—that's what the sapient species on this planet call themselves—were experiencing a push event when Prostallen's ship arrived. A virulent plague was devastating the population, doing serious damage to the social structure of their society. The exobiologists on board were able to determine that, before the plague, the Homines had been in a prolonged period of stagnation. So, the plague had an equal chance of destroying what they had or creating enough change for them to move forward "

"So?"

"The ship had a young and keen sapient-species specialist on board. His name is Derath. It was Derath's job, as you know, to determine whether the extraction process could proceed without violating The Will of the Giver, whether it could take place with no influence on the development of Homines. Prostallen allowed him to do his job," Greyling said.

"I don't understand," Barracute said.

"Under the circumstances, for Derath to do his job, certain small risks had to be taken. The Homines population had not evolved to the point where they were using any form of long-distance communication, wired or wireless, and so no form of digital or quantum data storage existed. Learning about them could not be done by hacking or listening in and so the young expert used animal mimics to gather data. This is standard procedure under the circumstances and it yielded the required information but..."

"But?" The bladder on the high priest's head looked as if it would burst.

"Derath did a rather poor job of designing the mimics and one them was discovered."

A silence settled over the room like deep silt. Barracute's ballow began the slow process of deflation. Greyling watched as the high priest studied the faces of each member of the counsel. He turned his attention back to Greyling.

"So, this push event, under the circumstances, will lead to this species moving forward at a rapid rate?"

"The probability is high, Your Holiness. Which will mean a high probability of resistance to the extraction. The proposal, as it currently stands, has the return expedition making use of a retrofitted military cruiser, with most of the military hardware removed to make room for a breeding population of the singers. That would make Agastin impaired and unarmed. So, if the song doesn't get him..."

Barracute held up his tentacle. He turned to the counsel. "When he arrives back on Centrix, we must ensure that this Derath, this sapient species specialist, never flies again. Do you all understand this?"

"Yes, Your Holiness," they intoned.

"Good. Within a few hundred years, and possibly before this council meets again, Chancellor Petar will head it. That should be a welcome change. I assume that each of you will give him all the help he needs. As you know, I must now enter the pre-down fast. I intend to spend that time in prayer and ask that you do not interrupt me. If you need to consult anyone regarding matters of faith, Occeane can assist you. I now call this meeting of the High Counsel to a close."

Barracute touched his breastplate and made the full open-clasped gesticulation over the other members of the counsel. Greyling caught the ripple in his gill slits just before he left the room. The others then swam out behind Barracute.

Greyling felt a twinge of guilt for sacrificing Derath in this way, but only a twinge. He had told the high priest and the others what they wanted to hear. There was no conceivable way a race as primitive as Homines could evolve fast enough to offer serious resistance. And the ship would be armed. Oh yes, it would be armed. In less than a millennium, Agastin would return, intact, with the biggest prize in the history of his company. And the lucrative relationship between Song Corp and The Chancellorship would continue.

Occeane

Teracia had not seen the Holy Son in 650 years and yet it was as if nothing had changed. He was still the quiet, dignified regal fahr she had known since childhood. Aging, if it had occurred at all, was minimal, few mottled scales perhaps, a few more winkles around the gills. She warmed at the sight of him.

"So, he feels indebted to you?" Occeane said.

"Prostallen believes I saved his life," Teracia confirmed. "All I did was to push him into the corridor outside the observation dome, where the filters were still functional. He would have survived in any case. He was wearing a personal."

"And he has no suspicion you later tried to kill him?"

"I provided him with the loop. I think he would have been angry had I made it safe. He wanted it to be as close to taste as possible. Perhaps I allowed a few too many of the problematic frequencies to remain but the damage was self-inflicted."

"Still that was unwise."

Teracia pinked. "It took Derath ten years to recover!"

"You understand that Prostallen is only a cog, a small piece of a giant machine that is easily replaced?"

"Yes."

Occeane studied Teracia. His gills began a slow ripple. "What's done is done. What matters is the perception and that perception strengthens your position. You warned him in advance that exposure to that environment could be dangerous and it was. Now you have his trust."

"It may not matter."

"Why not?"

"He was not in good health to begin with. Now he's seriously compromised. I doubt if he'll be on the extraction mission."

"But he's likely to recommend you. That's a good thing."

"Is it? I've heard Chancellor Agastin himself plans to be involved."

The Holy Son's gills flattened. "Is that already circulating? It's true, I'm afraid. The High Council wants to be rid of him. Agastin's been promoting instances of extreme public intoxication to increase his popularity. What's worse, while you were gone, he had a local municipal activist's diaphragm removed."

"Removed?"

"Yes."

Teracia's ballow blanched. "But why?"

"For suggesting changes in the Chancellor's Menagerie in the interests of public safety. That's when the High Council, and in particular the high priest..."

"Your father."

"Yes," Occeane said reluctantly. "That's when they decided they wanted to be rid of Agastin."

"But they can't get rid of him. He's the Chancellor."

"True, but he can abdicate. So, the whole question was what it would take to get him to do that. And then you brought back that song. The old lord played it perfectly. Now Agastin wants to take command of the return expedition, so he can expose himself to the virgin song in its natural environment. His plan is to abdicate while he does that."

"That song could kill him," Teracia said.

"That's what my father is hoping," Occeane said with an air of resignation.

"And this bothers you, Holy Son?"

"Doesn't it bother you? Our species is seven billion years old and we still haven't got beyond these petty political manipulations."

"Perhaps this as a good thing."

Occeane, the Holy Son, went into his silence, into his prayers. Teracia wondered if she had offended him. She waited. Hours.

"Tell me more about Homines," he said when the silence was over.

Thryke

Defense Minister Thryke studied the list of applicants on the wall screen before him. All were military fahr hoping to be assigned to the mandatory consignment on board the rumored Song Corp retrieval expedition. That was at least fifty years away and still a queue was forming, digitally at least. This was not about the chance to exercise one's military skills. It was a rare expedition that guaranteed taste but this one would, however dangerous that taste might be. This was about song lust. He reddened. How weak their species had become. Intoxication and lust had taken the place of honor.

Thryke felt the change in the current before he looked away from the wall. The resident herring school clumped into a silvery shadow and fled past the figure in the doorway. Chancellor Agastin floated into the room without so much as a gold-tinted ballow.

The defense minister pushed the purple forward, causing his ballow to pulsate and smooth over the reptilian military texture he wore as befit his rank. "Chancellor Agastin," he said. "I didn't know you were coming."

Agastin's gills shimmered and bounced, his mouth pursed, and a thin gold halo appeared, enclosing the kelp green of his ballow. He was clearly enjoying the effect his sudden appearance was having on Thryke. The minister of defense was wary.

"Defense Minister Thryke," Agastin said. "I'm so glad I caught you in!"

"And I'm glad you did too, Chancellor," Thryke said.

Agastin reached out with a single tentacle and touched Thryke's ballow. The point of contact went fear yellow before Thryke could control it. "Perhaps glad is the wrong word but at least you're here. That's the important thing." Agastin's member brushed down past Thryke's gills and then hung briefly in the water before the chancellor pulled it back in. The herring began their tentative return to the room.

Thryke said nothing.

"I suspect you know why I'm here," Agastin said.

"A cruiser for the retrieval expedition?"

Agastin's two tentacles spread wide. "These are large animals," he said.

"These ships are intended for military use," Thryke said forcing his ballow to display his military rank again.

"And when was the last time we had to do that?"

Thryke said nothing but his own tentacle moved toward his PDM. Agastin saw this.

"Not in your active memory or mine," the Chancellor said.

"It's a question of preparation, Chancellor. We never know what we might find out there." He felt his control returning.

"I do not have your grasp of military history, but I do remember these ships were built in anticipation of conflict with other interstellar species. Half a billion years ago, if I remember correctly, and since then we have encountered no such species."

Thryke allowed a hint of pink. "They have been useful in regional conflicts, battles within star systems, and there's the whole question of The Giver."

"The Giver?"

"The universal presence of DNA across the galaxy. That clearly points to a species capable of interstellar travel."

Agastin's gills rippled. "It's a good thing Barracute isn't hearing you talk like this. Pure heresy! But I agree with you, except we have no evidence for the existence of such a species apart from the DNA. That's why the mystics have had such an easy time with this. There's nothing out there to contradict them. But my point, Minister Thryke, is that these ships were designed to do something we don't need them to do. That being the case, and in the interests of good stewardship, they should be available for other tasks."

"But a pet expedition?"

Agastin flattened his gill slits. "Think of it this way, Minister Thryke, our race has not been militarily active for from forty to fifty long generations but, during that entire time, we have been seeking pets. It would seem the current priorities of our race are well established. Besides what I am talking about is the modification of a single ship, not the entire fleet. You might also give consideration to what the addition of a few of these beasts might mean to your own menagerie."

Thryke blanched in astonishment. He's trying to bribe me! "I don't have a menagerie, Chancellor."

"Oh, Yes. I'd forgotten you are divergent in that respect. Where is it you put your wealth? Ah, yes. Your little military museum. But it's not so little anymore is it? Supposedly, it contains quite a few items banned due to, now how was that put? Excessive lethality, wasn't it? Weapons considered unethical due to their tendency to be indiscriminate in what they kill? Wantonly destructive devices of various kinds all collected under one roof. Your museum exists for its educational value, to remind us of our uncivilized past. What is curious is many of these devices are operational? That would require a permit from the High Council. I don't remember such a permit ever being granted though I suppose that's a small concern. Arrangements can always be made."

Thryke sputtered. "I don't understand, Lord Chancellor. You are the supreme authority. You have absolute power. You can order me to do anything you want."

Agastin extended both tentacles into the room flexing his

claspers. "I'm sure you know that my son, Petar, will replace me the minute I set out on this expedition, giving him full chancellorship privilege. At the moment you are correct. I can still order you to do what I want. That is a hard habit to break but I will soon have to function without the benefits of absolute power. And over the millennia I couldn't help but notice how things get done among the rest of you, and since I'm about to join your ranks, practice would seem prudent."

"Practice?"

"Bribery, extortion."

Thryke's gills rippled. "But Lord Chancellor, you still have absolute power. I can refuse to be bribed by another. I can resist extortion by another. But you are the chancellor and you will still get what you want."

"Until I'm commanding that ship," Agastin said.

"Even then because, once the journey starts, you will be in command."

"With a set of restrictions on how that authority can be exercised."

"Does this concern you, Lord Chancellor?"

"No, not really."

Thryke studied Agastin. There were small waves of yellow green indecision rippling through his brow, vulnerability. "I know little about creating environments for animals," Thryke said.

"Lord Greyling will have his employees assist you in that regard. He stands to gain from this venture."

"And what about weaponry?"

"Weaponry? You are predictable, Minister Thryke, do you know that?"

"I've heard the planet has a sapient species."

"Homines. They're stage one terrestrial bipeds. Stagnant in their development and so unlikely to be much of a threat."

"But weren't they pushed?"

"They might have been. There's a strong possibility one of the reconnaissance mimics is in their hands. The exobiologists think it's unlikely they would understand what they have, but I suppose the possibility is there. Still, given the technological gap, I wouldn't concern myself about it. As long as we have the standard disarmament tools, we should be fine. Throw in a few of your toys if you like, but nothing that interferes with the modification."

After the chancellor left, Thryke went over the exact wording of what Agastin had said. "Throw in a few of your toys if you like." "Throw in a few of your toys if you like." He could do that, but he was the only fahr who would know how to operate such arcane weaponry. He wasn't about to teach those skills to anyone else, and most certainly no one else would get behind the controls of the Xburner.

Thryke had held sixty-seven occupations in his lifetime and sixty-three of them had been military. A lifetime dedicated to military ideals had taken its toll on him. He had never once seen true military action. His life had been sixty millennia of rehearsal for a part he would never play. He was in a terrible funk, so when Greyling brought The Song loop to Wrasse's party, Thryke had indulged. It had been by far the deepest arousal he had ever experienced, a wonderful bit of escapism, but when it was all over the funk returned, along with a new level of self-contempt for allowing himself to be tempted in the first place. Then he remembered what Greyling had said; the loop had been filtered, and The Song was lethal if experienced in its virgin state.

The following day he put his own name on the list. He would either see military action or he would see just how lethal The Song was.

Galileo

There had been rumors about the device and Fra Paulo had heard most. These rumors had been in circulation for six months,

Dutch spectacle makers coming up with a gadget that would make distant objects appear near. Then a travelling merchant appeared in Venice with one of these "spyglasses" offering to sell it and its secrets for 1000 scudi, an outrageous price considering the actual magnification was only three times. By then the rumors had also included speculations on how to make such a device, but no one as yet had increased the magnification. It was the kind of challenge likely to interest his friend, Galileo, and if the mathematician and instrument maker was successful, it might well secure him the Medici tenure he had been seeking.

Fra Paulo led the merchant to Galileo's quarters where they found the mathematician tinkering with a compass. The monk indicated the merchant should put the box containing the spyglass on the table and then withdraw from the room.

"What is this?" Galileo asked after the merchant had left.

"The rumored spyglass," Fra Paulo said. "All the way from Holland."

"THE spy glass?" Galileo said reaching for the box.

"You should know, before we proceed, that the merchant thinks you are a person of authority within the Medici court."

"Did you tell him this?"

Fra Paulo shook his head. "I am a man of the cloth," he said. "I would not say such a thing but, when he came to that conclusion on his own, I did not bother to correct him."

Galileo removed the spyglass from the box. It was a long slender tube, covered in leather, with a lens at each end. He pressed one end to his eye and pointed it at a tree in the yard. He frowned, looked through the other end, and then smiled. "So, I'm assuming he is hoping to sell this for significant gain?"

"1000 scudi," Fra Paulo said.

"A year's salary," Galileo shrugged. "It's a curiosity. Nothing more. The magnification is not great enough for it to be of any practical use. He won't get that kind of money."

"My thoughts, exactly. This current design is useless, but if one could figure out how to increase the magnification."

"Ah, so this is the real reason you are bringing this to my attention."

"I could think of no one better," Fra Paulo said. "And also," he admitted, "because our benefactor, Cosimo Medici, has an interest. He has asked me to deliver a package to you."

"A package?"

"Yes, and all he would tell me about it was that it was a da Vinci relic that would interest you. But I suspect it has something to do with Dutch spyglasses because that was what we were discussing when he sent it to you."

"Thank you for that, my friend. In the meantime, bring this to the attention of Cosimo, just so our merchant friend here doesn't feel cheated. You might also want to let our prince know, on the side, that I'm working on something better."

"I will talk to his Grace," Fra Paulo said with a smile. He gestured to the spyglass. "You had best do a quick study of this. I don't think we can leave the merchant waiting for long."

Later that day, Galileo picked up the plain wooden box that had arrived with Fra Paulo and carried it to the nearest window. In the improved light, he could see two oblong bits of machinery that looked like eyes at one end but stretched out almost to the length of his forefinger. On closer inspection, he saw what appeared to be a series of finely crafted lenses strung together with a kind of soft support system, keeping the lenses from touching each other.

"Da Vinci made these?" Galileo wondered aloud. He lifted one eye out of the box and examined it. The level of craftsmanship was far beyond anything he had ever seen.

Wrasse

Greyling had just been to see the menders, and the news was not good. At over one hundred millennia, he was dying and would not survive his next downing. He had known this was coming for some time but had hoped he would hang on long enough to see The Singer brought back to Centrix. That event was at least 600 years away and beyond any reasonable hope. It was time to think of his legacy, time to think about who would control Song Corp.

The Ministry of Pets was housed in a building that looked more like a giant coral bed than anything government functional. The entrance was an engineered ring coral that one had to pass through to get to the interior. Once inside Greyling found himself in a cavernous hall. Everywhere he looked he saw models of the less-significant singers Prostallen had collected on his last voyage. There were listening booths where one could sample the songs of each of them with the aid of government-approved loop players. Huge queues had formed in front of each of these even though the listening experiences would be filtered. It wouldn't do to have the Ministry of Pets turned into a place of public intoxication. Greyling was so used to unfettered access to virgin song that to see common fahr so giddy over mild titillation was almost depressing. Then he noticed a group of six or seven ministry fahrs moving towards him with a flotation harness. His gills rippled. Minister Wrasse had guessed the reason for his visit. There would be no waiting on this day.

Flotation harnesses were mobility assistance devices designed to help those who had either sustained a recent injury or who were too old to swim well. Greyling found himself tethered to the largest of Wrasse's officials and towed into the minister's presence. The remaining officials formed an honor guard, swimming in a semi-circle to either side and behind him. It was an instant spectacle and attracted the attention of almost every fahr in the place. Greyling was pulled forward toward the waiting Wrasse at the far end of the hall.

No matter how hard he tried, Greyling could not get used to Wrasse's new look. The minister of pets had become fond of scale implants. Normal fahr coloration ran along a continuum from muted greens to sludgy browns with the occasional muddy red. They blended in with the naturally occurring fauna in their environment and it had been that way since the dawn of their species. Genetic cosmetic changes were immoral; a violation of The Will of the Giver, so most fahr took care not to appear concerned with physical appearance. Wrasse, however, was an extreme exception, a huey if the rumors were true. He had undergone multiple scale implant procedures, and while these changes were not genetic and therefore legal, they suggested immorality. Wrasse modeled his look on a species of poisonous reef fish that announced its lethality with a display of gaudy colors. It was worse than that because, in Wrasse's case, the scales were programmed to turn off and on in pulsating patterns, something the fish couldn't do. He looked like bad advertising and gave others a headache if they had to spend too much time in his presence. What Greyling was about to do would not make him popular with Agastin, Thryke, and Prostallen or anyone else on the retrieval mission.

"Lord Greyling, my dear friend, how wonderful to see you!" Wrasse proclaimed with wild sweeps of his tentacles. These glinted, and it took Greyling a moment to realize the minister was also wearing several bracelets around each member. There was something mirror-like in the finishes of these rings that caught the pulsating patterns of the scales and further reflected them around the space.

"Minister Wrasse," Greyling said, with a slight nod in the minister's direction, but he couldn't help himself and closed his eyes to the visual assault.

Wrasse caught this. "I'm sorry, my friend," he said. "I suppose all of this is a bit much but I'm just so excited to see you!" With that, he touched a small button on his left shoulder and the pulsating stopped. The rings, however, continued to reflect the colors of the scales, but with less intensity.

"I'm glad the minister appreciates my visit," Greyling said.

Wrasse gestured big again, only this time the target was behind Greyling. "How could I not be excited to receive a visit from the fahr who is responsible for all this? For all these wonderful singers! We have all been blessed by the efforts of your company!"

A multi-voiced drone built. Every fahr in the hall was giving Greyling an ovation. What he intended as a simple meeting between the two of them was becoming a public spectacle. Greyling allowed his gill slits to flatten and his head bladder to redden and inflate just enough to show clear irritation.

"What I have to say to you, Minister Wrasse, has elements that are best discussed in private," he said just loud enough for Wrasse to hear.

The minister of pets looked at him for a moment. "Yes, of course," he said. He raised his tentacles one more time toward the assembled throng. "One more time, dear friends, let show our appreciation for Song Corp!"

The drone intensified and continued long after Wrasse had ushered Greyling into the ministerial chambers in the back of the hall. Once the door was closed, it was as if the drone had never occurred. Greyling and Wrasse floated, facing each other in total silence.

"I'm sorry," the minister said. "I was just feeling rather festive."

"Festive? About what?" Greyling asked.

"What Prostallen has already brought back and the retrieval mission to bring back the biggest prize of all, The Singer," he said.

"About the retrieval mission?"

"Yes, of course."

Greyling allowed his gill slits a small ripple. "I'm glad to hear that, Minister, because I have a small favor to ask."

"Anything," Wrasse said.

"Prostallen will be on that ship. He thinks he will be there to protect my interests and there is truth in that, but the main reason he will be on board is to insure they get to their destination. He's also there to mentor the femfahr and to keep Agastin from doing anything stupid. But I am not foolish enough to believe Prostallen will survive this journey; his health is too poor, and he will, eventually, succumb to his addiction. When he does it, it will kill him. So, I will need someone else on board to look after the affairs of Song Corp."

Wrasse blanched in stunned silence. "You want me on that ship?"

"Look at it this way," Greyling said. "If you go, you will protect Song Corp and your future controlling interest in the company. If you don't, there will be no controlling interest to protect. I don't intend to leave my stake to someone who will not go to any means necessary to protect its interests."

Summons

Derath had only one restriction. He could not leave the planet. He would spend the rest of his seventy-plus-millennia lifetime on Centrix. This restriction included other restrictions the big one being that any occupation requiring space travel was not open to him. Continuing as an exobiologist under the circumstances was not possible. He was mid-career and had given no thought to what else he might do. He needed research into this but doing it meant venturing out in public and being out in public was not an attractive option. Too many fahr knew what he had been convicted of and disapproved. They hissed at him.

The strobe on the wall scattered light around the room. Someone was at the entrance to his home. It flashed again. That someone was impatient. Derath swam the long green-slimed corridor to the entrance expecting to be hissed at again, but the fahr at the entrance was a government official. He carried a communications pouch from the Department of Religious Affairs.

"Exobiologist Derath?" the official said.

"Yes."

"This is a summons from the Holy Son," he said giving Derath the pouch. With that he swam straight up without another word.

Derath watched the official as he ascended. In the distance, silhouetted against the ocean's surface, was a government solar transport. Only the government had these. Light photoelectric motors powered these, and they moved at about ten times the speed of a swimming fahr. When they ran out of power, they floated to the surface for a quick recharge.

He turned his attention to the pouch. Now what? The bag was almost empty, containing nothing but a single shimmering communications loop. Derath would have to find his loop player, an item he didn't use much. He also wasn't especially tidy which meant - possessions floated around his home and could wind up anywhere, even out the front entrance where the prevailing currents could take them to the other side of the city. He hoped that wouldn't be the case here. His neighbor had stopped hissing at him but Derath wasn't sure he could borrow a loop player.

The data panel in his forward room was old and had lost some of its functionality, a software problem Derath couldn't be bothered fixing. The loop player was in a list of personal items and so he initiated a search. He knew it wouldn't find the loop player—that was the software glitch—but it should confirm if the item was still in the house and might trigger a strobe. It did both. Now all he had to do was swim around the place looking for a tiny flashing light. He found it bobbing near a gas pocket in the corner of the room.

He withdrew the communications loop from the pouch and studied it. "What could the Holy Son want with me?" he asked himself. He had already received the maximum sentence for pushing Homines, scapegoated by Lord Greyling and Song Corp, and dragged through the media as if he was some kind of moral deviant. What else could they do to him? All he knew at this point was that Occeane, the Holy Son, heir to High Priest Barracute, had sent him the loop. He knew little about Occeane. The Holy Son had a reputation as quiet meditative mystic, one who rarely interacted with the common fahr and who disliked giving song when he did. Derath fed the loop into the player.

"Exobiologist Derath," said the processed voice, filtered to remove all traces of pitch movement, "I am summoning you to meet with me tomorrow. A transport will arrive in the morning to bring you here. Do not be concerned. There is nothing about this meeting that will cause you further difficulties." Derath stared at the player as it ejected the loop and watched as the message dissolved in the water.

He spent the long Centrix night researching the Holy Son. His data portal yielded only the basics when him fed in the words. From this Derath learned Occeane was from the same gene pool as Barracute and he had been initiated in the reproduction labs during the last epoch of the previous High Priest's life to be the heir of Barracute. When Barracute became High Priest, Occeane was required to meet with him once a cycle to receive guidance. The only other time they saw each other was during meetings of the High Counsel where Occeane had observer status. Other than that, they had no contact. Theirs was not a familiar relationship.

To learn more about Occeane, Derath had to consult unofficial and less reliable sources. These sources gave the Holy Son the code name 'Poor Song.' This was a reference to the observation that, when Occeane gave songs in public, they were of inferior quality. Both their arousal and intoxication effects were mild, not worth the loops on which they were recorded. Feeding "Poor Song" into the data portal yielded stories mocking Occeane's religious devotion, some of them suggesting this misguided piety was the reason the Holy Son did not keep a menagerie and endless speculation about where Occeane got the loops he gave out. Much less frequent were stories about the Holy Son's kindness to fahr in distress, but they were there. Derath found this comforting.

The transport arrived early enough in the morning to avoid attracting too much attention. Derath could get in with barely a hiss from his neighbors, and the driver greeted him with rippling gills, the first friendly face he'd seen in years.

"The Holy Son awaits you," he said pleasantly.

Derath wasn't sure how to respond so he said nothing, but he was grateful the transport had tinted membranes.

"The Holy Son thought you would be more comfortable if you were not on display," the driver said as if he had read Derath's mind.

"The Holy Son is kind," Derath said.

"That he is, that he is," said the driver. "The journey will take a half day. I would offer you loops for the journey, but the Holy Son has requested you arrive unimpaired. There are visual distractions if you wish."

"Perhaps later," Derath said. He settled into a water pocket that made fin movement unnecessary. It was unclear to him how this worked. All he knew was water circulated in a manner that buoyed his body with a mild soothing pulsation. It was a luxury few fahr could afford.

Texts projected on the vehicle's inner membrane. They were so archaic most of them were unreadable. "The Book of the Gift?" Derath guessed.

"That's right," the driver said, but he offered no further explanation.

Derath tried to read the texts but the combination of ancient words and symbols made them incomprehensible. He knew "The Book of the Gift" predated "The Will of the Giver" by almost half a billion years, the most ancient of all Fahr religious texts. An old decision by the Department of Religious Affairs that it not be rendered into more contemporary language took it out of broad circulation over ten millennia ago. Only religious scholars knew what it contained, and they remained mute on the subject. Derath was vaguely aware of some controversy about "The Will of the Giver" and "The Book of the Gift" being theologically incompatible.

When they arrived at their destination, it was not where Derath expected. The Holy Son had an opulent official residence, but where they were now was a simple house only slightly larger than Derath's own home but in an isolated and barren part of the seabed. The driver caught Derath's surprise.

"The Holy Son lives simply," he said, "and alone. He has also chosen to trust you because few fahr know of this place."

The house, like Derath's, was sandstone arranged in interconnecting dune-like shapes. The entrance was the open oval common to most fahr homes but larger to accommodate the height of an elite fahr. It had inscription above it that was from "The Book of the Gift."

"It says 'All who enter here will be blessed,'" Occeane said appearing at the entrance.

Derath averted his gaze, but not before noticing the Holy Son was more than a head taller than he was.

"I remove the time of silence and free you to speak," the Holy Son said to Derath, gesturing with his right tentacle. He then spoke to the driver. "You may leave. Give us three days."

"Yes, Holy Son," the driver said getting back into the transport. It rose toward the surface.

"I'm surprised you got all the way here without a recharge," Occeane said watching it rise.

"It was a pleasant trip, Holy Son," Derath said.

"But slow?"

"Yes, slow, Holy Son" Derath agreed.

"I find that everyone who has been on an interstellar journey finds Centrix slow." Occeane regarded Derath. "I know that my position encourages the use of honorifics, but within my own home I prefer to be addressed as Occeane."

"Yes, Occeane."

"Well, come in. You must be hungry. I have fresh mackerel and kelp."

The contents of Occeane's forward room astonished Derath. It contained a large collection of khards, the ancient stone text poles of the first Fahr dynasty. Derath knew the Department of Religious Affairs had many in storage, but he did not expect to lay eyes on them ever. They were kept from the public.

"My father has no interest in texts from the first dynasty," Occeane said. "When I had them moved out here a half cycle ago, he didn't notice they were missing. He still hasn't noticed."

"I've always wanted to see them," Derath said.

"And study them, perhaps?" Occeane asked his gills rippling.

Derath did not respond.

"You are young, not yet fitted with a PDM and still at your intellectual peak, but I am half way through my life and not so quick of mind. When I was young and still living at the reproduction labs, they segregated me like all the elite. But there was one other young fahr with whom I was allowed contact, a femfahr. Because she couldn't be aroused there was no point in keeping her with others as they went through their song sensitivity training, so they put her with me. I believe you know her. Her name is Teracia."

With that, Teracia swam into the room, her gills rippling.

Derath was stunned. "Is this why you summoned me?" he said to Occeane and then turned to Teracia. "I didn't expect to see you again," he said as his ballow inflated blue joy.

"I explained to Occeane what happened on the voyage," Teracia said.

"There was nothing I could do about the verdict," Occeane said. "I only have observer status on the counsel. Nearly everyone on it has a menagerie and Song Corp supplies the singers. Lord Greyling gets his way, even with my father, though there is no love between them. It will be awhile before I'm able to change that."

"I told the Holy Son that you had an above average understanding of religious matters," Teracia said, "and I knew that you would have to change occupations."

"Yes, that's been a challenge," Derath said. "It's not as if employers are looking for fahr convicted of crimes against the Giver."

Occeane nodded. "I have need of an assistant to help with the study of these khards, many of them still need to be translated. That constitutes a huge gap not only in our religious knowledge of our distant past but also of our history. When you move an entire population to a new planet, it's not only the world that is left behind; it's also the physical history of the race. It's not as if we can go back to Aquafahr or even New Aquafahr and excavate the ancient sites. These khards are the only direct link with our past so studying them is crucial. I know it's not as stimulating as racing through space, but no one will hiss at you out here."

Derath was silent for a moment. "And what will you be doing?" he asked Teracia.

Teracia pinked and swam around the room. "You know that the menders saved Prostallen's life. That song should have killed him, but it didn't and now he thinks I saved his life. Song Corp asked Prostallen to go along on the retrieval mission as an adviser to Agastin, but he said he'd only go in the condition that I be appointed vice commander. Prostallen plans to mentor me in that position. And Song Corp thinks that's a great idea given what happened on the first expedition."

"Mentored by Prostallen and second in command to Chancellor Agastin and you agreed?"

"Given who's making the offer, it wouldn't have been an easy one to refuse. Agastin could order me to take the position. I thought it better to act flattered by the offer."

"Well, at least Homines will have someone with more authority looking out for them and not one who's so easily manipulated," Derath said purpling.

Occeane reached out a touched Derath's gills. "You were assaulted." The Holy Son gestured to his own diaphragm. "As long as we have these aberrations, we are vulnerable."

"Aberrations?"

"Did it serve you well?"

"No." Derath felt his ballow purple and morph into red. "Is not The Will of the Giver still in play? They used that to convict me!"

Occeane's gills rippled slightly and then flattened. "Agastin is no respecter of The Will of the Giver, though he has made a gallant pretense. He is obsessed with The Singers and will bring them back. I dislike the Homines' chances if they get in his way. But, even if they don't prove to be an obstacle, they will be pushed and pushed hard. I may not agree with The Will of the Giver, but I agree with non-interference with sapient species evolution."

Derath's gill slits stood straight up. "You are the Holy Son and you don't agree with The Will of the Giver?"

Occeane said nothing for a moment then he gestured to the khards. "Let's say that I am more comfortable with what is revealed here, but I would never say so in public. My father would seize these in an instant if he knew what I was thinking."

"But you're telling me..."

"Current theology has not served you well, has it?" Teracia said, "No."

"You are hungry and should eat," Occeane said. "We will have three days to explain ourselves before the driver returns for you. You can make your decision then."

Whale Prospector

Thomas Gardener was wiry and thin, possessed a mouth full of bad teeth, and wore clothes better suited to a bigger man. He was not a great fan of farm labor whether it was on his own rather pitiful piece of scrub or helping his neighbors. Their places were better because they had put in the effort to clear the land and work it efficiently. All he'd done was clear a few acres for tobacco, put in a good-sized vegetable plot, a pen for his three pigs, a hutch for the chickens, a hut to live in and a one-horse stable. With that, hunting and gathering, and occasionally hiring himself out to the neighbors, he could get by, as long as he kept himself away from the available women in the town. Marriage would not work with the lifestyle he wanted to live, haunting the bluffs along the coast.

If he could find a drift whale, one that was far enough outside the town that the townsfolk couldn't lay claim to it, and if he could get registered before anyone else did, then he could do well enough. He'd helped butcher one a few years back when a right whale had washed up and the finder got enough oil and baleen off the carcass to set himself up well. It had been one hell of an odor though, and Tom had retched more than a few times doing that job. Still the finder now owned a livery stable in town. That was worth a bit of retching.

Most of the time there was nothing to see, apart from the occasional whale spouts off in the distance, but there had been a huge storm the last few days, near hurricane level. The winds nearly blew down his chicken hutch and the birds were stressed and spooky. Sometimes, when there was a storm like that, the surge pushed weaker animals ashore. In the past he'd found dolphins, sharks and once a juvenile grampus, the latter too emaciated to have much value.

The beach was as usual, apart from an increase in driftwood, seaweed, and dead fish. The rocky bit beyond it, however, seemed to have increased in size. Tom found a path descending the bluff and clambered down. He was half way across the beach when he first caught a whiff. He knew that smell well enough. Here, however, it was much weaker than he remembered with the right whale. Something was dead in those rocks, but maybe not long dead. The question was what? The rocks themselves were black, so he was almost right up to them before he saw it, a large humpback lying flat on its stomach with its fluke buried in the sand. Finding a right whale would have been better, but this was still a substantial find. Humpbacks had less baleen but plenty of oil.

The trick was to make it into town and register the find before anyone else did. Then it would be his to process. Other whale prospectors may have missed it. The rocks partially hid it and the smell had not yet spread beyond the beach. That should give Tom an advantage, but he knew well that it was only a matter of time before increasing decay broadcast the animal far and wide. He spurred his horse on, but it was not a young animal and had limited speed.

Tom reached the town by midafternoon, hitched his horse to the rail, and made his way to the town office. His ears picked up nothing in the local conversation to indicate a whale find. He smiled. An animal of this size would have generated excitement, but everyone seemed relaxed. Maybe he'd made it on time. He walked in into the town office.

"I've come to register a drift whale," he said to the man at the desk.

The clerk who looked up at him had a pair of spectacles perched on his nose, a rare enough item since no one in the area had the equipment to grind lenses. His hair was longish, parted in the middle, and pulled into a grayish ponytail that disappeared into his collar. His face looked as if a flock of small birds had pecked it.

"A drift whale?" the clerk said.

"Yes. A humpback by the looks."

"Within the town's jurisdiction?"

"No, Sir." Tom said. "Well out. About fifteen miles down the coast."

"So, this is a claim?"

"It is, Sir. Has there been another?"

The clerk shook his head. "The last one was about a year ago." He smiled. "It's not likely the same animal. It appears the good Lord has seen to bless you." He pulled out the forms.

The carcass yielded forty-three barrels of oil, plus the baleen and the whalebone. With the proceeds, Tom bought new boots, tighter fitting clothes, a younger horse, a boat complete with harpoons, and a session at the Doc's to have his teeth yanked. His chewing days were over, but so were his farming and whale-prospecting days.

Reality

Teracia sought Prostallen out, arriving at the ex-commander's quarters after the cruiser had left orbit around Centrix.

Prostallen could barely get to the door. He floated awkwardly as she entered the room. "You've come," he said. "I was expecting this. Though perhaps it is I who should have come to you, now you outrank me."

"It will take me a while to get used to that," she said studying the former commander.

Prostallen's body was bent and distorted from his over exposure to Teracia's loop of The Song. "The Song" it was now called, even though the expedition had collected hundreds of other singers and songs and brought ninety-five percent of them back to Centrix. These were substantial finds under any other circumstances, but were now considered almost inconsequential, at least by those who knew of The Song.

The former commander now wore two belts fixed to his upper and lower torso. These he now attached to the wall to stabilize himself. Teracia watched this in silence and with a just a twinge of guilt.

"See what your condition has spared you," he said.

"Other fahr have managed," she said.

"Ah, your new rank has freed up your tongue. You will recall, however, that I could resist the temptation to expose myself to The Song in its virgin form."

"Self-preservation sometimes overcomes lust."

"All right, I'll grant I've earned your contempt," Prostallen said. "But even in this contemptible state I can still feel gratitude. You saved my life."

"And this is my reward, a few centuries of mollycoddling a spoiled ex-chancellor on a thrill-seeking expedition?"

Prostallen's gill slits rippled. "My, but we have attitude. A few points here. First, you took the job. You could have refused. Not that that would have been easy with Song Corp and an ex-chancellor involved, but you had a choice. Second, Agastin will be down for the middle part of the voyage—which overlaps with your own schedule I admit—but he won't always be around. Third, when it comes to our relationship, I do not have my collection with me. The collection that's not supposed to exist but does... I don't keep secrets well, do I?"

"No, you don't." But the loop of The Song will be on board. Agastin will make sure of that.

Prostallen raised a shaky clasper. "One's body gives one away.

I've given the collection to a library on Centrix since I'm too weak to use the loops now. That means that, while I will be of limited use to you due to my lack of mobility, at least there won't be issues regarding my judgment."

"Thank you for that," Teracia said.

"And I am aware of your real motivation here," Prostallen said. "Your fondness for Homines."

Teracia said nothing.

"I have always been a company fahr," Prostallen said, "even when I was serving in non-commercial occupations. Company profits have always been my top priority. And there are the associated perks. But I do understand the importance of The Will of the Giver. His DNA-seeding activities made pet collection possible."

"Save the spin, Commander Prostallen. It's wasted on me."

"It's an occupational habit. Though you may find this hard to believe, say something often enough and you believe it, at least at some level. The activities of the Giver have made possible the wealth and the life style I have enjoyed. This I do believe, though I may not have in the past. So, I do not want to see your Homines destroyed. And it occurred to me, once I saw Agastin's reaction to The Song, they could be in danger with the chancellor heading this expedition. Your position of vice commander is my way of trying to put in some insurance."

Teracia pinked. "He doesn't even know who I am. Why would he listen to me?"

"Because I intend to make him dependent on you. He can't run this expedition. All he's ever known is the court on Centrix and an endless supply of virgin song. His is a mission of lust not collection, which is why Greyling has me on board to make sure the latter happens."

"But I know nothing about running an expedition!"

"Ah, yes," Prostallen's gills rippled. "You're thinking of me as this old lamprey who can barely function when in command. There's truth in that, I admit. But without my loops I will at least be lucid, and you will need a mentor."

"You have to survive to mentor me!" She was rage red and didn't care.

"Yes, I will," Prostallen said, his ballow greening. "You should keep that in mind."

Teracia said nothing but her ballow deflated and bleed into yellow. If Prostallen noticed this, he gave no sign.

"By my calculations," he continued, "we will have at least one hundred and fifty years to get this right and I managed to re-enlist Baronth. With him doing the flying you won't have to pay much attention to the journey and we can focus on the logistics of running an interstellar ocean."

"The chancellor..." Teracia started to say.

"Agastin will either be down or aroused. Trust me, with the loops he has at his disposal he won't be paying much attention to the goings on around this ship."

"He is of the elite gene pool," Teracia said. "He has a natural resistance to..."

"Impairment? This is true but, as you've seen, The Song takes impairment to an entirely different level. He's lucid when he's listening to it but just barely. That will be to our advantage."

Teracia said nothing and swam around the room. "If he can ignore external things while he is listening to The Song, he can also pay attention to them. Despite his addiction there's nothing stupid about him."

"This is true," Prostallen admitted. "I'm not suggesting that we take him lightly. I'm just suggesting The Song gives us an advantage."

"Us an advantage? Us?" Teracia looked hard into Prostallen's eyes. "Do you have any idea how strange this alliance seems to me? You are the fahr who destroyed Derath..."

"I'm not pretending to be anything other than what I am, a company fahr. Derath was standing in the way of the exploitation of an amazing resource. He had to be convinced. We did convince him though I'm not sure we would do the same thing again. None of us had any idea how powerful The Song would be. Thank the Giver we were in orbit when that exposure took place. Distance saved his life."

"That and the menders," Teracia said. "And now he's been grounded."

Prostallen's gill slits flattened. "He is collateral damage," he said.

"What does that mean?"

"It means for the profits to continue, someone had to take the fall. During the investigation into the death of the crew members, it came out that one mimic released on to the planet was never recovered and there was a possibility of Homines contamination. There were only three fahr on board who could have been held responsible for that. I had just made the biggest find in company history, so they would not ground me. You had saved my life and were a hero. That left Derath."

"A sacrifice to the god of profit."

"Or the demon of profit. Take your pick."

"He's hissed at everywhere he goes."

"That will fade. By the time we return with The Singer, no one will remember."

"He will remember. I will remember."

Pointing a shaky clasper at her, Prostallen said, "The most useful perspective you can have on your current situation is that the collection of this Singer is the number-one priority. For the vast majority of fahr involved in this expedition, that is the only thing that matters, and it is huge. Derath or you or I we are all expendable. If you become a liability or even if there is some other profit-related advantage to eliminating you, you will be gone."

"Even if I'm the only one who knows how to run this ship?"

"Then you'd be an asset, wouldn't you? I suggest you pay attention to make sure that happens."

Teracia considered this. "So, who is the adaptive-species specialist on this voyage?" she asked.

"This is not a song-seeking expedition. It is a retrieval expedition. On a retrieval expedition it is assumed the adaptive-species issue has already been dealt with. Therefore, there is no requirement to have an adaptive-species specialist on board."

"Typical."

"Pragmatic," Prostallen said. "But on this mission Homines has you looking out for them; provided you remain an asset."

Teracia went red again. "To be an asset, I have to work to facilitate the very thing that could destroy Homines. Is everyone who works for Song Corp required to have this same set of ethically dubious values?"

Prostallen said nothing, but he watched as Teracia lost control of her ballow and inflated rage red.

"The company should not be seen as collection of fahr with ethical standards," he said. "It is not. It is best seen as an entity onto itself with profit as its primary motivation because the vast majority of its employees and investors will think like that. And this entity has a way of filtering out those who question its primary motivation, even if this questioning is for the most ethical of reasons, and especially if those persons are in positions of authority or influence. So, if you, who are now in a position of authority, want to save Homines you will have to do it in a way that does not threaten profitability. And do it in a way that cannot even be interpreted as such. Otherwise you will fail."

Teracia drew long mouthfuls of the room's yellowish water through her gills with deliberate slowness. The red bladder deflated.

"Better," Prostallen said.

Stasis

Agastin did not swim so much as drift around his quarters on the ship. The pre-down fast was five months long. It took the fahr body that long to metabolize the stimulants keeping it functioning during its 150-year awake state. As he got older, the fast robbed him of the energy he needed to do things, and in particular the energy required for arousal, but it did not allow him the oblivion of the down. It was almost as bad as the surfacing except that he could read or study, his mind being one of the last things to go.

High Priest Barracute always encouraged Agastin to pray during the fast but the Giver had always struck Agastin as, at best, an abstraction and, more likely, a huge cosmic joke the ancient fahr had played on their ancestors. Something or someone had seeded DNA across the galaxy, but it struck Agastin as a conceit that an entity of such obvious intellectual superiority would be interested in anything the Fahr, or any other sapient species had to say to it.

Then there was the whole issue of The Will of the Giver, a collection of ancient religious writings penned by mono-occupational mystics who had spent their entire seventy millennia lives in prayer. These prayers were mostly acts of listening, not speaking, and so the mystics claimed to have heard The Will of the Giver and to have written it down. Now these holy documents informed most of Fahr law, societal values, and behaviors—except when they didn't. The latter situation increased in frequency the further one got away from Centrix. There was a reason most freethinking fahr preferred to be on pet expeditions.

It was now over seventy years since the Fahr cruiser had left Centrix and Agastin was just days away from entering the stasis chamber. His thinking had slowed down to where he took several minutes to form a simple thought and a day or more to work through a complete idea. It was pointless to bother with strategic thinking at this stage because, even if he had a brilliant idea, he was impaired to where communicating that idea to anyone or even recording it for future consideration would be impossible. It was far better to allow himself the waking dream of hearing The Song in its virgin state. When they came for him, even gill rippling had been reduced to the occasional twitch.

Act Three: Interstellar Space

Radio Signal

The military cruiser was over twelve miles long, four miles wide, and half a mile deep. Receivers ran its the entire length and width and could pick up signals from the faintest of radio, optic, and digital sources. Vice Commander Teracia had left instructions the receivers be on continuous-scan mode in case anything came from Planet Song. Communications Officer Roont thought that unlikely, given the state of Homines technology half a millennium earlier.

They had programmed the ship's computer systems to flag any signal that had even a small chance of being artificial. This programming generated many false positives so most communications officers all but ignored the flags when they occurred. Nothing was more irritating and time consuming than trying to make sense out of a signal never intended to make sense in the first place. Roont's new choice of occupation was proving to be both frustrating and boring.

The first radio signals the computer flagged from Planet Song were ternary. They comprised short and long pulses with silences as the third element. For the first year there were just a few of these and there were significant gaps in time between instances. Roont ignored them, but when they became more frequent, he knew that he would have to bring them to the vice commander's attention. Unfortunately, they did not come to just her attention.

Agastin

Ex-chancellor and now Commander Agastin had been down for most of the middle part of the voyage. He had taken his down time early and pushed the surfacing, so he would be in full-command mode as they approached Planet Song's star system. He had also arranged for extra stimulants, so he would remain in a wakened state well past the usual 150-year limit. Given his age, the menders had advised against this but Agastin, as usual, ignored any advice he did not like. The combination of extra stimulants and his usual reaction to surfacing left him primed and ready to take the head off the first fahr he saw. He was not expecting Vice Commander Teracia.

She had arranged for a heavily filtered loop of The Song to play quietly in the background as he opened his eyes. It sucked the irritation right out of him, and when his eyes could focus, the first thing he saw was a display of his favorite foods. He was not hungry, but their presence still lightened his mood.

"They should have hired you to be part of my staff back on Centrix," he said once his tongue was loosened.

"Thank you, Commander," Teracia said. "Perhaps I'll try that as a future occupation."

"Am I being softened up because of bad news?"

"Bad news?"

"Has something gone wrong with the mission?"

"Not that I know of, Commander. We're making good progress toward our destination."

"Are we? I should check that out myself I suppose."

Agastin pulled himself away from the sponge restraining him and flexed his fins, propelling himself straight into the opposite wall.

"Are you all right, Commander?"

Agastin straightened himself but still looked wobbly. "I'm fine," he said.

"They said to tell you that coordination after a down returns more slowly in space," Teracia said. "They recommend taking it easy for the first few days."

"I'm fine, I said."

The COM system strobe flashed violet. Communications Officer Roont was using Teracia's discreet channel, which meant no one of lower rank would hear the communication. He wished the message to be heard by her alone. Agastin, however, was not of lower rank.

"Mamini," Roont said. "I may have detected a radio signal from Planet Song."

"An artificial signal?" Teracia asked.

"I think so, yes."

"And what is the nature of this signal," Agastin asked.

There was a long silence. "I'm sorry," Roont said. "Who is this?"

"Commander Agastin is here with me," Teracia said.

There was another long silence. "I'm sorry, Lord Chancellor," Roont said. "I didn't recognize your voice."

"You will not address me as Lord Chancellor. I no longer hold that position. From now on you will address me as Commander Agastin."

"Yes, Lord Commander Agastin," Roont said.

"The word 'lord' is not part of the address," said Agastin.

"I'm sorry, Commander Agastin," came the weak reply.

"Now answer the question."

"Question?"

Agastin looked at Teracia. "Who is this?" he asked.

"Communications Officer Roont," she replied.

"Communications Officer Roont," Agastin said. "I asked you about the nature of the signal."

"Nature?"

Agastin's ballow reddened.

"Communications Officer Roont," Teracia said. "Wait for us. We will come to you."

"Yes, Mamini," Roont said.

Teracia turned to Agastin. "For over sixty millennia, Commander Agastin, you held a position of extreme authority over all Fahr. No one is likely to forget that."

Agastin's ballow deflated. "Nor I, apparently," he said.

Voice

It took Roont several minutes to settle his gill slits and ballow. He needed to appear calm and in control. Commander Agastin and Vice Commander Teracia were both on their way, and he would have to explain why he had not alerted them earlier about the signals. He tuned the signals in again. It was clear to him now this was some kind of code; reinforced by the observation the signals now occupied several frequencies.

Then he heard it.

"One, two, three, four, is it snowing where you are Mr. Thiessen? If so telegraph and let me know."

The signal was faint, but the vocalizations had to be those of Homines. He was saved! He could now tell the commanders this was what he had found. No one would need to know about the ternary code! No one would need to know he had been sitting on that information for years! The Giver was smiling on him.

Roont knew it would take the commanders a while to get to him. Despite its size, the cruiser had no means of rapid transit within it. Its designers had concluded that the length of interstellar journeys would give crew members plenty of time to swim anywhere they needed to go. They also deemed this desirable for crew fitness. It would take Agastin and Teracia over an hour to get to the communications center from the surfacing chamber.

It was unlikely that Roont could translate the Homines' utterances before they arrived but engaging the vice commander's linguistic programs would at least make it look like he'd taken the initiative. He had made a bad first impression with Commander Agastin, of that he was certain. Doing something positive now couldn't hurt. He fed in the signal and waited almost fifty minutes.

Like all the computers on board, the voice was toneless, flat. "Initial evaluations indicate the language used is an evolved form of English, a language used on an island off the west coast of Planet Song's largest continent," it said. "Two of the words used are not in the data base. These are the words 'Thiessen' and 'telegraph'. 'Thiessen' is probably a name since the adult male form of address precedes it. The meaning of 'telegraph' is less certain bit appears to be a composite of two words borrowed from the Greek language. 'Tele' in that language means 'far off' or 'distant'. 'Graph' means 'written' or 'writing' but can also refer to a way of comparing numbers using pictorial representations. Since this sample was captured as part of a radio signal, the probability is high that 'telegraph' refers to distant writing. The word is a verb. This would suggest that to 'telegraph' is to write over a large distance, probably using coded radio frequencies. The sample size of the verbal communication, comprising only nineteen words, is too small for meaningful contextual analysis. The first four words are sequential numbers and so appear to have a function other than verbal communication, perhaps as a code or identifying marker of some sort, although, because these are spoken numbers, it makes it less likely they are part of the aforementioned-telegraph code. A larger sample size would be needed to confirm this including, if possible, actual samples of the telegraph code. None have been provided here. The actual size of the verbal message is therefore reduced to fifteen words. The first eight of these words are asking the receiver of the message about atmospheric conditions. They want to know if water, in the form of flakes, is present where Thiessen is located. The final seven words are asking the receiver to answer the question by using whatever radio means he has. The limited context, however seems to suggest either Thiessen lacks the ability of responding verbally to the question or, for other reasons, the unidentified sender wishes Thiessen to use the telegraph code, perhaps for security reasons. Given the size of the sample, the probability of a correct translation is 37.5 percent.

"Do you have samples of this telegraph code?"

Roont spun around quickly to find Commander Agastin and Vice Commander Teracia floating behind him. The question had come from Agastin. Roont had no idea how much of the linguistics analysis they had heard but quickly concluded that it would be pointless to lie. "Yes, Commander Agastin," he said.

"And how long have you had these?"

Roont forced his gill slits to lay flat. "The computers first flagged the signals a few years back. They were infrequent and insubstantial at the time and, given the percentage of false positives the system generates, I waited until I had something more significant to report. Then the signals showed up on more frequencies. That's why I called Vice Commander Teracia. I called about the code, not the vocalization. That just happened."

"Just happened?" Teracia asked.

"The vocalization, yes. While you were on your way here," Roont said. "I engaged the linguistic computer immediately."

Agastin and Teracia looked at each other. "The Homines were pushed," Teracia said.

Agastin turned to Roont. "Correct me if I am wrong, Communications Officer Roont, but are you not required to bring every instance of flagged radio signals from this planet to the attention of your superior officers?"

Roont head bladder inflated, yellowing. "I am, Commander, but..."

"The system is calibrated in a manner that gives a lot of false positives," Teracia said. "Communications Office Roont was acting out of experience."

Agastin inflated red."Vice Commander Teracia, what we're talking about is signals originating from a single planet. False positives or not, they should have been reported to us immediately." Agastin turned back to Roont. "Communication's Officer Roont, I relieve of your duties and confine you to your quarters."

"Yes, Commander."

Both Agastin and Teracia were silent for the first few minutes of their swim to the command center.

"Do we have others on board with Roont's level of communication's experience?" Agastin asked.

"Only one, Commander," Teracia said. "At least only one who's not currently down."

"And who is that?"

"Baronth, and he is flying this ship."

"Not an option then?"

"No, Commander."

Agastin was silent for a moment. "Then tell Roont to return to duty, but as a punishment he is to have no access to the ship's loop library, and I want a daily report on all signals coming from Planet Song. Afterwards, I want you to convene a meeting of senior officers. If the Homines have radio, then it is likely they also have telescopes and who knows what else. This retrieval expedition is about to get a lot more complicated."

Teracia swam in silence for a few moments. "Commander, under the circumstances, is it wise to collect these animals? It would be almost impossible for us to do so without damaging Homines. That would directly defy The Will of the Giver."

Agastin studied Teracia. "The damage is done, Vice Commander. And as for The Will of the Giver, I have had to play the role of religious adherent for sixty millennia. I intend to live the last few millennia of my life free of that hypocrisy."

Prostallen

It had taken the ship's computers several months to achieve even the most basic understanding of the ternary code and, even then, the error rate was high. Homines had made extraordinary progress since the Fahr had last visited Planet Song, but they were still intensely tribal, and each group had their own variations on the code and ways of using it. This left the translation accuracy rate at less than fifteen percent, but even at fifteen percent, the information gathered hinted at serious problems for the mission. The rate of change for Homines was increasing exponentially, but so far, they had made little use of their newfound abilities to transmit audio signals.

"What do we know so far?" Prostallen asked.

"Where do you want me to start?" Teracia replied.

"How about weaponry?"

"The advances have been mainly chemical, but that has broad implications. They have made significant improvements in their capacity to create and control explosions, including a wide variety of projectile weapons. At the moment those projectiles cannot be delivered beyond the low atmosphere, have a limited effective range, and no guidance systems. That would not normally be a concern, but the time it will take to collect these animals could leave us vulnerable to surface attack. Negotiation would be preferable but..."

"Which tribe would we negotiate with?" Prostallen finished.

Teracia said nothing.

"By now I'm sure you've realized that Agastin is determined to get these singers. He is not a military fahr, but given the technological gap, he wouldn't have to be. Your best hope is that Homines achieves planetary government by the time we get there." Prostallen's gill slits rippled. "In the meantime, I would investigate the possibility of reducing the effectiveness of those filters. You have experience with that and Agastin is more sanguine when impaired."

"And if they catch me, who would look after the interests of

Homines?"

"Point taken," Prostallen said.

Teracia regarded the old commander. "Sometimes I wonder if you're only in this for the intrigue."

Prostallen's gill slits rippled. "It is stimulating, and these days that's about the only stimulation I'm allowed."

Recruit

Agastin's personal assistant was a young fahr who had only been fitted with his PDM a few months before the ship left Centrix. Yarm had been naïve enough to idolize Agastin and had lobbied hard for the personal assistant position on board. The assistant was stressed, which Teracia attributed to his required presence whenever Agastin exposed himself to The Song. Yarm would have worn a personal filter but even though the filters were rated to be ninety-five percent effective, the remaining five percent when factored over multiple exposures to The Song had serious consequences. Add Agastin's bullying personality and that Yarm's down time had to coincide with the commander's, and you had one rattled individual. It didn't help that Agastin had opted for extra stimulants at his last surfacing to prolong his waking state. This had forced Yarm to do the same. Yarm was damaged, strung out and fearful and, in that state, highly irritating to Agastin.

Teracia had targeted Yarm as someone who might prove useful but meeting with him when he was not around Agastin proved difficult. Then, one day, she found him floating alone in the ship's kelp forest.

"Is the commander here?" She asked him.

Yarm inflated yellow. "Vice Commander Teracia," he said. "No. He's not here. He sent me away."

"Away?"

"He called me a clingfish."

"A clingfish? Well, you do keep him well groomed."

"He didn't mean it that way."

"You're sure?"

"Yes."

Teracia studied Yarm. "So, what is it like, being the personal assistant to the former chancellor of all Fahr?" Teracia asked.

Yarm did not respond. His gills flattened.

"You must be well compensated with such an important position."

Yarm looked at her blankly. "Compensation?" he said. "It's an honor to serve the most important fahr in the galaxy!"

"You're not paid?"

Yarm was slow to respond. "He feeds me, takes care of my needs. I have my own quarters."

Teracia nodded. "It is an honor to serve him."

"Yes, an honor," Yarm said, but his ballow was showing pink.

"They pay me too much," Teracia said. "By the time this mission is over I'll be able to buy a large home and have enough left over for a world-class menagerie."

"A menagerie, Vice Commander? What would a femfahr want with a menagerie?"

Teracia's gills rippled. "You're right. I have no need of that." She watched as Yarm first purpled into embarrassment and then tried to force a soothing green.

"My troubles are nothing," he said. "At least I can enjoy the songs."

"Do you?"

"Do I what?"

"Enjoy the songs?"

Yarm's gills flattened. "No. I get aroused like anyone else but... The commander is a member of the elite. He can handle so much more than I can, but I have to be there. I have to be there when he does it. I don't have time to recover. He keeps on doing it and he gets angry." Yarm stopped. Now he was gray.

"And you're not compensated," Teracia said.

"It's an honor."

"I was on the first expedition, you know that right?"

"You were the hero. You saved the commander's life."

"Prostallen, yes. But do you know the real reason I was on that mission?"

"Money?"

"I wanted to meet another sapient species, to study them."

Yarm blued, barely able to contain his excitement. "Oh, Vice Commander I've always wanted to do that. But the Will of the Giver prohibits contact. It's not like you can just meet them because there's always the risk something you do might push their development. They have to be protected!"

"That's the other reason I wanted to be on that mission, to protect any sapient species we might find."

"Protect them? The Will of the Giver..."

"Is not enforced one hundred light years from Centrix. Oh, they make a pretense, yes. But if they find a planet rich in song... Well let's say the sapient species will need more protection than The Will of the Giver."

"The planet we're going to has a sapient species."

Teracia studied Yarm. "Homines, yes. A very charming species."

Yarm said nothing. Teracia waited. "And you want to protect them?" he said.

"Yes, but I also want to help you."

"Help me?"

"On the last expedition I was a song chaser. It was a very successful mission, and I made a lot of money. That will happen again on this mission. I will have more money than I will ever need. You, on the other hand, do what you do simply for the privilege of serving Agastin. Noble but, in the end, you will have nothing but ill health. I can change that."

Teracia watched Yarm's bellow begin to yellow.

"I have a position of confidence," he said.

"And a master who calls you a clingfish and is no respecter of The Will of the Giver. All I want from you is any information you can glean about Agastin's intentions regarding the Homines. Nothing more. For that you will return to Centrix a rich fahr."

Yarm's ballow was now a fully inflated yellow. "He'll have my hearing!"

"The commander need never know. This is not a conspiracy. It's only me. And the commander already knows I have an interest in protecting Homines."

Yarm said nothing, but his yellow bladder deflated.

"Or you can choose not to do this, and our conversation will have never taken place."

"How will I get it to you?" Yarm asked. "I have to be with him constantly."

"Agastin will be a lot busier now we're approaching Planet Song. We will have our opportunities. Just be ready when they come."

She reached out and touched Yarm on his gills and watched as he greened. This was high risk. She could not even tell Prostallen.

Roont

Agastin punished Roont by banning him from the use of the ship's loop library. The restriction implied that getting loops from other sources was also a bad idea. Roont knew of song runners, fellow crew members who, for a price, could deliver high quality virgin loops and the means to get around the frequency filters in the loop players. But Agastin was now watching and Roont would have to work hard to get back into the commander's good graces. Complete withdrawal from song, however, was not something that would have to be endured.

Homines was one of the few sapient species that used radio

signals to broadcast singing. They weren't good singers and used irritating forms of instrumental accompaniment most of the time. The radio signals themselves were weak and noisy. They were, however, songs of sufficient length and variety to cause arousal and impairment.

Roont had a big problem. The signals provided him with a way of getting around the restrictions Agastin had placed on him. The temptation to do so was high, and he had already lost days to the songs, but he could not do his job while impaired. Using filters to stop the impairment flattened the tonal range of the signals so much they eliminated important parts of the bandwidth. The alternative was to feed the signals into the computers, but the songs themselves contained nothing of informational value. Yet, because they were in the same tonal range as Homines speech and formed artificial patterns, they continuously triggered false positives. This meant he would have to listen to the signals anyway to make the distinctions the computers could not make. He spent weeks trying to find the right level of filtration to allow enough of bandwidth through without, at the same time, becoming too impaired to make a judgment call. Finally, he gave up and called Vice Commander Teracia.

"You're impaired," was the first thing she said when she heard him.

"Yes, Mamini, I am. And that's why I need your help."

"Commander Agastin put severe restrictions on you; you were not to listen to songs in any form."

"But that's what Homines are broadcasting, Mamini, songs! It's all mixed up. They're talking, then they're singing, and then they're talking. The computers flag everything! I can't listen to it without drifting off. But you can. I know you're the vice commander and are very busy but you're the only one..."

"I'll be right there," Teracia said.

Xyros

The swim way to the communications center was long and wide. The only other fahr in it was impaired. Teracia watched him carefully as she approached. He was a young fahr whose ballow showed he was a low-ranking maintenance engineer, but it wasn't until she got closer that she recognized him. Xyros. The young engineer brazenly held up an illegal loop player as he sloshed right into her.

Teracia relieved him of the loop player. The young fahr seemed confused by his sudden lack of song. "Xyros isn't it? You were Navigational Officer Baronth's assistant on the last voyage, weren't you? The one who smacked the ship into the ocean?"

Xyros purpled. "I didn't like that occupation," he said.

"And it didn't like you. I'm surprised they let you talk your way onto this expedition, but I see that you now have an occupation more appropriate to your abilities." Teracia pressed the loop player against her abdomen. The recording was of virgin song, terrestrial, and of poor quality. Homines song? Was this what Roont had called her about? If so, it was already circulating on the ship.

"Xyros, you will return to your quarters and stay there until you are coherent. After which you will report to security and explain why you were in pocession of this loop player and where it and the loop came from."

Xyros looked at her blankly.

"Never mind," Teracia said. "Just return to your quarters. I'll send someone for you later."

"Yes, Mamini," Xyros said.

Teracia swam on a hundred feet or then looked back at Xyros. He had passed out and, because his swim bladders were still inflated, he had floated up to the ceiling of the swim way. There he bobbed up and down with his ballow randomizing and his gills rippling. Teracia called security and continued on her way.

Damage

Roont had turned off the sound on communications equipment before Teracia arrived but how long before she couldn't tell. He was still impaired but seemed coherent, floating calmly if raggedly before her, as if he knew whatever happened now was not something he could control and was resigned to his fate. Teracia saw serious damage. His tentacles floated in front of his body, occasionally twitching. It would take stasis time to repair that, but Roont was not scheduled to go down until they arrived at Planet Song. He had only surfaced sixty years earlier and had ninety years to go before his next down. Hopefully, the menders would have some kind of solution. She didn't think she could spare him at this point.

"Report?" Roont said with a slight ripple to his gills.

"You've crewed with Commander Prostallen," she said.

"No, never did, but he's a legend, isn't he? They tell me he was a hard bugger, but always gave taste. That's why I signed up; he always gives taste. But then I found out he wasn't commanding and now we have Chancellor Agastin. I used to be a niner when the chancellor gave song. I don't think the loops were even filtered. There were a lot of injuries and fahr going rogue. We were all wearing these constabulary-issue filters. Nothing got through."

"I'll need you to focus here," Teracia said.

"And I heard about you too, first femfahr song chaser ever!"

"Focus."

"Yes, Mamini."

"You said they were broadcasting songs?"

"Yes. It's strange. They discover radio and what do they do with it? Use it to broadcast songs. I've never heard of that before."

"There have been a few similar instances with other sapient species. It's usually a short phase, disappearing as soon as everything goes digital. And, of course, they have to be both singers and a species that puts a high value on distributing songs."

"Like us?"

"We don't sing, and we distribute songs for a different reason."
Roont's gills rippled wildly.

"Yes, well, perhaps you can show me what's going on here?"

"Yes, Mamini," Roont said reaching for the panel.

"Personal first," Teracia said.

Roont looked at her blankly for a moment, then his gills rippled, and he reached for his filter. "Yes, Mamini," he said. "But once I put it on, I can't hear what you're hearing. It makes it harder to tune in the frequencies."

"You have to put it on, Roont. I'll help you with the frequencies."

The shipboard personal filters were ungainly and held in place by straps that restricted movement. Roont had trouble with the straps. Prolonged impairment had reduced his motor control.

"Must be nice," he said once the filter was on.

"What?" Teracia asked.

"Never having to wear one of these things."

"Would you trade that for losing pleasure?" she asked. She knew Roont now heard her voice as a compressed monotone pitch.

"We live too long to be without song," he said.

Officers

The galactic observatory was the ship's executive meeting chamber. Such meetings were infrequent and so the ship's officers used the observatory as a place of relaxation. The main attraction was the domed ceiling screen, which gave 180-degree views of the cosmos. This could show any point within ten light years of their current location and with magnification far exceeding that of planetary-based telescopes.

In the center of the room was the fountain, Baronth's favorite item, a series of artificial vortexes and spouts. These provided comfort and support for the bodies of the ship's senior officers during the long meetings. It made swimming and floating unnecessary and also pushed water towards the gills to aid breathing. It was by far the most relaxing environment any fahr could be in and focused all energy on strategic thinking.

Baronth arrived early, hoping to have solo meditative time with the stars, but Wrasse was already there.

"Could you tell me," Wrasse said without a greeting, "which location on this strange contraption is the least conspicuous?"

"Least conspicuous?"

Wrasse turned and looked at Baronth. His scale implants had faded and frayed and only a few still flickered. He looked like the victim of some rare scale disease. "I should never have opted for extended stasis," he said. "They have no one on board who can fix this."

"Minister Wrasse, I presume," said Baronth trying to ignore the obvious. "My name is Baronth, chief navigational officer. To answer your question, the room's design makes each participant equally visible."

Wrasse's ballow showed the pinky hue of irritation.

"I'm sure the menders on board can find a solution," Baronth said.

"Oh, they have a solution, all right, wait for the implanted scales to all fall out and then grow new ones. That will only take about fifty years."

Baronth said nothing.

"I should take the cosmic view, I suppose," said Wrasse. "Fifty years is nothing except that I'll be awake and looking hideous for the whole time. And there are cameras, cameras everywhere on this slimy ship."

Defense Minister Thryke chose that moment to enter, swimming in with a broad gold sash across his chest. "Not in here, Minister Wrasse," he said clearly having trouble controlling his gill slits. "Executive protocol prohibits that. They record nothing that goes on in this chamber. It allows for the free exchange of views with no one having to worry about public accountability." Thryke's gill slits did a little mocking dance." Perhaps we could arrange for you to take up residency in here once the meeting is over?"

Wrasse said nothing as Thryke's gills continued to mock him. He swam toward the fountain, allowed it to pick up and suspend his body and then closed his eyes.

"Minister Thryke," Baronth said in greeting.

"Chief Navigational Officer Baronth," Thryke returned. "Not wearing your sash today?"

"Is this a military exercise?" One of Thryke's duties on board was to drill the crew on military procedures. He insisted on the wearing of sashes when he did so.

"No. But the subject of military action will come up."

"Then you have more knowledge of the agenda than I have," Baronth said.

Next to arrive was Prostallen, towed into the chamber by two menders. The ex-commander had gained weight, which surprised Baronth. Prostallen had always been slim, almost emaciated. Too much access to loops increased body metabolism. Could it be he was no longer using?

"Commander Prostallen," he said in greeting.

"Ex-commander," Prostallen corrected. "I'm glad to see you've elected to continue your occupation, Baronth."

"An easy decision, ex-commander. Who wouldn't want to be part of bringing The Singer back to Centrix?"

"Indeed," said Prostallen

"And where have you been hiding?" Baronth asked.

"Well, as you can see, mobility is now an issue for me. I have to be tethered, so it's easier to remain in my quarters. You should come by and visit."

"You're right, I should. I hear you've been mentoring Vice Commander Teracia."

"An easy task. She catches on quickly."

"She runs a tight ship," Thryke offered, "Not a military one, but a tight one."

"She does. She does. It's good to have you on board, Minister Thryke."

"Well, I can't allow my underlings to have all the fun," Thryke said.

The two menders had been patiently holding Prostallen up during this exchange. "We should get you installed," one of them said to him.

"Installed? Is that a medical term?"

"It means we can adjust the water pressures for individuals with disabilities to ensure their comfort level is the same as anyone else's." They led Prostallen to the fountain where they removed the ex-commander's tethers and placed him beside Wrasse. Wrasse opened his eyes.

"Prostallen," he said.

"Minister Wrasse," Prostallen returned.

The menders made a few more adjustments to Prostallen's positioning and then released him. "Are you comfortable, Sir?" the second one asked.

Prostallen squirmed and then sighed. "Nice," he said. "I don't suppose we could move this to my quarters?"

"It's not portable, Sir."

"Ah, well."

Prostallen reached out and lightly touched one of Wrasse's scales and then gestured to his own body. "Fellowship of the wounded," he said.

Wrasse looked away. Thryke and Baronth looked at each other.

Agastin and Teracia chose that moment to enter. One look at their ballows and Baronth could tell Agastin was not in any way impaired and that Teracia was worried. Baronth caught her eye contact with Prostallen and his slight nod in response.

Wrasse released himself from the fountain at Agastin's entrance but Prostallen could not do the same. Agastin looked at the ex-commander sharply but then realized the problem.

"Acknowledge!" Teracia commanded.

"Commander Agastin," the others replied in unison.

Agastin studied the faces of each fahr, a slight ripple to his gills when he saw Wrasse. He turned to the menders. "Is your business here concluded?" he asked.

"It is, Commander Agastin."

"Then leave us," Agastin said with a dismissive gesture. The menders left the chamber, and the door closed behind them.

The commander took his place at the far end of the fountain. Teracia was to his right and to her right, Prostallen. To his left was Thryke, followed by Baronth, a space and then Wrasse completing the circle beside Prostallen. Agastin gestured to the space. "Vice Commander Teracia will explain the absence of Communications Officer Roont."

Teracia seemed surprised by this. "Yes, well, Communications Officer Roont is indisposed."

"Tell them why," Agastin said.

Teracia took a moment to collect her thoughts. "Roont made the unfortunate decision to listen to the unfiltered Homines signals, which as you now know contain songs, and tried to control his own impairment by limiting his exposure. He failed and, by the time I learned of the problem, he had already done himself serious damage. He's in the care of the menders at the moment."

"So, we don't have a functioning communication's officer?" Thryke asked.

"We don't," Teracia confirmed.

"Anyone down we can revive?" Wrasse asked.

"Kiiam is in stasis, but he only went down fifty years ago," Teracia said. "He is scheduled to take over from Roont for most of the voyage home. If we revive him now, he'll only be about thirty percent functional; he'll be in a lot of pain and, considering his age, he'd also be at risk of terminal collapse."

Agastin looked at Baronth. "You have this in your PDM don't you?"

"I have, Commander Agastin," Baronth said. "Communications officer was my 29th occupation."

"Then who flies the ship?" Teracia asked.

"Wrasse," said Prostallen, his gills rippling.

"Wrasse?" Thryke said with contempt.

The minister of pets looked uncomfortable. His ballow was trying to inflate purple, but he was fighting it.

Agastin poked at Wrasse's PDM. "Is it even remotely possible you have navigation experience in there?"

"I have, Commander Agastin," Wrasse said. "From a long time ago, before my involvement in the pet trade. Not at a commissioned officer level, but it's there."

"Well then, it seems we have our solution," said Agastin. "Until Communications Office Roont can return, Baronth will take over as communications officer and Minister Wrasse, who as far as I'm aware, has no real purpose on this ship—apart from looking after Lord Greyling's business interests that is—can fly us."

Baronth exchanged worried glances with Thryke.

Teracia looked at Prostallen who gave her a slight nod. She turned to Agastin. "Commander Agastin, I think I should point out, first of all, that Baronth would have no more immunity to the impairments inherent in Homines song than Roont has. And the damage to Roont occurred over just a few years. So, if we put Baronth in that same position we risk compromising the health of our most experienced navigational officer. Secondly, we don't know, how long it will take Roont to recover, so if the same happens to Baronth we might..."

Agastin held up his tentacle. "I can see your point, Vice Commander. But we must have a communications officer on this ship, especially since those radio signals are our only source of information about Homines."

"We might work this another way, Commander Agastin," Teracia said.

"And what way is that?" Agastin asked.

"I agree we need to keep monitoring the Homines' transmissions. But there are only two fahr on this ship who can do that in relative safety, you and me. The trouble is neither one of us has any experience in communications. The other problem we have, and this is what I perceive Minister Thryke is so concerned about, is that Minister Wrasse has never been a chief navigational officer, and so we'd be putting the navigation of largest of all Fahr ships in inexperienced hands. Keep in mind; we're talking about the navigation of a ship with an eighty square mile surface area through a stellar system. I think even Minister Wrasse will agree that is not a wise choice."

"Oh, I concur. Yes." Wrasse said.

"But," continued Teracia, "we're not at the point yet where a navigational officer of Baronth's skill set is required and that gives us some time. My suggestion is that Wrasse take over from Baronth temporarily. In the meantime, Baronth can train you, Commander Agastin, on the basics of monitoring the radio signals."

"I am the commander of this mission, Vice Commander Teracia, not a communications officer!" Agastin said, reddening.

"I'm not suggesting we take your authority away from you, Commander Agastin," said Teracia, "but we have a logistical problem. The command decisions we will need you to make are a way off. The information you will need to make those decisions is only available through these radio transmissions as you, yourself, have just pointed out. You are genetically resistant to the impairment that has put Roont in the care of the menders."

"But you, Vice Commander Teracia, cannot be impaired and to my mind that makes you the logical choice to take this task," said Agastin.

"This would be true except for one undeniable fact," said Prostallen. "Vice Commander Teracia has spent considerable time studying the operational aspects of running this mission. She has been learning about this ship, its various capabilities, its staff, and how the whole command structure fits together. You have concerned with issues regarding the extraction of The Singers once we arrive at our destination. This is how it should be since our mission is to collect these animals, but it means you are uniquely qualified to be in command of the extraction process once we get there, while Vice Commander Teracia is better qualified to get us there."

Agastin said nothing. Instead, he studied the faces of every fahr in the room. When he got to Wrasse, he saw the minister of pets' gill slits rippling. "Do you find this funny, Minister Wrasse," he said.

"Oh no, Commander," Wrasse said. "I'm identifying with your position, wishing I was in it."

"And why is that?" Agastin asked.

"Because you can be aroused without being impaired. The Giver has blessed you!"

"The Giver had nothing to do with it," Agastin said, "and I am surprised, given your orientation, that you would see that as a blessing."

Wrasse purpled but said nothing.

Agastin turned to Baronth. "You have three months to get Minister Wrasse ready to fly this ship. Before you do that, I want you to go to the communication's room and make sure all signals from Planet Song are recorded for the period the post will be unoccupied. When all of that is done, you will report, and we will try to understand the communications system together."

"Yes, Commander."

"In the meantime, those radio transmissions have already told us certain things, the most important of which is that Planet Song's adaptive species, Homines, has been pushed. That is clearly unfortunate but what's done is done. I am of the opinion we cannot further damage Homines by extracting these animals and so I intend to do so."

Agastin scanned the room to make sure this announcement was having its desired effect. All gills were rippling though, in Teracia's case, this looked forced. Agastin seemed satisfied and continued. "Now as for what we have learned so far through analyzing these radio signals, I'll turn it over to Vice Commander Teracia for a summary."

Teracia looked up at the dome above them displaying the region of space in which they were currently traveling. Prominent in that view was their destination star. She looked back down at the expectant faces before her. "We have now been receiving radio signals from Planet Song for about fifty years," she said. "First of all, we need to remind ourselves the information we have is not current. And that may well be the biggest problem we face here. Homines appears to be evolving at such a rapid rate it's hard to predict what we'll be facing until we get to our destination. Here's what we know so far. There is evidence of terrestrial and oceanic vehicles that run off steam and fossilized hydrocarbons. There's even evidence of primitive powered flight. There is or was a major tribal war going on that seems to have involved most of the planet and used powerful chemical explosions. A single one of these destroyed an entire port and killed thousands of homines. The port was attached to a city called Halifax, which at the time of our last expedition, did not exist. Five hundred years ago, that entire hemisphere was sparsely populated with only a few significant cities. Now it has hundreds of large cities of which Halifax is an insignificant example. This points to a large population explosion, rather remarkable when you consider, when we last visited this planet, they were dealing with a virulent plague decimating the then-much-smaller Homines population."

"From that we can deduce some serious advances in medicine and in food production," said Wrasse.

"We can assume a major shift away from their stagnant superstitious past towards a mindset that embraces inquiry and research," said Thryke. "But this is happening so quickly that the wisdom needed to wield the resulting knowledge is lagging far behind. This planet-wide war is proof enough of that. We must be prepared."

Everyone was silent for a moment. Agastin removed himself from the fountain and swam around the chamber. Teracia and others watched him.

"What concerns me," he said, "is what all this means for The Singers. Greyling told me that, before they left Planet Song during the last expedition, they had detected a small tribal group of Homines called the Basque. This group was engaged in hunting whales."

"Whales?" said Baronth.

"It's a generic term," Agastin explained. "It refers to large aquatic mammals unique to Planet Song. The Singer is a species of whale. Most of the whale species sing to some extent, but The Singer is exceptional."

Teracia noticed a blood rush to Agastin's diaphragm even as he said this.

"The Basque were inefficient hunters and didn't prey on The Singers specifically, but that was almost 600 years ago, multiple generations for them," Agastin continued. "At the rate Homines are evolving, who knows what they might be capable of?"

No one said anything.

Whaling

"You handled that brilliantly," Prostallen said to Teracia. "With Agastin alternating between listening to loops of The Song, and monitoring the singing in the Homines radio broadcasts, he should be sanguine."

"He's right about the whale hunters, though," said Teracia

"How do you mean?"

"We've been focused on developmental issues, on whether Homines could put up much resistance, and not on analyzing the current relationship between The Singers and Homines. I checked into this after the meeting."

"And?"

"They have large fleets of ships dedicated to hunting whales."

"Including The Singers?"

"We're not sure. The information we've intercepted so far is not species specific," Teracia said. "We also don't know, the extent of the damage and why they're doing it. What do they gain?"

Prostallen was silent. "Food?" he ventured.

"Maybe," Teracia said, "but if so, they don't talk about it much.

We've yet to find any mention of whale meat in any of their food-related broadcasts, unless they have a word for it, we haven't learned yet. We do know whatever they're taking from these animals is being stored in barrels."

"Barrels?"

"Yes."

"Then it's liquid?"

"They also put solid food in barrels, particularly on-board ocean-going vessels."

Prostallen was silent again. "This adds more urgency to the mission," he said. "Does Agastin know about this?"

"I don't think so. Most of the information in the database came from deciphering the ternary code, not from audio broadcasts, and I had to ask specific questions of the computers to get that information. He would have to do the same which he will as soon as Baronth has taught him the system."

"And when he finds out, he will also know you've accessed the information before him," Prostallen warned. "You'd better tell him. You can play down the possibility of The Singers being included in the harvest."

"I doubt that will work," Teracia said.

Prostallen thought about this for a minute. "He'll want to accelerate the mission," he said.

"There's a limit to how fast we can go through an inner star system."

"Chancellor Agastin does not understand limits."

"He's not Chancellor Agastin, he's Commander Agastin."

"Legally, yes. Mentally, no," said Prostallen. "There's no off switch for 60,000 years of absolute authority."

Message

"Teracia," the message began.

She looked at the date, fifty-six years earlier. This is what passes for up-do-date messages from home when you were on a pet collecting expedition. She read on.

"Petar is following in his father's swimway. The loops he gives out are every bit as strong and are causing the same level of social upheaval. What's worse, he has reduced the level of filtration required of loops available through public libraries. Public intoxication and song addiction are increasing and so is his popularity. He has further endeared himself to the population by granting more access to the Chancellorship Monolith and reducing the waiting times and displaying none of his father's impatience. One wonders what level of welcome Agastin will receive if he returns from his misadventure. It may not be that easy for him to resume his position.

Derath and I have discovered khards revealing gene sequences from the original fahr DNA, those from before the First Modificate. This was quite a surprise since all khards were thought to deal solely with religious or historical matters. If we can find more of these, perhaps it may be possible to reconstruct the lost original genome.

We've been learning some of the original prayer patterns based on *The Book of the Gift*. A few of these are petitionary prayers, prayers in which one makes requests of the deity. I have no idea of the efficacy of such prayers, but I have decided I will use them to pray for you, your safety, and success. That way at least I will keep you in my thoughts."

It happened again, a full body flush, for only the second time in her life.

Yarm

Yarm's gills rippled. "For two months now, he hasn't been using the loops," he confided to Teracia. "And he doesn't want me around when he's listening to those broadcasts. It's given me time to see the menders and get some rest."

"He hasn't been using?"

"No, he's pretty focused on those broadcasts. Not too happy, I'd say. Pinking quite a bit but he doesn't tell me what he's thinking. Sorry about that."

"But he's stopped using..."

Yarm went yellow. "I shouldn't have told you that. It's not part of our bargain."

"It's not significant information. Don't worry about it."

"If I were to guess though, I'd say he's about to do something. And he's been meeting with Minister Thryke."

Teracia blanched. "Thryke? How frequently?"

"Just in the last few days."

"Have you heard any of those conversations?"

"No. That's another thing Agastin doesn't want me around for. It's kind of nice, actually. More time to relax. Why?"

Teracia studied Yarm before answering. *Could he be that thick?* "If we were to take military action against Homines, who do you think would be in command?"

Now it was Yarm's turn to blanch. "Surely that would not happen! It would completely defy The Will of the Giver!"

"What did I tell you about The Will of the Giver out here?"

"They could never hide an act that large!"

"They may not have to."

"I don't understand," Yarm said.

"Just tell me if Agastin has any more conversations with Thryke."

Urgency

When she arrived, Agastin hovered before the wall-sized communications panel.

"They're getting better at this," he said. "A lot less static in the broadcasts. And they sing well for terrestrials. It's a pity that gas-born song, when sung by sapient species, is almost always accompanied by instruments. Cheapens the song and the impact."

"Find anything else that's interesting, Commander Agastin?"

"Oh, yes. But before I tell you let me guess why you're here. You have found, through the analysis of the ternary code, that there has been an expansion of whale hunting."

"Yes," Teracia admitted. "But we don't know why. It doesn't seem to be for food, and so far, we have seen no evidence that The Singers are part of the harvest."

"They've broadcast long discussions on a wide variety of subjects," Agastin said. "Most of it is in English, which seems to be the dominant trade language at the moment, and so the computer is getting much better at interpreting it. I understand during the last voyage you had a hand in setting up a linguistic program?"

"Yes, two occupations ago, I was a programmer," Teracia said. It was recent enough that I didn't have to go into my PDM for that."

"Well, you've done a good job," Agastin said. He looked at Teracia. "It's the fat," he said, "which they render into premium grade oil. It is highly prized and has a wide variety of uses. There's a huge demand for it and that's fueling the slaughter." Agastin's tone was matter-of-fact, detached.

"Slaughter?" Teracia asked.

"Yes," said Agastin. "The Homines have not grown into their current level of technology. They have no sense of balance."

"And The Singers?"

"Included," said Agastin. He looked long and hard at Teracia. "I'm glad that you've maneuvered me into this little task. Homines singing has mellowed me and made me less prone to impulsivity, but we must act decisively in this matter."

Einstein

As he stood before the dome housing the Hooker telescope at the Mount Wilson Observatory, Albert Einstein couldn't help but get a sense of the historicity of the place. This was an odd feeling because he, himself, was older than the entire complex. He had spent a good deal of his life living in and around buildings and institutions many times its age. But, still, an astounding discovery had been made here. Through his observations and calculations, Edwin Hubble had proven that the Andromeda galaxy was outside the Milky Way. That discovery had shown the universe to be much larger than originally thought and much older. Perhaps it was this last bit that added to the perceived age of the place that the images the Hooker telescope had captured were from so long ago. It had taken 2.5 million years for the Andromeda Galaxy's light to reach them, and since then Hubble had found many more galaxies even farther away. He had also proven that the universe was expanding in every direction.

Edwin Hubble was standing to the right of him. Einstein could feel Hubble studying him as he, in turn, studied the dome.

"No clouds," Hubble said. "We should be able to see it tonight."

"I'm looking forward to it," Einstein said. He turned and looked at Hubble. "You know I have what one might call a well-deserved reputation as a non-conformist, a free thinker. That is an aspect of who I am that irritates many people. I usually don't care. But at the time I was publishing my theory I had no status to speak of. There was no reason for anyone to pay attention. There were certain implications to the theory I buried, actually changed, because they didn't seem to be consistent with what could be observed. I guess I didn't want to look too radical. But general relativity, at least as I originally conceived of it, allows for what you've discovered. Changing the original equations was the biggest blunder of my life, so thank you for bringing that correction."

Hubble laid his hands on Einstein's shoulders. "We all stand on these," he said.

That night Einstein saw 2.5 million years into the past.

Threat

Prostallen watched as Teracia swam in nervous little circles around his quarters.

"I've been to see the menders," she said. "They say Roont is at least six months away from even limited duties, probably much longer."

"Agastin seems to enjoy what he's doing," Prostallen said. "He is mellow."

"Mellow in the sense of less impulsive, yes. He has guessed that we maneuvered him into this position."

"Has he?"

"He said as much the last time we talked," Teracia said stopping in front of him. "He doesn't seem to be that bothered by it."

Prostallen considered this. "He sees himself as being in control. He's not feeling threatened by our actions, for the moment."

"And he's discovered that some homines are harvesting The Singers."

Prostallen blanched. "Through the radio broadcasts?" he asked.

"Yes. Homines have been discussing the subject on certain radio frequencies."

"And what does harvesting mean, exactly?"

"There's a huge demand for the oil found in the fat of larger whales, including The Singers."

"How huge?"

"Commander Agastin described what they were doing as slaughter," She said. "I'm sure he will order Baronth to increase our speed."

"As well he should," Prostallen said. "I'd be surprised if Agastin doesn't tell him to double it."

"Double it? Two-thirds the speed of light? Are we even capable of that? We can't travel at even a small fraction of that through a star system! The risk of collision..."

"We're not in the star system yet and won't be for a while. And this ship is capable of speeds approaching eighty percent of the speed of light in interstellar space. It is a military cruiser. And as for the star system itself, remember Thryke is on board, and while he may not be a pilot, he well knows of the capabilities of this ship. Its defensive capabilities include advanced hull reinforcement and space debris deflection systems. Thryke will know how to engage those. So, while we might not be able to operate at interstellar speeds within a star system, we can probably move much more quickly than a standard scout ship."

Prostallen paused and looked a Teracia. She was fighting not to display yellow. "Of course," he said, "such speed would come at a significant cost to the overall resources of the ship. It would be a terrible thing to arrive at Planet Song and not have enough energy left to collect the animals, especially if we have to subdue Homines to get at them."

"Thryke is not interested in The Singers," Teracia said.

"You're right, he's not."

"So, if Agastin consults with him..."

"The commander might not understand the implications of..." Prostallen thought for a moment. "I see your point," he said. "We've come a long way to collect these animals and if Homines are killing them..."

"Surely they cannot wipe out a species in a hundred years?"

Prostallen studied Teracia. "As I remember, Greyling hired you as an exobiologist, a song chaser, for our last voyage, but it turned out that your primary interest was in sapient species. So, let me ask you this. Have you ever, in all the research and study you have done, learned of a sapient species that has technologically evolved this fast?"

"No," admitted Teracia. "The speed of their advance is unprecedented."

"And have you ever encountered species that was less prepared for their own success?"

Teracia said nothing. Rapid technological evolution usually resulted in premature sapient species extinction. Everything she had studied told her this, but it also told her that each species had to find its own destiny. What she had witnessed on the last voyage told her that the Homines were special, worth preserving. But Prostallen was right. They were not ready for their own success.

"No," she said, "they are not prepared."

"Then you will have to agree the risk of terminal damage to The Singers is high. We cannot allow that to happen. This is greatest find in the history of Fahr song seeking. We cannot allow The Singers to be destroyed."

"Even if we have to destroy Homines to save them?"

"*Destroy* is not a word I would use, especially regarding our actions toward Homines. We can hardly see ourselves as their moral superiors and do that. We are here to retrieve The Singers, some of them at least. The hope is we can do that without causing further damage to Homines."

"Why am I not encouraged?" Teracia asked.

"Perhaps because you've seen the damage that's already done? Perhaps because you know what the primary motivation of this mission is?" Prostallen turned away from Teracia. "But we have had this conversation," he said. "I for one will not resist your efforts to help Homines but I cannot speak for the others. In the meantime, we need to get to Agastin before he talks to Thryke and Baronth."

He's already talked to Thryke, Teracia thought.

Speed

Prostallen used the word 'we' a lot in his conversations with Teracia. 'We' should do this, and 'we' should do that. But this was the royal 'we' that meant whatever action they decided on would have to be undertaken by her. She was the mobile part of the 'we' and so, once out of his quarters, she was on her own.

The ex commander may have thought intercepting Agastin before he went to Baronth was the wisest course of action, but Teracia wasn't so sure. In her last interaction with Agastin, he had made it quite clear he felt they had manipulated him. Was it likely he would listen to her under the circumstances? No. Going to Baronth was the better choice but she could not use the COM system to speak with him. Every use of the COM system was recorded and Agastin, as commander, was the one fahr on board who had access to all of those recordings. She, herself, as second in command could listen to any conversation not involving Agastin. It was not a privilege she used, but she wasn't sure about the Commander. The policy insured nothing of a questionable nature was ever discussed using the COM system, especially by lower ranking members of the crew, but even those of higher rank were reluctant. This was part of the on-board culture but Agastin was not a seasoned space traveler and may not have yet bought into that culture. Then again, he might well see his listening privileges as a means of control, as a means of getting intelligence. All of this meant Teracia would have to go to Baronth.

The chief navigation officer was not one for roaming about the ship. He was usually found in one of two places, either in the control room or in his quarters. Teracia tried the control room first because, if Agastin had already gotten to Baronth, that's where he would be. He was.

"Did you know this ship has a debris detection system that works four times as fast as the ones found in scout-class ships?" He asked as Teracia entered the room.

"You knew I was coming."

"Commander Agastin said I should expect you," Baronth said.

Teracia blanched. "Did he say why?"

"He said you would have concerns about our impending increase in speed."

"Did he?"

"Yes."

"And do *you* have concerns about that?" Teracia asked.

"The commander brought along Thryke," Baronth said. "Thryke, being a military fahr, knows all about the capabilities of this ship though he can't fly it. I knew that the ship was military grade and was capable of greater speed. So answering your question, yes, I was concerned about an increase in speed. Just because you can fly faster doesn't mean you should. The faster you go the more difficult it is to avoid obstacles and all that. So, I flew at a speed I was comfortable with, the same speed I use with the scout-class ships. Did I tell you I have a perfect operational record?"

"I've seen that record."

"It's not one I want tarnished," Baronth said. "Not that I would disobey a direct order if I were given one. But Agastin didn't do that. He brought along Thryke and the minister explained about the upgrades in the space debris detection system. It uses a quantum computer to calculate every probability of collision within this region of space. It does it in a nanosecond and continuously recalculates at the same speed. It also takes control of the ship to make evasive maneuvers if it determines, by a calculation of infinite probabilities, that the chief navigational officer, me, would not react quickly enough should such debris be detected in our path."

"Impressive," said Teracia.

"I don't trust it. I'm much more comfortable with digital computers. Quantum computers are, well, let's put it this way, they draw on supposed realities of which I have no experience. That's flying blind. But I agreed to try it to see how it goes. We're safe in interstellar space anyway, well protected against cosmic dust and radiation. There's not much else to hit. But we'll get to the Oort cloud soon enough and when that happens, we'll be reducing speed, or they'll be getting someone else to fly this thing."

"How fast will we be going until then?" Teracia asked.

"About two-thirds the speed of light. Commander Agastin should see some interesting compression in those radio signals."

Hiroshima

Agastin found the pace of the Homines' advance fascinating. It was impossible for a species to progress this quickly without destroying itself. A second global conflict had erupted, and the weapons were more lethal. This conflict extended the first with many of the same adversaries lining up against each other. But even though this second conflict had started only twenty-two years after the first, it was being fought by a different Homines generation. They lived such short lives that their horizons were tiny. How could they have a meaningful perspective on what they were doing to themselves and their planet if their entire lives were lived in what amounted to half of a fahr waking state? Seventy-five years. They would never survive as a species long enough to increase that life span.

This became even more clear with the next discovery. Agastin had been listening, with some considerable irritation, to a combination of overly orchestrated Homines songs and news of this war. There was a sudden spike in the radio signal, followed by a few days during which the finely tuned radio antennas had to be re-calibrated to compensate for increasing levels of background noise. Agastin had no idea what this was but suspected some new weaponry. He brought in Thryke.

"Play it again, Commander," Thryke said after he had heard the recording. Agastin did.

"There's something about this." Thryke mused.

"A weapon?" Agastin asked.

"I'm not sure, Commander," Thryke said. "I may have to go into my PDM, but which occupation should I to bring up? I was never a communication specialist so that can't be it. You said there was a lot of background noise after this?"

"For several hours afterwards, it was strong. Then it - weakened."

"And just one instance, Commander?"

"So far, yes," Agastin said.

"Can you still hear the background noise?"

"I had them re-calibrate the antennas and put in some filters, because the noise was interfering with most of the Homines' transmissions. The technicians showed me how to turn off the re-calibration though." Agastin gestured at the panel and the level of hiss jumped.

"And this is coming from Planet Song and not from somewhere else?" Thryke asked.

"As far as I can..."

The second spike was stronger than the first. Agastin and Thryke looked at each other.

"Commander, I don't know what this is but in my twenty-second occupation I was a military historian. I may have known back then."

"This development has only happened once before in any of the sapient species we have met," Thryke said. He was now speaking as a military historian, having downloaded the memories of that previous occupation. "It's keyed to rapid development. If you grow into this technology, if you wizen as you learn it, you will not weaponize it. The previous occurrence was in the early days of our interstellar explorations before we understood the risks of exposing less develop-ed species to our technology. We had shown this one species how to use nuclear power to prolong the lives of orbiting satellites. They took that knowledge and used it to develop destructive weapons, which they then turned on each other to solve a minor dispute about political succession. They destroyed three quarters of the surface of their planet, reduced their population to fifteen percent of its original number, and left that remaining population cancer prone and impoverished. A Fahr ship watched the whole thing unfold from an orbit far above the planet." Thryke's gill slits rippled. "Within a generation the mystics had a new set of revelations from The Giver. These forbade us from exposing any adaptive species to technology beyond that that they had achieved themsselves."

"And the whole pet collection process became that much more difficult," Agastin said.

"Yes," said Thryke, but he was thinking about something else.

"And the entire military lost its reason for being," said Agastin.

Pink shards flickered on Thryke's ballow and then disappeared. "There's no challenge in engaging in conflict when the results are always a forgone conclusion," he said. "We put on a show of force and get capitulation, every time. And when we don't, we immobilize them. Minimum casualties. We win, always. We are trained for wars we never fight."

Agastin studied Thryke. "Why did you sign on for this mission?"

Thryke said nothing.

"We have an under-armed ship moving towards a potential conflict with an adaptive species with nasty weapons. It almost looks like you've put this scenario in place, Minister Thryke."

"Everything we knew about this species suggested they were no threat, Commander. I could not have known, no one could have known, how this would unfold."

Agastin studied Thryke. "Yet unfold it has, Minister Thryke. And it continues to unfold, rapidly. Just so you know, Minister Thryke, I have every intention of collecting these singers. And with as little interaction with Homines as possible."

"Then you should hope they don't further use these new weapons before we get there, Commander. Because, compared to these devices, the whaling fleets you're so concerned about are nothing. There may not be singers left to collect."

Acceleration

How is it, thought Teracia, that Prostallen always seems to get sensitive information before I do? He spends ninety-eight percent of his time in his quarters, strapped to his wall, has less access to the COM system than I have, and has a lower security clearance. But was it actual information or was it informed speculation? Prostallen seemed certain that Agastin was about to increase the ship's speed again.

"But we're already travelling at the interstellar limit," Teracia said.

"We're only days from entering the star system. This is not about how fast we are going now, but about how fast we will go then."

"Surely Agastin does not plan to enter a star system at two-thirds the speed of light?"

"He will opt for a much more gradual slowing from our current speed than would be prudent, and for an eventual inner-stellar-system speed will be at least twice that of the normal .05," Prostallen said.

"But Baronth..."

"Perhaps, if you can get to him before Agastin does, the two of you can put up some kind of front, but don't count on it. Thryke has Agastin convinced that the Homines are about to blow up Planet Song."

Baronth

Baronth was in the control room, focused on the astronomical screen before him. Teracia wasn't sure he'd seen her enter the room. His right tentacle emerged from his abdomen and waved at the screen.

"Time to slow things down," he said. "It gets routine after a while. Everything gets routine if you allow yourself to be talked into repeating or extending an occupation." He turned to Teracia. "Are you planning to try this at some point, Vice Commander?"

"I hadn't given it much thought," Teracia said.

"It might be a come down after being a vice commander," Baronth said. "Personally, I don't make such decisions based on power considerations. It has to be an occupation that takes a while to master and evolves. Something that's not static. Something where the field of knowledge keeps expanding and keeps the mind engaged. That's what this has been so, when I was asked to repeat, I thought why not? Despite the repetition there's still lots to learn. But I hadn't counted on... I guess personal pride is an issue. I like to do my jobs well. So, when I'm told to endanger a ship..."

"Commander Agastin has already been here?" Teracia asked.

"He has, along with Minster Thryke. Apparently, our little Homines friends are engaged in a frenzy of self-destruction. They have developed a weapon powerful enough to destroy their planet, which means they have the power to destroy the thing Commander Agastin has come to collect." Baronth's gill slits flattened. "So, because of this, we're about the do something I've never heard of a Fahr ship doing before. We're about to put our safety at risk to collect a pet."

"You've agreed to this?"

"It's a question of rank, isn't it?" said Baronth. "At least that is how one is supposed to perceive it. And he is intimidating. He's not just the commander; he's the ex-chancellor of the entire race. Agastin has removed the diaphragms of those he doesn't like. So, it seems to me I have to balance the loss of my hearing against the loss of the ship. What would you do?"

"I cannot be emasculated," Teracia said.

Baronth's gills rippled. "All that means is he would have to devise a more appropriate punishment. But you get my point. Ethically the choice is obvious, but it cannot be seen as obvious. Not even by you, Vice Commander Teracia, which is why I intend to keep my own counsel from this point on."

The chief navigational officer turned away from Teracia and focused again on the navigation screen. They were about to enter the star system and Teracia knew the ship's speed, according to standard operational protocol, should be reduced to five percent of light speed. She watched as Baronth made the change to twenty percent.

"The deceleration will take 11.8 days," the ship's toneless voice said.

"The quantum computer worked well in interstellar space," Baronth said to Teracia. "No collisions or even close calls. We shall see how well it works within a star system."

Act Four: Jupiter

Course Correction

Baronth was in his quarters suspended in a qualuth; a body cleansing wedding precision laser technology with filtered song. The song he had chosen had been in honor of their entering the Planet Song system and comprised the clicking vocalizations of a small marine mammal that Homines called a spinner dolphin. In its filtered state, this produced a mild warming arousal and just enough impairment to mitigate the tiny zaps of the wall-mounted laser as it cleaned his scales. It had been a stressful time, and the qualuth was what Baronth needed. His eyes were closed, so he did not register the warning flicker of the strobe.

The jolt threw Baronth against the wall and snapped a small bone in his left fin. The pain flooded his system with stimulants and stopped the song's impairment. He pushed himself away from the wall, but the injury caused him to list the right. He pulled his left tentacle out, stabilized himself, and went to the COM system.

"What just happened?" he asked.

"I'm not sure but I think the quantum computer did a course correction," came the reply.

"Nothing hit us then?"

"No, Sir."

"Scan the area," Baronth ordered. "I want to know what we've just missed."

Teracia was in the observatory when the course correction happened. No other ship she had ever served on had such a room. She was curious about whether the view would be any different now they had transitioned between interstellar space and that of a star system. Nothing seemed to have changed apart from an increase in brightness in Planet Song's star.

The ship's warning strobe flashed. Something streaked across the sky and the ship lurched. She was thrown upwards toward the dome but had enough time to stop herself before a collision occurred. Then the ship's emergency lights flashed, and she rushed to the command center.

"A chunk of ice about the size of a fahr body," Baronth said.

Teracia looked at Thryke and then at Agastin.

"And how likely is something like that to happen again?" Agastin asked.

"About as likely as this was to happen, I suppose, Commander," Baronth said.

"You don't know," Agastin said.

"Our conventional sensors are not designed to operate at this speed and therefore we don't know what's out there. They designed the quantum computer's sensors to operate at this speed but detection and avoidance are simultaneous. They have to be. You will get no warnings," Baronth said.

"But we will hit nothing?" Agastin asked Thryke.

"We will hit nothing, Commander" Thryke assured him.

Agastin regarded his officers. "The good news is that our little bipeds have dropped none of their nuclear devices on each other. The bad news is that opposing sides are busy building more of them." He turned to Baronth. "We will continue on our present course and at our present speed."

Velocity

The menders had been busy. The quantum computer's abrupt course change had thrown fifty-seven crew members into walls, bulkheads, equipment, and other stationary objects. There were several broken bones, including the one in Baronth's fin, several sprains and abrasions, and one serious concussion. Roont, who was already recovering from over exposure to Homines song, had connected with the bulkhead with enough force to leave him unconscious for several days. The menders estimated that this would delay his return to duty by at least two months.

As Teracia swam into the communications center, she noticed Yarm in the corner. Agastin's personal assistant was putting away the commander's grooming tools and Teracia could see the sheen on Agastin's diaphragm. Personal grooming was done in one's quarters and was considered a private activity, even when one had a personal groomer.

The commander's attention was fixed on a grainy image on the center's screen. There appeared to be thousands of homines, dressed in white, swarming around an open space with a large black monument at its center. A solitary but beautiful voice was singing.

"Mecca?" Teracia asked.

"Yes, we finally get to see it and hear it. Astonishing isn't it?"

"So many of them..."

"Thryke did the math," Agastin said. "There are forty times as many homines on Planet Song than there are fahr in the entire galaxy."

Teracia let this sink in. "What have we done?" she finally asked.

"That's what I'm wondering. What happened six hundred years ago? A research mimic was lost that's all." Agastin gestured to the wall. "How does a robotic animal turn into this?"

The second jolt threw Agastin into the screen and Teracia into him. Mecca disappeared and the emergency lights flashed. Teracia gently pushed herself away from Agastin.

"Are you all right, Commander?" she asked.

"I'm fine," he said allowing himself to float back into an upright position.

Teracia studied Agastin for a moment and then went to the COM system. "Vice Commander Teracia here. Report."

"Another evasive maneuver by our friend the quantum computer," Baronth's voice said. "I think the obstacle was smaller this time."

The third jolt was much more powerful than the previous one. This threw both Agastin and Teracia into a wall sponge, but Yarm hit the bulkhead hard. The surrounding water clouded red. Agastin hit the COM switch.

"Commander Agastin here! Mender to the communications deck now!"

"Yes, Commander!"

Yarm floated away from the wall. His flukes were twitching, and his eyes were open but not responsive.

Remembrance

In a lifetime spanning forty thousand years Teracia had been to five memory rituals. When a species lived an average age of seventy millennia, deaths were rare events. Of the five rituals she had attended, only two could be recalled without accessing her PDM, the most recent being the mass remembrance for the thirty who had died due to The Song exposure on the first expedition. On Centrix, the Fahr did not die so much as fade out, while in stasis. The ancient would never surface, but the process of discontinuing would take 150 years. By then they were not missed or, if they were, so much time had gone by the emotional pain was minimal. The PDM was collected, added to the archives, and the body composted to feed the gardens. But in space the deaths were always sudden and jarring.

The bodies of the five crew members were put in active stasis chambers as if they were expected to revive. They attached each one, so the various elements of their physiologies could go on. There was life, after a fashion, but no sapience. The PDMs had been removed.

Prostallen had been asked to officiate because Commander Agastin had no experience in such matters. Agastin kept a low profile in the corner of the room. *A wise decision* thought Teracia. She watched as the crew members swam past him, struggling to control their ballows.

The menders had constructed a support system allowing Prostallen to remain upright while addressing the crew, most of whom now floated before the stasis chambers. The chambers themselves had opaque green coverings and were labeled. The bodies were present but could be seen only in outline. Prostallen's ballow inflated gold. Everyone went silent.

"It is the Will of Giver that we should each do a remembrance of those who have been taken from us," Prostallen said. "That we should ease them into the next stage of their being. Their bodies have been connected so that that which can live does and can be eased into death. But their minds are gone and with those minds any relationship you may have had with them. So today we will speak our memories. Each of you will approach that which lives from each of them and speak your memory over it. Speak only that which you presently contain, not that which you have stored in your PDMs. If you do not currently have a memory for one of them, then pass that one by. When you have finished speaking your memories, exit this chamber in silence. May The Will of the Giver be done by each of you."

By tradition, the memories were spoken in reverse order of rank, leaving the highest-ranking officers until last. No one would be in the room to hear what Agastin had to say and only he would hear what Teracia had to say. Recordings were made of all the re-membrances for the archives.

Yarm's stasis chamber was on the far right. Few of the crew

spoke memories over it. He was regarded by most as the property of Agastin and avoided for that reason. Teracia kept her silence until only she and Agastin were left. She spoke a few memories over each of the chambers and then went to the one containing Yarm.

"I remember your dedication to serving the needs of Commander Agastin and your self-sacrifice in doing that," she said. Then she turned to leave the room and let Agastin have his say, but he followed her out. She looked at him.

"I have no memories to speak over them," he said and continued on his way.

Draft Dodger

Robby Saunders was thirty-two years old, growing his hair long and wearing tie-dyed everything. He had a horn, a cheap imitation of the Martin trumpet Miles Davis had played on the "Kind of Blue" album. He had no case for it, so it hung on twine from a belt loop on his Levies. When he was hungry, he would stand on 5th Avenue or in some conspicuous place in the Village and play the entire album with his cap on the ground. Sometimes he would play Dizzy too if the mood struck him, but unaccompanied, so no one could hear the changes that grooved between his ears. This resulted in staccato bursts and lines punctuated by street-corner silences as he remembered the performances from the records he'd worn out and waited for his solo to come around. The coins were few. When things got tough, he'd drop a tab of acid, ride his thumb back to Atlanta, and work for a few months driving a truck for his uncle Ben's cement company. He was there when the yellow letter came: drafted.

The following day he was stuck in traffic with a spinning load of concrete. As he drummed his fingers on the wheel, he noticed a promo for a bus tour to Niagara Falls, Canada in the window of a travel agency. Simple enough, he thought. He finished the week, collected his pay, got a haircut, pawned the horn, and got on the bus. Hidden in his jeans was a final tab of acid, which he planned to take once he'd crossed the Canadian border. The falls would be amazing stoned!

At first Robby paid little attention to who his fellow travelers were but soon he realized his dilemma. He was the only single person. Everyone else was paired up and most of the couples were older. He heard snatches of conversation that told him this was largely a group of second honeymooners and realized he would stick out when it came time to go through customs. If they were looking for draft dodgers, they would find him. But there were a few young couples on the bus, probably just married and on a budget. He wondered if he could get paired up before they reached the border.

The trip's itinerary had them overnighting at a motel in Columbus, Ohio. That would give him eleven hours to find a desperate woman and get her on the bus. Time to unleash the old Robby Saunders charm. He took a shower in the motel room and then studied his naked self in the mirror. There was munchies flab around the middle and his teeth showed stain, the latter from coffee and pot since he didn't smoke tobacco. Over all, he looked good, especially once the jeans were on. He reminded himself that the goal was not a prom queen, just a woman, any woman.

The night manager told him there were two bars within walking distance of the motel. Did he want country, or did he want rock? He chose country. More alcohol, fewer drugs. In his experience, stoned women were a great deal less predictable. He wanted as much certainty as he could get.

He got rowdy instead, even though it was only nine when he walked into the place. Already a scuffle had broken out, some guy hitting on some other guy's girl. The bouncer stepped between the two and warned them off as Robby took a place at the bar. The girl was pissed off at her boyfriend for being so possessive. She was sulking in the corner.

Robby ordered a beer, determined to nurse it and keep his wits about him. The guy beside him at the bar was staring down at Robby's feet. Robby followed his gaze. Sandals. He was wearing sandals in a country bar. This was Columbus not Dallas! Why would that matter? But it did. A quick look around told him that everyone else was wearing either cowboy or work boots, even the sulking girl. It was a bad start.

"Buy you a drink, my friend?" he said to the guy beside him.

The guy grunted and smiled.

"Give him another of whatever he's drinking," Robby instructed the barkeeper.

The guy kept smiling.

The band had been tuning up when Robby came in. Two telecasters, a bass, and a small kit: Pure Buck Owens without the Buck, good old toe-tapping stuff. The dance floor filled, except the sulking girl who stayed where she was. Her boyfriend was not being persuasive. It took a few moments before the other guy noticed this. He made a broad gesture for the girl to join him on the dance floor. She did, followed by a right cross from the boyfriend. Two broken chairs and three smashed beer glasses later, the bouncer threw both into the street. The girl was back at her table in the corner. There was an extra chair. Robby walked over as if his sandals were cowboy boots. She grinned at him.

"So, ever thought of going to Niagara Falls?" Robby said to the warm bit of nakedness cuddled up to him.

"Niagara Falls? You mean up near Buffalo?"

"I was thinking of the Canadian side. Supposed to be a lot more beautiful."

"How d'you know?"

"Know what?"

"About me being Canadian?"

"I didn't. Are you really?" Robby asked.

"You're supposed to be able to tell. You know, the way we say 'about' and things like that. I've had to try hard not to say 'eh' 'cause that's a dead giveaway. I'm not supposed to be here. No green card or anything."

Robby laughed. "I can't believe this," he said. "How d'you wind up in Columbus?"

"A hockey player," she said. "He came up here to play with the Columbus Checkers. That's this really bad minor pro team that doesn't have any fans." She shrugged. "Anyway, it didn't work out, and I didn't have the money to get back. So, I've been, you know, couch surfing and doing odd jobs and stuff."

Robby couldn't help himself. He had the biggest grin on his face. She looked at him.

"You're gonna help me get back, aren't you?" she said stroking his leg.

"Well..." He looked at her and gestured.

"Angela, my name's Angela."

"Well Angela, I think we might be able to work something out. Fancy getting married?"

Angela's entire family turned out to be a single alcoholic mother living in Sudbury, Ontario. She was more than happy that her only daughter had married a guy she'd met a week earlier. She even helped Robby find an under-the-table job driving cement trucks. This he did for about four years, fathering sons Jeff and Reb during that time. Then in September 1973 Robby became a landed immigrant through the Canadian Adjustment of Status Program. Two weeks later, he emptied their meager savings account, bought a vintage Martin Custom C trumpet, and disappeared.

Assignment

Minister Wrasse had been summoned to the navigation room. He had not been there since his brief time at the helm, taking over while Baronth instructed Agastin on the intricacies of running the communications array. Afterwards, Wrasse had done his best to disappear, staying in his quarters where he nursed the slow regeneration of his scales. The menders had changed the chemical content in his quarters' water, adding some kind of circulating healing balm but this didn't follow him into the common areas. So, if he wanted some semblance of a normal appearance he had to spend as much time in his own quarters as possible. No one seemed to notice his absence, but he had not been forgotten. No doubt he would be assigned some task; the question was what?

"Minister Wrasse," Baronth said as Wrasse swam into the room. "You keep yourself hidden. Were you injured?"

"Chief Navigation Officer Baronth," Wrasse said with a slight ripple to his gills. "Concern about my wellbeing? How nice. My quarters are too small, as you know, and I was there for all three instances. So, I wasn't thrown far. Nothing but bruises and more scale damage. Not that I needed any more of that."

"You weren't at the remembrance."

"This is true, but the whole point of that is to offer one's memories of the deceased and I knew none of them. Given my rank that meant I would have had to float for hours while everyone of lower rank spoke his memories and, when it came time for me, I would have nothing to say. That would have me away from the healing balms in my quarters for no real purpose." Wrasse forced his gills to ripple. "You, I hear, broke a bone?"

"A small one," Baronth said. "I was lucky to be near a wall brace when the third one hit and could grab hold. Also, there were no issues with my staff apart from the same bruises and abrasions everyone else experienced. Some other departments weren't so lucky."

Wrasse's gills laid flat. "Five dead and two injured badly enough to require a prolonged down time for healing. I'm assuming we've slowed down?"

"I've received no such orders."

"So, we're still..."

"Racing towards Planet Song? Yes. If the path was direct, which it isn't, we could make it in about fifteen years at our current speed.

But we'll have to deal with the magnetic pull of four large planets and their respective moons, not to mention that belt of rubble between the fourth and fifth planets. Even if we left this quantum computer in control, it would have no choice but to slow us down. Either that or continue throw us around the inside this thing until it kills us all."

"Prostallen would survive," said Wrasse.

"The only one of us without a bruise," Baronth said his gills rippling. "I guess there are certain advantages to being suspended from the wall of your quarters."

"Acknowledge!"

Commander Agastin, Vice Commander Teracia, and Minster Thryke arrived together along with a fourth fahr Wrasse did not know.

"Are we all here then?" Agastin asked as he entered the room.

"Roont is in the care of the menders and Prostallen's mobility issues have restricted him to his quarters," replied Teracia. "Those who can be here are here."

Agastin studied both Baronth and Wrasse, but he lingered on Wrasse. The commander's gills did a small knowing wave, and Wrasse knew he would not like what was coming. Agastin turned away and addressed the group.

"Joining us today is Tunar," he said. "Tunar is part of our military contingent and has, in the past, done some programming for the quantum computer. He has been working on an algorithm to help us get past our current difficulties. I'll let him tell you what he's been doing."

Tunar, Wrasse could see, was fighting not to display mauve or yellow, but both were fringing around the base green he was trying to maintain. Tunar gave a forced gill ripple.

"First some background," he said. "The quantum computer we have on board is a rare item having restricted use only on military vessels of this size. Its intent is to give the military an extreme form of mobility in high-speed conflict situations. It was thought, at the time of its design, that its use would be restricted to actual conflict and for short durations. The designers understood that an abrupt change in direction could imperil the crew members, but this had never before happened. There have been few instances where it was used, and the durations of those instances were short. Before this, the quantum computers had never made any abrupt course changes even when this specific algorithm was engaged. So, this situation is unique."

Wrasse searched Tunar's eyes for some hint of inner retinal projection. Tunar was reading from a prepared script but nothing was visible, not even a glint off the eyes.

"Minister Thryke has asked me to modify the algorithm," Tunar said, "so it will take into account the physical wellbeing of the crew members when making course corrections and speed decisions."

To this point Tunar had both tentacles retracted but now he extended his right one. The digits held a disk that emitted a soft pinkish glow. He gave this to Baronth. Baronth studied it for a moment and then presented the disk to the navigation panel.

"Program received," the ship's voice said. "Modifications to speed and procedures will take 5.8 days."

"Does that mean we still have to take precautions until then?" Wrasse asked Tunar.

"It means things on board will get safer over the next 5.8 days."

"So, for the next little while we should take precautions? Fine. In my quarters I was safe. I'll stay there." Wrasse moved towards the door.

"This meeting is not over," Agastin said.

"Oh. I'm sorry, Commander Agastin. Forgive me. I thought..."

"Am I right in assuming that, since your time at the helm, you have been unoccupied?" Agastin asked.

"Well I uh, I've been undergoing therapeutic treatments in my quarters, Commander Agastin."

"Therapeutic treatments for your scales?"

"Yes, Commander Agastin."

"Which means you're not impaired, just unsightly?"

"Well, Commander Agastin, it does involve social impairment."

"At the moment, Minister Wrasse, we are down eight crew

members on this vessel, which means we don't have the luxury of personal vanity. My personal assistant, Yarm, was one of those whom we lost. You will take his place."

"I...?" Wrasse could not restrain the immediate reddening and inflation of his ballow. "I am an elected senior minister in the Fahr Government. I am no one's personal assistant!"

"Really, Minister Wrasse?" Agastin said. "Then perhaps I should drop the honorific. Because the only source of authority on this ship is its commander, and that commander has just demoted you."

Course Change

Baronth's gills were in a state of shimmer, of deep satisfaction. Teracia was happy for him. The new algorithm Tunar had introduced to the quantum computer slowed the ship to only a .65 percent increase over that of standard operating procedure. They now moved towards Planet Song at .050325 of light speed rather than .05. They would arrive at their destination only a few weeks earlier than planned; the ship would be safe, and no one would be hurt.

Teracia expected Agastin to be annoyed by this turn of events, but, if he was, he gave no sign. He entered the room displaying a contented kelpie green with a few streaks of gold as if everything was going as he'd hoped. Thryke and the now taciturn Wrasse followed him.

"We will change course," Agastin said to Baronth.

The chief navigational officer floated back from the helm and looked at his commander. "A change Commander?" he said. "We're already on the most direct route and travelling at optimal speed."

Agastin's gills flattened, and he ceased all movement. "Chief Navigational Officer Baronth, you are indispensable to this mission as I'm sure you are aware, but we will not require someone of your unique skill set to get us back to Centrix once this operation is over. I suggest you keep that small thought in the back of your mind."

"I will, Commander," Baronth said. The shimmering stopped.

"Minister Thryke will explain the reason for the course change."

Thryke extended his right tentacle into the room and opened its claspers. Within them was a disk similar to the one Tunar had brought earlier, but the glow was a soft yellow. "We will go to the fifth planet, the one the bipeds call Jupiter, and into orbit above its largest moon. We will synchronize our orbit there so the moon will always be between us and Planet Song."

It's a military maneuver, thought Teracia, *a stealth move, so we won't be seen.* "That will delay our arrival, Commander," she said. "I thought the idea was to get there before they blew up the planet and killed all The Singers."

Thryke answered. "The leaders of the various tribes seemed to have realized, at least temporarily, that a conflict using weapons of this nature would result in no victors. But they still have the weapons, so we will have to deal with them."

"As for The Singers," Agastin continued, "Homines has arrived at a planet-wide consensus to put a restriction on hunting them, at least for now. Wisps of maturity seem to be drifting over the chaos."

"Which means," Thryke continued, "we have time to monitor Homines from a safe distance while we decide how best to engage them."

"Engage them?" Teracia said. "Have we decided on a military option already? Will there be no attempt to talk to them?"

"Talk to them, Vice Commander?" Agastin said. "With whom would we talk? The Pope perhaps? The American president? The Chinese or Russian leaders? The Dalai Lama? A shaman from the Kalahari Desert is a possibility, I suppose."

"If you attempted to talk to one, the others would just resent it," Thryke said. "This is their pattern."

Teracia spoke to Agastin. "Commander, you just said they had reached a planetary wide decision to stop hunting The Singer. That, at least, points to their ability to cooperate. They may do so again once they become aware of us."

"This is true," Agastin said, "but, once we leave the orbit of that moon, we will be there quite quickly by their standards. How long would you say that last bit would take us, Baronth?"

"There is a massive orbiting debris field between the fifth and fourth planet," Baronth said. "We would have to slow to get through that without endangering the ship. It would take us from fourteen to twenty days to get from the fifth planet to Planet Song."

"There, you see," said Thryke. "They would not have enough time to unify their government before we arrived, even if they detected us as soon as we came out from behind that moon."

"Would they detect us?" Teracia asked.

"This is why I suggested we hide behind that moon," Thryke responded. "They have already detected moons orbiting the fifth planet much smaller than our ship. If their telescopes are pointed in our direction, they will see us."

"But would they recognize us for what we are even if they see us?" Teracia asked. "What degree of resolution do they have?"

"They'll know the minute we move," Baronth said. "Nothing within their system moves as fast as we can. They won't know what we are, but they'll know we're not natural."

"Which only means they'll be frightened," Teracia said. "It doesn't mean they'll form a world government for negotiation. They will not understand what they're dealing with."

Thryke's head bladder inflated red. "Are you suggesting that we reveal our presence to them well in advance? If we do have to engage them that makes no sense!"

"Correct me if I'm wrong, please, Minister Thryke," Teracia said, her own bladder matching his, "but we're on a mission to collect Singers, not to make war on another sapient species. We've already pushed them to where their development is out of control. I say we give them a chance to make a wise choice here."

"Have you seen any evidence of wise choices in these bipeds?" Thryke asked.

Baronth spoke up. "Commander Agastin, if they do hit us with one of those devices, and assuming we survive such an attack, this ship will be in no shape to carry The Singers back to Centrix."

Thryke had reached rage red. "There is no conceivable way they would have delivery systems capable of attacking this ship!"

"Yet," Teracia said.

Agastin had been watching the exchange. "All right, we will not hide," he said. "We will orbit the fifth planet in full view of them and before we get there, we will transmit radio signals, so they will know we are coming. They will expect us."

"But what will we transmit, Commander Agastin?" It was the first thing Wrasse had said.

Agastin's gills flattened. "A while back I recorded a song off their radio broadcasts, one that Homines sang about the slaughter of The Singers. When they hear it being played back to them, they will know why we are coming."

Pioneer 10

"Anomaly detected," the ship's voice said.

Agastin looked at the communications screen but there was nothing displayed apart from a frequency range.

"Why is this an anomaly?" he asked.

"The signal is weak, does not originate from the target planet, and is not natural in origin," the ship responded.

"State the source," Agastin said.

"The source is a primitive mechanical scientific probe. It broadcasts on a frequency range typical to those used by Homines. The device is too small to contain a life support system and, given its speed and assuming an origin of the target planet, it has been on its current trajectory for at least thirty years. It is experiencing gradual power loss and so the signal is weakening. It is travelling outwards from the star and will leave the star system if it stays on its current course. However, it will lose all power to its internal systems before then."

"This is probably the Pioneer 10 space probe they've been talking about," Agastin said to himself. "How close it is to us? How much time will it take us to intercept?"

"It is approaching us at a 67.83-degree angle from the star. We will be equidistant with it from the star in about 3.145 days, but the degree value means it is .78431 of a light year away. Time to intercept would be 14.1763 years."

"So, it's on the other side of the star system?"

"Yes."

"Is there any point to us intercepting this?" Agastin asked Thryke and Teracia.

"How old is it?" Thryke asked.

"If it's their Pioneer 10 probe, then it's thirty years old," Agastin said. "It was launched to explore the two largest planets in their stellar system and its trajectory will eventually take it into interstellar space."

"At their current rate of technological advance, that would make it obsolete," said Thryke. "And, if its purpose is interplanetary research, then it may contain nothing of strategic value. Intercepting it would also delay us, perhaps by as much as fifteen years."

"Then we ignore it?" Agastin asked.

"Maybe not," said Teracia. Both Thryke and Agastin looked at her.

"The probe is still sending signals back to Planet Song, it is not?"

"Much weakened but yes, it is still sending," said Agastin.

"And someone is monitoring those signals?" Teracia said.

Agastin studied the vice commander for a moment then his gills rippled. "I think we've found our frequency for communicating with Planet Song."

Thryke pinked. "Delaying the inevitable," he said.

NASA

Trent Proctor was a balding redhead with a perpetual sunburn. The last thing he ever thought about when he went into town was picking up sunscreen. He didn't like the feel of the stuff in his thinning hair anyway, so he opted for a hat, whenever he remembered to put it on, which wasn't often. So, he peeled in the desert sun, tiny little wisps, which floated above the surface of his red skin. He ignored these and their carcinogenic implications whenever he glimpsed them reflecting off his monitor.

He frowned. "When was the last time we received a signal from Pioneer 10?" he asked into the room.

A few other geeky heads popped up from behind their respective monitors. No one was sure who was being asked the question. They all worked for NASA's Deep Space Network in Goldstone, California. Their job was to track communications between the Earth and the various satellites and space probes NASA had launched.

"I'll check the logs," Diana McLean said, "But I think it was at least a week ago. We can barely detect them now, anyway. It's running out of juice. Why?"

Diane was a curvaceous fortyish woman who over dressed for the desert heat. Her pantsuits were always creased, and she was a smoker. This took her outside periodically where the desert heat blessed her with sweat stains on her blouses and just enough body odor to leak through her deodorant. This was only a problem if she got close to you and that only happened if you were the flavor of the month. Trent had been that in the past and had no wish to repeat the experience.

"Because we're receiving a strong signal from it at the moment," said Trent. Now he had everyone's attention.

"Not possible," said Billy, the resident Goth. The NASA dress code kept him from wearing his black leathers, but he still had the piercings, tattoos and gelled black hair. "It's on its way out of the solar system so the signal has to be weak, very weak."

Trent shrugged. "I'm just telling you what I'm seeing," he said.

Everyone moved on mass to his screen. Trent changed the view to that of a waveform.

"Jesus," Billy said. "That is strong. Can't be from Pioneer then. Some cross frequency interference. Has to be terrestrial."

"Our filters would catch that," Diane said.

"Put it on audio," someone suggested, and Trent flipped the switch.

The room filled with wordless human harmonies, so gorgeous everyone stopped to listen. When the initial vocals had finished, there was short instrumental part with whale song in the background and then a return to singing, this time with lyrics decrying the hunting of whales.

"The tree huggers have hacked into the system," Billy said. "Tricky getting through that firewall."

"But why us?" Trent said. "Why would they go to all that trouble to get into NASA's Deep Space Network? It's not as if NASA is out killing whales."

"Crosby and Nash," said Diane. "*Wind on the Water,* off their second album I believe. It's been a while since I've heard that. Came out in the '70s. Reminds me of good times."

"Whatever," Billy said."The question is how did they trick the system into identifying it as coming from Pioneer 10? We'll have to call Jacobs. He'll want to know about this."

Cadets

Angela Saunders sat on the Sally-Ann sofa with a glass of scotch in one hand, a cigarette in the other, and a half-empty bottle of Hennessy leaning against her thigh. She had splurged, but she could see that Reb did not appreciate it. Her eleven-year-old son had stolen one of her cigarettes and was defiantly blowing smoke rings at her from across the room.

"Why don't you go outside and play hockey or something," she slurred.

Reb gave her the finger.

"I thought you liked hockey?"

"Yeah, with a puck and on ice," Reb said.

"You know I can't afford..."

"What did that cost?" Reb said pointing at the bottle.

"I was celebrating."

"Celebrating what?"

"The trumpet. The fuckin' trumpet! Ten years ago, today that was!"

Angela poured herself another glass and toasted Reb with it. Her son ground the remains of his cigarette into the arm of the chair and stormed out the front door. A few seconds later, another whiskey bottle, this one empty, came crashing through the picture window. Angela instinctively protected her drink from the flying glass. She looked at the still-intact bottle, now resting on the carpet in front of her. Crown Royal. Cheap stuff. She took another drink of her Hennessy.

The following morning, after sweeping up the glass and making the kids pancakes, she called Atlanta. "I think you'd better come and get them, Ben," she said. "I can't do this mothering thing anymore." It was a moment of clarity in an otherwise foggy life.

Ben was sixty years old, with two failed marriages and no children. He had sold his cement business and had planned to spend his retirement hunting, fishing, and playing golf. The local chapter of the NRA had also been pressuring him to run for president. Now he had to rethink things.

Jeff was thirteen and Reb eleven. Both were fit, despite not having played any organized sport or being involved in anything else organized. The resentment was palpable. Ben knew he would have to work on that, but the first order of business was to get the kids involved in the things they had been missing. They tried baseball, football, and basketball. Neither boy had played any of those sports and they were well behind the skill level of other boys their age. Then came army cadets.

What appealed to Ben about army cadets was that the boys had to be at least eleven to be involved. That meant Jeff and Reb wouldn't have to play catch up the way they would with other activities, but the cadets were fussy about discipline. Jeff and Reb had a way to go in that department, but it was worth a try. To Ben's surprise, both boys loved it and wanted to sign up.

"One thing though," Ben said as they were filling out the forms. "I wouldn't mention that your dad was a draft dodger."

"We hate him," Reb said while his older brother nodded. "We don't talk about him at all. You're our dad now."

"And our mom, " Jeff added.

They would never see either parent again.

Wall

The train was almost two-thirds the way across East Germany before the transport *polizei* made an appearance. Andreas Huber tensed but the two men, dressed in dark blue uniforms with gold sashes, seemed casual and chatty. They took little more than cursory glances at the papers and passports presented to them and wished everyone a good trip before moving on to the next car. There was a collective release of held breaths.

"Fucking blueberries," Andreas said just loud enough for everyone in the car to hear.

"Something's going on," said the lady across the aisle from him.

"They've been more relaxed lately," a tall whiskered man in a tweed jacket said and shrugged. "I take this train twice a week, and recently it's been almost pleasant."

"Probably Gorbachev is going on," Andreas said. "Probably Honecker is listening to Gorbachev for the time being, but I don't trust him." His foot nudged the dirty blue duffel at his feet. The top layer he'd filled with smelly gym clothes, disgusting enough to discourage further investigation. Beneath that was a layer of Sea Shepherd propaganda he planned to hand out in Berlin once he got there.

Andreas had long greasy brown hair and a face bearing the traces of a major adolescent battle with acne. He was slight of frame, green of eyes, and bore little resemblance to the Hollywood depiction of Aryan good looks. He nudged the duffel again as if, by doing so, he was keeping it and its contents safe. The *polizei* had gone through, so the next problem would be his father.

Werner Huber was thicker than his son and he had a short blond brush cut and blue eyes, a late middle-aged Aryan. He greeted Andreas with a cap-toothed smile, a slap on the back, and a grunt as he hefted the duffel into the Volkswagen's trunk.

"What have you got in there? Dutch beer?"

"Brochures," Andreas said knowing his father would find out anyway.

"Brochures?"

"Sea Shepherd stuff."

Werner sighed and shook his head. They got into the car.

"Did you meet him?"

"Who?"

"Paul Watson, the criminal."

"No, and he's not a criminal. He's an activist. There's a difference."

"He rammed a whaling ship. That's a criminal act."

Andreas said nothing.

"So why the brochures? I thought you wanted to get on board?"

"They know nothing about me. And I'm not a seaman. I thought

I'd prove my worth to them in other ways. Increase my chances."

Werner shook his head again. He pointed to a long line of people outside of a MacDonald's. "East Germans," he said. "The wall will come down soon, but it has not happened yet. They are opening more crossing points though. We've given each of them about fifty dollars to spend." He laughed. "They are imprisoned for thirty years in a communist state and what do they do when they get out? They line up to buy fast food."

The city was in full party mode. People were drinking and dancing and singing and everyone was smiling, everyone except for Erich Honecker. Reagan had told Gorbachev to tear down Honecker's wall, but no one was waiting for Gorbachev. Dusty Germans carried around chucks of cement and stone, some of which still had traces of wall art. One man pushed a wheelbarrow with a large slab of concrete in it. On the slab there was an intact painting of someone tangled in barbwire.

"I lent it to the wall," he explained. "Now, I'm taking it back."

Andreas tucked a Sea Shepherd brochure into the wheelbarrow. "Something for you to think about when all this is over," he said. He adjusted the strap on his backpack and passed out another brochure. He had passed out hundreds but now, as he made his way back to his father's flat, he noticed many of them were just lying on the street.

Werner greeted him with a huge smile. "Normally in times of chaos the criminals thrive," he said. "But perhaps not today?"

"You're wrong," Andreas lied. "People were engaged."

9/11

There was fire, smoke, and chaos. But in the overall scheme of things, the aircraft impacts on the two towers did not seem to be that large an event. After all the various bombings of the Second World War had been much more destructive and had taken many more homines lives. Commander Agastin knew different. The events had taken place in the largest city of the most powerful nation on Planet Song. The United States of America had a huge stockpile of nuclear weapons. It had come close to unleashing it a generation and a half earlier over a minor squabble on a small island off its southern coast. This was a much bigger provocation, a direct attack on their soil. What would they do?

He placed the intercepted signals on every display on the ship. The broadcasts continually replayed the crashes of the two aircraft, the collapses of both buildings and images of dusty bipeds wandering their city in a state of shock. The newscasts were stoking the emotions of the country's inhabitants, preparing them for war. And if there was a war, and if they used the nuclear weapons, they had at their disposal, then the retrieval mission might as well head back to Centrix. They were too far away to intervene and there would be nothing to collect in the aftermath. Agastin wanted the crew to have a full understanding of the situation and he wanted to be sure he understood it himself. They could reduce the greatest prize in the history of song seeking to radioactive pulp before they had a chance to to collect it.

Honi

Kale placed his feet with exaggerated care as he walked around the fire pit. One other time, when he had been less than attentive and had also consumed a few too many Fire Rock Pale Ales, he had slipped and burned the side of his leg on one of the cooking stones. He still had the scar and was imbibing the same ale. It made him wary.

The cousins had arranged the luau to celebrate the successful defense of Kale's PhD thesis; a study of environment factors in the production of humpback whale song. It had been an intense few weeks, but it was done, and it was time for some serious loose letting.

Kale had had almost no social life for most of the past few years, but when he had gone out, Ka Pua was almost always in the company of his cousins. He couldn't help but notice. Ka Pua was not a cousin—not a close one anyway—and so she was fair game. He had even been told she had grown up in Honolulu, which made it even more unlikely they were genetically close. His cousins would never have worried about such things, but Kale had spent too much time in the presence of scientists obsessing about the dwindling genes pools. *What the hell,* he thought, *she's cute.* He held out his bottle and clicked it against hers.

"To King Kamehameha the Second," he said saluting her.

"Who?"

"He was the king who first allowed women to eat with men at luaus," Kale said.

"Really?" she said.

Kale could already see this was not going well. He could break whale song into its component parts and even recreate it using synthesizers, but he could not talk to women. It didn't help that he wore XXL floral print shirts that still stretched around the middle and was attempting dreadlocks. Ka Pua was not interested. She was scanning the crowd behind him, looking for a way out.

"Hey, congrats on your thesis," she said with a forced cheeriness. She waved and made her way to another of Kale's cousins.

"Thanks," he said holding up the bottle again as she passed.

The scream behind him nearly made him drop his ale. He turned to see several cousins rushing to a small prone figure at the bottom of a coconut palm. It was Honi, the daughter of one of Kale's older cousins, and his favorite in that generation.

"Oh my God! Oh my God!" shouted one woman. "She's not breathing!"

Kale pushed himself through the gathering crowd and got down on his knees beside his young cousin. Honi was breathing, but in tiny panicked gasps.

"Let me through, please. I'm a nurse!" Ka Pua shouted.

Honi was awake but only her eyes and mouth were moving. The crowd let Ka Pua through and then closed around them. Kale acknowledged her and got out of her way. She did a quick once over of Honi and then turned to Kale.

"Get an ambulance now!" she commanded. "And tell them it's a possible broken neck with serious respiratory complications, and that you got that from an emergency-room nurse who's on the scene. They'll want to know who made that assessment."

Kale nodded and ran to the house to make the call.

No one thought to take the pig out of the fire pit until well after the ambulance had left. It was overcooked, but no one cared. They drifted away in twos and threes until only a handful remained doing clean up. Kale stared out to sea, looking for whale breeches where none were likely to be.

"Is she your sister?"

Kale looked back to find Ka Pua standing behind him on the beach.

"No, a cousin. A second cousin if you want to get technical." He gestured out to sea. "She loves the whales. Can't get enough of them, so she's naturally drawn to what I do. Is she going to be all right?"

Ka Pua shuffled her feet and followed his gaze out to sea. "She's got serious trauma, but she's young. You never know how they will respond if they get the right care."

"A careful answer."

"Would you prefer a rash one?" she asked.

"No. I'd prefer hope in whatever package you want to offer it. I'm thinking about making my way over to the hospital in a few minutes."

"They won't let you in. She'll be in intensive care and that's immediate family only. For first few days, anyway." They stood for a while watching the waves. She reached out and touched his arm. "I've got to be going," she said.

"Thanks for coming," he said. He turned and watched as she made her way back to the parking lot. She had just the right number of curves, fit but not fat while not looking like she was on a perpetual diet. He, however, needed to get on one, but he didn't know how many times he'd told himself that without ever following through. And every time he got on the scale the task was bigger than it had been the previous time. No wonder he studied whales.

Canada

Paul Watson did not take Andreas on board the Sea Shepherd. It would have helped if Andreas had not gone into the interview stoned. He had bumped into some friendly sailors on the dock whom he assumed were part of the Sea Shepherd crew. They were not, but they were generous with their weed. So, on the assumption he was partaking in Sea Shepherd culture, he joined in. Watson was not impressed.

On the rail trip back to Berlin Andreas thought about Canada, about the pristine north, about battling big oil and mining companies.

"You were not invited to join the criminals," his father said over coffee the following morning.

"They had no openings," Andreas lied.

"But they interviewed you, anyway, making you come all the way from Germany?"

"In case there were openings."

"But there are not?"

"No."

"They wasted your time and your money."

Andreas said nothing.

Werner put his hand on his son's shoulder. "There are other ways to be involved in these issues."

"I know. I'm going to Canada. I'm going to emigrate," he said.

"Canada?" Werner said removing his arm.

"It's your fault. You took me there."

His father nodded. They had been on a hunting trip to northern Canada when Andreas was a teenager. "There are worse places," Werner said. "What will you do?"

Andreas shook his head. "I don't know."

"It's the North, right? That's where you want to go?"

"It's beautiful and still untouched." He didn't want to bring up the oil and mining companies.

"You will need a skill that's useful there. They have regulations. You can't just emigrate because you feel like it. Make yourself attractive to them. Otherwise they'll just refuse you."

"I can be a guide, an outfitter," Andreas said.

"Perhaps, after you get to know the terrain and get experience but remember there are many people serving as guides and outfitters up there who know the land. If you put that on an immigration document as your intention, they won't let you in. Why should they? They already have much more knowledgeable people doing that. You will need a skill that will get you into the country."

Andreas sighed.

"A pilot's license. Learn how to fly the bush planes. I remember talking to a pilot when we were there. He was Swedish. He told me he had gone through some kind of bush pilot school."

"In Canada?"

"It's much easier to get a student visa there. When he finished, he popped over to Alaska, applied for landed immigrant status showing he was a graduate from that school, and they took him because they were short of bush pilots."

Andreas looked at his father suspiciously. "Why are you being so helpful?"

Werner shrugged. "My son has been refused membership in a criminal organization. What father wouldn't want to steer his son on to a straighter path given the opportunity? Besides, it would give me an excuse to go bear hunting again."

"You didn't shoot a bear the last time we were up there."

"I did, using the Bolex."

"So, we're talking about film here and not guns?"

"No. Not guns. I don't know what I was thinking: killing endangered animals for sport. After all these years, it's still embarrassing."

B-25 Mitchell

Jeff Saunders was a Republican, but he hated George W. Bush. Right now, he was on his way over to his brother's place for the third time this week. Nancy had called again and said Reb was out back of their place bayoneting trees. She said he hadn't been drinking. Maybe not, Jeff thought, but he was into something. A sober Reb did nothing but stare at TV.

Their uncle Ben owned few acres outside Tifton, Georgia; he'd bought on spec, though what he'd been speculating about wasn't all that clear. He'd let Reb park a trailer out there and had put in a phone, power lines, a satellite dish, a septic tank, and had even sunk a well. The situation was livable if isolated. The rural school bus didn't come down their road so Nancy had to load the two girls into the pickup and drive them to and from school every day. She welcomed it because it got her out of the house and away from Reb.

Jeff found his brother in the backyard straddling a canvas camp stool and smoking a thin cigar. At his feet lay the old M1903 rifle with the bayonet attached and splinters of wood still clinging to it. Reb had found the World War I rifle, complete with a blade, in the back of a closet after he'd bought the trailer from a much-older vet. He had never fired it but fixed the bayonet and used it to attack trees.

"How's it going, eh?" Jeff said.

Reb laughed. "You've got to lose that Canadian accent," he said in his cultivated Southern drawl. "Everyone around here thinks you're some kind of pinko." Jeff, being the older brother, had kept his Canadian accent. His younger brother had lost his, becoming a Southern boy.

"Canadians are pinkos?" Jeff asked.

"Got socialized health care, don't they?"

"Can't argue with that, I guess," Jeff said.

"You know you can wait ten years up there for a hip replacement?"

Jeff shrugged. "You can get it done in Atlanta in a week, *if* you pay big insurance premiums or have a shitload of money."

"*If.* Well our system ain't perfect, that's for sure."

Neither of them said anything for a moment. Reb used his foot to flick a splinter off the bayonet.

"Kill any trees?" Jeff asked.

"Better than watchin' Oprah," Reb said.

"Nancy called me."

"So, this isn't a social call?"

"She's pretty concerned."

Reb dropped the cigar butt and pushed it into the damp soil with the heel of his boot.

"You get any sleep last night?" Jeff asked.

"Night's when the best TV's on. Old war movies."

"So, you didn't sleep?"

"It'll pass, Jeff. It'll pass. I got to give it time that's all."

"They've got programs, good ones from what I hear."

"I'm not going through any of that veteran's psycho bullshit," Reb said. He picked up the M1903 and walked back to the trailer. "There's no point in you coming out here," he said over his shoulder. "It's not makin' anything better." He opened the door to the trailer, entered, and slammed the door behind him.

Jeff stood in the yard for a few moments studying the splintered tree trunks. "I need air time," he said to himself. He made a modest living giving flying lessons at the Henry Tift Myers Airport just outside Tifton. During the Second World War, the place had been a training facility for the Air Force, so Jeff looked at it as a kind of continuity.

It wasn't. Flying a single-engine recreational aircraft was nothing like dealing with F-16s. You flew a lot slower with a lot fewer instruments, and you weren't packing ordinance and killing people. Not that you actually saw anyone die in an F-16; you were too far away to see that. Not like Reb, not like house-to-house urban combat, not like Fallujah. Nearly everyone in his unit was dead or maimed or messed up. And there weren't any weapons of mass destruction, just a crazy dictator and a lot of oil. The Iraqis didn't like democracy, anyway. They were too busy offing each other to participate.

Jeff pulled his Jeep into the flight school's parking spot and got out. Everyone he could see was looking skyward. An old B-25 Mitchell bomber was circling above them, not something you saw every day. Jeff watched as it made its approach and heard the distant screech as it put down. It taxied to within a few hundred feet of the terminal and stopped. It was poetry. A small crowd gathered, veterans and few younger vintage aircraft keeners. Some of them he knew by name, others only by sight. He joined them.

"Hey, Jeff. Didn't know you were interested in history," one of them said. He wore a John Deere baseball cap and had straw clinging to his work boots.

"Hey, George," Jeff said shrugging. "It's just cool seeing old machines that still work."

"This one's stock, a beautiful restoration. They'll take you up if you want. They're always looking for pilots they can train, especially vets."

"Yeah? I suppose most of the folks who know how to fly one of these would be long in the tooth."

"Lots of young folks want to learn but these guys are picky. Looking for seriousness of purpose, people who understand. Show 'em your veteran's card."

Jeff did just that. The old man who met him at the ramp squinted at the card and then studied Jeff. "Welcome aboard, Captain Saunders," he said in a soft voice. "You can call me Willy. I was just a bombardier back in the day, so you outrank me, but I've been out of the services for too long to stand on ceremony. I hope you don't mind."

"Not at all," Jeff said.

"But the Major, when you meet him, he'll want proper respect. Let me show you around the aircraft. It's a bit cramped as you'll see."

The B-25 was one hundred percent WWII functional so, even though it had the updated communications system required by modern aviation standards, the original radio was still functional. It was like stepping into his grandfather's era.

"Your dad went down with the Arizona?" Willy asked.

"My grandfather. So, I never met him."

"And you flew over Iraq?"

"I did."

"Flying this thing is a bit different from what you're used to."

"I'm up for the challenge."

"Well it's not me who has the final say. That'll be the Major, but you look like his kind of person. He'll like the Arizona connection, that's for sure."

"Impressed with legacies, is he?"

Willy nodded. "He's got his own. A million stories. You'll see."

Ganymede

When Teracia arrived at the observatory, the menders had already installed Prostallen. The ex-commander now had more restraints than and it was easy to see why. Spasms were now clear in both his fins and his tentacles. He did not appear to have noticed her when she entered, his gaze involved with the giant spectacle of Ganymede projected on the dome above them, but he had noticed her.

"Did you know this moon has liquid water," he said, still staring at Ganymede. "Imagine that. This far out it should be frozen solid, but apparently geothermal processes heat it. Have they tested it for life?"

"Yes, and there is none," Teracia said. "And if there were, it would be due to secondary seeding. Perhaps it hasn't yet occurred to Homines to try that."

"Maybe it's still beyond them," Prostallen's gills rippled. "Or maybe it's because it's not inherently destructive."

"They're learning."

"Not fast enough. And there was never a response to our message."

"It was met by general confusion. Their instruments told them that the signal came from the Pioneer 10 spacecraft, but the song itself dates from several years after its launch. They've been going on the assumption that someone on the planet has made a terrestrial signal look like it's coming from the edge of their stellar system. They were obsessive about it. NASA is supposed to have a secure system, so naturally they want to know how it was breached. We stopped sending it. It was pointless."

"So we're within striking distance and still nothing's been communicated?" Prostallen said.

Teracia gestured to the dome. A small bright dot to the left of Ganymede became highlighted. "That is Planet Song," she said. "We can see them, but they can't see us."

"We're a lot smaller than a planet, or a moon," Prostallen said.

"Yes and detecting us this close to Jupiter is unlikely. The scattered light from the planet itself and this moon makes us invisible even if they had advanced frequency filters and they don't. But we're bigger than several of the moons they've discovered orbiting Jupiter further out. That's where we must be if we want to be seen, away from the glare. Even then they'll have to be looking for us."

"And they will be," said Commander Agastin entering the observatory, "we'll send that song again, this time from Jupiter, on several frequencies and in a manner that gives no doubt where it came from."

"Acknowledge!" Teracia said as Thryke, Wrasse, Baronth, and Roont, followed Agastin into the observatory. The latter had a wobble to his swim and did not look well.

Thryke looked right at Teracia. "We've consulted the menders and Communications Officer Roont has been cleared for limited duties."

Teracia studied the minister of defense, her rage building into red. She knew nothing of the mender's decision and, as vice commander, she should have known about it before Thryke. Roont was listing even as he floated before them, his gills rippling bravely. He was in no shape to resume duty.

"Perhaps, I should consult with the menders myself since staffing issues are my responsibility," her ballow now inflated.

"Actually, Vice Commander," said Agastin. "It was I who consulted with the menders and they have given the Communications Office Roont clearance to resume his duties at the communications console. He will have time limitations, but his presence will allow me to get on with the business of extracting The Singers."

Teracia studied the other officers. Baronth avoided her gaze. Wrasse was staring straight ahead. Prostallen had flattened his gills and appeared to be studying the projected image of Ganymede. She looked back at Roont who was fighting to keep his stability and losing control of his ballow. This was shifting hues. She said to him, "Could you teach me to operate the console? Can you manage that?"

"Vice Commander Teracia, what are you talking about?" said Agastin.

"Commander, you are about to extract The Singers. My job was to get you into a position where you could do that. That I have done. You are here. Right now our most pressing need is for accurate up-to-date information about what Homines is doing."

The observatory went silent except for the ever-present sound of circulating water. Agastin and Thryke looked at each other and then back to Teracia. Neither spoke.

"And we both know this fahr," she said pointing to Roont, "is in no condition to resume his duties. Especially since exposure to song again will further compromise him. I have the advantage of being song dead. Providing Communications Officer Roont is well enough to give me a working knowledge of the console, I think this is best. If he is not well enough to do that, he will also fail you as communications officer."

Prostallen's gills were rippling. Agastin looked at him. "You find this amusing?" he said.

"I am dying, Commander," he said. "I will not survive this voyage. It's quite liberating in a way because it removes concern for one's future." He gestured to Teracia. "She's right because there is enormous risk in sacrificing Communications Officer Roont in this way. If he fails, you yourself will be the only backup which would effectively put the whole mission into the hands of a fahr who wants war more than he wants The Singers."

Thryke's ballow had swollen red. "I am here, like everyone else on this mission, to extract The Singers!"

"So you say, Minister Thryke," said Prostallen, "but I wonder to what extent you were involved in this decision to reinstate Roont, and why the decision was made without consulting the vice commander. This may well be Commander Agastin's intent, but, if so, it is my duty as adviser to point out the implications."

Agastin studied Thryke and then Prostallen. "You have performed your duty, Prostallen." He gestured to the cushion. "We should take our places. This promises to be a long discussion."

Each of them took their respective places but Roont, who had never been to a meeting in the observatory, seemed uncertain both about his place and how to install himself. He floated awkwardly above the cushion until Teracia swam over to help him.

"You are the junior officer here Officer Roont," she said to him. "This is your place." She indicated the space between Baronth and Wrasse.

"Thank you, Mamini," Roont said and maneuvered himself into place. Once there his gills rippled.

"Nice, isn't it," Prostallen said to him.

"Yes."

"I will begin with the obvious," Agastin said. "We are orbiting Ganymede, the largest of Jupiter's moons. We will not remain here. The astrophysicists are calculating an orbit around Jupiter much farther out and away from the planet's glare. And Minister Thryke has a device we can set off once they're looking in the right direction. It creates a burst of protons that will make us much brighter from Planet Song than we would normally be. That combined with our hijacking of all their space probe radio frequencies should bring us to their attention."

"And so, Commander, the plan is to rebroadcast that same song?" Prostallen asked.

"Yes, but this time there will be no doubt about the song's origins."

"And why are we taking that action, specifically?"

"You mean as opposed to a direct contact approach?"

"Well, we have already sent that song once, from the edge of this stellar system, and my understanding is it was met with general confusion. They concluded not that it was a communication from an-other sapient species, but a breech in their own security protocol. Why would it be any different this time?"

"Because we'll be doing it in concert with their discovery of our ship," said Thryke. "They will know where it's coming from."

"But it's their own song," said Teracia. "I'll grant you it talks about the problems with their harvesting of The Singer, but it says nothing about our intentions and it is not our content even if we agree with the sentiments expressed."

Agastin studied the vice commander and his gill slits rippled. "I may be occupying the position of commander on this ship, but my reality is that I am an elite-level fahr. I have spent most my existence as a mono-occupational concerned with matters of governance." He tapped his PDM. "Within this I have the memories of my exhaustive studies of every available text on matters of diplomacy. One of the guiding principles of diplomacy is, if one wishes to communicate with another sapient species, one should use methods of communication with which the other species is familiar."

"But, Commander Agastin," said Teracia, "this is not communication. This is reflecting back to them what they, and not us, have created."

"This is true, but this reflection has to be seen in context. From their perspective, an alien species has just sent them one of their own songs on a specific theme. And we will have done it twice. From that they should be able to infer we are concerned about their treatment of The Singers."

"I don't understand how that, alone, would make them form a planetary government."

Thryke answered. "That we are here means we are much further advanced than they are. To deal with us they will have to unite. If they don't, then the extraction process will get a lot more interesting."

Despite her efforts to control it, Teracia's ballow was reddening. "Minister Thryke, with due respect to your status before coming aboard this ship, I addressed that question to Commander Agastin, not to you."

The sound of the observatory vortexes and spouts got a lot louder and most of the focus seemed to be on Ganymede. Wrasse's gills were rippling as he looked at Roont beside him. "Oh my," he said.

Roont had fallen asleep, his head lolling to one side.

"He has been under heavy sedation due to his injuries," Teracia said.

"It doesn't matter," said Agastin. "We'll revive him later, but it is now clear we can't use him as the communications officer." He looked at Teracia. "You are the logical choice to replace him. Have the menders bring him around and see what you can learn from him."

"Yes, Commander," Teracia said.

Thryke had no visible reaction to this but Prostallen's gills rippled. He looked at Teracia and then returned his gaze to Ganymede. They would talk later.

"We are looking at two broad scenarios here," Agastin continued. "The first, and I believe less likely of the two, has our little bipeds uniting and forming a provisional government for negotiation. In that event, we could offer them some small advances in technology for The Singers. This goes against The Will of the Giver, but the damage is done. The second and more likely scenario is that we extract The Singers without their agreement."

"So," Teracia said, "we behave in an agressive manner toward them hoping, by our example, they will behave in a less aggressive manner towards each other?"

Again the vortexes and spouts got much louder. The ballows of both Agastin and Thryke were reddening. A stream of bubbles came out of the mouth of the sleeping Roont and he sank further into the fountain. Wrasse plucked a diseased scale from his torso, released it, and watched as it circled above the sleeping officer.

Agastin spoke slowly. "It will not come to war," he said.

Kale

There was a family legend. Some distant great-great-grandparent was supposed to have escaped from a tsunami by riding on the back of a whale. No one knew what kind of whale, but everyone in the family seemed to agree that Kale's interest in humpback research was hereditary. His uncle, Mikala, called it being driven by genes.

Kale cultivated the deep bronze skin tone of his Hawaiian ancestry by going shirtless on the boat. His feet were bare, always. He had dreadlocks hanging well past his shoulders that moved like a sodden mop. His fondness for reggae music and his dislike for anything connected to ukuleles made him a source of amusement among his cousins. But he still wore the Hawaiian shirts, loud and proud, and was tattooed in the traditional manner.

While on the boat he allowed himself two beers a day, one in the afternoon while the water shimmered in the sunlight and the other in the evening, after they had lowered the hydrophone into the water. He held up his afternoon beer in greeting to a passing boatload of tourists. A few of them snapped his picture. There was little point in putting the hydrophone into the water during the day. Half of what it would pick up would be engine noise from the whale-watching boats. These were an economic fact of life, not only for the local economy, but also because they funded his research. Every spectacular humpback breech threw more money into the till.

The boat with his uncle in the wheelhouse pulled into the Kona dock. Kale reached for the coil of rope on the deck and lifted it chest high. He started the motion to throw it on to the pier when he felt a tug that stopped him. He looked down. One of his dreads was caught in the coils.

Mikala grinned at him. "Dreads are a Jamaican thing, not Hawaiian."

"It's an island thing," Kale said extracting his hair.

"Definitely Jamaican," said another voice.

Kale looked down at the pier. His sixteen-year-old cousin, Honi, grinned up at him from her customized wheelchair.

"Hey Cuz, been waiting long?"

"Just a few minutes."

Kale jumped down from the boat, secured it to the dock, and then kissed his young cousin on the forehead.

Honi beamed.

"So how's it going?"

"Good, good," Honi said. "I've been working through Thewissen's paper again. You know the one where he argues that hippos are more related to pigs than whales?"

"Are you buying the argument this time?" Kale asked.

"He doesn't deal with the DNA evidence; that's the problem. It's basically a morphology argument. That's old school paleontology. These days you have to deal with DNA."

Kale shrugged. "There are a lot more old bones around than old DNA." He grinned.

"Oh, come on, Kale!"

Kale laughed. "Listen, Honi, let's get you on board and then we can talk, OK?" He gestured to Mikala in the wheelhouse.

The old man slowly emerged, pushing his considerable bulk sideways through the door and puffing over to the ramp. He lowered it to the pier and gave Honi a little noncommittal wave. Mikala didn't like the idea of taking someone so impaired out on the boat.

The ramp was barely wide enough to accommodate the chair. Kale got behind it and started to push.

"Please don't," said Honi. "I can handle this."

"You sure? I don't like the idea of fishing you out of that soup."

"Yes, I'm sure."

Mikala and Kale looked at each other. Mikala shook his head, but Kale stepped back from the chair. Honi studied the ramp and then took the narrow black tube into her mouth. The chair moved back and forth in small increments until it lined up perfectly with the ramp. Then she scooted up so quickly Mikala had to leap out of the way. She stuck her tongue out at him.

"Ah hah!" said Kale clapping his hands together with glee. Even Mikala looked pleased.

When she was on board Honi was always the spotter. She could see the humpbacks at a distance much further away than Kale could.

"That's seven to one and you have the binoculars," she said with a grin.

"You win again. We should probably get out of this heat. Want to listen to last night?"

"Of course!"

Mikala was sleeping on the bench opposite the computer equipment when they moved into the cabin. He was on his side. If he rolled over, Mikala could produce sounds that would easily compete with whale song, both in volume and in pitch, but for now he was quiet.

"Should we wake him?" Honi asked.

Kale shook his head. "He'll probably sleep right through it."

"How does anyone sleep through *kohola* song?"

"I don't know, but he does."

Kale selected the wave file, jacked up its frequency range by a couple of octaves, and they settled back to listen. Most of his colleagues used digital filters to search for changes and variations in the songs, but Kale preferred using his ears.

Honi closed her eyes.

She is so beautiful, Kale thought. It broke his heart to see her all strapped in like that.

He turned his attention back to the recording. Kale had been listening to *kohola* song for over twenty years and usually knew immediately when anything had changed. And it did change, incrementally, over time. The songs he had first listened to as an undergrad twenty-five years earlier had now been almost completely replaced by new structures and forms. These changes had happened slowly, in much the same manner that human music evolved over time. To Kale, this was a sure sign of advanced intelligence. Creativity was at work here, creativity and purpose. The question was what was the purpose?

The song as it currently stood was about fourteen minutes in length and repeated several times during the night. At the eight-minute mark of the fourth repeat, there was a small variation, a lengthening of a deep vowel sound followed by a few stuttered clicks.

"There, did you hear it?" Kale said.

Honi's eyes flew open. "Hear what?"

"There's been a change, a sequence that wasn't there earlier."

Kale put the cursor on the wave file and scrubbed it to the left. He replayed the deep hollow vowel sound and the stuttered clicks."

"That's new?"

"I've never heard it before."

"So it could be a change?"

"Maybe. We'll have to see if the other whales pick it up. If they do, you've just heard *kohola* song evolution in action."

"Evolution?" Honi said brightening. Humpback evolution was her thing. She read everything she could find on the subject.

"You know what they're doing, right?" Mikala said behind them.

"You're awake," Kale said.

"It's hard to sleep with all that praying and hymn singing going on."

"Praying and hymn singing?" Honi said.

"That's what I think they're doing."

Kale smiled and shook his head. "Praying and singing hymns. Well, that's a new one. What makes you think that's what's going on?"

Mikala shrugged, "I'm an Anglican. There's this passage in the book of Job: 'But ask now the beasts, and they shall teach thee; and the fowls of the air, and they shall tell thee: Or speak to the earth, and it shall teach thee: and the fishes of the sea shall declare unto thee. Who knoweth not in all these that the hand of the Lord hath wrought this?'" Mikala looked smug.

Kale laughed. "That would mean that humpbacks have a concept of God."

"Not bloody likely," Honi said.

Mikala gave Honi a dirty look and then turned back to Kale. "You said they were intelligent. Look at the whole bubble-net feeding thing. You have to be pretty smart to come up with something like that and then get others to join in." Mikala crossed his massive arms. "I think they're praying and singing," he said.

Kale shook his head and grinned. Honi looked disgusted.

The computer beeped. The upper right-hand side of his monitor showed a new email message. Kale saw that it was from the

Intersea Foundation and clicked on it.

"Speaking of bubble-nets," he said. "I've just been invited to spend the summer doing research aboard the Acania."

"In Alaska?" Honi asked.

"Yeah. They range a little further than that, but it's mostly in Alaska."

"You going to go?"

"If I can arrange it. Nice opportunity."

Mikala laughed. "You won't be going barefoot on that boat."

Kale looked at his toes and wiggled them. "No, I don't suppose I will," he said and then noticed that Honi was tearing up.

"Hey, it will only be for four months."

"Yeah, but..."

"Uncle Mikala can take you out," Kale said watching his uncle reluctantly nod.

"She's getting a little too attached to you, you know," Mikala said after they had driven Honi home.

"I know. But what do you want me to do about it? It's not like she has a lot of options in her life."

"That's just it. She shouldn't be seeing you as an option. She's sixteen and she has hormones raging through that battered body."

"What are you suggesting?"

"Just be careful, that's all."

"My God, Uncle, I'm nearly three times her age!"

"I'm not saying it's rational."

Kale sighed. "Did you know she reads all my papers before I send them out and makes comments? How many kids her age can interact with post-doc stuff?"

"Not many, but that's not the point."

"Maybe me going to Alaska is a good thing."

"I think so."

"And you'll take her out?"

"I'll take her out."

Kale sighed and drove on in silence.

Jovian Pulse

Diane McLean had been kicked upstairs. Everyone thought she had slept her way into Jacob's position when the old man retired. So now NASA had a woman running Goldstone. From Trent Proctor's point of view, this was a good thing, not because she was a great boss, but because she was now focused on the demands of her position and away from the young men at the monitors. The downside was she had to be in the loop for almost everything. Forced interaction.

They had never resolved the *"Wind on the Water"* incident. For three years they had received a strong signal, which the software said was coming from Pioneer 10, and which played the Crosby/Nash song repeatedly. They could not track the actual source and then it stopped. Trent had seen the wave forms so many times he had them memorized. And now they were back, ten years later. And they showed up on his monitor. His. Just like the last time. Maybe whoever was perpetrating this had some kind of personal issue with him.

"Jesus," Billy blurted out.

Trent looked over at him, surprised. Billy had stopped taking the Lord's name in vain months ago. The former Goth was transitioning to the mainstream, but there was a lot to undo. Away from work Billy now wore floral print shirts, cargo shorts, and sandals. His sandy-colored hair had grown back but still had little black tips. The tongue, lip, nose, and ear piercings were all gone, but some holes persisted, particularly in his ears where the piercings had been large. A plastic surgeon was dealing with the tattoos, so Billy had bandages on both of his arms. His new Southern Baptist girl friend had insisted on this. A wedding waited completion of the transition.

"It's back," Billy said.

"Here too," said another.

"Yup," came a third.

"Are we talking about the same thing?" Trent asked.

"Wind on the Water," said Billy.

"We're not all monitoring the same frequencies. How can that be?"

Everyone shuffled around looking at each other's monitors. The stations showing missions outside the moon's orbit had the song, anything closer did not.

"Jesus," Billy said again.

"I guess we'd better call Diane," Trent said.

"She's outside communing with the cacti," someone said. It was the group euphemism for Diane's tobacco habit.

"I'll get her," Trent said. The others looked at each other with raised eyebrows.

Trent found Diane puffing away in the shade of the radio dish. She watched Trent's approach, put on a brief warm smile, and then switched to professional concern when she saw the look on his face.

"What's up?" she said.

"You remember that whale song thing of a few years back?"

"The Pioneer 10 interference, yes."

"Well it's back, as strong as ever, and on every mission frequency outside lunar orbit."

"Every frequency?"

"If the signal comes from a mission farther away than the moon it's now playing that song. That's all we've got coming in right now on those frequencies. At least it's overpowering everything else."

"Jesus," said Diane stomping out her cigarette. "Whoever this guy is, he has got to be stopped."

"How do you know it's a guy?"

Diane looked at Trent. "Trust me, this is a guy. Maybe a woman put him up to it, but this is a guy."

"Nice," said Trent. He followed Diane back into the building.

"It's only broadcasting on the frequencies currently being used," Billy said as they entered.

"What do you mean?" Diane asked.

"Well, watch this." Billy adjusted the frequency on his monitor. He had been tracking an aspect of the Mars Odyssey mission, now he moved off that frequency: static. "See. No Crosby/Nash," he said. He gestured to the other monitors. "Same with all the other distant missions. Move off the designated frequencies and you lose the song."

"All of them?" Diane asked.

"Everyone."

"Well, the first thing that tells us is whoever is doing this knows the broadcast frequencies of all those missions," Diane said.

The control room became silent. Everyone was looking at everyone else.

"Oh, my," said a thin high voice in the corner. Everyone turned and looked at Fatima.

Fatima was a slim and coppery young woman of Pakistani descent. She was American born, her parents having fled Pakistan when their liberal views drew too much attention, but Fatima continued to wear hijabs even when her own mother dropped the practice. She had beautiful ones all hand-sewn and imported from Egypt. Nothing seemed to please her more than receiving compliments whenever she wore a new head covering, but the men were careful with their praise. Fatima would stiffen up if any man showed interest in her.

"Jupiter just stopped." she said.

"Stopped?" Trent asked.

"The Jovian radio signals," Fatima said. "They've stopped." She had been studying L and S bursts from Jupiter, among the strongest naturally occurring radio signals in the solar system. "We're not picking up anything," she said.

"Put it on audio," Diane said.

Fatima obliged. At first, they heard nothing. Then they heard the Crosby and Nash harmonies, but even as they heard them, they faded to silence.

"Jesus," Billy said for the third time. "He's even hacking Jupiter."

Diane turned to Trent. "See, even Billy thinks it's a guy."

Trent ignored her. "The Jupiter signals are broader spectrum; you can hear them between 15 and 40MHz." He approached Fatima's workstation. "May I?"

"Of course," she said moving well away from the monitor.

Trent sat down and adjusted the frequency range. Nothing.

"It's gone," Billy said. "Maybe it was a random thing."

"Was the pulse due?" Trent asked Fatima.

Fatima checked the clock on her screen. "Yes. It was due just then." She brightened. "Maybe that was it?"

"We'll know in about forty-five minutes," Trent said.

"Forty-five minutes?"

"He's referring to the next hot spot pulse," said Diane. "Jupiter's a radio pulsar, remember? We get a pulse from there about every forty-five minutes. Let's see if we get the song instead."

"Why would that be important?" Billy asked.

Trent answered. "Because it would be pretty damn difficult for the hacker to simulate Jovian radio pulsation. If the source is terrestrial, it won't pulsate."

"And if we hear the song then?" Fatima asked.

"Then either he's exceedingly clever or we have a problem of a different magnitude," Diane said.

Forty-five minutes later Diane was on the phone to D.A. Phillips, the administrator of NASA.

Diane

"And you suspect this interference is coming from Jupiter?" Phillips asked.

"We don't know what to think, Sir, but the time delay on the Jovian pulsation is consistent with that conclusion."

"Time delay?"

"Radio signals from Jupiter take anywhere from about thirty-three to fifty-four minutes to reach the earth depending on where the planets are in relation to each other. Right now it's about forty-five minutes but, because the Earth and Jupiter are moving closer together, that time is decreasing." Diane explained. "The thing is all the signals from the other missions are taking the exact same time to reach us, whether the mission is closer to us than Jupiter or further away. And we've talked to the Europeans, Japanese, the Russians, anyone with a mission beyond lunar orbit and they all have the same problem. Whoever or whatever is doing this has replaced all those mission signals with this song about whales but do it with the same ever-changing time delay as the Jovian signals."

"The Spartan mission is there. Are the signals coming from it?" Phillips said.

"All signals from outside the lunar orbit are being affected. The replacement of all the other mission signals is constant. If you tune in those frequencies, you will get a continuous playback of that song, but if you tune in the Jovian radio pulsar, you only get it for a second or two while the signal is pulsing, barely long enough to recognize it for what it is. It's almost as if we were meant to discover the Jovian origins of this interference."

Phillips said nothing for a moment. "I don't know. This seems far-fetched or a clever prank. But we have to get to the bottom of it because we're losing valuable data here."

"So is everyone else, Sir."

"Yes, that's the part that doesn't fit. What do you need from me?"

"Well, sir, I have the authority to bring in the security IT folks. That's already happening." Diane stopped and sighed. She knew how this would play. "It would be nice to get images," she said and winced.

"Images?"

"Some up-to-date photographs of Jupiter and its moons and maybe a survey of that part of the sky. Just in case there's something out there."

"And Spartan?"

"Can't use it. The SpartanCam only captures images in a set direction and the other thing is the quality will take a nosedive soon. Damage from the planet's radiation. And we can't communicate with it because of the frequency high jacking."

Phillips laughed. "So we'll be looking for little green tree huggers who like listening to David Crosby and Graham Nash." His tone became serious. "Go find your hackers, Diane, and I'll see what I can do."

Mikala

Over the years, Kale had become accustomed to waking to the gentle rocking of the boat. It got so waking up on land seemed stifling somehow. He always allowed himself a few minutes to drift in and out of sleep while being moved gently from side to side. Back on land, the old family house still contained the wooden rocking crib where he had spent his earliest nights. Kale wondered if he had been conditioned by that crib to sleep best when he was rocking.

With any luck, his uncle Mikala would already be up and have the coffee on. But on this morning, everything was quiet. His uncle's bunk was empty but there was no sound of rummaging in the galley.

"Coffee on?" Kale shouted but there was no response. He pulled himself into a sitting position and let his bare feet dangle just above the floor. The cool of the early morning was the only time he was tempted to put on socks. He never did. He stood up, bent over, and attempted to touch his toes. "Six inches to go," he told himself as he straightened up.

There was no sign of Mikala in the galley, so he'd have to be out on deck. *Probably has a line in water trying to catch breakfast,* Kale thought. He reached out and touched the kettle resting on the gas burner. Still warm. That was his uncle's pattern: get up early, fix himself a cup of instant for that immediate caffeine fix, and then put on the filtered coffee. There it was, green light glowing to show it had done its job. Kale poured himself a cup. As he lifted it to his lips, he noticed a brown spill on the deck just outside the galley door, and then the cup that had spilled lying beside it. He pushed through the door onto the deck.

His uncle lay crumpled on the deck just a few feet from where they'd hung the hydrophone. His right hand still held the baitfish he was trying to put on the hook. The rod itself lay across his body with the hook swaying lazily in the wind just above his head. It was a picture Kale would never forget.

Mikala was still warm, but Kale couldn't get him to respond. The race to the docks proved futile when his uncle was pronounced dead on arrival at the hospital. It wasn't until two days later when Kale realized, that in his haste, he had failed to pull up the hydrophone. Dragging it at high speed through the water had ruined the instrument. It had been a bad day.

The Hawaiian state flag is unique among state flags because it incorporates the Union Jack. That portion of the flag covered most of Mikala's face, as his body lay wrapped in it on the deck of Kale's boat. This was how his uncle wanted to be buried, at sea wrapped in the Hawaiian state flag. Mikala had been 1/16th British, a paternal great grandfather. He never talked about it, referring to his ancestry only as native Hawaiian, but he had also attended an Episcopal church. Mikala disliked the word "Episcopal" and always called himself an "Anglican," so maybe this was what he wanted. Kale wasn't about to argue with his uncle's wishes, but he was getting long looks from the cousins.

Honi looked grim but contained. She had never been close to Mikala, but he had agreed to take her out while Kale was in Alaska. Now that would not happen. He wondered which part of the loss she felt more.

Eighty-nine people saw Mikala's body committed to the sea. Twenty, including the rector and Honi, were on Kale's boat. The rest were on two other boats owned by Kale's cousins. They all stood more or less at attention as the rector read his brief homily and two cousins read remembrances. Then, just as they were about to tip his body into sea, the humpbacks arrived.

At first, there were only a few animals and they came up some distance from the boats, a common enough occurrence. But by the time the body entered the water there were upwards of thirty humpbacks at the surface.

"It is a hymn," Honi said to Kale as Mikala's body disappeared beneath the waves.

New Moon

A favor, D.A. Phillips had asked for, a favor. Just drop everything you're doing, take pictures of Jupiter and do a sky survey in the planet's vicinity. Just like that. No explanations other than they should look for anomalies, anything unexpected. What the hell was this all about? Daniel Nylander, the head of the Keck Observatory, frowned. He massaged his left thumb joint, something he did both to sooth the arthritis there and because the action seemed to push him into a more analytic frame of mind. The staff looked on.

"NASA wants Jupiter," he said to the gathered scientists.

"Jupiter?"

"Yes, just drop whatever you're doing and image Jupiter, and anything in the vicinity. A full sky survey. They're calling in a favor; one they say we owe them. I don't remember that, but Phillips seems intense about this so guess we'd better humor him, for now at least."

"What are we looking for?"

"That's part of the problem. They don't know: anomalies, anything unexpected. That's all they said."

Five days later they had it, a sudden bright flash that immediately faded. But even after the flash was gone there was something there. Whatever it was was larger than Callirrhoe, one of Jupiter's smaller and more distant moons, twice its size. And then it flashed again. What was this and why the flash? They tracked it for several days until they determined it was also in a distant orbit around Jupiter. Was it a new moon perhaps, or a captured asteroid? But what was the flash: a collision? No because collisions didn't repeat. Was it a volcanic eruption? The moon was too small for seismic activity. And how the hell did NASA know they would find this?

Demotion

Teracia arrived at the communications center well before Roont. When the communications officer came, two menders accompanied him. They led him into the room as if he were blind. Roont looked worse than when she had last seen him in the observatory. He floated from side to side and he had still not regained control of his ballow. His gill slits rippled randomly.

"Communications Officer Roont, stay here for a moment," she said swimming with the menders into the hallway.

"Was he actually approved to resume duties?" she asked them.

They were silent; their gill slits flattened and their ballows neutral beige.

"You approved him?" she asked again.

"When the chancellor of all Fahr asks you a question," one of them said, "you answer with what he wants to hear."

"He is no longer the chancellor. He is the commander, and you are required to give him accurate information."

"And who should we fear more, you or him?" the other said. They both turned and swam down the hallway.

Teracia watched them retreat and then turned and swam back into the communications room. Roont had gained more control.

"Perhaps, Mamini, if we studied the computer protocols first." Roont said.

"Yes," Teracia said, "let's do that." She knew he was trying to avoid exposure to Homines' songs.

"Using the computer might be better given the time constraints," Roont intoned. He reached out for the panel and then, just before he made contact, his tentacle twitched. He pulled it away, held the clasper in front of his face, studied it for a moment, and then with some effort retracted it into his abdomen. He turned toward Teracia. "I'm sorry, Mamini, I..." Roont drifted sideways making slow motion contact with the wall behind him. He had lost consciousness.

Teracia hit the COM button and barked a command. "Vice Commander Teracia here. Menders return to the communications room! Now!"

Silence.

She tried again.

No response. She thought for a moment and then tried again. "Communications Officer Teracia here," she said. "Mender to the communications room."

"Acknowledged," came the response.

Teracia's ballow expanded red into the room. She sucked water through her gills in a long stream and then forced them to lay flat. She had been demoted. Calling Prostallen was not an option because Thryke could now listen in to her communications. And he would. There was no doubt that he would. There was nothing Prostallen could do, anyway. She tried to force beige onto her ballow and it came reluctantly, but the ballow remained inflated with little swirling eddies of red appearing and disappearing so there could be no doubt about her true state of mind. It didn't matter. Only the menders would see her, and they'd be expecting her wrath.

Teracia had no medical training, but she knew allowing Roont to float freely away from any of the walls would be best until the menders arrived. She pulled him into the center of the room and released him. He had stopped twitching, so his drift was minimal. She watched him as she reached again for the COM button.

"Vice Commander Thryke, this is Communications Officer Teracia," she said.

"Report!" said Thryke in his best military voice.

"I thought you should know, *Vice Commander*," she said

putting as much exaggerated emphasis on his new title as she could, "that Communications Officer Roont is too ill to train me on the equipment down here. The menders are on the way to get him."

"What's wrong with him?"

"Officer Roont is unconscious and is currently in a free float in the center of the communications room."

"But the menders said he was fine to resume limited duties."

"The menders, *Vice Commander Thryke*," she again over emphasized the pronunciation of his title, "told Commander Agastin what he wanted to hear. They admitted as much a short time ago."

Thryke was silent.

"So, under the circumstances, *Vice Commander Thryke*," she was enjoying this, "I will have to access the computer training to become proficient on this equipment. This is likely to slow my progress somewhat and I'm not all that sure I'll achieve the level of... "

"We don't have time for you to master the communications through computer training!" Thryke said.

Teracia had mental picture of Thryke's ballow inflated deep red and his gills standing straight up. Her gills rippled. "I understand you feel a certain urgency with this situation, *Vice Commander*, but at the moment, apart from Commander Agastin himself, we have no one proficient with this equipment. I think you agree it would be unwise to proceed without someone knowledgeable monitoring the Homines' communications."

The same two menders appeared in the hallway with floating harnesses and other medical equipment.

"I'm sorry, *Vice Commander*, but the menders have arrived. Given the sensitive nature of what we're discussing, it might be best to resume this conversation after they leave."

"Agreed," Thryke said reluctantly. "Reconnect after they've gone."

"I will do that, *Vice Commander*," Teracia said again with emphasis. She hit the COM button.

The menders now displayed contrite purple.

"He lost consciousness a few moments ago," she told them.

They took particular note of her inflated ballow.

"We may have to put him in stasis," one of them said. "It may be the only way we can help him, but we must have the commander's permission."

"I have no influence at the moment. I think you know that," Teracia said and then watched as they strapped harnesses around the unconscious Roont and swam him from the room. She hit the COM button again.

"Vice Commander Thryke, this is Communications Officer Teracia, again."

"Acknowledged," Thryke replied. He sounded calmer.

"Perhaps you could ask Commander Agastin to give me a quick rundown on the algorithms he set up for monitoring Homines' broadcasts. I'm sure that would be faster than me trying to come up with my own."

"He's busy," Thryke said.

"He also wants to collect The Singers," Teracia said, "and this is crucial to that being accomplished. Unless you want to go in blind."

"I already know all I need to know."

"Do you, *Vice Commander Thryke*? And what exactly do you know? How to start a war or how to collect The Singers? You may have usurped my position, *Vice Commander Thryke*, but you have not yet changed the mission. The goal of this mission remains the collection of The Singers, not the starting of a war. Commander Agastin has made that clear."

Thryke was silent. "I will ask him to help you," he said and then disconnected the conversation.

"An enemy made intentionally is an enemy known," Teracia said to herself. She had read that somewhere but wondered about the truth of it.

Internet

The door to the communications room was ajar when Teracia returned for her session with the Commander. She could hear the strains of *Wind on the Water* leaking into the swim way as she approached. But this was the filtered version, with most of the impairing frequencies reduced. It was odd that Agastin would choose this. She stopped just outside the door, took a long pull of water through her gills, and willed her ballow into a controlled and focused shade of green. Agastin would see the speckles of red, but he could hardly expect her to be happy with the demotion.

She entered the room and found Agastin floating relaxed amid a mixed school of reef fish; odd because the room contained no coral and none of the nooks and crannies these fish favored. He must feed them, she thought. Two large jellies hung ominously in the corners, their tentacles low enough to brush the floor. A few hapless fish were tangled in these.

"I don't think I've ever heard a gas-born song I like as much as this one," Agastin said to her. "I almost wish they were an aquatic species. One wonders what they could produce in the right medium."

"It's filtered," Teracia said.

"I'm resistant to impairment, not immune to it, and we have serious work to do. You'll need me at my best if you are to understand this system." He turned away from the panel, looked at her and then reached out and touched her ballow.

Teracia felt herself redden.

"Not all decisions are easy," he said.

Teracia said nothing.

Agastin turned back to the panel. "It is unfortunate the menders regarding the true state of Officer Roont's health misled me. I will deal with that indiscretion in due course, but for now I must teach you this system."

"You're changing the subject," Teracia said, her gills flaring.

"Subject?"

"I wasn't even told about the demotion. I had to find out by having the COM system refuse to respond."

"Thryke needs your level of authority to do what I've asked of him. You, on the other hand, volunteered to be the communications officer."

"I volunteered to do what needed to be done, not to be demoted. Vice commander was the position I was offered when this mission began, not communications officer."

Agastin pushed away from the panel and studied Teracia. "Did you or did you not volunteer to do this work?"

"I did but..."

"It wouldn't have mattered. Your solution was the best one and I would have seen that as soon as the true state of Roont's health had been revealed. You will not need the authority level of a vice commander to do this work. Thryke will need it to do what I require of him. You will not lose income and your position will be restored as soon as this operation is complete provided that you don't become an obstacle to the mission."

"But Thryke..."

"This discussion is over, *Communications Officer Teracia*." Agastin inflated red. "I will need you to focus on the system. Are you able to do that?"

"Yes, Commander," Teracia said. She felt herself blanch.

"Good. Now watch." Agastin gestured toward the panel.

The room exploded with color and three-dimensional depth. Frightened fish scattered everywhere. Teracia took a long pull of water through her gills and closed her eyes. When she opened them seconds later, she found intricate interweaving lines and shapes that seemed to be in a state continual flux around her. It was as if she were swimming among them. The most prominent of these resembled stars in that they were bright and spherical and seemed to radiate into the surrounding space, making and then breaking connections with smaller objects as far away as the other side of the room.

"This is a small part of what they call the Internet," Agastin said. Here you're looking at a visual representation of the digital information available on The Singers."

Agastin stopped, almost as if he had forgotten what he wanted to say. Teracia caught the change in his diaphragm, the simmering beneath the surface that showed arousal. *He's so close to his goal.*

The commander looked down at himself. "Yes, well..." He shook himself, flattened his gill slits, and got the shimmering under control. "I had the system render this three dimensionally because I found it easier to see the various connections that way. The brightest spots are the locations of information currently attracting the most attention from various homines individuals and organizations connected to the system. What you need to remember here is that what attracts the most attention is not necessarily the most useful. It is the content that individual homines find most engaging."

"So the bright spots are indications of intense interest?" Teracia asked.

"Yes, although compared to most other subjects, intense interest in The Singers among the overall Homines population is low." He gestured toward the top of the panel.

The room filled with what looked to Teracia like a million blazing stars, almost one on top of another. She closed her eyes again.

"Yes, this can take getting used to. I'll tone down the intensity." Agastin moved his claspers away from the panel and the brightness dropped to a comfortable level. "Their original sexuality is intact and they express it a lot. Their Internet is full of this kind of material. It's everywhere."

Agastin reached out and touched one star. The rest of the stars disappeared replaced by a two-dimensional rectangular grid further sub divided into smaller rectangles. These were images of the homines without their usual body coverings.

"This, if you like, is their version of our loop library. But it's much more extensive and less controlled than what we have."

"But it doesn't impair them?" Teracia said.

"Not in the physical sense, no. But many of them become obsessive about it so, in that sense it can become addictive. This is why their merchants of this material do well and why the Internet has so much of it. It is useless for our purposes. And therein lies the major problem. This medium of communication, over the last twenty years, has become so widely used for various Homines obsessions that one wonders at their sanity. They seem to have so little discernment about what is important and what it not. I've been watching the growth of this since the beginning, so I've learned where to go to get useful information. But you have no such experience, and this can be overwhelming. I have put procedures in place, some algorithms that filter content using known reliabilities of the various sites and protocols. These reduce the information down to the most important facts. The problem is this medium of communication is evolving so quickly it's difficult to keep on top of the changes. An algorithm that works now may not in a few weeks."

Agastin gestured again at the panel. The rectangular grid disappeared and Teracia again found herself again amid The Singer material. The commander reached out and touched one star. Everything flattened to display a grainy two-dimensional image of a deceased juvenile singer lying on a sandy beach beside a body of water. A large group of homines was standing around the body. A tangled clump of fibers was off to one side and the carcass had deep cuts toward the rear of the body and on the fluke.

"That one will never sing," Agastin said, his ballow reddening.

"Is this common?" Teracia asked.

"Common enough. What's good about this is that some homines are concerned about the fate of these animals and they are seeking changes. They've had some success but much more needs to be done."

"Where did this happen?"

"A small community called White Rock in a country called Canada. The country is insignificant except for its physical size and its proximity to the proposed collection site," Agastin said. "It's the country south of it that poses the greatest threat."

"The one you'll be negotiating with if they can't form a planetary government?" Teracia asked.

"There is no *if*," Agastin said. "An agreement with America that would allow us to extract The Singers would not be an agreement with any of the other nations. The rest would be capable of resisting us. Homines will need a planetary government to negotiate with us. Otherwise negotiation will be futile."

Teracia reddened "Negotiations are never futile."

"I know your concerns," said Agastin. "I have a bigger picture, a picture that's uncluttered by theology. I know what all of this will look like when we take these animals back to Centrix. The religious ones will hiss and ask for our diaphragms for all of our supposed violations of The Will of the Giver. It's inevitable, but what is even more inevitable is that these Singers will take pleasure to a level far above what any of the common fahr have ever experienced before. They will love us for it! They will love us!"

Teracia swam to the corner of the room right under the largest of the two jellies. As she turned to face Agastin, she felt the creature's tentacles burn across her back. She didn't care. "This is what matters to you?"

"We will all be heroes, far more appreciated than I ever was as chancellor, and I gave out a lot of song when I held that position."

"This is about popularity, Commander Agastin?"

"It's about survival, surely you understand that."

"Survival? Survival of whom?"

"Or what?" Agastin countered. "Homines will survive and, we will give them time to grow into their technologies. Or perhaps they will form a world government and negotiate with us, which would be preferable and a step forward. But I think you and I both know that is unlikely to happen. They fight about everything. Will they put that aside and unify? Unlikely, but we'll give them the opportunity. As for us, we will give the Fahr population what it wants. More importantly, we will give the merchants what they want. And because of that we will survive and survive well. I'm looking forward to a life bathed in The Song."

"How many homines will die?" Teracia asked.

"Perhaps you should ask yourself the question how many of them would have to die before the species loses its viability? Before their culture—or cultures as things currently stand—would be endangered? Given the absurd population down there that number might be as high as ninety-five percent. Our goal is not the eradication of the Homines species but rather the collection of The Singers. We will do only what is necessary to achieve that end and no more. Their losses on a relative scale will be minimal. We will, however, set them back technologically and give them the time they need to think through their options going forward. Whether they do that will be up to them. I think it's possible to argue that what we're planning here amounts to an attempt at preservation of a species."

"This is not about the preservation of Homines. Ethical spin, however well-reasoned, will not reduce the collateral damage. But, in the end, that doesn't matter does it?"

Agastin was silent. "No other fahr has ever dared to speak to me like that." His gill slits rippled. "You are refreshing. Did you know that? But here's the thing. Ultimately, spin becomes the belief system. You believe what you need to believe to achieve your goal. And ethical considerations are what you can justify. There's an element of entitlement to this, I realize. I've spent my life being entitled to everything I have without having to work for it. Now I'm working for it. It's quite invigorating."

Teracia felt as if she was sinking into herself. *Why did I ever hope to succeed against these odds?*

Agastin gestured to the screen. "The homines are polyps. As a species, they have existed for less than two fahr generations. The Fahr were in their second epoch when Planet Song formed around this star. And what makes that notable is that we have survived seven billion years in a slow and steady swim toward the stable society we have today. We've earned it by overcoming what was destructive in our own past. We are entitled to the small distractions we enjoy today. Homines will earn its own entitlements once it proves its worth."

"And in the meantime, you intend to get in their way?" Teracia said.

"I intend to get what I came for, The Singers. It is that simple. Now, enough of this, I have a lot to teach you."

SETI

Benjamin Stofi had followed the coverage of the original *Wind on the Water* incident. Like everyone else, he dismissed it as a clever prank by someone in the environmental movement. The previous Bernard M. Oliver Chair for SETI had directed her staff to ignore it, and he had been part of that staff. Now he had her position.

NASA had waited for the whole thing to go away. It helped that the Pioneer 10 mission had slipped from public consciousness, that it was a space age anachronism, noteworthy for its early imaging of the larger planets and its leaving the solar system on a journey to the stars. It was fun to speculate what would happen if at some distant future date an alien civilization found the Sagan-inspired golden disk it contained, but that was about the extent of waning public interest. the hijacked transmissions stopped but this had taken almost three years, and, during that time, NASA never found out the source. Now Pioneer 10 was silent and too far away to respond to signals. Goldstone had lost contact.

Diane McLean, Goldstone's head, was now sitting across from Bernard in his office. With her was Trent Proctor, one of her senior staff.

"So the latest thing," Diane was saying, "is that Jupiter appears to have a new moon, for want of a better word, and this moon flashes."

"What do you mean 'flashes'?"

"It emits a pulse of light about every forty-five minutes."

"So it's regular?" Benjamin asked.

Diane nodded. "It's not only regular, it's synchronized."

"Synchronized? To what?"

Proctor answered. "To the Jovian radio pulsar."

Benjamin took a minute. His face flushed. "My God," he said, "the same pulsar that's supposedly broadcasting tiny snippets of that Crosby/Nash song?"

"Exactly," said Diane.

Benjamin sank into his armchair. "Jesus," he said.

"So I think we can rule out environmental extremists," Diane said.

"At least terrestrial ones," Proctor said.

"Jesus," Benjamin said again. He studied the faces of his two guests. This was why they had asked to see him. "And the song is a lament about the fate of whales at the hands of the whaling industry?"

"Pretty much," Diane said.

"Aliens concerned about the fate of whales. Can't say I saw that one coming," Benjamin said. "And there's been no other communication?"

"Not on any of our frequencies," Proctor said. Both he and McLean studied Benjamin.

"No," Benjamin shook his head. "We haven't picked up a thing, but then we're focused on radio sources from outside the solar system." He reached forward and picked up a pad from the top of his desk. "Let's get down what we know," he said, trying to steady himself. He jotted several things with Diane looking over his shoulder.

"You're assuming this moon or satellite is a spaceship?" she asked pointing to an item he had written.

"And you're not?" asked Bernard. "Can you think of another explanation for this synchronized pulsation and these hijacked signals all coming from Jupiter?"

"It would have to be a large ship," mused Proctor.

"The other thing is it's safe to assume they've been monitoring our radio signals for a long time, long enough to have acquired some understanding of our languages."

"Unless the choosing of that song was random," Diane said.

"Well, there are two things mitigating against that," Benjamin said. "The first is that they're trying to get our attention and the second is they've sent the same song twice. they got the song from our radio signals. They had a lot of other choices. They didn't have to send the same song again, but they did so, with a ten-year gap between instances."

"So you think they might understand a message if we sent them one?"

"Maybe, but it wouldn't be us who would send them a message," Benjamin said. "That's the problem. Who speaks for the Earth? It's not like we can just pick up the phone and call them."

"Who speaks for the Earth," Diane laughed. "Yeah, right, as if we will sort that one out anytime soon."

"We may have to," Procter said. "I'm guessing they can get here pretty damn quickly."

Benjamin and Diane looked at Trent and then at each other. "What do you mean?" Benjamin asked.

'Well," said Trent, "it was about ten years ago when we first received the song on the Pioneer 10 wave length, right?"

"Yeah," said Diane.

At the time we got that last legit signal, Pioneer 10 was on heading out of our solar system. And that's when they hijacked it. So, if we assume they used that frequency because of an encounter with Pioneer 10, that would have put them close to the edge of the solar system. Yet here they are orbiting Jupiter ten years later."

Benjamin caught his breath. "That would mean..."

"That they were travelling far faster than any technology we have. They could theoretically travel from Jupiter to the earth in under a month," Diane finished.

They sat in silence.

"How long have they been in orbit around Jupiter?" Benjamin asked.

Trent shrugged. "We know they've been interfering with transmissions for 103 days, but we didn't find the moon, spacecraft, whatever, until about a month later and didn't make the connection about the synchronization until a few days ago. Who knows how long they were out there before they broadcast that song."

"The question is," said Diane, "do they know that we know that they're there?"

Benjamin nodded. "Because as soon as the aliens know we're aware of them they will expect a response. Who else knows about this?" he asked Diane.

"That depends on which 'this' you're referring to," Diane said. "Pretty much the entire planet knows about the Crosby/Nash song interfering with mission radio signals. That's been on the news quite a bit as we've been cut off from all our interplanetary probes. A lot of fist pumping is going on in the environmental community, though they're not taking credit for it. The discovery of a new Jovian moon was announced to the broader scientific community, but the details of its flashing haven't been reported. I think the community is uncomfortable about talking about it until they can come up with some kind of plausible explanation. The discovery of the moon itself didn't create much of a stir largely because over the past fifteen years a lot of smaller Jovian moons have been discovered, mostly by Scott Sheppard and his team at Carnegie. I believe this brings the total of all known moons to 69, so a new one is passé. As far as the synchronization is concerned knowledge of that is Deep Space Network only. We brought it to you first."

"There's been no attempt to inform anyone else through electronic means?"

"We've thought of the implications," Trent said. " Whoever these aliens are, they can hear and interpret conventional radio signals, and they may be able intercept and decrypt digital ones. We don't know but I don't think we can risk wireless transmission of any kind about these issues until we know what we're dealing with."

"Proceeding with this will be old school, face-to-face," Diane said. "No cameras, microphones, or anything else that can be recorded and put out as content on the web."

Benjamin shook his head. "We can contain this for a while but not for long. It will get out. It's just a matter of time. Especially since the United States can't act unilaterally with something like this."

"Can't or shouldn't?" Diane said.

President

It was a rare occasion when Maria Alatorre, the first Hispanic President of the United States, was not told in advance about the precise reasons for a meeting. All she knew about this one was it involved national security and NASA, and that an old friend D.A. Phillips would be there. Even her chief of staff knew nothing more than this. Phillips had only told the chief the issue was sensitive, and the president should come alone, with appropriate security but with no other advisors. The secret service didn't like this, but they did not have the final say.

The location of the meeting was a puzzle, NASA's large radio array in Goldstone California. They wanted Alatorre to come there rather than them coming to her or arranging for a meeting closer to the capital. Could this have something to do with the hacking of NASA's space probe communications, the Crosby/Nash song everyone was talking about? It hardly seemed to be an issue important enough to require presidential involvement, let alone a secret meeting, but maybe the situation had escalated. She doubted that D.A. Phillips would initiate such a meeting for anything trivial.

Alatorre was glad she'd kept her hair short. The wind from the copter blades would have made short work of any well-coiffed hair-style but had little impact on hers. Still the wind kicked up desert sand, depositing some of it in both her hair and her mouth. There was nothing the secret service could do about that. The three of them led her across the parking lot to a building shaded by an array. She spat the sand before entering, very unpresidential. She glanced at all three faces. There was no reaction. One of these days she would fart in an elevator with those guys.

They were trained to look for any kind of threat and she had learned to let them tell her when and how to move. Here they opened the door and let her in, remaining outside. Four other secret service agents had arrived earlier to ensure the place was secure. She was happy to see that, as per her instructions, all four were female. They still had a long way to go but progress was being made.

The room she entered was full of computer monitors and workstations; it would have housed a good-sized staff. The monitors were all on, displaying a variety of data streams, grids, and waveforms. There was a low-level ambient sound: a mixture of air conditioning, computer fans, and the now overly familiar refrain of Crosby and Nash's *Wind on the Water*". She wondered if they ever turned that off. Talk about an earworm.

There were four non-secret service people in the room, but she knew only one, D.A. Phillips. Phillips was the administrator of NASA, whom she had appointed. His wife called him David, but everyone else called him Dah. He was a tall, stooped man who had an external metal brace around his right knee. He called himself an old-fashioned cripple. Dah had Ph.D. in astrophysics but had spent most of his life as an administrator, keeping the costs down almost everywhere he went. Even the Republicans liked him. He and Alatorre had been undergrads together three decades earlier.

Dah came forward and shook her hand. "Madam President, we're glad you could come."

"It's good to see you, Dah," Alatorre returned warmly.

"Let me introduce the rest of our small party," Dah gestured to the three persons behind him. "First this is Diane McLean, who is responsible for this facility."

Diane did an awkward curtsey and then extended her hand. "Madam President," she said.

Alatorre shook her hand. "So you're the person who has to listen to that song all day?"

"I'm one of them, yes."

"And this is another one," Dah said pushing Trent forward. "Trent Proctor was the first person to hear the signal."

Proctor's suit was too big on him. He bowed to her. "Madam President, it's an honor, Ma'am," he mumbled.

"Pleased to meet you, Mr. Proctor," Alatorre said.

"And finally, Madam President, this is Benjamin Stofi, the Bernard M. Oliver Chair for SETI."

"SETI?" Alatorre asked Dah.

"Yes, Ma'am."

Alatorre shook Benjamin's hand. "Please to meet you Mr. Stofi," she said and turned to Dah again.

"SETI?" she asked again.

"This will take some explaining, Ma'am," Dah said.

"I'm sure it will," said the president.

Alatorre took off her jacket and handed it to a secret service agent. The building from which she and Stofi had just emerged was air-conditioned, but it didn't matter. She was sweating. In the distance, one of the radio dishes was silhouetted against the desert sunset. The image was both beautiful and ominous. She'd bummed a cigarette from Stofi, the first she'd smoked in ten years.

"And your facility didn't pick up anything?" she asked Stofi.

"Our arrays are listening for signs of intelligent life. Why would we monitor NASA's signals?" he asked with a grin.

Alatorre smiled.

"These days we start with the basic assumption we're it as far as the solar system is concerned. We're listening for signals from interstellar space. So we wouldn't be listening for local signals anyway and wouldn't have any reason to eavesdrop on NASA frequencies. We knew about *Wind on the Water* but like everyone else assumed it was a clever terrestrial hacker. It bothered me that the initial instance went on for three years without resolution; it wasn't our problem. And it wasn't much of an issue for NASA either when you consider that Pioneer 10 was way beyond its useful lifespan. The original data stream no longer existed, so it wasn't as if they had to solve the problem to get their data stream back. It was an irritant and security concern. And then it went away for almost ten years." Stofi shrugged. "Case closed, it seemed," he said.

"So when did they bring you in?" Alatorre asked.

"Right after they discovered the synchronization between the flashing moon and the Jovian radio pulsar."

"And there's no way this could a naturally occurring

phenomena?"

"You've heard the explanation, Madam President, what do you think?"

"Unlikely, I suppose." Alatorre took the half-smoked cigarette out of her mouth and ground it into the sand. "And you think we should respond, send a message back to whatever this is?"

"We may not have a choice. Think about this. The first instance likely came from the edge of the solar system. If that's true, then it points to an interstellar origin for whoever or whatever sent that signal. They've mastered interstellar travel. Second, they can intercept and interpret our various broadcasts. How much they know about us is an open question, but it's more than we know about them. And they can rebroadcast those signals with a level of control beyond anything we can manage. Third, they appear to be in a deep orbit around Jupiter, which means they got there in ten years or less from the edge of the solar system. At that speed, they could reach the Earth in less than a month. And finally, they've created a flash from that orbit so bright we can detect it from here and they're doing it every 45 minutes, which is beyond our current technologies. They're signaling us. We have to respond."

Alatorre took out a handkerchief and wiped her brow. She looked up and saw that Diane, Trent, and Dah now approached from the building. The secret service folks had already taken notice.

"What do we say?" Alatorre asked Stofi as the others arrived.

"That may not be the most important question," Stofi said.

"What would be more important?"

"Who speaks for the Earth?" Diane replied.

The Alatorre nodded and wiped her brow again. She had taken office confident in her ability to negotiate with anyone. Three years of confrontations with intractable Republican ideology had taken some of that confidence. Now she would need it back.

G9

Stofi and Phillips had done a masterful job. It now went any lingering doubts that American President Maria Alatorre had carried forth from Goldstone. The lights, florescent and harsh, were now back up to their original intensity as the image of Jupiter faded from their monitors.

Across from the president at the conference table sat the British prime minister, Jeffery Harrison, and the French and Russian presidents, André Lambert and Vitaly Gulubev. Both presidents were late middle-aged but Lambert looked older, a wisp of white hair dancing with the ceiling fans and amber plastic glasses he was forever pushing up his nose. He had made little time for exercise in his routine so there was a certain middle pudginess about him and he smoked electronic cigarettes, a lot. Gulubev had cropped and dyed dark brown hair, azure blue contact lenses, a high level of fitness, and a glossy black suit tailored to show this off. In his youth, he had been a junior member of the Soviet Red Army hockey team, which put him in his sixties, but he seemed much younger. He had an intensity making him look as though he were waiting to pounce on unsuspecting prey, perhaps what was left of the Ukraine or Georgia.

British Prime Minister Jeffery Harrison did not have a suit, wearing instead a light brown Harris Tweed jacket, and darker brown pants that almost descended into a polished pair of brogues, a middle shade of brown. He was approaching seventy but did not wear glasses or contacts as far as the American could see. Harrison had an air of infinite patience.

The only other person in the room was a Russian interpreter: a perfectly quaffed minion who did his best to be furniture unless called upon. Gulubev could understand most English but had trouble speaking it.

From a separate monitor mounted on the wall peered out the

concerned face of Zhao Hui, the Chinese president, a black-oiled-hair kind of man who could have passed for Ronald Reagan if not for his eyes. He had an affable fatherly manner and was the most popular Chinese leader in a generation. He received interpretation at his end.

Alatorre expected a muted reaction but not total silence, and this went on for quite a while. The sideways glances ping ponging around the room told her that her colleagues were in the same state of shock she had experienced a fortnight ago.

Harrison shook his head and spoke. "It can't be one of us," he said to everyone else in the room.

"You're convinced that this is real?" Lambert said to him.

The Brit pursed his lips. "It's convincing, I think. Otherwise we're looking at a ten-year-long brilliant fraud."

"Or someone who had picked up on a ten-year-old unexplained incident and built a new fraud on top," the French president said.

"All three Deep Space Network observatories have confirmed the flashing moon and its synchronization with the Jovian pulse," Alatorre said. "And there have been multiple confirmations through triangulation that the hijacked signals are coming from Jupiter."

The Russian interpreter relayed all of this to his president and a similar thing was happening halfway across the world in China.

Gulubev spoke in halting English. "This is important," he began and then grew frustrated and spoke in Russian.

"He says it must be one of us because there may not be time to reach a consensus," the interpreter said.

They waited for this to be translated for Zhao. Once he understood he spoke and this time they had to wait for the Chinese to be translated, first into English and then into Russian.

"I have concerns about how the rest of the world will react if we try to communicate with these creatures without talking to the other world leaders first," came the translation.

"No time," Gulubev said again in English.

"Tell me again how much time the scientists thought it would take the alien craft to get to the Earth," Harrison asked Alatorre.

"It could be as little as two weeks," she said. "That's a guess.

This is all physics, which is not my strong point, but the people I've spoken to assure me the speed they're capable of would far exceed anything we can accomplish. They could certainly get here in less than a month."

"*C'est fou, c'est fou, c'est fou,*" Lambert said under his breath while the American's words were being translated. He then stood up. "The problem with all this," he said, "is it goes against the old idea that the simplest explanation is best. And the most likely explanation is this is an elaborate hoax. We are the leaders of the five most powerful nations on the Earth and we're talking about attempting communication with little green men because of a pop song. We all have better and much more important things to do!"

"Ten years ago this was about a pop song," Alatorre said. "It is not about that now. I think the presentation makes that clear. You are at liberty to disagree. But if you choose not to take part in this, I hope we can count on your discretion."

"Discretion," Lambert said reluctantly and with the French pronunciation. He sat down.

"So we must speak for the planet even if the others would not like it and should do so without them knowing about it?" The Chinese president asked.

"No time for consensus," the Russian said again, this time without translation.

"And how big do they think this spaceship is?" Harrison asked Alatorre.

"Well that may be a problem," the American president said. "The moon in question did not show up in any previous sky surveys and when it showed up, they estimated its surface area at about forty square miles, at least the side of it we're seeing. If it is that large then, when it moves toward the Earth, it will only be a matter of time before the whole planet knows about it."

"Especially if it keeps flashing," Harrison said.

After all the translation, the French leader spoke. "Then we will need to keep it where it is if we hope to control the situation," he said.

The others all looked at each other, exchanging smiles. "And how do we do that?" the British leader asked.

"Spin," Lambert said with a grin.

"Spin?"

"Of course," Lambert said. "We tell them what they want to hear in order to keep them where they are." He looked smug.

"But we don't know what these creatures want to hear," Zhao said once the translation was complete.

"Whales. They are interested in whales," the Russian said.

"We don't know they want to talk about whales," said Alatorre said. "We only know they've chosen that song. It might even be a random choice. We don't know."

Lambert gestured into the air. "If what we are seeing here is real, if this is not a hoax, then we have to assume advanced intelligence. Whoever they are, they are sophisticated enough to commandeer NASA's and everyone else's radio signals and use them for their own purposes. And they have been listening to our broadcast signals for at least ten years, probably a lot longer. If they are sophisticated enough to interpret even a small amount of what they are hearing, then they already know vastly more about us than we know about them. And I think it's also safe to assume they were intentional in their use of that song. From that we can presume they are concerned about the welfare of whales."

"Wow," said Harrison, "a minute ago you were..."

"I know, I know," said Lambert. "Sometimes I take a while to see the whole picture. It is, how do you say it? A tragic flaw."

"It's only a tragic flaw if it leads to something tragic," Alatorre said and then noticed Zhao looked baffled. She gestured to the screen and everyone waited until for the translation on the other side. When it was the Chinese president laughed, and everyone else joined in.

"OK, OK," said Lambert waving his hands in surrender, "So, if we think these aliens are concerned about the whales, then when we communicate with them, we should tell them we are concerned too."

"So you think the first message we send to these aliens should be spin about the whaling industry?" Harrison asked.

"No, of course not!" the Frenchman said. "You are a politician and you would ask such things? We do not even mention the whaling industry. It does not exist. We are, however, very concerned about these animals. We have that in common with the aliens and that should help us be friends. But first we greet them and welcome them to our solar system."

"I think they know the whaling industry exists," Alatorre said. "The song is about the evils of the whaling industry." She caught, out of the corner of her eye, Zhao conferring with his interpreter.

"We should talk, of course," the Chinese leader said, "but we should also prepare in case the talking does not go well. We don't know what they want but we know they have come a long way to get it. Maybe they are just curious but that is a very expensive curiosity."

Each person in the room began a slow nod.

"But how do we prepare for something we know nothing about?" Harrison asked. "All we know at the moment is that they're good with broadcast signals, they have a large fast ship that can generate bright flashes, they probably came from outside the solar system—if the first point of contact is any sign—and they seem to be interested in whales. That's not much to go on. We don't even know what type of creatures they are. They could be insects for all we know or some other form of life we haven't even conceived of."

Gulubev spoke to his interpreter. "I doubt they're insects," the interpreter translated. "What interest would an insect have in whales? But they may be aquatic, a species that lives either in or close to water. They might even be a kind of whale. That would make sense of their concern."

Everyone waited for the Chinese president to receive his translation. He laughed again. "Whales on a spaceship, snakes on a plane. We're making an American movie, right?" But then his face became more serious. "We have to find out more about them before they come," he said.

"Which is why I agree with what André said earlier," Alatorre said. "We have to keep them where they are and learn as much as we can about them before they come. We will need to decide on the content, the language, and the speaker."

"French is the international language of diplomacy," said Lambert.

"But is it the intergalactic language of diplomacy?" asked Harrison.

"English," said the Russian. "We use English."

"Why?" Zhao asked, once he had the translation.

Gulubev conferred with his translator. "Because, if they have been intercepting Earth's transmissions for any length of time, much of what they have heard will be English. There have been more English-language broadcasts historically than anything else. It will be the language they are most familiar with."

"But standard Chinese is the most spoken language on the Earth," Zhao responded.

"Yes, but will the aliens have intercepted more Chinese language broadcasts than English over time? Or would they have received more broadcasts in Russian? I am not arguing for my language here. I'm trying to be practical."

The room was silent while the Chinese leader considered this. He nodded his head. "I could argue about this," he said, "but we need to move on. We have only two native English speakers and we have to choose one. Then we must do the most important thing and decide what he will say."

Harrison and Alatorre looked at each other.

"Although I was born in the U.S.," Alatorre said, "Spanish was my first language, not English."

"But you have spoken English since you were a small child and that makes you a native speaker," Harrison replied.

"I would grant this technicality. But, we in the U.S. have a well-deserved reputation for self-righteous and self-serving international meddling. Both of my predecessors and I have tried to change this but have failed. The perception is still there."

"And so you would instead give this role to the leader of a nation whose primary reputation is as a culture-destroying colonial power?" Harrison responded. "And our current international reputation is not much better than yours."

Gulubev gestured to Lambert and Zhou. "We should vote," he said. "With three of us there will not be a tie."

"All right," Lambert said and Zhou nodded his approval. "Show of hands. Who would like the American president to speak for us?"

Zhou raised his hand.

"And who would like the British prime minister to take our words to the aliens?"

Lambert and Gulubev both raised their hands. Alatorre breathed an audible sigh of relief. Everyone looked at her. "Congratulations, Mr. Harrison," she said.

Jeffery Harrison opened both of his hands and looked at them. "That's bloody brilliant," he said. "I thought it was bad enough I had the fate of the British economy in these hands but now I may also have the fate of the planet."

"Remember the time delay," Alatorre said. "We'll have plenty of time between transmissions to collectively compose a response to anything they might say."

"We all have countries to run," Zhou said. "How will we do this?"

"We'll need some kind of reason for the five of us to meet together," Lambert said.

Gulubev shrugged. "North Korea," he said and then spoke through his interpreter. "They're threatening western countries with nuclear weapons."

"I cannot do that, no," said Zhou when he heard the idea.

"Pakistan then?" Harrison suggested.

Alatorre gritted her teeth. The Asian nation was a foreign policy nightmare for her administration. The drone attacks had made the Americans extremely unpopular with the Pakistani people and their government, but they were the only things keeping the Taliban from taking over the country and having access to that country's nuclear arsenal. She needed such a meeting for discussing this and not as a front for dealing with the aliens, but she would take what she could get. Harrison knew, of course.

"We could use that I suppose," Alatorre said as nonchalantly as she could.

"Pakistan?" Gulubev said. He spoke through his interpreter again. "As long as we remember this is a front and we will not be discussing that issue at any length."

"But enough to have something to say afterwards," Harrison said.

Gulubev shrugged. "I have nothing to say. This is an American problem. But I do not object to it being used as a front for our real purpose."

"Pakistan then?" Harrison said to Zhou and Lambert.

"Of course," Lambert said and Zhou nodded his approval.

"I can host this," Lambert said. "Say in a week's time?" He turned to Alatorre. "Madam President, is it possible you can do something that will make this meeting take on a level of urgency?"

"Urgency?" Alatorre said.

"He means that gathering the five of us together with such short notice will give rise to questions about the meeting's real purpose if there isn't something serious happening on the ground in Pakistan," Harrison said.

"I see," Alatorre said. *It falls on me to do something provocative.*

Pakistan

The truck had stickers, photographs, tapestries, plates, reflectors, quotations from poets and the Koran, folk art paintings, and hundreds of glued-on bits of colored plastic, all arranged in the gaudy symmetry of Pakistani truck art. Inside a selection of household goods, food items, and cheap electronics filled most of the boxes.

The driver, an American soldier of Indian decent, wore a light *shalwar kameez* and a *taqiyah*. He piloted the truck joining the queue of vehicles waiting to supply the local mountainside market. The soldier turned off the ignition, got out, stretched, and then studied the distance between his truck and the off-load ramps. Satisfied, he lit a cigarette, took two long drags, shuddered, dropped the cigarette and flipped open his cell phone. The resulting blast killed forty-three, injured fifty-seven, and threw debris to within meters of the steel reinforced inner doors.

The Americans were not supposed to know of the location of this part of the Pakistani nuclear arsenal, but they knew. And now it would appear that the Taliban knew as well.

Message

A certain opulence laid claim to any high-level meeting. It went with the territory, but Jeffrey Harrison was a man of simple tastes. His preference for pub food was well known in Britain and he never quite knew what to do with the culinary spreads that always appeared whenever the French hosted an event. He couldn't identify half of what was on the plate and always worried that he'd get indigestion just before a crucial negotiation. On this day, however, he didn't have much of an appetite at all. He nibbled on a baguette, sampled runny cheeses, and had a spoonful of an intentionally cold and carroty soup.

Across from him, Maria Alatorre finished everything on her plate. If anything, Harrison figured Alatorre should be the one with no appetite. Earlier that morning MI6 had informed Harrison that the suicide bomber who had attacked a nuclear facility in Pakistan was an American soldier, a second-generation immigrant from India. He had taken the mission in the mistaken belief he would deal a fatal blow to a Pakistani nuclear weapon's facility. But the bomb was never intended to be that powerful and only resulted in the soldier's death and that of fifty-seven innocents.

Alatorre caught Harrison's gaze and then glanced around to see that the others were engaged in their own conversations at the other end of the table. "My orders were that they create an incident large enough for us to justify this meeting," she whispered. "I had no idea they would do this. I plan to get to the bottom of it, of course."

"I'd be worried about setting a precedent for the future," Harrison said.

"There is no way anything like this will happen again, not on my watch." Maria Alatorre wiped her face with a napkin.

"They briefed me this morning," Harrison said

"MI6 is good at what they do. And that includes getting intel on your allies."

"And you're not watching us?"

"We are. We watch everyone. It's not hostile, it's just..."

"But if we can find out that quickly then..."

"It may not matter."

"Why not?"

"Well, it took the Pakistani Taliban a while to react, but do you know what they did about half an hour ago?"

"What?"

"They took responsibility for the bombing."

"You're joking," Harrison said.

Alatorre smiled.

"Why would they do that?"

"Prestige, probably. And no one else came forward. I suspect their leadership wasn't all that sure about what their various cells were up to. This was, after all, one driver and one truck. It could have been one of their cells. So, with something this big, why not take credit?"

Harrison shook his head. "So you don't have to worry about compensating anyone."

Alatorre picked up a spoon and passed it back and forth between her fingers. "That's the whole thing, isn't it? This just messed up many people's lives. I think we should compensate them but how do we do that without pointing the finger at ourselves? More aid programs I suppose though anything we do over there is suspect as far the locals are concerned."

"The whole idea was to make the Taliban look bad wasn't it?"

"No, the idea was to give us a reason to get together that wasn't about talking to aliens. The Taliban doesn't need our help to look bad. I mean they took credit for this. What does that say? Anyway, their willingness to do that took the stress down a couple of notches."

"And that's why you had an appetite tonight? Relief?" Harrison asked.

"Unlike you, I've known about this for about three days. And I didn't feel much like eating during that time." She shrugged. "It looks like I'm enjoying myself, but I'm ravenous."

The two of them shared a silence that was then broken by laughter from the other end of the table.

"Are you ready for this?" she asked Harrison.

"How do you prepare for something like this? It will be like putting a message in a bottle. We'll have no idea who will respond, when they'll respond, or even if they'll respond."

"If they do it will be quicker, though. It should be anyway. Somehow, I don't think we'll be waiting for a bottle to wash up on the other side of the solar system."

Lambert had all his IT people working 24/7. They had a portable studio set up to record audio and video, a closed loop of computers with multiple layers of encryption, wall-sized monitors and a secure link with the Institut de Radioastromomie Millimétrique (IRAM) in Grenoble. That was how they would send the signal to Jupiter.

But there was still no agreed-upon message.

"How about something simple like 'welcome to planet Earth?'" Lambert said.

"They're not here. They're orbiting Jupiter," Zhao said though his interpreter. "That is where we want them to stay, remember? We don't want to encourage them."

"We could always send the song back to them and add a

greeting," Alatorre said.

"What would that accomplish?" Lambert said.

"It might draw them out," she said.

Gulubev was nodding his head. "I like it," he said.

"Why don't I greet them, tell them who I am and ask them who they are?" Harrison said.

"That would be direct," Alatorre said. "That way if they answer we'll at least know who or what we're dealing with."

"Or we could send them an actual whale song," Lambert said. "That seems to be what they're interested in."

"What would that communicate?" Alatorre asked.

"They're being obtuse with us. I thought..."

"We know nothing about them," Harrison said. "For all we know, sending us a song might be a direct form of communication in their culture. They might not understand it as being obtuse."

"But they sent one of our own songs. They communicated nothing." Lambert said. "We would just be doing the same."

"Except we wouldn't be sending them one of their own songs, now would we?" Alatorre said.

"Unless they are also whales," Gulubev said in English and grinned.

"So we should be equally annoying right back at them?" Harrison stood up and pointed his finger at Gulubev and then Lambert. "Do I need to remind you we're dealing with an advanced civilization here? Do I need to remind you they know infinitely more about us than we know about them? Do I need to remind you by provoking them you might well bring them to our front door? I thought we'd already agreed we wanted to keep them where they are until we knew more about them."

The silence that followed allowed Zhou's translator to bring him up to speed on the conversation. "No, we do not provoke them," the translator said as Zhou glared at Lambert and Gulubev. "Prime Minister Harrison should only greet them, tell them his name, and ask who they are. We need not do anything more than that. Prime Minister Harrison knows how to be polite, and he should do that."

They decided to shoot Harrison's greeting before a green screen. That way they could have him standing before an added high-resolution image of the Earth in space. A small blue thing, Harrison thought, remembering an old song by Suzanne Vega. He couldn't remember what the song was about, but it seemed apt somehow. Now he stood in front of a mirror adjusting his tie, aligning his Harris Tweed jacket, and combing his hair. Would they even notice if he weren't well turned out?

"They're ready for you," Lambert said.

"Right," Harrison said, running his tongue across his top front teeth. He took his place in front of the green screen.

"Mr. Prime Minister, we have the text of your greeting on the teleprompter," the technician said, gesturing to the monitor at his feet.

"I won't need it," Harrison said composing himself.

"Begin when you are ready," the technician said. "We're taping."

Harrison looked up and saw the other four leaders standing in perfect line about fifteen feet away. *I'll address this to them*, he thought. It would be easier than trying to imagine a group of concerned aliens on the other side of the lens.

"Hello and welcome to our small part of the galaxy. My name is Jeffrey Harrison and I am speaking on behalf of the inhabitants of planet Earth. Please tell us who you are."

Alatorre gave him a thumbs up and the others looked pleased.

Message Received

"Communications Officer Teracia to Commander Agastin."

"You have my attention, Communications Officer Teracia." Agastin replied.

"We have a response from Planet Song, Commander," she said. "Shall I send it to you?"

"A response? Interesting. Yes, send it to my quarters."

Agastin looked over at Wrasse who floated quietly in the corner.

"Do you want me to leave while you watch the response, Commander?" Wrasse asked.

"No, stay," Agastin said.

"Stay?" Wrasse asked, surprised.

"We won't continue this," Agastin said. "You're ill-suited to this role."

"I thought you couldn't find anyone else, Commander?"

"Do you actually believe that?" Agastin said.

"No."

"What do you believe?"

"That power is not an easy addiction to overcome."

Agastin's gills rippled. "On these expeditions there are no passengers, Minster Wrasse. If you don't make yourself useful, a use will be found for you."

"I didn't choose this voyage, Commander."

"No, I don't suppose you did." Agastin reached out and touched Wrasse. ""Your scales are growing in. Have you noticed?"

Wrasse gave Agastin a blank look.

"You haven't had time to fuss about them, so they've taken care of themselves. Look at your reflection."

Agastin gestured to the wall and Wrasse swam before his own healthier reflection. He said nothing.

"We have no time for vanity here," Agastin said. "Besides, I will soon need your particular expertise, Minister Wrasse"

"That's twice you've called me Minister Wrasse."

"That's who you are, isn't it?"

Wrasse studied Agastin. "Is he dead?"

"Who?"

"Lord Greyling."

"Greyling is back on Centrix. How would I know that?"

"Transmissions travel at the speed of light," Wrasse said.

"Well, I haven't heard anything. Come, let's see what the bipeds have sent."

He gestured to the wall and Jeffrey Harrison backed by Planet Song appeared.

Response

The response to Harrison's message had taken a little over two hours.

"We are the Fahr. And you are Jeffrey Harrison, prime minister of Great Britain, the leader of a small island nation off the coast of Europe. Have you been elevated to planetary leader? If not, we wish to speak to the person who occupies that position."

It was a straight text message with no sound or accompanying image.

"Jesus," Alatorre said. She was trying another cigarette.

"They are not giving us much," said Lambert.

Gulubev spoke through his interpreter. "We know what they call themselves: The Fahr. We now have confirmation they know a lot about us. We know they won't accept Prime Minister Harrison as the Earth's spokesperson because they know him to be the leader of only Great Britain, and they expect or want someone to be declared planetary leader."

"Which means they want to negotiate something," Harrison said, "and whatever that is involves the entire planet."

"What do we do now?" Zhou said.

"We find out the stakes," Alatorre said. "We send them another message."

Second Message

"Greetings to the Fahr leadership from Jeffery Harrison, prime minister of Great Britain. You are correct that I am only the leader of Great Britain. We do not have a planetary leader. Our planet is divided into 196 countries, all of which have independent leadership. These countries meet in a large organization called the United Nations to discuss matters of international concern. Why is it important to you that we have planetary leadership?"

Agastin's gill slits rippled when he read the response. There was a bleed in his diaphragm telling Teracia he was impaired — mildly, because of his resistance—but impaired nonetheless.

"He's not the most practical of leaders, is he?" he said to Teracia.

"Where I in his position, Commander, I might have asked the same question."

The commander's gill slits flattened and his ballow flashed red. "Tribalism is in our distant past, Teracia. This is not a question any advanced species would ask. It means they have a bias toward the primitive status quo, despite all their recent advances. How do you negotiate with such a species?"

"You are asking a lot, Commander. Tribalism is in their biology, consistently manifested throughout their history. But they are on the verge of stage two. They've already mapped their own genome and have manipulated that of other species. They're on the right path. It's only a matter of time before they can fix themselves."

Agastin's tentacle made a dismissive gesture. "This is the most impulsive sapient species we've ever encountered. They're - predisposed not only toward tribalism but also towards rash decisions. Their technology far outstrips their maturity level."

A small crab skittered across the sand in front of them too close to a waiting anemone. It disappeared into it.

"Fifty years ago, when that Cuban island incident happened, we thought they wouldn't survive until our arrival," Teracia said. "When those towers came down, we thought the same thing. Homines is still there. And so are The Singers. They've preserved them and increased their numbers."

"But not before nearly wiping them out and, for that matter, nearly destroying their own planet. We're fortunate not to be looking at a radioactive cinder."

"But we're not, are we Commander Agastin?"

"Give them time, give them time."

"Precisely. That's what they need: time. Not to destroy themselves but to grow as a species. Commander, every fahr lives an average of seventy millennia. What is a thousand years in a lifetime that long?"

Agastin pinked. "I was not required to take a sapient species exobiologist on this voyage. This is, a retrieval mission and experts can be so annoying. But I got you, didn't I? Teracia, the champion of Will-of-the-Gods morality. A femfahr who cannot experience arousal and therefore cannot understand what we have here. I'm glad you've found this little passion that makes an otherwise dull life worth living. But you cannot seriously be entertaining the notion I would turn around and head back to Centrix without The Singers, just to give Homines a millennium to grow up? Leaving aside the likely outcome of such a move on the future availability of The Singers, I have expectations to fulfill here. Song Corp has spent a great deal of money on this expedition and is expecting a return. And I have given up my position as Chancellor to take on this little challenge. If I were to return without The Singers, what would I be returning to? Hostility? Anger? A feeling of betrayal on the part of Song Corp and the Fahr citizenry? So put aside the faint hope you have that this extraction will not take place."

Teracia said nothing. She studied the text of the Homines' response on the screen. "So what will you say to them, Commander?"

Mask

Agastin looked across the control room at Thryke. The vice commander, despite his new rank, was still wearing his military finery, if one could call it that. It comprised a gold mesh sash that looped over one shoulder and descended to just above his diaphragm. The shimmering purple rectangle of his rank floated chest high, tethered by some invisible wire or other tailoring trick so it moved with the sash without ever seeming to touch it. It was more interesting than the sash itself but still looked pretentious. Agastin preferred the days when military rank was indicated only by the hue and texture of the lower third of a ballow.

"We'll mask the ship now, Vice Commander Thryke," he said.

"The communication is over with Homines, Commander?" Thryke asked.

"They were baffled by the request, as you said they would be. They asked why it was important they have planetary leadership."

"And what did you say?"

Agastin gills rippled. "I told them we could not have a relationship with 196 countries, as if that wouldn't be self-evident, and they should unite."

"Not much likelihood of that," Thryke said.

"No, but the channels are open in the unlikely event they pull together. We will not be initiating further communication. We've stopped broadcasting the song and your photon device. What did you call it again?"

"It's a protonova, Commander."

"Yes, that's it. Anyway, it's been retracted into the ship."

"All right then, Commander Agastin, I will mask the ship."

"How long will that take?"

"By the time they realize that the ship is no longer flashing, they will not be able to find us. All the surfaces on the ship will absorb rather than reflect light," Thryke said. "We will be invisible."

"And how effective will that be?" Agastin asked.

"They will look for us. This ship is large enough to block the light from distant stars, smaller moons, and bits of orbiting space debris, but we will move quickly, and those effects will be fleeting. They would have to have their telescopes pointed in the right direction at the right time, and they would have to guess correctly what is blocking the light. Since they do not know we have this technology that's unlikely. However, the closer we get to Planet Song the more light we will block so, eventually, they will figure it out. By then, we should be no further than a few days away, perhaps as little as a few hours."

Agastin studied Thryke. The former minister of defense had a great deal of self-control but there were minute scatterings of hue in his ballow, tiny flashes of red and silver. Thryke was in a state of heightened anticipation. Most fahr would have missed this, but Agastin's diplomatic experience had taught him to look for such things.

"I'm counting on you to ensure this extraction is as painless as possible. The nature of this mission will cause us enough trouble when we return to Centrix. I don't need a sapient species genocide on my hands."

Thryke took a minute to respond. "If you don't mind me saying so, Commander, you're allowing the concerns of the lone femfahr member of our crew to get to you."

"The two of you swim in different currents, both of which are dangerous to this mission. I need you because of your military ex-pertise and I need her because, once The Singers are on board, we will be carrying the most dangerous cargo in the history of our race. She is the only fahr on this ship who is immune to their power. That makes her indispensable, but, once the extraction is complete, you will not be. Keep that in mind, Vice Commander Thryke."

"I will, Commander."

Ultimatum

"It is not practical for us to establish relationships with 196 countries. Unite."

"Nothing! They are giving us nothing," Lambert said. "We know nothing about them!"

"I would see that as a veiled threat," Alatorre said.

"I agree," said Harrison. "It is a clear demand but there is no timeline and no stated consequence. We couldn't take this to the world even if we wanted to. How would we explain the need for world government based on a single word? Unite. Why should we unite? Just to have a conversation?"

"This isn't about having a conversation," Alatorre said. "Whatever their motive is, it's bigger than that."

Zhou turned to Gulubev. "Don't you have a spacecraft?" he said. "We must find out more about them."

Gulubev listened to the translation. "Nothing we could send into interplanetary space. Even if we had such a thing, it would take years to get there."

Alatorre's cell phone beeped. "It's NASA," he said looking at the tiny screen. "The song is gone. They've stopped sending it. Everything at NASA is back to normal."

"About forty-five minutes ago then, with the time delay," Harrison said, gesturing to the screen. "About the same time they would have sent us this." He turned to Alatorre. "See if NASA has re-established contact with Spartan."

"For the SpartanCam, you mean? I'm not even sure it's still working, and even if it is, you can't aim it."

"But it might have accidentally captured something while the high jacking was going on," Harrison said. "Any information is more than what we have now."

"All right, and while I'm at it, I'll ask them if the moon is still flashing," Alatorre said and thumbed a message back to NASA.

"I've always wondered why American presidents use such old phones," Lambert said.

"I inherited it from my predecessors. While in office, they developed extra layers of encryption that made it very secure. It still is, which is why I've now got one too. Comes with the job and I didn't have to learn a new operating system."

"Something to be said for that," Harrison said. "Last Christmas my daughter got me an iPod Touch because, she said, it was stupid I was carrying around a CD Walkman everywhere I went." He gestured into the air with his fingers. "You have to do all these squiggly things on the screen and half the time you're accidentally turning on apps you don't want or lose track of what you do want. I now hide my Walkman beneath my underwear whenever I travel."

When Zhou got the translation, he laughed. "You're afraid of your daughter?" he asked Harrison.

"NASA says the flashing has also stopped," Alatorre said.

"They're coming," said Gulubev.

"We don't know that," Harrison said. "They may have just turned everything off because they've got our attention."

"NASA has asked for another sky survey," Alatorre said. "That should tell us if the moon is still there. In the meantime, they're downloading the images from the SpartanCam," said Alatorre.

"How long will all this take?" Lambert asked.

"I don't know," Alatorre said. "I'm new to all this astrological research stuff. I didn't have much interest in it until two weeks ago."

"We may have to let the world know about this," Zhou said.

"Eventually, yes," Harrison said, "but not yet. As soon as we open this up, things will get much more complicated."

"But the longer we exclude the others, the more difficult it will become to include them when the time comes. There will be much resentment," Zhou said.

"If we know the Fahr are coming, we will tell the world. They'll find out soon enough anyway," Harrison said.

"But by then we can do nothing," Zhou said.

"What can we do now? Harrison said, "We have no information."

"We can position our weapons," Gulubev said. "They will have to orbit the planet. We are the only countries with the technology to engage them there." He gestured to the five leaders. "It will be our fight, anyway."

"You have such technology?" Zhou asked.

"We all have such technology," Gulubev said.

The Chinese president did not respond.

Alatorre's Blackberry beeped again. The president frowned as he read the message. "They know," he said.

"Who knows?" Lambert said.

"Soon, everyone," Alatorre said. She ground out her tenth successive cigarette. "More scientists have made the connection between the Jovian pulsar and the flashing moon. There's growing speculation on the web about the nature of the connection. It's only a matter of time."

"But it's stopped pulsing," said Gulubev.

"It doesn't matter," Harrison said. "The data is still there. This will get out of hand quickly. I know what I said earlier, but we may have to go public with this to have any hope of containing it."

Lambert sighed and made a slicing gesture with his hands. "I present my head for the guillotine," he said.

Act Five: The Extraction

Weapon

The bowels of the ship had storage areas with encrypted locks. There was a kind of respected antiquity attached to them not unlike the rooms in a museum where collections were kept when not on display. The Fahr ships were ancient, and they had their secrets. No one much cared any more what those were, but Thryke cared. What he had placed behind those encrypted locks during the retrofit was old and dangerous.

He led Commander Agastin and Communications Officer Teracia down the long scummy corridor. They floated before the first door as the reader above it scanned Thryke's ballow. The door slid open. Even the water was old. It had a metallic sterile quality and little dissolved oxygen. There were no fish, arthropods, or anything much in the way of multicellular organisms, but a thin layer of microbial extremophiles coated the floors and walls.

"Wait here," Thryke said.

They floated on the brink while the floor released the gas and they were temporarily blinded to the room's contents as the bubbles rose. When the bubbles had dissipated, Thryke gestured for Agastin to enter.

"Now you can breathe," he said. "Some of what I have put in here is fragile because of its antiquity, so I take the maximum precautions. Nothing much can live down here."

Agastin swam into the room. "These are the toys you've chosen to bring along?" he asked, surveying the various crates.

"This is but a small fraction of what I have back on Centrix, Commander," said Thryke. "I brought a few items along that we might need."

"A few?" Teracia said. "This looks like an arsenal."

"I prepared for any eventuality, as any good military commander would do," said Thryke.

"The Fahr have not fought a war in generations. There's been no need," she said.

"The reason there's been no need is that all opponents have been over matched." Thryke's gills rippled and he turned to Agastin. "As soon as they realize we hold a superior position the conflict is over, especially since it's usually about the collection of pets. Most adaptive species are not willing to risk war with us over the loss of a few animals, and we make sure we leave viable populations behind."

"So why did you bring these weapons?" Teracia asked pointing at a group of archaic machines.

Thryke ignored her and continued to address his remarks to Agastin. "All of this depends on the maturity of the civilization. The problem with Planet Song is Homines are still stage one. They have no global leadership and no ability to see beyond the immediate consequences of anything they do. They might well choose to fight despite the odds."

"But you said we could disarm them." Agastin said.

"Easily," said Thryke. "But the speed of their development could throw a few surprises our way."

"Surprises? Is that why you brought that little item?" Teracia said, gesturing to the collapsed-wing atmospheric flyer on a pad in the far corner. It was contained within a transparent plastic gas bubble. "An Xburner isn't it? If memory serves me correctly, it is a strictly offensive machine."

Teracia caught the look of surprise on Thryke's face. He was not expecting any non-military fahr to have knowledge of ancient weapon systems, but Teracia had been through Thryke's museum back on

Centrix.

"The homines are terrestrial bipeds," he said. "They live their lives exposed to their planet's atmosphere. Under the circumstances it would be imprudent for us not to have access to rapid atmospheric transport."

"Rapid atmospheric transport?" Teracia said. "Surely you had other choices. An Xburner reduces anything to ash. Your own museum presentation said as much."

Thryke's gill slits rippled fast and he pinked. "I'm glad you took the time to visit the museum, *Communications Officer Teracia*," he said over emphasizing her rank. He turned back to Agastin. "This device has a rather nasty history, but for the burning to happen one must first engage the weapons system. And what rarely gets discussed by the military historians is that this flyer also has excellent surveillance capabilities."

"Surveillance capabilities?" Teracia said to Thryke. "The Xburner is ancient technology. It was developed when the Fahr race was only about half its current age. Its surveillance capabilities might have been significant during that time period but compared to what we have on this ship they are nothing."

Thryke said nothing and Teracia could see that all of his energies were going into the control of his ballow.

Agastin studied both of them. He turned to Thryke. "This Xburner will not be removed from this room without my prior authorization, understood?"

"Yes, Commander."

Thryke was good at controlling his ballow. Even so, Teracia could see the red rage circulating beneath the beige surface.

Bandwidth

There was an enormous risk in sending Homines an unauthorized message. The system would record and date any transmission she sent and alert both Agastin and Thryke the message had been sent. Unless...

Teracia checked the logs for the messages they'd sent ten years earlier on the Pioneer 10 bandwidth. Yes! The messages had been automated and sent out over a three-year period. The last thing Agastin wanted was to be informed every time the song was sent, so he had the alerts disabled.

Teracia had a frequency she could use, but would anyone be listening on the other end? It had been ten years since the last time NASA had received a message from Pioneer 10.

Linguistics was not her forte, but she dared not involve anyone else in this. Keep the message simple and urgent.

"Unite. We are coming. Talking is better than war."

Goldstone

Diane wasn't sure if she should be relieved or concerned. All her missions were back, seemed in good working order, and *Wind on the Water* was gone. The same was true of all the other space agencies but the mystery had deepened. The flashing moon, the spaceship, or whatever it was, had vanished. It was as if none of this had ever occurred, but it had. They had hundreds of hours of audio recordings, sky surveys showing the flashing moon, and President Alatorre had told her about their brief and enigmatic correspondence with the Fahr.

"Unite," they had said, a one-word command and then they disappeared, or rendered themselves undetectable, which Diane thought more likely. They were either waiting for humankind to make some bold political move, or they were on their way. Either way, more direct contact was unavoidable. She tried not to think of this negatively. It might be a good thing but, somehow, that final one-word command did not bode well.

"Did you send the SpartanCam data off for analysis?" she asked Proctor.

Trent shrugged. "I did but they will not find anything. The SpartanCam took pictures of the Jupiter's storm clouds, so every shot is going be dominated by the glare from the planet. The alien moon, or whatever it is, was a deep orbit around the planet so, even if it's in the frame, it will be a speck washed out by the planet itself."

Diane took a cigarette out and put it in her mouth. She took out her lighter and then realized she was still inside the building. She put the lighter back into her pocket and took the cigarette between two fingers. "I'm just doing what I'm told, that's all."

"You think it's still out there, right?"

"Yes," said Diane. "What's scary is they can make themselves bright one moment and invisible the next, and they're doing so deliberately so we can detect this."

"Or not detect it," Trent said.

"Come out and talk with me while I smoke this," Diane said gesturing to the door with the cigarette.

Trent gave her a wary look.

"Jesus, Proctor, get over it please. I made a mistake that's all. That was a long time ago."

Proctor put his hands in his pockets and followed Diane out the door. It was late afternoon and hot. The more distant of the radio dishes were shimmering in the heat. Diane stopped in the shade of the closest one and lit up. She studied Trent.

"You know, within six months of our marriage Bert was hitting on and bedding much younger women?"

"This is not my business," Trent said.

"No? Well here's the thing. He was a cheater, but no one ever called him that. He was just this oversexed charming guy who strayed a lot. Me? I act like that and I morph into this cat, this predator who picks on younger men, who makes them uncomfortable. It's been over for years, but I'm still Diane the cougar, Diane the predator. Just so you know, I didn't sleep with anyone to get this position. I got it on merit."

"You're good at what you do," Trent admitted.

There was a long silence.

"You're the best I've got, you know," Diane said. "I'm just pissed that I..."

"What about radar?" Trent said.

"What about it?"

"Well, it would be a way of searching. We could scatter the signals and hope we hit something."

"Needle in a hay stack," Diane said.

"But at least we know the needle is in the hay stack. And the closer they get to us, assuming they're coming, the more likely we are to hit something."

Diane nodded. "I suppose it wouldn't hurt, but it's just as likely as finding images of their spaceship in the SpartanCam data." She shook her head. "I can't help thinking we're over-matched here. Did you ever see '2001'?"

"The Kubrick film, you mean? Yeah, I've seen it." Trent said. "It would be hard to find anyone in this line of work who hasn't seen that."

Diane smiled. "As a kid I had seen all these sci-fi movies where the aliens looked like lizards and were shooting at us with ray guns. And then Clark and Kubrick come along, and their aliens are completely incomprehensible, so advanced we can't get them. I've always thought their portrayal was more realistic."

"Those aliens were benign," Trent said, "but you don't think that's what's going on here?"

Diane shook her head. "They want something. The question is what?"

"Hey!"

They both looked at Billy standing in the doorway. "They're going public with this thing," he shouted.

"Public?" Trent said.

"Yes, they have a live telecast scheduled for two hours from now. The details are in the email." He gestured for them to come back in. "Get in here."

"Who are they?" Diane asked Billy as she entered the building.

"The permanent members of the Security Council," Billy said.

"Sounds like our colleagues couldn't keep their mouths shut," said Diane to Trent.

"I'm surprised it took this long," Trent said. "Security is such a myth on the Internet, and there were a couple of hundred people in the loop."

Diane read the message on the screen. "They say some scientists figured it out independently, at least the synchronization between the Jovian pulse and the flashing moon. And then I guess there was a leak about the attempts at communicating." She sighed. "They want us to fill in the rest of the scientific community once they've gone public," she said.

"Who is *us*?" Billy asked.

"I don't know but I'm not touching any of this before I hear from Phillips. I'm not sure I'm going to touch it, anyway."

"Quick, run and hide," Trent said reading over Diane's shoulder. "I'd say you've got forty-five minutes tops once they've gone to air. The Deep Space Network will be front and center on this. I'd be contacting someone about upping the security level fast."

"No need," Billy said looking out the door. "Security's already here."

Diane looked out to see several trucks full of soldiers from Fort Irwin disembarking in the parking lot. "Obviously they were contacted before we were," she said.

"Do they even know why they're here, I wonder." Trent said.

"If they don't, they will soon enough." Diane said. She sighed as her cell phone rang. She looked at it. "Phillips," she said raising the phone to her ear. "I'll take it outside."

She walked out the door and stood beneath the radio dish, watching the soldiers arrange themselves in little clumps on the asphalt.

"Hello, sir," she said into the phone.

"McLean?"

"Yes, sir."

"Are the troops there yet?"

"They're unloading in the parking lot as we speak, Sir."

"Are they all there?"

"I don't know, Sir. How many are there supposed to be?"

"About two hundred, I think." He didn't sound sure.

"Really, sir?"

"It wasn't my idea. And you can stop calling me Sir. Call me Dah and I'll call you Diane."

"Sir?"

Phillips didn't respond.

"All right, Dah," Diane said. "I don't think there are two hundred. Maybe sixty, seventy."

"Well uh, the rest are probably deployed further down the road. Listen, Diane, stay inside. That way you'll be safe."

"Safe?"

"We're, uh, we're not taking any calls until after the telecast. That's in about two hours' time. We'll, uh; we'll set up a video link. I'll take most of the questions but, uh, if it gets technical, if it's something you can answer better than I can, I may defer to you."

"How technical? I mean, who is this for?" Diane asked.

"Oh," said Dah. "I see what you mean. This is supposed to follow the telecast which means it's for mass consumption, I guess."

"So you don't actually need me?"

"Well, not for the press conference, I guess. But I, uh, I want you to be available, just in case."

"Dah, forgive me for saying this but, if this is for mass consumption, then there probably won't be questions you can't handle."

There was a silence on the other end of the phone. Diane looked at it as if, by doing so, she could get some visual clue as to what was going on. She could hear Phillips breathing. "Turn the video on, Dah," she said.

"No. No I'm not going to do that." His breathing picked up.

"Jesus, Dah, what's going on?"

Phillips said nothing.

"You're worried about the scientific community, right?" Diane said. "Because a lot of them have been kept out of the loop, right? And there might be some hostility? But the thing is, it's not you. You were acting on protocol and we didn't have that much to tell them anyway, did we? And they made the same connection we did with the same information. All we did was to make a connection earlier and then, when we made that connection, we took it to our superiors. That's what we're supposed do in that situation."

"They're coming, Diane," Phillips whispered.

"Who's coming?"

"I didn't think this was real. Not really. I enjoyed the speculation but..."

"The Fahr? We don't know that, Dah. We don't know anything."

"That's the problem, isn't it? They've got us right where they want us. We know nothing. If they were friendly, don't you think they share more about themselves?"

"Dah, this is not helpful."

"I know but I just can't..."

Diane heard a sob, then another.

"Let me handle the press conference," she said. "Tell the president that I'm going to do it because I have the expertise. OK? Just don't tell her what you're thinking right now. Don't tell her, O.K.?"

"I'm the administrator of NASA."

"Which means you have the authority to delegate. Let me handle the press conference."

"The president appointed me. She will expect me to..."

"She will respect your judgment. Leave this with me. Tell the president I'm going to do this, OK?"

"OK," Phillips said almost inaudibly.

"Tell the president what we're doing here and then get some rest, all right?"

"Thanks, Diane," Phillips said and closed his phone.

Diane looked up to see Billy and Trent watching her from the doorway. "I'm doing the press conference," she said.

"What!" Billy said.

"But you just said you didn't want any part of this," Trent said.

"Things have changed," Diane said

"What things?"

"You don't want to know," Diane said, storming past the two men and into the building. "And get me Stofi if you can find him. I'm going to need all the help I can get."

Broadcast

Reb Saunders was coming around. He'd stopped abusing trees, was sleeping through the night, and was even being a father to his girls. But not all was well. There was still the whole question of the alcohol and the rages he would sometimes fly into, especially when watching the Fox news coverage of the continuing problems in Iraq. Jeff wished his brother would watch CNN or ABC and get some balance, but Reb wanted no part of "liberal" news.

They were sharing some Buds one night when Reb piped up, "When you gonna take me up in the B-25?"

Reb had never expressed much interest Jeff's new hobby before. "Didn't know you wanted to," Jeff said.

"They had *30 Seconds Over Tokyo* on Turner Classic Movies last night," Reb said. "Looked kind of cool. Made me want to check it out."

"Really?" Jeff said. He'd seen the film and found it typical of the WWII era propaganda films. It did, however, show the B-25s in a positive light.

"So what version of the B-25 are you flying?" Reb asked.

Jeff smiled. "You've been doing more than just watching *30 Seconds Over Tokyo*," he said.

"Did a little research online," Reb admitted.

"It's a B-25J," Jeff said.

"Whoa! That's a serious gunship." Reb said. His grin was a mile wide.

"You have been doing your homework."

"Everything in working order?" Reb asked.

"As far as I know, yeah." He studied Reb. "But we don't fly with ammunition," he said.

"Can you still get it?"

"Why? You want to go up there and fire off some rounds?"

"Might be fun," Reb said with a grin.

Jeff shook his head. "I'll take you up, but we won't be using the guns."

The two of them were sitting in front of Reb's TV when the piece came on, Maria Alatorre sitting in a room with her Russian, Chinese, French, and British counterparts. By then the media had been abuzz with rumors about space aliens orbiting the planet Jupiter and those same aliens being responsible for the musical hijacking of NASA's radio communications. To Jeff, this fell into the same category as all the old Area 51 and alien abduction stories, pure bunk. He couldn't believe how gullible some people were. That the heads of the planet's five most powerful nations now played lip service to these rumors was troubling, if not downright weird.

"Here it is," Reb said. "This ought to be good." He pulled the tab of a Miller and settled back into his Lazyboy.

"Not too often you get these five together co-operating about anything, let alone a joint press release," Jeff said, opening his own beer and then reached over to dim the lights.

"Good evening peoples of the world," Maria Alatorre said.

"I should have known she'd have something to do with this," Reb said.

"Shhhh!" said Jeff.

"We will begin this evening's presentation with a short video," Alatorre said. "It's a compilation of material I, myself, was only exposed to seventeen days ago. I showed my fellow heads of state this video a little over a week ago. That meeting was arranged at short notice because I knew four of the five of us were scheduled to be at G9 meetings and President Zhao could be made available by video conferencing. Many of you may feel resentment that I did not include your own heads of state in this meeting, but I think you'll see that I had to move quickly. That is even more the case now considering recent developments."

"Bitch," Reb said.

"Let's just watch, OK?" Jeff said.

The video took twenty minutes. When it was over, the British prime minister addressed the camera.

"Presidents Zhao, Lambert, Gulubev, and I first learned of this by watching the same presentation you've just watched. Like you, we had many questions, but it became clear to us that a superior extraterrestrial intelligence was out there in the vicinity of Jupiter and they were trying to communicate. We sent them a simple greeting and asked them who they were. I was the one who spoke that message. They responded by identifying themselves as 'The Fahr' and identifying me as the prime minister of Great Britain—they knew who I was—they had that information—and they wanted to know if I had been elevated to leader of the entire planet. When I replied that I had not been elevated, and that we on this planet comprised 196 independent nations, they responded it was not practical for them to establish relationships with 196 nations. Their message concluded with a single word, a command: 'Unite.' Since then we have had no further communication from them, and perhaps more significantly, they have disappeared. NASA's radio signals are no longer being affected, and the object detected in deep orbit around Jupiter is no longer there, at least we can no longer detect it. We do not know where they are or what they expect from us, but we believe putting some kind of provisional world government in place might be in our best interests."

"Nice scam," Reb said. "Of course they've disappeared. They were never there. Some computer hacking asshole is laughing his head off right now. Trust Alatorre to fall for something like this. The woman's an idiot. Come on. Let's go shoot some pool."

"It's kind of strange that she dragged the others in with her, though," said Jeff, picking a cue of the rack. "And all those scientists too."

"Trust me, big bro, this is as bogus as a three-dollar bill," Reb said.

"Yeah, but how the hell do you get this moon to show up on all these different telescopes?"

"They're all on the same network, that's how. Think about it, Jeff, how likely is this?"

"Not very, I guess."

"Be cool if it was true, though," Reb said, racking up the balls. "Give us a real enemy to fight."

Twin Otter

It was Friday and Andreas had a load of petroleum geologists and their equipment behind him in the Twin Otter. They were chattering about their latest MacBook Pros, their cars, their iPhones, even their apartments in Edmonton. The company, stipulated by the consultancy contracts they had all signed, leased everything for them. It also provided all the gear and clothing they would need in the camp. Andreas wondered what they did with their high six-figure incomes, what they spent their money on.

This was the tenth time he'd landed on the lake and there had been no problems. Though shallow, it was more than deep enough to handle the Twin Otter's floats and the aircraft could get quite close to shore. The shore itself was rocky, so he couldn't lower the wheels in the floats. One of the early crews had constructed a wharf, short and stable, from wood and pontoons he'd brought in. Nobody was in the camp now. He'd flown the last crew out two days earlier.

As he approached, he could see one tent had blown over. It lay collapsed, still pinned to the ground, flattened over a table inside. They'd have it back up in two minutes. He did a quick pass over the lake studying the surface for any new obstacles, but it seemed the same as he'd left it. A quick glance over his shoulder told him most of the passengers had done this before. There were no anxious faces.

Andreas liked to think of himself as an Olympic diver. Divers got extra points for a smooth entry, for as little splash as possible, so when he set the aircraft down, he was always trying for minimal wake. On a larger lake like this one, he could do it, provided the wind cooperated, but not today. They had too much weight. He brought the Twin Otter in and watched as the wake bounced the wharf. The men were all high-fiving each other as if they had just scored the winning goal in some championship game. Maybe they were anxious. He waited for the wharf to settle and then taxied up to it.

The men scrambled out of the aircraft and then set up an eight-person fire line, passing the equipment, baggage and food stores one to another until they had it all stacked on the shore. Then they waved him in. There wasn't anything for him to take back—he'd done all that when he picked up the previous crew—but he had a pattern of having a coffee and a bite to eat before heading back. He wanted to be on his way, to get this thing done, but he also didn't want to break the pattern. He wanted nothing to look suspicious, not at this point. That would come soon enough. He clambered out of the Otter, secured it to the wharf, and followed the men into camp.

He hated the whole idea of the place. Petroleum geologists searching for oil, searching for more fossil fuel to burn, for ways to exploit, taint, and destroy this glorious wilderness. The mining companies were no better, setting up big operations to pull gold, diamonds, and uranium out the ground, scarring the landscape. The caribou herds were crashing, the sea ice was melting—stranding starving polar bears—and the natives were being driven away from their traditional way of life. Nothing about this was right. None of the companies denied the warming anymore; they just didn't care.

The worst part of it was he had been in the service of these clowns for the last ten years, flying them in and out of their various camps and operations. He loved the North, and the money was good, but the hypocrisy of it was eating him up. What finally pushed him over was an insect, a bloody hornet. One had stung him on his first visit to the camp. The natives didn't have a word for hornet because they had never seen one this far north. It had never been warm enough for hornets before.

The geologists found the stash of dry wood and kindling left by the previous crew and had a fire going in no time. Andreas plopped himself down on a campstool and accepted a smoky on a metal fork from the camp cook and a cup of lukewarm thermosed coffee. He passed the meat in and out of the flames as everyone around him talked of rock formations and the results of previous tests.

"Hey Andreas, the idea is to cook the thing, not incinerate it," the cook said.

Andreas brought his attention back to the smoky, now in flames on the end of the fork. "I like them charred," he said accepting a bun from the cook.

"You're going to love that then," the cook laughed.

Andreas slid the smoky off the fork and into the bun. He added a few caramelized onions from a pan on the fire and some mustard. He took a tentative bite. It was not only blackened, it was dry. "I guess I over-cooked it," he said.

"Here," said the cook holding out another smoky. "Give it another go."

Andreas stood up. "No, I'd better be on my way. I've got to get the plane back."

"You sure?"

"Yeah, I've got to be going. Thanks anyway."

"Thank you for flying us out here," the cook said. Several other voices agreed.

He shook half a dozen smoky-greased hands, turned and walked back to the aircraft.

Andreas was scheduled to refuel the Twin Otter at the Fort Nelson Airport and spend the night in the town, so that's what he would do, except for the refuel and spend the night parts. He brought the aircraft down, taxied in, and parked it far enough away from the buildings. The fuel gauges in both wing tanks were showing less than a quarter, exactly where he wanted them to be. He told the airport administrator he'd refuel in the morning and he was going into town to get some shuteye. He set the timer for twenty-four hours before he left the aircraft.

The guy with the F-150 was meeting him at Dan's Neighborhood Pub. He had listed the truck on the Prince George Craig's List, but said the vehicle was in Fort Nelson. Perfect. Andreas told the seller he would pay the asking price in cash, sight unseen, provided it came with a full tank and if the guy was willing to wait a few days before changing the registration. He'd be into town too late to get to the registration office, he explained. The seller was hesitant about that until Andreas offered him an additional five hundred. There was still some reluctance, but they agreed to meet that evening at Dan's. The owner would wear a scruffy Saskatchewan Roughriders ball cap. If it didn't work out, Andreas could always go back, disarm the bomb, and continue on until he had another opportunity.

He found the seller and wished he hadn't. The man was about six foot five, three hundred pounds, with a braided beard, and a Harley-Davidson motorcycle tattooed on his left cheek. The cap was on backwards over a swath of dirty blond hair. This guy could leave with both the truck and the money.

"A Rider's fan in northern B.C.?" Andreas asked in greeting.

"A lot of us up here," the man said in a soft voice. "You Carl?"

Andreas knew he couldn't use his real name, but he also knew he couldn't hide his German accent. Choosing an Anglo-Saxon sounding alias didn't make much sense under the circumstances. "That's me," he said.

The big guy reached across the table and shook Andreas's hand. "Ben, Ben Johnston," he said. He smiled revealing capped gold teeth in the front.

"Like the poet?" Andreas said.

"He wrote all Shakespeare's stuff, you know," Ben said. "You want a beer?"

"I guess one wouldn't hurt, "Andreas said. "I've got a long drive ahead of me."

Ben gestured to the woman behind the bar. "What do you do up here anyway?" he asked. "Haven't seen you around."

"I'm in the bush. A naturalist. I run around the forest collecting bear scat."

"Really?" Ben's laugh was much bigger than his voice.

"There's a lot we can do with poo," Andreas grinned. The beer arrived.

"So where are you going tonight?"

"A wedding in Edmonton," Andreas said. "It's tomorrow afternoon and I'm supposed to be the best man. Then I'm coming straight back. We can change the registration on Monday."

Ben studied him. "You're paying me an extra five hundred bucks just to delay changing the registration for two days? Seems like a lot of money for a small favor."

"Yeah, well I have a delivery to do too," Andreas shrugged. He had to at least appear to be straight with the guy.

"A delivery?"

"Yeah. Just some stuff I've got to drop off on the way."

Ben stood up. "Nobody's going to use a vehicle registered in my name to deliver drugs," he said.

"Sit down, Ben. It's not drugs."

Ben sat down. "What then?"

Andreas sipped his beer and regarded the big man. "You a tree hugger, Ben?" he asked.

The big man huffed. "Give me a break. I've been involved in forestry all my life. I'd string those guys up if I could. They've cost me wages several times. Not sure if they've got anything to do with what's currently going on but I wouldn't be surprised." He looked down into his beer. "That's why I'm selling the truck," he said. "I've been laid off.

It's supposed to start up again soon but right now I got cash flow issues." He looked up and grinned. "And I need some party money before the aliens show up."

"Been following that have you?"

"A bit," Ben said.

Andreas could tell that it was more than a bit. This whole thing had many people spooked. "I figure if those aliens were coming, we'd have seen the ship by now," he said. "They say the thing is ten miles across. You'd think one of those telescopes would have seen something that big by now."

Ben shrugged and took a long pull from his beer.

"Anyway, it's bear parts," Andreas said softly.

Ben gave him a look of complete non-comprehension.

"The Chinese will pay a lot for the gall bladders. They use them in traditional medicine. I have a large cooler full of frozen bear meat to throw in the back of the truck, and the bladders are part of that. I'll be dropping that off at a friend's in Grand Prairie on the way through. That's all. It's perfectly safe."

"You shoot them?" Ben asked.

Andreas shook his head. "Trophy hunters. They shoot the animals and just take the head and mount it. They're not big on bear meat but it looks bad if they don't do something with it. So I provide a service by taking the carcasses off their hands. I call it research and mostly it is. I just make some money on the side that's all."

Ben looked unsure.

"I have the cash, Ben," Andreas said.

Ben looked around to see if anyone was listening to the conversation. No one was. "All right," he said. "Don't you even want to see the truck?"

They paid for the beers and went out to the parking lot.

Andreas was an hour down the road before he allowed himself to believe he'd pulled it off. He was grateful the big man hadn't asked to see the cooler. All he had in it was a half a dozen Red Bulls, two sandwiches, three hard-boiled eggs, and an Alberta plate. Ben would have ripped his head off. As it was, Ben hadn't even set up a time for them to meet on Monday, just took the cash and left as quickly as he could. Andreas had watched him pile into the passenger side of a rusting Honda civic. The driver was a scrawny woman with bad mascara. She was rolling a cigarette around in her mouth. She checked Andreas out in the side-view mirror as she pulled away from the curb. He had given her a little wave that was not returned.

Now he was heading toward Abbotsford B.C. in a truck that smelled like an ashtray. Ben had done a cursory job of cleaning the vehicle, but one of the first things Andreas found was a roach clip on the floor of the passenger side with its tiny jaws still clamped on to a charred bit of roll-your-own paper. He hadn't smoked pot since Amsterdam and wondered if the device was now old school. He rolled down the window and flicked it into the ditch, hoping there weren't any other nasty surprises. The last thing he needed was to be pulled over and busted, but then again, he'd be busted anyway if he got pulled over, especially after he put on the Alberta plate. He would do that in a couple of hours. Andreas made a mental note to remind himself to remove the front B.C. Plate. In Alberta, they only had back plates.

It was eighteen hours to Abbotsford, but he'd be there before the thing went off.

It would be noon before the airport realized he was a no show. Then they'd call the company, but it would be at least a day before they could get a pilot to Fort Nelson. By then the Otter would be a pile of rubble. He figured Paul Watson would like that even if it weren't quite as dramatic as ramming a whaling ship.

He was just outside Prince George listening to the CBC when he heard the report, an explosion at the Fort Nelson airport. A fucked-up timer, obviously. Now they'd be looking for him sooner than he expected. He pulled off down a logging road and changed the plates on the truck. He doubted if Ben would say anything. The big guy would look like an idiot if he did, especially since they hadn't done the required change in registration.

Andreas grinned. They'd get him, he knew. But he was looking forward to the thrill of the chase and the following environmental martyrdom. He'd sent a letter to the CBC explaining why he done it, but the whole idea was they'd get the letter long before the police got him. Now that might not happen. The National would cover it and he'd get his fifteen minutes of fame. Before all that, he was hoping to take in the Abbotsford Air Show. His online buddy was flying in with an old WWII B-25 Mitchell and had promised to take him up.

Ordnance

The Abbotsford Air Show in British Columbia had put out a call for vintage WWII bombers for their upcoming show. Jeff and Reb were contracted to fly the B-25 up to the Paine Field Airport in Everett Washington and use that as a base for the short hop to the Abbotsford. They took along two of the old guard, veterans who had crewed the B-25 during the Korean War.

One of these was Whispering Willy, a bright-eyed wispy-haired eighty-year-old who came by his nickname because of his tendency to whisper, a trait that made him inaudible when the aircraft was in the air. The B-25 was loud to the point of leaving one's ears ringing after a long flight. As a former bombardier, Willy had no real on-board duties, so it didn't matter. His inclusion in the crew had more to do with his historical credentials than it did with any operational need.

The second vet was retired Air Force Major Roderick Evans, who had piloted the plane during the Korean War and who had flown Lancaster's with the British during WWII. Technically, he was in command. He knew the aircraft better than anyone, but he was also ninety-four and blind. His bald head had a quarter-sized circular scar he claimed was a souvenir from a bull run in Spain. He wouldn't elaborate beyond that, but it looked like the puncture one might get from the tip of a bovine horn. Evans also had several other marks on his head, running sores Jeff was sure were cancerous, and he had a pacemaker. The Major installed himself in the co-pilot's seat, from which he gave Jeff a series of B-25 history lessons and frequently nodded off. When he woke, he repeated the lessons, almost word for word.

Jeff knew the Flying Heritage Collection in Everett also had an operational B-25 and wondered why Abbotsford wasn't using that one. He brought his B-25 in on a runway slick with light rain and felt a slight skid as it touched down. There was a small welcoming party composed of retired vets with a few young men. They walked around the parked B-25 several times and climbed inside for a look around.

"She's even cleaner than ours," said one vet.

"Where is yours?" Jeff asked.

The man wore a Boeing Cap over yellowing-to-white long hair. He had an unlit Camel tipping precariously out of the right side of his mouth. "We scrounged a couple of Wright R-2600s from a warehoused Mitchell in Kansas," he said. "They weren't never going to fly that thing, or even show it off, but the engines were in good shape. So we made an arrangement. Better to extend the life of a functioning aircraft and have it available to the public. Once we get the R-2600s in, we should get another ten years out of her, but right now she's in the hangar."

Jeff looked out the cockpit window and noticed Reb and one of the younger men were having an animated conversation down on the tarmac. Jeff shook his head. Reb had been quiet and sullen during the long flight, leaving his older brother to the mercy of The Major. Now Reb was all smiles.

The Major and Willy were pretty bagged. It was time to get them to the motel. They'd need a good night's rest before tomorrow. The welcoming party had all come in a small shuttle bus with the Boeing Saturn logo on the side. They all piled into this and, within a few minutes, were at the motel. The welcoming party said their goodbyes. Willie and The Major retired to one room with Reb and Jeff to another. Through all of this, the smile never left Reb's face.

They'd had a few beers before turning in, so Jeff was sleeping heavy. He woke once during the night and noticed Reb wasn't in his bed, but there was a light showing under the bathroom door, so he turned over and went back to sleep.

In the morning they all opened their suit bags and put on the WWII B-25 Mitchell flight crew uniforms recreated by a tailor back in Tifton. They had opted for the tropical-weight khaki cotton shirts and pants with the traditional flight caps. The Major had shoulder straps on his shirt. Jeff had had one extra made for Andreas, a B-25 enthusiast he'd met on line. Andreas was a Canadian bush pilot who was meeting them at the Abbotsford airport. Jeff had promised to take him up. The Canadian had sent his measurements, so he'd look like a crew member even if he were only a passenger. That was bending the rules, but Jeff didn't think anyone would care.

He was wrong.

"Who's the extra uniform for?" The Major asked when he saw it.

"Do you remember, Sir, that we're picking up a passenger at the Abbotsford Airport?" Jeff responded.

"So this is for him?"

"Yes. I thought it would give us a consistent look."

"Is he an enlisted man? An American Air force vet?"

"No, sir, he's a Canadian bush pilot. Got plenty of air time though."

"Then he doesn't wear the uniform," The Major said firmly. "We'll take him up, but he doesn't wear the uniform."

"I just thought..."

"There's a protocol to these things, boy, and if you're not military or a vet, then you don't wear the uniform. It's that simple."

"Yes, Sir," Jeff said.

"Reb shouldn't even be wearing it because he's a Marine vet, but we'll let that one pass," The Major said.

Jeff glanced over a Reb. The uniform fit him perfectly. He was still wearing the same grin from the previous night, but his eyes looked bloodshot.

The same Boeing shuttle from the previous night picked them up and took them back to the B-25. Only one of the original welcoming party met them this time, the same young man Reb had been talking to on the tarmac the night before.

Willy was always the first to climb on. For him it was a slow climb, and he didn't like having anyone behind him on the stairs, so he always went up well before the crew to settle in. The rest of them were all still standing around on the tarmac when he reappeared at the hatch.

"We've got ammo!" he said in his loudest whisper. His face was flushed, and he looked unsteady on the top of the stairs.

"What do you mean we've got ammo?" Jeff said.

"There are belts loaded into the guns in the front turret," Willy said gasping for breath.

Jeff looked at Reb. His brother was nodding.

"Where the hell did you get that?" Jeff demanded.

"You can find most anything online if you look hard enough," Reb said. "They had some in storage right here in the museum."

Jeff looked at the young man from the previous night's welcoming party who was also nodding. He looked back at Reb.

"That's where you were last night?"

"I left the light on in the can in case you woke up," Reb said.

"Jesus," Jeff said. "We can't take live ammunition to an air show!"

"Well, it would make us more authentic wouldn't it?" Reb asked.

"It's an issue of public safety, Reb!"

"It's only dangerous if somebody fires the gun," the Major said smiling. "And that's not likely to happen now, is it?"

Press Conference

Alatorre looked at her watch, less than ten minutes to show time. They arranged the five of them behind a kidney-shaped table facing the cameras. Technicians were busy fastening lapel microphones, checking levels, and focusing cameras.

The members of the press were still outside the auditorium waiting to enter. Usually it was the other way around. The media folks would be in their seats waiting for the featured speaker or speakers and those persons would enter once the press were seated. But there would be eight people on stage, including the two interpreters who had come with Zhou and Gulubev, and an additional interpreter for the local media. The French technicians and security people wanted everything and everyone in place before the curtains opened. Alatorre found it hard to collect her thoughts in all the chaos.

Harrison sat beside her. A technician was trying to get a small alligator clip around the thickness of his Harris Tweed. He finally gave up and clipped the microphone to the prime minister's shirt. Harrison turned to Alatorre. "It's remarkable how often people miss the most obvious solutions to small problems," he said.

"You ready for this?" Alatorre asked.

"No."

Alatorre nodded.

"All right, everyone," Lambert announced. "They will close the curtains and then let the press in. Remember that you're on microphone. These should not be live, but you never know so say nothing you don't want overheard."

Alatorre felt behind her lapel mic, found the switch and turned it off. Harrison watched her do it and then did the same.

"Just remember to turn it back on," Alatorre said.

Harrison nodded. "Tell me again how I got drafted for this?"

Two layers of curtains began a slow crossing in front.

"We all agreed that Great Britain had done the fewest internationally stupid things over the past few years," Alatorre said with a grin.

Harrison laughed. "Ah, yes, and I remember thinking that I wished I could use that in my next election campaign, because that certainly isn't the perception back home."

"Anyway, you just have to talk about your interaction with the Fahr. The video will explain most of the rest of it and I'll introduce that."

"And then the questions. I'll get the bulk of those."

"Lambert will try to spread those out."

The curtains were now closed, and they could hear the muffled din as the media filed in. An argument broke out, a mixture of French and English curses. Alatorre looked over at Zhao. He was the only one of the five to have his water glass replaced. Instead he held a commercial clear plastic bottle containing some kind of amber liquid. Tea? Alatorre couldn't tell. The label was printed in Chinese characters. Zhao was struggling to open it. When he did, he took a long pull and then noticed that Alatorre was watching him. He smiled and then spoke to his interpreter, who in turn spoke to a stagehand. Thirty seconds later the stagehand was presenting Alatorre with a bottle of the same amber liquid.

"This is a kind of ginseng tea," the stagehand explained. "He said to tell you it is good for the nerves."

"Thank you," Alatorre said, first to the stagehand and then to the Chinese president.

Alatorre wasn't sure she wanted to put anything new into her stomach at that point but didn't want to offend. She removed the top and took a tentative sip. It was an acquired taste, strong and bee-honey sweet.

The din on the other side of the curtains increased. There were more arguments, a muffled crash, and more bilingual swearing. Her colleagues were all exchanging nervous glances except Gulubev, who stared straight ahead, his jaw set. He looked like he was about to lead troops into battle. A member of the security team came on stage and consulted with Lambert.

"There will be a short delay," Lambert said. "They're having to remove people from the auditorium."

"Brilliant," Harrison said.

"I'm wondering if they'll have the patience to sit through that video presentation," Alatorre said.

There was another crash with more shouting. The security person rushed off stage. Someone tried to open the curtain from the other side. Alatorre glimpsed a bearded man being tackled by security and heard the zap of a stun gun.

"*Allāhu akbar!*" someone shouted.

"*Allāhu akbar!*" came the chorused response.

The curtain suddenly pushed inward, the shape of a body pressed up against it and then another and another. The security person rushed back onstage. He gestured for everyone to follow him.

"No one was armed," the French president said. He laughed. "I think they planned to strangle us."

"Who were they?" Alatorre asked still holding the bottle of ginseng tea that Zhao had given her.

"We think they were part of the local Algerian community," said Lambert. "They had that kind of accent, but they all had Al Zezeera press passes. That's how they got in."

"How many?" Harrison asked.

"Only three," Lambert said. "Big guys though. Maybe wrestlers? I don't think we were in danger, at least not from them."

"And they made all that noise, just the three of them?" Harrison asked.

Lambert conferred with security chief. "He says no. There were quite few agitated people, a lot. It wasn't even the Algerians they were trying to remove at first: two Italians, a South African, and someone from Brazil. There was a lot of anger in the room."

"This was a bad idea," Gulubev said.

They waited for the interpreter to translate for Zhao.

"Then we go to the U.N.," the Chinese leader said. "We should have done that to begin with."

There was a general resignation and nodding of heads.

"And then we think about how we will defend this planet," Gulubev said.

United Nations

"As Prime Minister of Canada, I would like to announce that Canada intends to recommit itself to the United Nations. It is our intention to be an active member and to support the various initiatives that are agreed upon by this body. And, while we do not generally agree with initiatives that challenge the sovereignty of member nations, we think this current situation may require flexibility on that front. We have seen the evidence and we believe prudence may be the best course of action in this situation. I see no reason why the temporary position of world leader cannot be created for communication with the Fahr. We intend to support any resolution to that effect."

Maria Alatorre watched as Pierce O'Malley, the Canada's prime minister, sat down to muted applause and grumbling. His rock star status had been wearing thin of late, the selfie seekers had retreated and the grays in his blond hair, once hidden, were on full display. He was becoming a statesman and boring like the rest, but she liked him. Too bad his support would count for nothing in this crowd. Maybe it would have a few years earlier but not now. Now he was just another progressive fighting to resist the rising tide of conservatism in his own country.

The chancellor of Germany was the next invited to speak. He was one who was also losing that battle, the German electorate turning against the Syrian refugees his party had so compassionately let in. They had not become German in their thinking and, while many of them had adapted and become productive citizens, an equal number were struggling and continuing to require help. Some of these were resorting to crime. It was these that got all the attention in the German press and now a right leaning and anti-immigration party was leading in the polls. It was unclear what they would do if they gained power but most of Europe was nervous. Alatorre was sure they could count on German support. The Chancellor stood up.

"I would like to suggest that calling an emergency debate in this body to discuss what amounts to science fiction is a serious misuse of the resources available to this international body. And, even if the threat was credible, asking us to put our individual sovereignties on hold is outrageous. Most of us put a great deal of energy into maintaining our sovereignties and for some of us this is a never-ending and costly struggle. But no, the five permanent members of the Security Council want us to just hand our sovereignties over to them so they can better deal with this phantom menace. This alien entity, this Fahr, as you call them—if they exist—and I will state the obvious one more time for the benefit of anyone who missed it. We cannot find this moon or spaceship or whatever it is supposed to be— it seems to have disappeared—if it ever existed. The most eminent scientists in the world cannot find this thing but we are supposed to turn over our sovereignties to one of these five nations in case it exists? And which of them would speak for us? It's not as if they occupy an ideologically common ground. No. I tell you that the government of Germany does not believe the Fahr exist. And if they do exist, then they will just have to deal with the reality as it is on the ground on this planet: we have 196 independent sovereign states here."

Alatorre's mouth dropped, accompanied by wild applause and cheering for the German Chancellor. He had killed any chance for temporary world leadership, any chance for dialogue with the Fahr, but he would probably be re-elected.

Flickering

Darryl's wife had argued spending several hundred dollars on their son's fleeting interest in astronomy was excessive and she had been right. Within a month Andrew's interest waned, but during that same month Darryl learned to operate the telescope and now he was hooked.

Mars had two small moons. Finding and viewing the red planet had never been a problem but viewing the moons was. The light from the planet would wash them out. The trick was to place a thin occulting bar across the center of the lens and position it over Mars to block its light. Then the moons were easier to see.

Darryl fashioned the bar out of copper wire and wrapped it in aluminum foil. It took a while to adjust it and get it into place, but when he did, he was rewarded with a clear view of the two moons in all their glory. Well, hardly glory, since they were barely visible but at least he could see them.

At first he was so fixated on the two small dots he failed to notice his field of view was darkening from the left side. When he noticed, the obstruction was about a third the way across. Darryl looked up from the telescope to see if there were cloud cover but it was a clear night. He could see Mars with his naked eye and then it blinked out. He looked through the eyepiece again. Now the field of view was two-thirds obstructed and he could see the edge of whatever it was drifting toward the right side. Then the stars on the left side of the field of view reappeared. He looked with his naked eye again. Mars was back but now the stars to the right of it were flickering in and out.

Probably a satellite, he thought, and went back to studying the Martian moons.

Coquihalla

The Coquihalla was a fast road. To this point, the roads Andreas had driven on his long journey down from Fort Nelson had been winding and curvy; the kinds of roads requiring focused driving with a lot of speeding up and slowing down. This was good because it kept him alert, but the Coquihalla had been constructed for speed with wide lanes, increased speed limits, and long downhill grades where one's speed naturally crept up. Andreas was tired. He'd been on the road now for almost sixteen hours. He let it creep up.

The flashing red and blue lights caught him by surprise. Where had the cop come from? He looked in his rear-view mirror and thought through his options. Running was not one. The police cruiser was much faster than the pickup and the officer would know the area. Nor was acting against the lone cop. Andreas was not armed, and the officer was. He rolled down the window and grinned up at him.

"You're from Alberta, eh?" The cop asked.

"Yes, sir."

"Ever driven the Coquihalla before?"

"No, sir. This is the first time I've driven in B.C."

The police officer cocked an eyebrow. "Really?"

"Well, you can probably tell from my accent I wasn't born here. Flew in a year back to take a position with Suncor. It's been intense so when I got a few weeks off I decided to relax and explore."

"Well, OK. You were well over the speed limit. That happens a lot on the Coquihalla because of those long downhill grades. It sneaks up on you. So you need to pay attention to your speed. All right?"

"Yes, sir."

"I'll let you go this time. But just so you know, the speeding tickets here are about double what they are in Alberta. So pay attention to your driving."

"Yes, sir. Thank you, sir."

"You're welcome."

The cop stepped back, wrote Andreas's plate number on a small pad of paper, and then walked back to the cruiser. Andreas got out of the truck and pretended to rummage around in the box, opening the cooler and removing a sandwich. All the while he was watching the cop to see if he would enter the plate number into the system. If he did, then the gig was up. It would flash the stolen plate. But the cop threw the pad onto the seat beside him and pulled back onto the road.

Andreas looked at the sandwich in his hand. He had crushed it, bits of tuna salad coating his fingers. Abbotsford was still two hours away.

Warning

A quarter of the ship's complement pressed into the observatory, a room never intended for such a large group. In its center, Agastin swam in tight little circles around the senior officers with his diaphragm engorged and his excitement high. Teracia could see his anticipation mirrored in the diaphragms of most of his audience.

"There are, as you know, two elements to our operation," Agastin said. "The first of these involves the disabling of Planet Song's defenses. Vice Commander Thryke has already spoken to you about this. The second involves the actual extraction of The Singers and I will speak to that now."

Gills rippled wildly in the room; the engorgement of the diaphragms increased to collective shimmer. "Taste, taste, taste," the chant began.

Teracia blanched. They want it even though it will kill them.

Agastin raised his claspers to silence them. "As you know, eighty percent of the mass of this vessel is ballast water. We will do a controlled release of this as we enter that atmosphere and it will cool the ship during our descent. Most of you will also have noticed we have been maximizing the ship's battery power. This is to allow us to sustain and preserve the vacuum we will have once the ballast is released. We will hover over the extraction point where The Singers are gathering to feed and use the vacuum to draw those close to surface into the ship. We expect to collect between fifteen and twenty-five individuals along with several cubic miles of the ocean they inhabit. This will include their primary food sources and other environmental elements necessary to their immediate survival. Afterwards, our biogenetic engineers will get to work to put the elements in place to ensure their survival during the journey home."

"Taste, taste, taste, taste," the chant resumed.

Agastin waited for the chants to stop. When they didn't, he inflated red. Everyone stopped. He gestured to Teracia.

Teracia swam forward and surveyed the group before her. "You're all aware of what happened to the crew during the last voyage here,"she said.

"Some of them died, Mamini," an officer spoke up.

"Correct, and how did they die?"

"Exposure to The Singers' virgin song," the officer answered.

"And yet this is what you want to do to yourselves?" she asked.

"You're a femfahr. How could you know?"

The voice was anonymous, part of the crowd. Teracia had no idea who had spoken.

"I know there is a certain mentality that seems to accompany fahrs who go on pet expeditions. Let's call this what it is, lust, the seeking of virgin song. And you're right. I cannot know how that feels, but this virgin song will kill you."

Agastin took over. "The entire containment area has been baffled so the song cannot move throughout the ship. Do not put yourself on the other side of that baffle. Do you understand?"

"Yes, Commander Agastin," came a chorus of responses.

"Are there questions?"

The room fell silent but Teracia knew that did not mean agreement.

Ayers Rock

A full moon hung above Ayers Rock, blue and mottled with just enough wispy red cloud to make the image a study in near primary colors. Gymea had the camera on a tripod set to video. She would go through it later, isolate stills, and mount them in frames for tourists.

The camera was set to silent, allowing her to attend to the wind whispering through the sparse grass. She pulled the blanket around her and closed her eyes, letting the device do its thing. When the wind dropped off her ears tuned in to smaller sounds, the scamperings of lizards and rodents, the slitherings of snakes, the scratchings of insects. It had taken her years to gain those listening skills, to learn to identify each creature. They were her family, her intimates.

Silence.

She waited for this to pass but it did not. Something was wrong. She opened her eyes. A large rectangular bite advanced across the moon.

Her first thought was that it would ruin everything, all that video taken on a perfect night. Then she wondered what it was. It was black, and that made little sense. Any satellite in that position would also reflect the sunlight from just beyond the horizon, but this was blocking the moonlight, a right-angled eclipse. It was also larger than any satellite she'd ever seen, much larger. Gymea let the camera keep on shooting. The tourists may not pay for this but perhaps someone else would.

Diane

The Fahr were gone. They had disappeared, and Diane was on the verge of joining the vast majority of scientists who doubted if they had ever existed. This was now the twelfth of the tri-weekly series of

NASA press conferences at which she would be skewered. *Damn you, Dah Williams!* She took her place behind the microphone. Her boss was at home recuperating from what his doctors described as an "upper body injury."

At least Benjamin Stofi was there. The chair for SETI was used to people thinking he was a little off and did not seem bothered by it. The problem was few of the media questions came his way. NASA had put forward the idea that aliens were orbiting Jupiter, and it was to NASA that most of the questions were directed. That meant Diane.

Had they found the alien ship?

No.

Had they found the person who had hacked into NASA's computers?

No.

How much money had David Crosby and Graham Nash made from the insane popularity of their song?

She didn't know.

Were they perhaps behind the whole scam?

She doubted it.

Does the alien ship have windshield wipers?

Towards the end of each conference it always deteriorated like that.

The problem was she had no new information to give them. But there was one question in which the members of the media were intensely interested.

"How long did your scientists calculate it would take for the alien ship to reach Earth from Jupiter?"

Diane studied the face of the woman who had asked—young, intense, bleeding mascara—definitely not the same person who asked two days earlier. Stofi gave Diane a look of tired resignation.

She sighed. "This is speculation," she said carefully. "It's based on the assumption that when the aliens first encountered the Pioneer 10 probe, they would have been at the edge of the solar system. That's pretty far out, about half a light year from Jupiter. That was ten years ago. The next time they contacted us, fairly recently, they were near

Jupiter. To do that they would have to travel at the five percent of the speed of light. At that speed they could reach the Earth from Jupiter in less than a month."

"The solar system is that big?"

"Yes, it is," Diane replied.

"So how much time is left?" the woman asked.

"Do the math," Diane said and regretted it. She was losing the ability to be civil.

"So any time now?" the woman asked after a pause.

Diane caught Trent making a throat slashing gesture off stage. He seemed agitated.

"I'm sorry," Diane said, "We must cut this off now. Something's come up that needs our attention. We'll meet again for an update in two days." She ignored the sudden barrage of questions and gestured to Stofi to follow her off stage.

"What's up," she said to Trent.

"You know how we stopped monitoring the Pioneer 10 frequencies years ago?"

"There was nothing to monitor. Why?"

"I did a random check about fifteen minutes ago," he gestured for Diane to look at the monitor.

"Unite. We are coming. Talking is better than war."

"Shit! When did this come in?"

"Twenty days ago," Trent said.

"But that makes little sense. Why would they use that frequency when all the other messages came through Grenoble?"

"I don't know."

"It's too late anyway," Stofi said pointing to his laptop. The screen showed a large rectangular-shaped object passing in front of a full moon. "Australian outback, about half an hour ago."

Diane let out a long breath. "So they do have some kind of stealth technology," she said.

"And we have no world government," Stofi said.

Diane could hear the gasps and shouts coming from the media as the same information appeared on their laptops.

"Someone or something on that ship is on our side," she said.

Stofi nodded. "But not in a position of power. If it were, it would have found a more direct means of communication."

IEMP

Thryke chose six crew members to disarm Planet Song. Only the two primaries were needed. The other four followed the Fahr military convention of double backups. They floated behind the primaries as secondaries and tertiaries, little more than observers.

The primaries floated in front of the control panels watching displays.

"IEMP ordnance ready for descent," said the second primary.

"Stand by," Thryke said. There were twelve IEMP devices in high orbit around Planet Song, fewer and more vulnerable than their satellite-killing counterparts. The IEMPs carried intelligent electro-magnetic pulse generators, timed to go off simultaneously at preset locations around the planet. But not before the satellite killers had done their work. These would attach themselves to Planet Song's satellites and await a signal from the ship.

"Satellite killers in place," said the first primary.

"All of them?" asked Thryke.

"Yes, Vice Commander, 1087 killers in place."

"Deploy," Thryke said, his gills rippling. Over the next few minutes, they would vaporize every operational satellite in Planet Song orbit. Once they did this, the Fahr could deploy the IEMPs with less risk. With the satellites gone, it would be harder for Homines to detect them.

"Thirty-seven percent of mission," said the first primary.

Thryke watched the indicators blink off on the control panels.

It would take the radio signals longer to reach the satellites in deeper orbit.

"Eighty-two percent of mission," said the first primary.

They all watched as the remaining eighteen percent blinked off.

"Deploy IEMPs," Thryke said. Those bipeds on the night side of the planet might see them fall, tiny streaks against the night sky. They would then detonate, producing electro-magnetic pulses that would seek out and fry ninety-five percent of the circuit boards, chips and electrical grids on Planet Song.

"IEMPs are one hundred percent," the second primary said after twelve flashes on the screen.

"Good. Well done." Thryke swam over to the COM system. "Commander, it is finished," he said.

"They're neutralized?" Agastin asked.

"Yes, Commander."

"Then the time for the collection has come," Agastin said, ending the communication.

Thryke stared at the COM controls before turning back to the six crew members. "We will begin the descent shortly," he said. "Sponge in."

He watched as the crew members allowed themselves to be pulled in by the large shock-absorbing sponges growing out of the walls. Then he swam off quickly, heading for the bowels of the ship.

Thryke had little doubt that Homines would offer resistance and, when they did, he would be there to meet it.

Offline

It took the Fort Irwin troops only fifteen minutes to expel the media, most of whom were demanding the resumption of the press conference after the appearance of the Fahr ship. But no sooner had they left than a new problem arose.

"We're losing the satellites," Trent said peering at his monitor.

"Which satellites?" Diane said.

"All of them."

"What? Are they hijacking the signals again?"

"No," Trent said. "They're just gone. As if they were never there."

"All of them?"

"Yes."

Diane looked over Trent's shoulder. "Jesus," she said. "Find out if the other agencies have the same problem."

Trent typed in an IP address and entered it.

"You are not connected to the Internet," he read from the screen.

Diane stared at the screen. "If we've lost connection with the satellites, that would affect the Internet too. We'll have to call them."

"Same problem," Trent said. "No satellites, no phones."

"Unless you're on a land line," Diane said.

"Even the land lines are routed through satellites," Trent said.

"So we have no way of getting a hold of anyone," Diane said.

"Not until this comes back up," Trent said.

The monitors flickered off and room went dark.

"Great, now we get a brownout," Diane said.

"This is weird," Trent said, looking around. "The emergency lights should come on automatically."

"You're right," Diane said. "They're all on independent battery systems. They should be on, at least some of them."

"But they're not."

Diane pulled her cell phone out of her pocket. "I can use this as a flashlight in a pinch," she said.

It was dead.

Trent pulled his out and got the same result.

"OK, what the hell is going on here?" Diane said.

"I don't know," Trent said. "But I'm not sitting around in the dark. Let's go outside."

In the parking lot, an officer and a soldier from Fort Irwin had popped the hood on a Humvee and were trying to get the vehicle started.

"I don't understand, sir," the soldier said. "It started just fine this morning and there seemed to be plenty of juice in the battery."

"Probably the starter then," the officer said. "I'll call it in."

Diane and Trent looked at each other as the officer fished his cell phone out of his pocket.

Defense

Within a few minutes of the ship's appearance, they were all on the phone to each other.

"They're in a deep orbit," Alatorre said. "Anything we launched against them would be seen from a long way off."

"We have nothing that could strike at an object that far away," said Lambert.

"We could hit it, but the weapon would be too small," said Zhao.

"Our situation is much the same," Gulubev said. "But I say we strike, anyway."

"We have to assume their technology is much superior to our own," Harrison said. "That they could get this close to us with such a massive ship and remain undetected is proof enough, never mind what went on before that. I think it would be foolhardy to initiate conflict. We could be seriously over-matched."

"So we sit here and do nothing?" Gulubev said.

"We don't know what we're dealing with," said Harrison. "We must wait until we know more."

"But they've already demonstrated an unwillingness to reveal much about themselves," Lambert said. "Can we assume that's about to change?"

"They're here, they're visible, and they're a big target," said Gulubev.

"But they also know they're a big target and, as you and

President Alatorre have already pointed out, you can't launch a weapon at them they wouldn't be able to detect from a long way off. If they have any means of intercepting such a weapon, then it would be useless, anyway. But they would see it as an act of..."

The line went dead. Harrison looked at the phone and then at his assistant. His assistant shrugged.

"Do something," Harrison snapped at him.

Lambert put the phone down and walked to the window that overlooked the gardens. "Let me know when you've re-established the link," he said to the woman behind him.

Zhao watched as all the monitors in the room displayed static and then went dead. He handed the phone to his assistant and then looked up at his minister of defense. "Get all the important people into bunkers," he said.

Gulubev studied the phone and then set it down. "It's time for decisive action anyway," he said to the general in the room. "It's no longer time for talk. Prepare the weapon."

"Yes Mr. President," the general said. He pulled out his own phone, looked at it and then showed it to Gulubev. "Also dead," he said.

Gulubev frowned as the lights flickered and died.

Maria Alatorre looked at her chief of staff. "What do you mean all the phone lines are down?"

"That's what they're telling me, Ma'am."

"Turn on the television," Alatorre said.

Gerald Garneau flicked the remote. Static. Every channel.

"Satellites," Alatorre said.

"Satellites, Ma'am?"

"If you wanted to disrupt communications on the entire planet, what would be the best way to do that?"

"Oh, I see what you mean. You think that..."

The television went black. The lights flickered out. Alatorre became aware of her own breathing and that of Garneau's. All the ambient sounds hissing in the background were suddenl" gone: no air-conditioning, no fans, no humming lights. Alatorre and Garneau looked at each other.

"If they've knocked out the satellites, Ma'am," said Garneau, "how would that affect the...?"

There was a tire screech, shouts, and a huge crash. Flickerings from outside flames played across the walls. Alatorre and Garneau raced to the window. What remained of a helicopter was burning on the White House lawn. Cars in the distance had either run into each other or stalled. A woman was screaming. The president pulled out her cell phone and looked at it. Dead. She checked her watch. The second hand had stopped.

"Get someone out there to help these people," Alatorre told Garneau.

"What just happened?" Garneau asked.

"We lost the war, that's what happened," Alatorre said.

"Lost what war?".

"You've heard of electromagnetic pulses?"

"Of course," said Garneau. "Nuclear bombs exploded high enough in the atmosphere can fry electrical connections for hundreds of miles in any direction." His mouth dropped open. "Destroy the communications and the electronic infrastructure. You think this is worldwide?"

"I'm guessing it will be awhile before we know," Alatorre said.

"But our crucial electronic and communications systems are protected from EMPs," Garneau said.

"From known sources and strengths of EMPs, yes. But what if they have a way of getting around those defenses?" the president asked.

The doors to the room burst open and several secret service agents entered.

"Madam President," an agent said, "there's been some kind of attack. We have to get you to safety."

Alatorre nodded, and they escorted Garneau and her from the room.

Descent

Commander Agastin floated before the COM system.

"Minister Wrasse," Agastin said.

"Yes, Commander."

"This is where you earn your passage. Make sure that everything is in place to receive The Singers."

"It is, Commander," Wrasse said.

"Good," said Agastin. Next, he contacted Teracia.

"Are Homines reporting any damage?" Agastin asked.

"We destroyed their entire communications system, Commander." Teracia said coolly. "There's nothing to intercept."

"Nothing?"

"Well, there are snippets of panic being broadcast on the few surviving circuit boards and on outdated equipment," Teracia said.

"Equipment without circuit boards? How much of that is out there?"

"Not much, Commander. And electrical power grids are down. A lot of that older equipment still has to be plugged into newer power grids so..."

"Keep me informed," Agastin said.

"Yes, Commander." Teracia said.

"Navigational Officer Baronth," he said.

"Yes, Commander."

"Bring us down."

Wish

Teracia made her way to Prostallen's quarters.

"You look distressed," he said as she entered.

"I am not dying," she said.

"Is that a reference to me or what's going on down there?"

Teracia studied Prostallen. He was fading fast. The ex-commander could no longer swim, could only move along a series of magnetic tracks, and could not keep most of his various members from twitching. "Both," she said.

"Do you plan to ride out the descent here?" he asked.

Teracia answered by presenting herself before Prostallen's wall sponge. It pulled her in.

"Well, I guess my restraints will keep me safe enough."

Teracia said nothing.

Prostallen's gills rippled. "Ah, you've come to talk but not to talk. Interesting."

The descent timer appeared on Prostallen's wall, set to zero. Teracia looked at that.

"Perspective," Prostallen said. "There are more homines individuals alive in New York City right now there are fahr on the entire planet of Centrix. We're doing them a favor. Ninety-nine out of a hundred homines will never see their full potential because of the size of their population."

"Stop," Teracia said, her ballow reddening.

"Ethics are guidelines, nothing more. We want to be seen as behaving ethically, and we will do the right thing if it is not too costly, but ultimately ethics, ultimately The Will of the Giver, is situational. If the potential profit is high enough, then the cost of achieving it, however unethical, will be paid. The Fahr, all fahr will want this Singer and this Song."

"Not all," said Teracia.

"All is too strong a word, perhaps," Prostallen said. "But for the vast majority of the residents of Centrix, the fate of Homines will be a distant abstraction that has no impact on their lives. The acquisition of The Singers, however, will be celebrated for millennia to come."

Teracia said nothing.

"You have not failed, Teracia," Prostallen said. "Thanks to you, Thryke has failed in turning this into a full-scale military conflict. He wanted a war, and you have deprived him of that."

"We have just destroyed their communications and electronics infrastructure. As a result, many homines have died and many more will die. How is that different from engaging in war?"

"It's a lot less costly, and it's limited. The action taken was to facilitate the most efficient means of collecting The Singers. That was the intent, not to kill homines."

"But the action was taken with the foreknowledge it would cause death and destruction."

"A business plan that includes a foreknowledge of collateral damage is still a business plan, as long as the cost of that collateral damage is considered."

"The cost for whom?" Teracia said.

"What did I tell you when you first signed on for this mission?"

"That was three hundred years ago. I don't remember."

"I think you do," Prostallen said. "I told you it is best to think of the company as an entity onto itself. It has the maximizing of profit as its sole motivation. It will behave ethically only if ethical behavior is a means to greater profitability. So, believe it or not, Thryke had to be controlled for reasons of profitability. An all-out war would have been costly, might have endangered The Singers, and most certainly would have reduced profitability. You turned out to be useful to Song Corp."

"Not dangerous?"

"Manageable risk. I wanted you included. I argued for you because I knew the return trip would be hazardous. We will have a cargo that could kill every member of the crew just by singing. We've taken precautions to shield the crew from the cargo, but something could go wrong. If it does, then all profit is lost. But you are immune. You saved my crew on the last voyage and you might save this one. It wasn't hard to argue in your favor even with your save-the-Homines mentality. And that mentality proved useful in restraining Thryke."

Teracia said nothing.

"The company does not care about Homines. It cares about profit; the only costs it cares about are its own. So when Homines turned out to be much more advanced than we expected, Song Corp chose the least expensive method to deal with the problem. We disabled them to where they were incapable of resisting the extraction. Many of the homines have died and will die because of this, but the vast majority will survive and there is no doubt they will continue on as a species. They will rebuild but Song Corp doesn't care because that is unlikely to affect profitability."

"Sometimes you talk about the company as an 'it' with a mind of its own and other times you talk about it using 'we' as if the decisions made were our decisions. Which is it?"

Prostallen's gills rippled again. "Both but for your purposes it's more helpful to see it as a single entity. You may convince a single fahr to behave ethically because he will have a conscience allowing for such an internal debate, but the company is only concerned about profit and that's because the vast majority of the employees and investors agree with that emphasis. You, yourself, will arrive back at Centrix with a huge bonus. You will be set for the rest of a long life. That's an attractive thing for most fahr, which is why it's easy for them to push away concerns about Homines. That may not be true in your case, but it pits you against the corporate entity in a battle you can't win."

"You agree with that corporate agenda," Teracia said gesturing the Prostallen's restraints, "and look at what it's done to you."

"It's true," said Prostallen, "I've spent my life in service to this corporate entity and my reward is a premature death. But premature by what standard? We live fifty times longer than any other sapient species in the galaxy. Fifty times! And what do we do with all that living? We study. Our lives are measured in occupations. Our PDMs are filled with accomplishments we can no longer recall and which we wear below our necks as if they actually mean something. If not for the songs, our race would have gone mad a billion years ago. I do not regret my loyalty to the company, or what I have done to myself. We have given the Fahr race a reason to go on."

Teracia studied Prostallen. "And yet for what you're planning you'll require my help. The only fahr on board who, according to you, does not have a reason to go on?"

"Yes, I will need your help."

The ship lurched, and fish raced in a panic around the room. Teracia felt herself being pushed further back into the sponge and the descent timer began its count.

Xburner

Agastin could have ordered the destruction of the Xburner but he had not. Thryke took encouragement from that. The commander saw value in preserving military history even if he didn't want it used. Defying Agastin would be simple enough. The commander would be preoccupied with the landing and would not be watching for or expecting the ejection of a single flyer.

Thryke swam quickly down the narrow barnacle-infested passages of the ship's bowels and up to the door. The reader scanned his ballow and opened the door, releasing oxygen into the water. He swam into the compartment and to the Xburner. Thryke strapped himself into the flyer and hoped that securing himself in such a way would make up for the lack of shock-absorbing sponges. Descending through Planet Song's atmosphere would be a bumpy ride.

The Xburner had to be ejected from the ship while the ship was still well up in the atmosphere and not when it was hovering over the extraction point. If he waited too long, the flyer would be propelled into the ocean rather than into the air and rendered useless. Or, if the flyer was ejected too early, he might wind up halfway around the planet from the extraction site. Xburner's guidance technology was too old to interface with the ship's so Thryke would have to trigger the ejection manually. He had done calculations, and all that was left was the descent.

He felt the entire ship shudder. The two restraints pulled him back against the wall of the cockpit. They were hard, cold, and ungiving. His gill slits flattened from the pressure and he had to force them open to breathe. Then the shaking started. It was much worse than he expected. He had never descended through a planetary atmosphere without the sponges and his ribs were taking a pounding. One snapped and then another. He had to stay focused on the task, but pain was intruding on every thought. Then the shaking stopped. He looked at the time, less than a minute to ejection. The rib pain increased as he extended his clasper, grasped the control, and pulled. Again he was thrown back against the wall of the cockpit, this time smacking his head.

His eyes closed with the pain. When he opened them, he was outside the ship in free fall. The Xburner was spinning and tumbling through the atmosphere. He was dizzy and unable to think. The control panel was a blur. Because of the age of the flyer, most of the controls were mechanical, not controlled by gestures but by actual physical contact. He flicked a switch, and the Xburner leveled off. A few moments passed as he composed himself and then he reached for the craft's main control lever.

The priority was to find the ship. If he would defend it, he had to stay close. He saw the trail of smoke and fog. It was already a long way off. The ship was ejecting water as it descended to make room for The Singers and their environment. The water vaporized, creating a dense fog behind the ship and rendering it invisible from behind. Thryke found another switch and turned on the Xburner's archaic radar system. It told him that the ship was several hundred miles ahead. Unlike the ship, the Xburner was designed for atmospheric flight. Catching the ship would not be a problem. He had timed the ejection perfectly.

Abbotsford

They flew into Abbotsford the night before so the B-25 would be on the tarmac when the gates opened. This would allow the crowd to get close to the aircraft before the actual flying demonstration.

The Major and Willie handled most of the questions, steeped as they were in the history of the aircraft. Jeff studied the crowd, scanning the faces and comparing them to the one Andreas had sent to his phone. The German-Canadian looked like the clichéd backwoodsman, straggly long hair and beard. But, apart from two fellows wearing Hells Angels colors, Jeff saw no one who was even close to that image. Andreas had said nothing about membership in a biking club and the two men in question did not approach him.

"Looking for me?" said a soft German accent.

Jeff turned and stared into the face of a man with short dirty brown hair, a week's worth of stubble, gray dress pants, a light blue shirt, and a clip-on tie.

"Sorry," Andreas said. "I should have sent you a more recent picture, but I figured I'd be able to spot you with no trouble."

"Andreas?" Jeff asked.

"Yeah." He shook Jeff's hand. "You must be Jeff."

"That's me."

Andreas gestured to his clothes. "I hope these are all right. I got your message about not being able to wear the uniform, but I was piggy backing on someone else's Wi-Fi at the time and they disconnected before I could respond. I don't have a data plan. They're useless up north. But I thought if the rest of you will be in uniform, I'd better try to find something better than jeans."

"You look fine," Jeff said.

"This is the bird, eh?" Andreas said looking at the B-25.

Jeff laughed. "My brother will love you. He spent years teaching himself to drop the Canadian "eh" when we moved down south. Thinks it's a liberal thing, so he's always trying to get me to drop it too."

"Well, I'm about as liberal as they come," Andreas said smiling. "Are you Canadian? I sort of assumed if you were flying this in from Georgia, you'd be an American."

"I was born here, back east, but we moved to Georgia when I was in my early teens. I still have my Canadian citizenship, but I flew F-16s over Iraq with the American Air Force. Reb was there too, on the ground though."

"Rough business," Andreas said.

"I came through it all right."

They both stared at the aircraft in silence.

"I've seen two of these before," Andreas said. "They weren't operational. They have one in a museum in Soesterberg in Holland that I saw before I immigrated to Canada. Then they have one in the Reynolds Air Museum in Wetaskiwin and I visited there a while back when I was living in Edmonton. I always wondered what it would be like to go up in one."

"They're noisy as hell. I'll tell you that," Jeff said. "By the time we're finished our flight your ears will be ringing. Come on, I'll introduce you to the others."

There was a sudden rumble in the crowd and a wave of people moved toward the terminal.

"It's here!" someone shouted.

"Oh my God! It's real!" shouted another.

Reb appeared from the other side of the aircraft. "What's going on?" he asked.

"I don't know," Jeff said. "Better see I guess."

By now there was almost no one left near the B-25. All were pushing towards the terminal building. A woman wept, then another and children joined in. Jeff passed a man fingering a rosary. Everyone looked shell-shocked. Then he saw it.

The monitor in the terminal was showing a dark rectangular mass passing in front of a full moon.

"These images were taken half an hour ago in southern central Australia," the commentator was saying. "NASA is estimating the object's size at about 200 cubic kilometers and they're saying it is artificial."

"Jesus," Reb said. "The damn thing is real!" There was a huge grin on his face.

"How the hell does something that size get this close to the Earth without someone seeing it before now?" Andreas said.

"Maybe it didn't want to be seen," Jeff said. "Maybe it has some kind of stealth technology."

"Only one reason to do that," Reb said. He gestured to the B-25. "Let get that bird into the air."

"What?" Jeff said

"They will be scrambling planes all over the planet," Reb said. "Might as well join in."

"In a World War II bomber?" Jeff said.

"It's a gunship and we've got ammo," Reb said.

"Runway's clear," Andreas said.

Jeff looked at the B-25 and noticed The Major had already climbed on board and was gesturing for them to join him. Then he noticed Willy lying on the ground with two Saint John Ambulance attendants working on him.

"Get up here," The Major was shouting. "They'll take care of him."

Jeff, Andreas, and Reb ran for the aircraft.

"Who's this guy?" The Major asked as Andreas entered the aircraft.

"This is Andreas," Jeff said.

"The bush pilot?"

"Yes."

"I'm sorry but this not a good time."

"Major, with all due respect, you're over ninety years of age and you will not be commanding this mission. If you want to stay on board as an adviser that's fine. But I need another experienced pilot on board and that's Andreas. He knows this aircraft."

"He does?"

"Yes."

The Major looked dubiously at Andreas. The German kept a

straight face.

"Major?"

"Yes?"

"Take a seat in the radio operator's compartment," Jeff said.

The Major looked as if he might object, but then turned and took his place.

"Andreas, take the co-pilot's seat."

"What about me?" Reb said.

Jeff just looked at him.

Reb nodded. "Front turret," he said.

Once they were airborne, Andreas turned to Jeff. He almost shouted. "You're right. This thing is loud. Just so you know, I don't know squat about this aircraft."

"You're a pilot," Jeff said. "The Major fell asleep in that seat several times on the way over, often in mid-sentence. Trust me, I'd rather have you in that seat."

"Where are we going?" Andreas asked.

"I don't know. We'll listen to the radio chatter and then decide."

"Radio's dead," The Major said a few minutes later.

"Dead?" Jeff said.

"Nothing, not even static."

"It was working fine when we took off," Jeff said.

"It's dead now," The Major said.

"Jesus, will you look at that," Reb said.

They were flying to the north of Vancouver. Smoke was rising from multiple locations in the downtown area, but they were too high to see much.

"Has it been attacked?" Andreas said.

Jeff said. "Let's take her down and have a look."

"I, uh, I don't feel well. Something's wrong," The Major said.

"Major, are you all right?" Jeff asked.

"Something's wrong."

"Andreas go check on him and see what's going on."

Andreas undid his seatbelt and scrambled into the radio operator's compartment. The Major looked pale and was holding his chest. "I think my pacemaker has just stopped working," he said.

"Your pacemaker?"

"Yes, I don't think it's working because my heart is slowing down and speeding up. Mostly speeding up. It wouldn't do that if the pacemaker was working."

"Will you be all right?" Andreas asked.

"I, uh, I don't know. I've had one in for almost twenty years. I don't know how I'll do without it."

"All right, well stay calm and we'll radio ahead and let them know we have a medical problem on board, so they'll have someone there when we arrive."

"The radio's dead," The Major said.

"Yeah, right," said Andreas.

"I'll just sit here, and you guys carry on. We have an enemy to engage." The Major took a deep breath and straightened himself up in the chair. "I'll be fine," he said. "You go back to your station."

"You're sure?"

The Major gritted his teeth. "Go," he said.

Andreas reinstalled himself in the co-pilot's seat. "His pacemaker has failed," he said to Jeff.

"Is he all right?"

"I don't know. Said his heart was racing. I told him to stay calm."

"That's all we need," Jeff said. "Keep an eye on him."

"Sure."

"I will definitely do a fly over of Vancouver now," Jeff said. "I think I may know what's going on."

Andreas looked at him.

"Reb!" Jeff called out. "See anything in the sky right now? Any other aircraft?"

"Nothing," came the response.

"This is a busy chunk of airspace around here," Jeff said to Andreas. "Doesn't it strike you as odd that there's nothing else up here?"

"Yeah, come to think of it, that is strange," Andreas said.

"Confirms what I'm thinking," said Jeff, "but I'll need to see what's going on on the ground."

He pulled the B-25 around and dropped altitude. The source of Vancouver's fires became clear. Most of them were traffic accidents; everything was at a dead stop, even the light rail transit. Then he noticed more things: no lights, no power, people streaming out of buildings and filling the roads.

"Holy shit," Reb said. "Look out in the water!"

An airliner was down in Georgia Straight, the bigger pieces sinking just beyond Stanley Park.

"EMP," Jeff said.

"EMP?" Andreas said.

"Electro Magnetic Pulse," said Jeff. "A big one set off in the atmosphere can fry circuit boards and electrical systems for hundreds of miles in any direction, yet it's silent and has no impact on living tissue. Explains everything. The cars are all stopped, the power grid is dead, the airliner is down, and people swarming into the streets."

"But we're still up," said Andreas.

"No circuit boards in this thing. It's vintage World War II. Except the radio."

"And the Major's pacemaker," said Andreas.

"That too," Jeff agreed. "We should all check our cell phones."

Andreas pulled his out. "Dead," he confirmed. "But wouldn't we see a nuclear blast or something?"

"Could be a solar flare or..."

Andreas and Jeff looked at each other.

"Holy shit!" Reb shouted. "Holy, holy, holy, holy shit!"

The cockpit darkened as if night had fallen suddenly, but there were also flames. A huge slab of what looked like burning black rubber passed overhead. Then came the turbulence and the boom. The B-25 shook violently.

"Get us down!" Andreas shouted but Jeff was already putting the aircraft into a steep dive.

The tops of Vancouver's buildings were now perilously close. Jeff leveled the B-25 about fifty feet above them. The black slab was behind them now heading north fast, trailing a plume of black smoke and fog.

"That thing is fuckin' huge!" Reb shouted.

Andreas remembered and looked behind him. The Major's eyes were wide open and blank, a thin stream of spittle running from the corner of his mouth and down his chin. "The Major," Andreas said.

Jeff nodded as Andreas made for the fallen officer.

"I'm going after it," Jeff said. He banked the aircraft around and followed the plume.

A few minutes later Andreas slumped back into the co-pilot seat. "He's gone," he said.

Jeff nodded again. "Hopefully we can get him back for his family. Lot of history back there."

"Did you know him well?"

Jeff shook his head. "No. He was old-school Air Force. Mostly he told me stories about this plane and others like it. He never talked about his family or anything personal and I never saw him away from the airfield. He served in Korea and in World War II that much I know."

The object they were following was receded quickly disappearing into a thick fog.

"That thing's got to be travelling at least Mach two," Andreas said.

"We can follow the smoke and the fog," Jeff said.

"What's with the fog?" Andreas said. "I mean is it normal something descending through the atmosphere would generate fog?"

"I don't know," Jeff said, "but hopefully we'll catch up to it before we run out of fuel. Depends on where it's going, I guess."

"How far can we go?"

"She has a range of about 1350 miles and we had full tanks when we left Everett, but we also landed in Abbotsford and took off again. We can remain airborne for a few hours."

"Depending on whether or not we engage that thing," Andreas

said, "and where that happens."

"Everything's a blank slate. We have no idea where we're going or what will happen when we get there. And there's no way we can get any information without landing."

The two of them sat in silence staring at the trail of black smoke and fog.

"This is bloody surreal," said Andreas shaking his head. "Half an hour ago you and I hadn't even met."

Jeff said. "I'm not likely to forget you, I'll tell you that."

"Yeah, well," Andreas said. "I suppose I should go up front and introduce myself to your brother."

"Good idea," Jeff said. "And while you're at it, have him fire off a few rounds. Those guns haven't seen live ammo in a while."

"Does he know how to handle them?"

"He's a marine. They can fire any gun," Jeff said.

Haida Gwaii

Kale and two of the divers from the Acania set out in the Zodiac about midafternoon after they had spotted a group of humpbacks bubble net feeding earlier in the day. They had told him the humpbacks always came to the surface in the same configuration, but he wanted to see that for himself. He would take pictures on the surface while they did the same in the water.

The divers had been in the water for only about five minutes when Kale noticed the camera's L.E.D.s were not glowing. A battery issue, he wondered? Whatever it was, the camera was not working. Then he noticed the silence on his radio set. Nothing was there either. Was it another battery failure? What were the chances that both devices would go at the same time? Were the divers able to communicate he wondered? If not, they'd have to come in: safety protocol.

He scanned the surface for their bubbles and saw they were directly under the Zodiac. Then the bubbles suddenly increased and circled the boat. Herring jumped out of the water in a panic, one of them landing in his lap. He grabbed one rope just as the surface of the water erupted and eight gaping humpback mouths burst from the sea.

The Zodiac was thrown into the air where it did a complete 360. It came down a few seconds later, miraculously upright but missing most of its contents. The whales had already dived. Kale pulled himself into the boat, his left arm feeling as if it had been ripped out of its socket.

The next thing he noticed was the smell, the lingering putrid breath of whales, mainly blowhole breath but something else too. Kale had never been close enough to a living humpback when it had opened its mouth to know what that would smell like. It added a fishy briny element to blowhole breath. It was not an improvement. He scanned the surface of the water. It was calm with an oily sheen and bits of dead and dying herring.

He looked for the telltale sign of scuba bubbles and saw nothing. Where were the divers? He looked back into the boat. The only thing left was his camera lying in an inch of water at the bottom of the craft and the Zodiac's outboard. He attempted to start this and failed.

Out of the corner of his eyes he saw movement. The Acania was off in the distance and someone was waving flags at him, semaphore. He struggled to remember the code. It took several tries before he understood. Everything onboard the Acania was dead: the radio, all other electronic devices, electrical power, and the engine. They could not come and get him. He tried to signal back to them, but he couldn't raise his arm above his shoulder: rotator cuff probably.

He looked again for the scuba bubbles. Nothing. Where were the divers? Something was wrong. Everything was wrong.

Kale caught a flash in the sky. It was a floatplane, and it was falling. He watched in horror as it hit the water's surface and then heard the sickening smack about two seconds later. He panicked and made several more attempts to start the Zodiac's outboard. Nothing. The oars were gone, but he could see at least one floating about thirty yards away from the boat. He'd have to get to it. He breathed deeply to calm himself down. There was nothing to paddle with except his hands and the Zodiac was large enough to make that difficult. And he had an injured arm. He'd have to try though. Kale began hand paddling the boat towards the floating oar, his shoulder screaming.

The sky darkened. A few minutes earlier there hadn't been a cloud anywhere. Now the sky was darkening? He looked to the southeast and saw a dark form coming over the coastal mountains. It contained what looked like sparks. Lightning? No. No, it was fire. There was a fire in the sky. Was it a volcanic eruption? He tried to remember if there were active volcanoes off the coast of Canada. Then he stopped. Too many strange things were happening. He had to be hallucinating.

God, he thought, maybe one of the Acania's hippy crew members had slipped him a tab of acid. That had to be it. He'd been drugged! Then all of this would be fine in a few hours. He just had to get the oar, but did the oar actually exist? Maybe that was part of the hallucination? Kale dropped his hands back into the water and paddled again. The pain was real enough; his hands felt like they were pushing water and the Zodiac seemed to advance ever so slowly.

Engage

"It appears to be descending," Jeff said. "Where are we?"

Andreas studied the charts. "About fifty miles south of Prince Rupert."

The fog had dissipated, becoming more like a wide vapor trail. The smoke was gone, just a few wisps and sparks. Jeff could now see the spaceship, if that's what it was, a massive coal-black slab, a lumpy version of the monolith in "2001, A Space Odyssey." It looked about as aerodynamic as a pizza box, yet it moved as if it were not encountering any wind resistance. Smooth.

"If it's landing, where is it landing?"

"Has to be the ocean," Andreas said. "You couldn't put anything thing that large down anywhere else around here."

"Bogey, twelve o'clock!" Reb shouted.

Jeff looked up. Whatever it was looked like a giant housefly. It flashed and a glowing stream of what looked like volcanic lava passed to the left of the B-25.

"Engage!" Jeff shouted but Reb was already firing on the thing.

Thryke had missed with his first shot. Not surprising given his lack of practice. The Xburner simulators stored in the ship's library were as old as the flyer itself and not that well designed. But there was little cause for concern. The aircraft below him was an obsolete design, even by Homines' standards, which paradoxically was probably why it was still in the air. There was nothing in its design for the IEMPs to fry.

Then he heard a pop, a small sound, but the panel immediately flashed a warning about a breach in the environment containment system. The Xburner was leaking water. He'd been hit. So whatever this aircraft was, it had offensive capabilities. Thryke's gill slits rippled. He had waited millennia for this.

The B-25 only had one functioning turret in the front. That meant for them to engage the alien craft, Jeff had to keep the B-25 pointed almost right at it. This was not the most maneuverable of aircraft by modern standards, so this would be tricky.

The Xburner, because of its antiquity, could not access the library on board the ship. Thryke had studied Homines weaponry enough to know the aircraft below him was unlikely to carry missiles. It looked like part of a class of aircraft designed to drop chemical weapons on ground-based military targets, but then he remembered such aircraft also carried weapons designed to protect it from other attacking aircraft. Thryke suspected they were using this weaponry to attack him, which meant small metal projectiles. These could be dangerous, but it would take several them to do the Xburner serious damage. He, however, would need only one accurate shot to turn his enemy to ash.

"I think I hit it," Reb said.
"Keep shooting," Jeff said, "It's still up there."

Thryke wanted a fair fight. It wouldn't be if he moved himself out of range of the homines weapons and incinerated them from a distance. That would be too easy. He moved the Xburner closer to the aircraft. He'd wait for them to fire on him before destroying them. He'd give them a chance.

The alien craft moved closer to the B-25 but stayed in Reb's line of fire. They either didn't understand the danger they were in or thought they were immune.

"Bring it down," Jeff told Reb, "but save some ammo. We still have to go after that ship."

Jeff was now close enough to see several bullets hit the alien craft.

Thryke felt a sharp pain in his diaphragm. One of the metal projectiles had made it through the Xburner's hull. The panel was now flashing urgent messages about multiple breaches in the environmental containment system. He was losing water fast, and he was injured. That was enough fair play. He fired at the homines aircraft and again missed. More of the projectiles hit the Xburner. He felt the firing mechanism go limp.

Reb got a glimpse of the creature: brownish with two eyes, a circular mouth and a forehead that looked like an inflated yellow balloon. He fired again.

The Xburner's controls were not responding. Sixty millennia of preparation for this and he had lost. Thryke looked down at his bleeding diaphragm just as it screamed pain. A few seconds later the Xburner smacked into the shallow waters off the island.

Extraction

The target group of Singers was feeding off the northern coast of an island that Homines called Haida Gwaii. It was a stretch of ocean large enough to accommodate the ship and rich enough to allow the extraction, not only of The Singers, but also of the nutrients. It was Baronth's job to position the ship a few feet above the water.

The ship creaked and shuddered as it struggled to keep itself from collapsing. The huge vacuum created by the atmospheric expulsion of the ballast water was pulling at the ship's bulkheads and supports, but that same vacuum, aided by the ship's pumps, would also draw The Singers and much of their surrounding environment to the hold. Huge cultivated sponges stood along its wall to cushion and restrain The Singers as the water rushed into the ship. It would not do to have such a valuable cargo damaged.

Baronth settled the ship above the water and threw the ship into hover mode: a procedure he knew would rapidly drain the ship's energy resources. He calculated the ship could only maintain this for twenty-three minutes. Any longer than that and they would lack sufficient energy to escape Planet Song's gravity during takeoff. It meant that the extraction had to be done quickly.

He felt the ship sag and knew the water was rising into the hold.

It was then the screen flashed a warning. A single homines aircraft was approaching.

Baronth reached for the COM system.

"Turn hull amplifiers on," he said.

Ship

The alien ship appeared to be hovering off the northern end of Haida Gwaii. Jeff was astonished by the sheer size. *This will be like a gnat attacking an elephant.* He looked down at the fuel gauge. They were running low.

He looked at Andreas and pointed to the charts in the German's lap. "See if you can find a place to put us down once we're done here," he said.

"You're worried about landing?" Andreas gestured to the ship. "That looks like a much bigger problem."

Jeff nodded. "Yeah, you're right, but unless we can figure out where it's vulnerable, firing the remaining belts of ammo into that thing would be like keying a car in a parking lot. It might piss off the owner but it's unlikely to do much more."

"What if we crashed into it?"

Jeff looked at Andreas. "Feeling self-sacrificial, are we?"

Andreas said nothing.

"That might work," Jeff said.

He scanned the horizon for any sign of help. The sky was empty. Nothing. Not even more of those lava-throwing insects. Help might be on its way, but without a functioning radio, there was no way to know for sure. It was best to assume they were on their own.

"Reb!" he shouted up to the turret. "Keep an eye out for more bogies. I'm going to take us in for a closer look."

"Will do, Bro!"

"Now's when we find out what kind of defensive systems that thing's got," Jeff said to Andreas. "Ever been in combat?"

Andreas shook his head.

"You're cool for a civilian."

"Nothing to lose," Andreas said. He pointed to the ship. "What is that, a waterfall?"

Jeff looked. There was some kind of water turbulence happening beneath the ship, but it looked more like the water was flowing up than down. "It's sucking up water," he said.

"That's what they've come for then? Water?"

"I don't know but I think we may have just found out where they're vulnerable. There has to be an opening there."

Jeff looked at Andreas. "You ready for this?"

The turret exploded with gunfire.

"No! Reb! No!" Jeff shouted, his voice drowned out by the loud ricochet pings coming off the surface of the ship.

Reb kept firing.

The pings got louder with every reverberation. They were now both dropping and increasing in pitch. The surrounding air roared and the B-25 shook. Sound waves were buffeting the plane and slowing it. His ears shrieked. Jeff released the yoke, covered them, and screamed. He glimpsed Andreas doubled over with fingers rammed into both ears. The aircraft was coming apart around them.

Zodiac

It dawned on Kale this was not a hallucination. Before he had left for the dive, he'd heard some Acania crew members talking about some huge object that had eclipsed the moon over the Australian outback, but he was too busy preparing his equipment to pay close attention. Now he realized the same massive object might be lowering itself on top of him and the Zodiac. Was this the alien spacecraft the media had been speculating about for the last month? There was no other explanation, but real or not, it had a nightmarish quality.

The spacecraft, if that's what it was, was generating a wind that pushed down on him in the Zodiac. This intensified until it pinned him to the bottom of the boat and forced the air out of his lungs. He struggled for breath until he felt himself fading. Then the surrounding water became a wall rushing upwards. He was behind a waterfall moving in the wrong direction. He gasped as the air returned to his lungs. The boat rose with the water.

Kale squinted at the dark hole opening above him, but the salt spray forced him to close his eyes. When he opened them, it was dark, and he could feel the Zodiac spinning as if caught in a vortex. He grabbed for the rope, wrapped it several times around his wrist, and held on. Suddenly, the water crashed down on him from above and he was submerged. His ears ached, and he knew he was well below the surface wherever that was. It wasn't clear which direction was up but then a tug on his arm told him the botent Zodiac was heading in that direction.

A few seconds later, he was pulled to the surface beside the overturned boat. Up did not show sky but a strange ambient light emanating from a gray ceiling. Then he smelled whale breath. A humpback was fifteen feet away, a frightened cetacean eye looking right at him. Hale looked around. There were several more whales at the surface. They were not moving much and seemed stunned.

The Graham Nash song *Wind on the Water* came to him. This is why they came, he thought, to get the whales? That's why they sent the song, because of their concern. But what were they going to do with him? He flipped the Zodiac over, climbed in, and looked again at the humpbacks.

"Pray, my giant friends, pray."

Author's Notes

"Planet Song" is the first book in The Fahr Trilogy. The second book, "Alpha Tribe", was published in late 2018 and is available in both digital and paperback editions. The third book in the trilogy "The Will of the Giver" is under construction and should appear in late 2019. To learn of its actual publication date and for a chance to ensnare a free advanced review copy and other swag, subscribe to the newsletter at http://tkboomer.com/contact/. To learn more about T.K. Boomer and the Fahr visit the website at http://tkboomer.com. There you will also find purchase links. Please review "Planet Song". Indie authors depend on reader reviews and word of mouth. It's through your efforts that we survive, write books, and keep prices low. Thank you.

If you are curious and want to know more about the Fahr, a short appendix follows.

Appendix

Physical Appearance

A Fahr is best described as large fish, about the size of a beluga whale but with scales, fins, and gills. The gill slits are large and flank a small circular mouth in the lower third of the head. This head connects at a right angle to a discernible neck, making the creature's natural posture upright rather than horizontal. The brain is over twice that of any comparably sized cetacean, with an enlarged neocortex making up most of that difference. Fahr eyes resemble those of a predatory mammal, forward facing with a wide field of view. Above these is an inflatable bladder (ballow) which expands from and contracts into a concave forehead. The Fahr have two retractable limbs, half way in appearance between an elephant trunk and an octopus tentacle, except each ends with four opposable digits. The final obvious feature is a large oval diaphragm on the lower abdomen. This feature functions as an ear, a vibrating surface for creating sound, and when engorged as an organ of pleasurable stimulation. The rest of the body is fishlike, accept that the fins are adapted to keeping the creature upright rather than horizontal. As a result, the Fahr are slow swimmers.

There is one other important feature, an almond-shaped pad a few inches below the neck. Its color and texture blend in with the scales around it but the feature is non-organic, a digital memory archiving device allowing the fahr to store memories externally. The necessity for such a device will become clear, but for now it is enough to know gaining access to the contents of one of these is the principle reason we know what we do about this alien race.

What follows is from this Fahr digital memory archive.

The Modificates

A brief history of Fahr physical modifications

Sexuality in the epochs before genetic manipulation was an intoxicant, giving rise to violence, destructive competitiveness, social upheaval, and war. To ensure survival of the species, the Fahr genetically engineered their own species away from sexuality and took reproduction into the lab creating an exclusively male population. This became known as the First Modificate.

For a while, Fahr society became more stable and peaceful, and then the leadership noticed productivity and innovation slowing. Soon a great lethargy had set in. A few generations later the suicides began, and within a millennium the Fahr population was less than half the pre-modificate numbers. The geneticists set to work again. They reintroduced arousal not as a response to sexuality but to song. This became known as the Second Modificate. The Fahr had genetically re-engineered themselves to receive intense physical pleasure and intoxication from songs, songs they themselves could not produce. Instead, the songs were sung by carefully regulated pets.

Over time, this gave rise to a third problem. The Aquafar stellar system, where the original Fahr home world was located, had three planets on which life had evolved, but this still limited the number of singers. The Fahr population became bored with these. To find more singers, interstellar travel would be necessary, but this idea was fraught with problems. Chief among them was the time necessary for such journeys. The solution was the Third Modificate, a massive increase in Fahr life expectancy. Through a series of genetic changes, timed stasis interventions, and digital memory archiving, they increased the average Fahr lifespan to seventy millennia.

Religion

Early in their history, the Fahr had gone through a series of - religious ideas, moving from early animistic tribal beliefs to various forms of monotheism. These too received widespread rejection in the Fahr population as scientific atheism took hold. For much of the middle period of Fahr history, atheism ruled supreme until its own rigidly dogmatic scientific approach encountered a problem: the DNA molecule. Every life-supporting planet they found had it, or the viral RNA form. These were universal and little conclusive evidence existed for their independent evolution on any one planet. These complex molecules seemed to have arrived on each world intact and ready to adapt to whatever environment they found themselves in. The Fahr concluded something or someone was seeding DNA on a galactic scale. They called this entity the Giver of the Double Strand, usually shortened to The Giver. Over time, a succession of mono-occupational mystics developed religious codes around the central idea that DNA driven evolution itself was sacred. These codes became a sacred text called "The Will of the Giver".

The Archiving of Fahr Memories

Keeping a member of their species alive for upwards of seventy millennia involved more than just the artificial lengthening of life spans. No amount of genetic reprogramming and stasis reconstruction could produce a brain capable of storing seventy millennia of worth of memories. They found that four millennia was the upper limit and when this limit was reached, the Fahr brain began an irreversible deterioration leading to dementia and cognitive death.

The solution lay in introducing a personal digital memory (PDM), a hyper-efficient memory archiving system involving a neurological digital interface and almost unlimited storage. PDMs stored memories in one-millennium chunks, referred to as "occupations" because of the Fahr tendency to focus on specific skills sets for that length of time. When Fahr brain capacity approached its limit, a stasis intervention occurred, removing the oldest adult occupation from active memory and placing it in this archive. With an older fahr, this meant up to ninety percent of his accumulated memory was stored in his PDM. Access to these memories involved initiating a digital download through which the older memories, one occupation at a time, transferred back into active memory. For this to happen, however, a quarter of the brain synapses had to lay fallow to allow room for such downloads. This gave rise to a situation where younger fahr, those not yet old enough to need a PDM, had a higher mental capacity than their elders did.

Stasis

Once in every 150 years, each fahr enters a time of stasis, equivalent to their waking state. During stasis their bodies are rebuilt. The Fahr referred to entering stasis as "going down" and emerging from it as "surfacing." Stasis is used to repair, replace, and rejuvenate bodily structures, all while allowing a natural but slow aging to occur. Older fahr were, therefore, healthy but less robust than their younger counterparts. Eventually, this process becomes less effective, resulting in an average life span of about seventy millennia. As in the human population, life-style choices play a role in individual longevity.

The Display of Emotion

The Fahr have two primary non-verbal means of displaying emotion and these work in tandem. The first is a set of gill slits flanking each side of the mouth. They use these organs for much more than breathing. Each gill slit has individual muscle control, which allows flattening, standing erect, quivering, pulsating, and waving. Each of these elements, when used alone or in combination with the ballow and diaphragm, can communicate an infinite variety of emotions. The simplest of these is gill rippling, the intensity of which can display anything from the human equivalent of a subtle smile to a huge laugh. Continuous gill rippling is a sign of intense pleasure. The flattening of gills slits is the Fahr equivalent of a frown.

The ballow, an inflatable bladder in the concave forehead of the Fahr is a much more complex organ. It can display a broad pallet of colors and textures, often several at once and in infinite pattern combinations. Each of these colors and combinations have meanings understood by other Fahr. They can be and often are displays of emotion, but they can also be status displays, allowing their fellow fahr to know their station in life. Red is the color of anger and, depending on its intensity, can mean anything from mild irritation (pink) to rage (deep red with the ballow inflated). Inflation of the ballow is an intensifier of the status or emotion. An inflated gold ballow shows not emotion but high rank. An inflated purple ballow - shows extreme embarrassment or humility and is often interpreted as an apology. A rippling cascade of rainbow colors is a sign the individual fahr has lost control of his ballow and is in a state of extreme intoxication.

Here is an additional list of color meanings in the Fahr ballow. Beige is neutral and most fahr try to maintain this in day-to-day interaction. Green is similar except it adds the element of confidence and self-assurance to the person displaying it. Blue shows a state of well-being or joy. Yellow is fear. Gray is depression or sorrow.

A ballow display will be accompanied by some gill movement to add layers of subtlety to the emotion expressed. Diaphragm vibrations and tentacle movements also contribute. Reaching out and touching a fellow fahr's gill slits is a sign of great affection.

About the Author

T.K. Boomer lives in Sherwood Park Alberta, Canada with his wife. He has a degree in theatre and has had several stage plays produced. In 2014 he published a mainstream fiction novel, "A Walk in the Thai Sun", written under the name G.J.C. McKitrick. Over the years he has been a professional musician, a songwriter, a puppeteer, and a mailman. He has always loved science fiction and, on his retirement, decided he would devote his remaining days to writing it. He has chosen to self-publish, despite the interest of traditional publishers, because of the freedom it affords him.

www.ingramcontent.com/pod-product-compliance
Lightning Source LLC
Chambersburg PA
CBHW071109250626
47159CB00002B/671